TITANS *of*

Chaos

TITANS *of*

Chaos

John C. Wright

A TOM DOHERTY ASSOCIATES BOOK

New York

TITANS OF CHAOS

Copyright © 2007 by John C. Wright

This book is printed on acid-free paper.

Edited by David G. Hartwell

A Tor Book
Published by Tom Doherty Associates, LLC
175 Fifth Avenue
New York, NY 10010

www.tor.com

Tor® is a registered trademark of Tom Doherty Associates, LLC.

Library of Congress Cataloging-in-Publication Data

Wright, John C. (John Charles), 1961–
    Titans of chaos / John C. Wright.—1st ed.
        p. cm.
    "A Tor book"—T.p. verso.
    ISBN-13: 978-0-765-31648-6
    ISBN-10: 0-765-31648-X
    1. Orphans—Fiction. 2. Immortalism—Fiction. 3. Boarding schools—Fiction. 4. Kidnapping victims—Fiction. 5. Great Britain—Fiction. I. Title.
    PS3623.R54T58 2007
    813'.6—dc22

                                                                                    2006100535

First Edition: April 2007

Printed in the United States of America

0 9 8 7 6 5 4 3 2 1

CONTENTS

Contents

ACKNOWLEDGMENTS

The fragment used of the "Homeric Hymn to Pythian Apollo" is the translation by Hugh G. Evelyn-White, based on the edition of T. W. Allen.

DRAMATIS PERSONAE

The Students

(Primus) Victor Invictus Triumph ❖ Damnameneus of the Telchine
(Secunda) Amelia Armstrong Windrose ❖ Phaethusa, Daughter of Helios
    and Neaera of Myriagon
(Tertia) Vanity Bonfire Fair ❖ Nausicaa, Daughter of Alcinuous and Arete
(Quartinus) Colin Iblis mac FirBolg ❖ Phobetor, son of Morpheus and
    Nepenthe
Quentin Nemo ❖ Eidotheia, child of Proteus and the Graeae

The Staff

Headmaster Reginald Boggin ❖ Boreas, of the North Wind
Dr. Ananias Fell ❖ Telemus, Cyclopes
Mrs. Jenny Wren ❖ Erichtho the Witch
Miss Christabel Daw ❖ Thelxiepia the Siren
Grendel Glum ❖ Grendel, son of Echidna
Dr. Miles Drinkwater ❖ Mestor of Atlantis
Taffy ap Cymru ❖ Laverna, Lady of Fraud

The Olympians

Lord Terminus ❖ Zeus
The Great Queen, Lady Basilissa ❖ Hera
Lord Pelagaeus, also called the Earthshaker ❖ Poseidon

The Grain Mother ❖ Demeter
Lord Dis, also called the Unseen One ❖ Hades
The Maiden, also called Kore ❖ Proserpine
Phoebus the Bright God, also called the Destroyer ❖ Apollo
Phoebe, also called the Huntress ❖ Artemis
Lord Mavors ❖ Ares
Lady Cyprian ❖ Aphrodite
Trismegistus ❖ Hermes
Tritogenia, also called Lady Wisdom ❖ Athena
Mulciber ❖ Hephaestus
Lady Hestia
Lord Anacreon, also called Lord Vintner and the Vine God ❖ Dionysus

OF THE FOUR HOUSES OF CHAOS

The Dark rule dreams and phantoms of Old Night;
Cimmeria their land, Morpheus their king.
The Fallen rage in Tartarus, lamenting lost delight,
And that virtue, which, betrayed, lost them everything.
The Lost fall through th' Abyss, silent and serene as rain,
Typhon is their eldest, and nothingness his whole domain.
The Telchine are their serfs on Earth,
Ialysus their golden isle, rich-laden with treasures fine.
The Nameless live before all birth,
In Labyrinths of Thousand-walled design,
And, prelapsarian, still laws recall
That Uranus knew before his fall.

TITANS *of*

Chaos

SHIPS OF SABLE, DARK AND SWIFT

1.

It was our fault.

We fled the old gods; fleeing, we drew our pursuers after us, so that the frail and mortal men we hid among were in the shadow of destruction meant for us, to be whelmed by the fury of heaven, and malice of the deep.

Here was the great luxury liner *Queen Elizabeth II,* an engineering marvel of seventy thousand tons and nine hundred sixty feet, as wealthy as a palace afloat, more opulent than what antique kings in Nineveh lavished on their splendors. For many idle days we five children lolled among the passengers, giddy with freedom as if with wine, and the equatorial sun hovered, weightless gold, above calm, blue Atlantic waves.

That was then. Now it was night, and the stars hid, and the wind howled, and trumpets sounded, echoing across the black abyss of storm-lashed waters. Clouds like boiling floodwaters fell past overhead, and waves like thunderclouds rose and trembled and collapsed down below.

The gods we fled did not want men to see them. The *Queen Elizabeth II* was struck with slumber: As if that archangel who had entranced Adam on the day when Eve was born without pain from his side had shaken dark wings above the ship, the mortals were drowned in oblivion. No one, young or old, could stir, but lay where chance tumbled him, in cabins or passage-ways, or heaped at the bottom of ladders.

No one human. I was alert, gripping the broken rail and staring out into the utter darkness.

2.

"Why did you two come back?" I shouted. "I ordered you to abandon ship! We will all die if we don't follow orders. My orders! Didn't you vote for me as leader?"

I have heard that there are grown-ups who do not take seriously the ideas about voting, obeying authority, or acting with purpose and discipline. Lucky them. What soft and comfortable lives they must lead! Lives without foes.

Vanity Fair was shorter than me, a dress size smaller, but with more generous hip and bust measurements. We were closer than sisters, having been raised in the same, well, you can call it a jail cell, since that's what it was. The freezing rain had plastered her hair to her head, and her thin coat tight to her body. She was shivering. Her real name was Nausicaa, of the mythic land called Phaeacia, beyond Earth's shore, but our real names had been taken from us in youth and, until recently, we had only the names we chose for ourselves as children.

"You are not going to run away and get killed!" She was a green-eyed redhead, and her eyes seemed to glow like emeralds when she was angry. I could see only her silhouette, but from her tone of voice I knew her eyes blazed.

"If the leader orders a retreat, you retreat!" (I was screaming louder than regulation for a British military officer, but I was still new at this, and was outshouting the storm-wind.)

Colin mac FirBolg was blue-eyed, with unruly hair and ruddy skin, built like a wrestler. He gave me a stiff-armed Roman salute. "*Sieg Heil, mein Obergruppenfräulein!* But we thought you were dead! Didn't Echidna kill you?"

Vanity hissed, "Stupid! No matter how far away, she hears whenever her name is spoken! Speaking summons her!"

Colin shrugged. "Is she going to get through that fleet?" To me, he said: "Besides, Leader, we came to report that your dumb order could not be carried out. We are entirely surrounded, cut off, doomed, so we can't retreat! There may be time for a quickie, though, so if I can suggest, without seeming insubordinate, ma'am—I mean, you don't want me to die a virgin, do you?"

Thunder drowned out any words I might have spoken back. I slapped him. I could hear the smack of my palm on his not-quite-shaven cheek even above the storm.

"Thank you, ma'am! May I have another!" he barked out, unperturbed, still holding his Nazi salute. His real name was Phobetor, son of Morpheus, and he was a dream-lord of Cimmeria, the sunless world.

Even if he meant it in mockery, his stiff bearing reminded me I had no time for anger. We were within minutes of recapture, and if I was the leader, I had to invent the plan and give the orders.

If we failed, we failed under my leadership. It would be my fault.

3.

Giddy with freedom, we had been! Because all our lives had been spent on the orphanage grounds, behind pitiless walls, under strictest watch, beneath the tutelage of Boreas. He could pass for human, but Headmaster Boggin, as we called him, had been the North Wind himself. My real father, a sovereign of some ulterior dimension, never knew his daughter, did not raise me: Boreas, my enemy, did.

A flash of lightning lit the sea for a frozen moment, dazzling, burning.

I was expecting to see Echidna. Echidna, the mother of all monsters, who had dragged the giant luxury ship into these unearthly waters, had been looming over the rail just a moment ago, her beautiful maiden's face cold with tearless grief and scaly snake-tail swollen with scorpion poison. She had raised that sting to kill me, but had spared my life because I shed a tear for her dead son. Then, she turned and dove beneath the waves when I whispered the name of the war-god who had slain him.

Perhaps she was somewhere in the deep, brooding on revenge, her huge bulk drowned in fathoms below fathoms, her long snaky body, furlong after furlong, writhing. But my special powers were blind, and I did not see her.

Instead I saw the fleet. There were at least a dozen barges, larger than oil tankers, built like stepped pyramids, with shields on every deck, and cannons, arbalests, catapults, and ballistae behind every shield, and both upper and lower decks had raised gangplanks with iron teeth built along the bottom, like a siege-tower at sea. The barges were made of some black wood or metal that shone darkly in the lightning flash, mountains of iron. Even from here I could hear the drumbeats counting time for the oars. At the apex of each tall barge, strung between two tall poles that jutted up and diverged, was a triangle of storm-beaten cloth. The cloth was black and on its field, in red, was a circle with an arrow coming from it at an angle.

It was the armada that Lord Mavors, whom the Greeks worshipped as Ares and the Romans as Mars, sent for us. Perhaps he was here, and Echidna hunted him; perhaps it was merely his men, and the unearthly flesh-eating Laestrygonians.

Between these barges and the ocean liner, slender as spears in the water, was a flotilla of black ships. They were as light and swift as racing sculls, but each one held fifty men or more, with shields hung along the rail, Viking-style. Each one had a sloping nose ending with an iron-beaked ram, and red eyes painted on the narrow hulls to each side of the ram.

4.

Boreas raised us, I should say, in a second childhood. Either by magic, or by science unknown on Earth, we had been forced out of our original forms and made into children. Having robbed us of our memories and homes, the Olympians held us hostage against uneasy peace with Chaos. The plan would have worked, except that we adapted to human shape too well; the impersonation was so perfect that normal human biology, normal emotions, began to grow in us. The plan would have worked, except that we grew up.

The orphanage had been designed to contain monster cubs from Chaos: five children. It could not hold five adults, raised as human, with the dreams and ideals of humans, but armed with the strange powers of adult chaoticists. We grew up. We wanted our freedom. By stealth and cunning and violent battle, we had won it.

And the first thing we did when we won our freedom was . . . Well, we took a cruise. (Come on. Wouldn't you?)

We should have just fled to a desert island. All these humans were about to die, and it was our fault.

My friends were about to die, and it was my fault.

5.

I said to them, "Where are Quentin and Victor?"

Colin said, "Ma'am! They took off in a lifeboat, like you said!"

Victor had always been the one in charge, back at the orphanage, back when we were young students together. (How long ago had that been? A week? Less?) He was the logical one, cold-bloodedly brave, dispassionate, determined. Somehow I had won the last show of hands, and the group was now counting on me. So I had to be Victor.

So get a grip. Square your shoulders and start barking out orders. They don't have to make sense; they just have to get the group moving. Tell the troops the leader is leading. Say something.

So I said, "Vanity! Call your magic silver ship over to the other side of the liner. Once the three of us are on your ship, have her find the lifeboat Victor and Quentin are in. If they haven't been captured already."

She could summon her ship by thought alone. The Phaeacian ships had neither pilot nor rudder, but understood the unspoken wishes of their masters, and sped as swift as winged falcons, swift as thought, to their destinations. Vanity had discovered the *Argent Nautilus* was her very own ship, a Greek trireme with painted eyes port and starboard, and she did not need to be aboard to give commands to her.

Vanity said, "I don't know. The ship goes where I tell her. But if I say, 'Find Victor,' can she find Victor?" Vanity shook her head sadly and, for a moment, looked very sober and grown up. "We should have performed experiments, found out what we can and cannot do, instead of spending New Year's Eve on a cruise ship, living it up with the money you stole from Taffy ap Cymru!"

Taffy had been one of the staff at the school, a member of one of the several factions of Olympians seeking to take possession of us away from our headmaster, Boreas.

"I didn't steal it!" I protested. "I blackmailed him fair and square! Her. Whatever."

Taffy was a shape-changer like us: her real name was Laverna, the Roman goddess of Fraud. She had been the henchman (henchwoman?) of Trismegistus, the trickster god the Greeks worshipped under the name Hermes.

But I hadn't actually blackmailed the money from her. She had scoffed at my attempt and given it to me. Strange. That had happened just after Lamia, the Queen of Vampires, had attempted to murder Quentin. As if Laverna had wanted to help us escape. Why? And was she really working for Trismegistus or Mavors? Did Mavors want us to escape?

At some point, when I had time to think, I should puzzle that one out.

I turned to Colin. "Are your powers working?"

"Locked and loaded and ready to rumble!" Colin grinned, flexing his big rawboned hands as if eager for mayhem. Who understands boys?

Who, for that matter, understands any of us?

6.

We each came from a different version of Chaos, a different paradigm. Our minds somehow interpreted the supernatural with mutually exclusive explanations. What looked to me like fluctuations of mind-body monads of time-space in the fourth dimension, Colin saw as passions, Quentin saw as magic, Victor saw as matter in motion.

We each could manipulate the Unknown in our own way: Colin's anger made him strong, his elation made him fly, and his disbelief made him able to unmake deadly wounds and brush them away; Quentin summoned up fell spirits from the night world with words of power, and bound them to his service in circles of chalked sigils and the scents of talismanic candles; Victor could electromagnetically reorganize matter and energy in his environment; I could deflect gravity, walk through walls, or send my many senses ranging through the higher dimensions.

Each one could negate one other. I could reach through the fourth dimension to alter the internal nature of any atoms Victor programmed, and he could neither see nor understand what I did. His Newtonian universe did not even have words for the relativistic principles I used. An azure ray from Victor's third eye could banish Quentin's thaumaturgy as quickly as a skeptic's question quiets a table tipper. With a wave of his charming wand, Quentin's unseen familiars could banish Colin's passions. And Colin could simply will my powers to stop.

Vanity was different. She was not a princess of Chaos held hostage, but a princess of allies the Olympians did not trust, an ancient and immortal race called the Phaeacians. She (and, we had reason to believe, her people) could find secret doors through solid walls, and passages beyond leading to distant realms. These secret paths always looked as if they were natural and contemporary, as if they had been built there long ago: And yet I suspected they were made, as suddenly as the details in a dream are made.

And the laws of nature varied from realm to realm, and the Phaeacians could erect barriers to prevent one set of laws from being enforced out of its realm, or part the barrier to permit it. One other power they had, stranger than the others: Phaeacians could tell when someone was watching, no matter what means were used.

Yet even all these superhuman, supernatural powers did not make them supreme of the races of Cosmos. They were a conquered people.

The Olympians could manipulate destiny as adroitly as the Phaeacians manipulated space. A god of Olympos need only decree the outcome he desired from the future, and somehow the step-by-step details, the coincidences needed to bring that chain of events about would be created to suit. With this power, they could dictate the desired outcome of battles and love affairs, the progress of industry, the direction of philosophical and scientific inquiry, the verdict of trials or negotiations . . . anything there was for a god to control, they could control. They conquered lesser races who had powers like ours, cyclopes and sirens, maenads and meliads.

In the same way I could overrule Victor's paradigm, so could a siren; in the same way Victor could negate Quentin's powers, so could a cyclopes. We were really safe only when we were together and used all our talents in combination.

Which meant that the first order of business was . . .

Colin. He was the only one whose powers worked here, now. Colin was our best hope.

There was a sobering thought.

7.

"Colin! We need to find the others, if we have any hope of escaping this blockade. That means flying."

He blinked at me. "So? Can't you pop out those energy wing-thingies of yours? Oh, wait. We are not in the waters of Earth any longer, are we? We passed over a boundary when Echidna pulled the ship off course. Like when one dream turns into another, and a flying dream becomes a falling dream. Am I right?"

Instead of answering, I said, "If I run and jump off that rail, is your inspiration enough to turn into something that can fly, so that you can grab me before I hit the water and die?"

I started running for the rail without waiting for an answer.

Colin took five huge steps and threw his hand around my waist. "Never mind!" he said. "I feel pretty damn inspired as it is. Upsy daisy!"

He tossed me up onto his shoulder Tarzan-carries-Jane style, so the world was all dizzy and upside down to me, and my rain-soaked hair was slapping his firm little butt. He had his hand pretty near the top of my thighs, and creeping higher, so I said, "Watch the hand!"

"Oh," he said, and, "Sorry!" And he clamped his hand to cup one cheek of my buttocks instead.

"Hey!"

He said, "Kick your legs. It looks cute. You've got great gams."

Gams? Colin had been corrupted by Yank terminology.

Colin now came after Vanity. From the confused view I was getting (sort of a Colin's lower-back-eyed view) it looked like she was backing up and had her hands out in protest.

Colin said, "Leader! Will you tell the redhead to hold still so I can grab her? There is no time for games right now."

I am certain that my dignity as a leader could not be questioned while I was being hauled around, helpless and bottom proudly held high, like a cavewoman on the shoulder of your friendly neighborhood Neanderthal.

I said, "Vanity! Let Colin grope you! No time for games right now."

I saw Vanity biting her lips in disgust, but she came forward and held up her arms. Colin stooped (dizzying from my point of view) and put his shoulder into the small of her stomach. With a *woof!* of effort, he straightened, two fair captives slung like booty over his back. (Actually, one fair and one redheaded.)

I put my arms around his waist (an odd sensation, since his belt was upside down to me), and Vanity did the same. The bare skin of our arms brushed up against each other. As well as we could in that reversed position, she and I huddled.

I turned my head so that my other cheek was pressed against Colin's back. Vanity was now hanging head-down only inches from me, her longer hair, also wetted and limp in the rain, slapping around Colin's knees. She was breathless. Her emerald eyes were so wide, so close to mine, and so alarmed, that for a moment, whatever the real purpose of letting Colin pick us up this way had been was lost to me.

For a moment, a moment with no context of before or after, I actually felt like a cavegirl who had been captured. I could feel the tense, strong muscles in Colin's body where I was pressed up against him, I could smell the clean, masculine scent of him, a young, strong animal, innocent and ruthless.

I am sure Vanity was only afraid of the prospect of being carried through the air by Colin, who had not flown before. But that is not what I saw. I saw a girl, like me, my friend, being carried off by a strong young man, frightened at her own helplessness in the face of his savage will and lawless lusts. Seeing it in her communicated it to me. In that one mad moment, I was certain with terror that Colin was going to carry us off to some place of his own choosing and ravish us, first one, then the other, then both.

A silly fear, and it was gone the next moment. But even after it faded, the echo left behind made me feel small and delicate.

Colin spoke, and sounded so pleased with himself that I somehow knew Colin knew my fears and inner feelings, and he smiled in his masculine pride, relishing the sensation of my vulnerability: as if, by carrying me, he had gained the power to know what quaked in my fast-beating heart.

Colin said, "Okay, ladies! We'll do the games later. Please! More kicking and squirming! Now, concentrate! Remember, girls, your job here is to inspire me, right? You are both Roxanne to my Cyrano, got it?" And I felt him rub his cheek first against my hip, then against Vanity's.

"Hey!" exclaimed Vanity, who began kicking and squirming in earnest, and pounding her fists into his back. I do not think of Vanity as being all that weak, and there are places on a man's back where one can do serious damage. I was sure he was going to drop us.

Instead he laughed. I felt his arm that clamped my legs, his hand that clutched my buttocks growing stronger, almost as if I could see muscles swelling, bunching up, growing like the limbs of a giant.

And suddenly we were not in Colin's arms anymore. The talons of an enormous eagle—or I should call it the bird from the Sinbad tale, the Roc— the talons of the Roc were around our waists, and his wings threw out hurricanes in a frenzy of beating.

There was no transition to it, no logic. Colin was gone and the Roc was here. We moved from being over his shoulders to under his talons all at once.

The deck dropped away down—or from our point of view, fell up and away from our heads. I could have kept my cool and been delighted with the sensation of flying, even in this foul weather, if Vanity hadn't screamed.

Vanity let out a piercing shriek, and suddenly I was not Amelia the leader being carried by loyal Colin, I was the helpless cavegirl again, except this time, it was not the Neanderthal who was carrying me off to the cave for some savage mating ritual; it was the pterodactyl monster who was carrying me off to eat me. (I realize that pterodactyls and cavegirls were not actually contemporaries, but I am saying how I felt.)

Well, I screamed, too. She screamed, I screamed, and the Roc raised its terrible cruel beak into the lightning storm and let out a shrill and blood-freezing cry that echoed from the clouds.

We all screamed. It was just a screaming sort of moment.

The Silvery Ship, luminous in the rain-swept dark, and winged with streaming foam, came darting like an arrow into view below us.

The Roc folded his wings, and suddenly we were without weight. Down we plunged. Vanity ran out of scream-gas, or maybe the talons, the zero-g fall, or the prospect of instant death by splattering drove the breath out from her. I do not think I was screaming at that moment, either, although I would not testify in a court of law to that fact. I was paying somewhat more attention to the silver deck that was shooting upward at terminal velocity toward me. *Terminal.* There is the operative word in the sentence.

But I heard more screams. Someone was answering the Roc's fierce challenge cry. It was horns: shrill horns and trumpets. The men on the swift black ships were shaking the air with horn-calls and challenges of their own, horns so loud that even the storm seemed quiet.

The black ships were leaping like sharks over the waves toward the silver one. If our *Argent Nautilus* was as swift as an arrow, they were at least as swift as javelins.

Had she been required to stop or slow, or even to drive through the waves in a straight line, surely the speeding black ships, racing on white trails of high-flung spray, would have overtaken her.

But the Roc cupped its titan-wings, creating a gale to catch us, and dropped to the tilting deck even as the silver ship jumped across the air from one mountain-size wave crest to the next.

Sploosh! Foam and cold spray showered in every direction, and I would have fallen, or been flung overboard, except that Colin (where had he come from?) had one strong arm around me. I was standing tiptoed on the deck, my face pressed into the neck where it met his shoulder, still weak and trembling with fright. Vanity was clinging to him, too, crushing her body into his, her arms tightly around him and tightly around one of my arms that was trapped under hers, since we were both using the selfsame man's torso as our anchor point. Vanity was screaming, still. Take two girls who have never been on a roller coaster before, sit between them, and make sure they are not brave when it comes to heights, and you will get an idea of the situation. We clutch and scream. It's a reflex.

"Ta-da!" exclaimed Colin. I could not see his face in the dark stormy air, but his tone was cheerful. "Nor rain nor storm nor dark of night, will stay this messenger. Whaddya think? Wasn't that great?"

I would have let go of him, except that the ship chose that moment to leap like a dolphin in the sky and jump to another rolling wave in the distance. I heard something scrape the hull below. In the confusion and gloom, I was convinced we had just passed over the masts of a pursuing ship.

In terms of keeping my footing, imagine having four Russian acrobats in tights grab the section of floor you are standing on and toss it to their cousins, who are also Russian, and also wearing tights, some hundreds of feet away. Being Russian, of course, they are morose acrobats, and do not care much one way or the other if you live or die.

Vanity said, "I hate you, Colin mac FirBolg!" And then she screamed again and grabbed him tight.

I held on to him, too. "How come you are not falling over?" I called out to him.

He replied in a loud, calm voice: "I do not want to fall over. And I am psychokinetic, or something, remember?"

He put his arms gently around us, hugging the wet, soaking girls in their wet, clinging, see-through shirts to his manly chest. Yes, yes, I bet he was inspired to stay upright. Very upright.

"Psychotic, you mean!" Vanity said. "Get us out of here!"

I assume the first comment was meant for Colin, and the second for *Argent Nautilus,* because the ship launched herself across the waves like a bolt from a crossbow, and we skipped like a stone from wave to wave.

Suddenly the storm grew quiet and the sensation of motion dampened. I could still see with my eyes that the ocean was bucking and leaping like an untamed horse, but the magic spell or the forcefield or whatever it was that had been protecting us from our own supersonic speed had appeared around the ship, enfolding us like a blanket.

I saw the light from my hypersphere. The laws of nature I knew had just turned back on. We had crossed back out of the ward. These were the waters of Earth.

Colin, answering Vanity's comment, said, "I am sure there is a place to go to get out of this rain."

She was still huddled up against his shoulder. I did not hear her muffled comment, but I heard Colin's reply: He laughed a loud laugh and said, "This is a Phaeacian ship! Do you really think there are no secret passages aboard?"

Vanity looked up, a glint of surprise in her eye.

I was about to ask Colin (now that the ship's bucking and jumping were no longer affecting us) to let go. His warm, strong, protective arm was still trapping my shivering body against his, and I wanted him to let me go. I think I did.

I never got the chance. Vanity smiled and moved her foot. Her toe clicked some hidden switch. Maybe it did not exist until she looked for it.

However she did it, Vanity made a trapdoor open beneath our feet. We all screamed, except Colin, who laughed, and we fell from a seven-foot-high deck twelve feet to a large chamber that was simply too high and too wide to fit in a ship as small as Vanity's. With a loud *poof!* we landed on a mattress, which jumped and puffed around us.

There lay Colin, looking up as the leaves of the trapdoor clattered shut and cut off the rain, in the dark, two girls pressed up against him, still clutching him and shrieking (roller-coaster reflex, remember?), with his arms around us, in the dark. On a mattress.

Colin said in a voice of perfect satisfaction, "This is the best day of my life. Ever."

8.

I did not even bother to try to move out of Colin's grasp. Instead I said, "Vanity, have the ship bear toward Victor and Quentin. If she cannot see where they are, have her go"—I pointed—"that way." With my powers back on, I could see strands of moral energy, perhaps representing the mutual obligations of the group, streaming off in that direction.

One of the objects that had been kept from me during my youth and imprisonment was a child's toy from my home, which could unfold from a point, to a line, to a disk, to a globe, to a four-dimensional hypersphere. It gave off, not light, but some heavier particle of hyperspace, which allowed me to sense the over-reality around me with senses that can barely be explained in three dimensions.

Hyperspace is dark. Energy falls off, not as an inverse square of distance, but an inverse cube. Hyperspace is thick. Each particle has both volume and hypervolume, and therefore has much more mass crammed into a smaller area than its 3-D counterpart. Sound and light don't travel there very far.

But I had four new sense impressions, because the subject–object relations are very different in overspace. If an object was useful to my will, I could see the distortion in the time-energy caused by that object having more futures than a useless object had: Vanity's silver ship was ablaze with possibilities.

Likewise, if a person had a reciprocal moral obligation with me (for free will also distorted the time-frames), I could see it like a thread tying us together. Immoral acts were visible as tangles or snarls.

Every object had an internal nature: I could see the drunken anger of storm clouds, or the gentle melancholy of deep water, the placid ferocity of fish.

Every object-energy-event combination had a monad, a unity of mind-matter that could be rotated along four axes to produce more free will or less, open up pearly gray shining zones of quantum uncertainty, or collapse into hard bright lights of no-probability.

I did not try to open the hypersphere into its five-dimensional aspect. I have three additional senses operating there, fit for the harder-than-neutronium density of that environment, which can detect extension, relation, existence.

9.

Looking "past" the hull of the ship, I could see we were in a vest-pocket dimension attached to the slim hull, in a little bubble of wood (containing the air and laws of nature of Earth) surrounded by the waters of the dream continuum, where distances and directions had no fixed measure. The intersection back into normal space was contiguous with the area of the trapdoor above us.

Outside, the seas of Earth met the seas of some other sphere of existence, and storms raged through both. There was no light, but I could dimly sense, at the far end of the strand representing the group, two internal natures: one methodical, self-controlled, calm, virtuous, fearless, tinged with a mild humor; the other quiet, thoughtful, resourceful, intuitive, confident. Confident . . . ? Quentin's internal nature had changed since last I had seen him. Humor . . . ? Victor was changing, too.

Both of them had an aura of masculine power, which had not been there before; it was a nature that at once both sought to cherish, and sought to dominate; it was both gentle and fierce in a way I cannot describe. It was more forthright and forceful than anything I knew in myself, bold to the point of madness. There was something frightening about it. To think of the placid, icy-calm Victor or the polite, mild-spoken Quentin charged with such vehement, masterful, potent nature, not merely for a moment or two, but at all times, made me feel awed and aghast, and secretly delighted.

Colin said, "Leader! Can you see the black ships?"

Oops. In my voyeuristic peep into the male inward parts of Victor and Quentin, I had forgotten the danger.

"There are five of them closing in on us. One is within a score of yards, and men—lizard-men, really, Laestrygonians—are casting grapples. Have the ship jump to the starboard, now! Wow . . ."

"What are you seeing?"

"Those black ships are as fast as we are. Like speedboats. There are also men in the water. They are in green and blue and ultramarine scale mail, and they swim merely by pointing their toes and having space-time bend around them. Atlanteans. They are pretty fast, too. I just saw some go past Victor's lifeboat. . . . That's funny. I bet they cannot see them."

Colin said, "Vanity, can you ask your ship to stop glowing in the dark? That has got to be the only reason why they can follow us—"

I shouted, "Vanity! Hard to port! Damn—"

Vanity said, "What happened?"

"One of those black ships shot past us while we were sliding down a pretty big wave. It shot over our heads like a rocket. I think we did that to one of them a moment ago. Boy, that looked scary. Oops! There are Atlanteans aboard! Four of them! No—jeez—eight. They are swarming up the side, negating the distance to climb in one bound . . ."

Colin said, "Vanity, can you turn off the force field around the boat?"

Vanity said, "It's not a force field. The boundary for the laws of nature—"

"Can you?"

"Yes. It's done."

I said, "Two of them just got swept overboard."

Colin said, "Leader, with your permission, I'd like to go topside and repel boarders."

I said, "Granted. Don't get yourself killed, or your one-fourth of Chaos will attack the universe—"

He bent his head and kissed me.

He kissed me. Just like that.

It was warm and nice. His internal nature was as dark and fierce and masculine as any of the other boys' (I suppose I should call them men, considering) but he had a streak of loyalty, of wolf-pack love of comrades, that made his male power gentler than the others'. You would never guess it by looking at his outside, but Phobetor, the prince of dreams, had the soul of a poet, an almost feminine desire to be caught up and swept away by his emotions.

I yielded to that sweet hot kiss, and, before I knew what I was doing, I was pressing up to his hard, stern body with eager hunger, a yearning to surrender to him. There was a long, low moan in my throat I could not believe came from me. Only girls in movies, during kissing scenes, made that noise. Didn't they?

He kissed me till I was out of breath, and then he relaxed his arm, so that I collapsed onto the mattress, too warm and too happy to move.

I do not know if he was using a magic power on me to make me feel this way, or if all good kisses have magic in them.

Wow. I sort of forgot that I didn't like him.

Be careful about looking into the inner nature of people you know. It might surprise you. Close your eyes when kissing, and your higher senses, too.

I did close my eyes for a moment.

My lips were tingling. So was my whole body. Wow.

"Now, you," I heard. Then, a kissing noise.

I sat up. I sort of remembered that I didn't like him: "Hey!" I said, outraged. What a cad. What a slap in the face.

I heard the noise of a slap in the face, right at that moment. "Mm-mmmph! Get off! Get away! I belong to Quentin!"

"Oho. Never mind. Just hearing any girl say 'I belong to' is inspiration enough. Open those topside doors, Vain One, before I leap and make a hole through them."

"Hey!" I said. "I am not done yelling at you—! Bloody git! How dare you kiss me—!"

The doors opened and rain splashed down, and the laws of nature of Earth, including such things as momentum, must have splashed into the room as well, because suddenly we were shaken and pressed against the mattress by some wild acceleration, as if the ship were doing an Immelman.

I could see Colin in the splash of silvery light from the deck. The laws of momentum were not affecting him. I suppose he could stand upright in a roller coaster doing a loop-the-loop, without getting his hair mussed, if he were inspired.

I saw the flash of teeth from his devil-may-care-but-Colin-does-not grin, and heard the chuckle in his voice: "There now, lass. Keep yourself simmering for me. I'll be back to claim my reward when I'm done knocking heads together."

And he jumped, in one leap, fifteen feet or more in the air, straight up and out of the hold. It did not look like a jump. It looked like a superhero taking off, or warrior angel taking wing, rushing to fight with the rebel angels.

(What am I saying? Colin Iblis mac FirBolg would be fighting alongside the fallen angels, not against them.)

2

FIGHT AND FLIGHT BY SEA

1.

The battle was exciting for everyone but me. It was over before I did anything; not that I mind not being exposed to more danger, thank you. Staring into the eyes of Echidna might not seem like much compared to what else the others did during those next ten minutes, but it was enough for me, that day.

Our Silvery Ship came upon (and sped past) the lifeboat containing Victor and Quentin in the waters of Earth. They had rowed to outside the ward, and their powers had come back on.

There were black ships burning to every side of Victor. I think he was precipitating pure oxygen out of the atmosphere or up from the water, and gathering trace amounts of phosphorous together from the glowing lamps of the undersea torches carried by the Atlanteans to make an incendiary. There was apparently enough chlorophyll in the plankton for him to make chlorine gas, and streamers of poison were issuing from the boiling water around him, green and horrid in the light of the burning ships. The trace chemicals in the enemy ornaments and weapons had been disintegrated out and recombined to make toxins and acids.

Despite all this, I did not see the moral energy snarls one would expect to see from committing murder. The Atlanteans were staying well away from the areas of water frothing with poison, and it looked as if the Laestrygonians aboard the burning ships were immune to fire. All this visible horror and destruction Victor was shedding was distraction. His real attack were groups of small molecular packages distributed widely over the area, which, if inhaled, influenced the central nervous system to send panic and fear signals to the brain, release adrenaline, cause selective shutdowns in the cortex and higher-reasoning centers. Apparently, there was a mechanical cause for determining which way a flight/fight reaction would go, and he was setting it to "flight."

Quentin was invisible—in all this confusion, he still was carrying the ring of Gyges, which Colin had handed him to perform his astronomy experiments. I never saw what he did, and he did not talk about it later, but I do not think he was simply hiding and letting Victor do all the work. Once or twice I saw a shadow moving on the black ships, silhouetted by the flames Victor was spreading, and it bent over any Laestrygonian whose helmet contained more plumes than the others. Those to whom the shadow spoke did not look at it, but cast their weapons away and jumped into the sea. Every time I tried to look at the shadow, my higher sense bent away, and I lost sight of it.

And Colin—it really was a good day for Colin. He picked up the first Atlantean he came across by the legs and used him like a baseball bat to knock the others reeling. They shot arrows into his arms and legs and he just laughed and ignored them, plucking them out and wiping away the red ink from his untouched limbs. They threw nets on him and he threw them back; they belabored him with truncheons and he plucked the staves from their hands and broke them over his knee. He was like one of those absurd characters from Irish folklore who doesn't need armor, cannot be hurt, and can toss around trained soldiers like dolls. He threw them off the ship one after another, shouting out my name each time he made a throw. I had become his battle cry.

They were not trying to kill him, and he returned the favor. Tossing Atlanteans into the water would not drown them; they were amphibious. I do not think he ever broke any limbs, except on people whom he recognized as having climbed back up the gunwales more than once.

Colin got his hands on the commander of the squad, or, at least, an Atlantean with nicer looking blue-and-green scale mail than the rest, and was holding him up in midair, shaking him by the throat, shouting at him.

Storm-winds and thunder crashed all around him as he paced the reeling, rain-washed deck, hauling the struggling man toward the rail. Then Colin mounted the prow, dangling the man over the water, shouting again at him.

This time, the thunder was less, and I heard what the shouts were about. Was it something like, *Call off your men?* No. Nothing so sensible.

"WHO IS THE PRETTIEST GIRL IN THE WORLD? SAY IT! SAY IT! SAY THE NAME I TOLD YOU TO SAY!"

"A-Amelia! Amelia Windrose!"

"PRETTIER THAN YOUR GIRL?"

"Ye-yes sir! Much prettier!"

"GOD BLESS YOU FOR AN HONEST MAN!" roared Colin over the storm. "YOU GET TO LIVE!" And he threw the man headlong into the raging sea, a hundred yards if it was an inch.

How sweet. I mean, really. It was sweet.

2.

If you are wondering why, during all this, the Atlanteans and Laestrygonians did not unleash horrific magic upon us all, or blast us with space-age weapons from some futuristic parallel dimension, or even unlimber their deck-guns and blow a hole into our ship, the reason (as far as I can tell) is that Vanity saved us.

The Silvery Ship was skipping like a wild dolphin from wave-crest to wave-crest, and the sleek black ships were darting like dark sharks in her wake. But the moment we crossed the invisible line (invisible to all but me) separating the waters of the other sphere from the waters of Earth, the ward blocking our powers was crossed, and the green stone hanging around Vanity's neck began to glow. It was beneath her shirt, and only I saw it, I, whose vision was not stopped by merely three-dimensional surfaces.

It was glowing when she and I, wrapped in Colin's arms, fell through her secret trapdoor and landed on that mattress. It was glowing when Colin tried to molest her and she slapped him, and he went bounding like a super ninja movie hero on wires up out of the hold to battle the Atlanteans.

Before another word was spoken, Vanity, without bothering to stir from the mattress, clasped both hands to her bosom and bent her head, concentrating. The Silvery Ship skipped back across the ward, shutting down my powers; I went blind. I could hear the noise of rushing waters, and felt the bucking and leaping of the deck beneath me, and that was all.

Then, on again. The Silvery Ship was once more in the waters of Earth, and our pursuit, streaming fans of spray rushing from them as they passed the speed of sound, came bearing down on us. But, at the moment, the ward was between them and us. They were still in the waters of the other place.

Vanity did something. I saw lines of energy fold and sway; the intersection of the two universes quivered. Beyond that, I was not sure what it was she did.

Vanity said, "When they cross, their powers will shut off. I just did to them what Echidna showed me how to do."

"Will it slow down their ships . . . ?"

"I cannot do that without slowing down this one. I can make the gunpowder forget how to burn when it crosses from one jurisdiction to the next."

"How?"

"It is all based on attention. I can feel something look us over when we cross the line. It is something that makes objects act the way they are supposed to. The something gets confused when you cross things from one jurisdiction to another. It does not know which laws to apply. During that moment of confusion, I can make the decision for it."

"Jurisdiction . . . ?"

"Um. Dreamscapes? Universes? What do you call a set of laws of nature?"

"Continuum. Can't the Atlanteans do the same thing?"

"If they have a stone like this, I suppose. And they would have to get in the first shot. Watch me. Did it work?"

"I can't tell. What am I looking for?"

"Are the bad guys using guns or casting spells?"

"No." I peered through the walls. I could see Colin and Quentin in the distance.

"Then it worked. Do you think they can beat us just with normal weapons?"

Guess what the answer to that one was.

3.

Five minutes later, we were all up on deck. Victor dropped down out of the sky, his chain mail crackling with ozone, and Quentin faded into view, twisting the gold ring on his finger. The storm was behind us, slowly shrinking backwards over the horizon, and we were skimming along the water surface under the moonlight.

Off our port and starboard stern, like arrows with fletching made of white foam, came the black ships of the Atlanteans.

Colin said, "They are gaining, Leader. I suggest we let them catch up and we trash more of them." He was panting and shining with sweat and rainwater, happy as a player who has crushed an opposing team after a hard game. His eyes danced. He needed only a bottle of champagne to pour over his head to make the picture complete.

Even Victor seemed in good spirits. He stood on the stern, hands clasped behind him, watching the moonlit pursuit with a tiny smile on his lips. "Leader, I suggest not. We must assume that Mavors the god of war is somewhere among them, and we have no experience to tell us how to overcome his powers."

Quentin was leaning on his white staff, his dark cloak flapping and folding around him in the sea-wind like the wings of a bird of shadow. He spoke without raising his head, "Leader, our defeat is inevitable. I have seen the signs. When I was in the air, in the storm cloud, one of the thunder-children turned and spoke to me. Lord Mavors can control fate. There will be ships ahead of us, no matter which way we turn."

As if his words had summoned them, tall black triangles appeared on the horizon ahead, the mountain-shaped barges of the war-god. Dimly, in the moonlight, I thought I saw rippling trails of white foam issuing from ports along their bases, the slim black ships of the Laestrygonians cutting like torpedoes through the waves.

I sat down on the bench at the stern of the ship with my elbows on my knees and my fingers slowly massaging my temples.

Think, Amelia, think. It is like a game, like a puzzle. There are certain moves you can make, and certain moves your opponent, Mavors, can make. Unfortunately, one of the moves he could make was something like bribe the judges of the contest to fix the outcome no matter what you do.

I said, "Idea number one: If Mavors is controlling fate by means of something, a little 'bad luck elf' named Murphy or something, then Murphy has to see or sense us to do his dirty work, right? Maybe a combination of Vanity's powers and the ring of Gyges can deflect whatever sense impression Murphy is using to zero in on us."

Quentin said, half to himself, "I suspect Murphy's real name is Clotho, Atropos, or Lachesis."

"Idea number two: You all grab hold of me and I step into the fourth dimension."

Colin said, "Dark Mistress, idea number one is much better than idea number two. When you step into your 'fourth dimension,' you are only creating an illusion, and you haven't really gone anywhere. If he has got anyone like me among his staff, he can just penetrate the illusion."

I said, "Grendel's dead."

"Maybe. But if a low-level god like Boreas can have a psychic on his staff, are you telling me the God of Strategy and Winning Battles is not smart enough to go find someone who can trump your powers when he is setting out to hunt you down? Come on. Seriously, guys. All these gods must travel in packs of four, just like Boggin and his four flunkies. Jeez, even if he can't get Grendel, don't you think he can get a recording of Miss Daw's music?"

Victor said, "Leader, we have to assume the enemy has taken reasonable steps in calculating their tactics."

He still had that look of good humor on his face. Now I knew why he was wearing it: because he was not leader, and he did not have to make decisions in the no-win situations. Bastard.

I looked out at the ships. Closer now. Coming as fast as the fastest bird can fly—faster, even.

I said, "Idea number three: We put the ring of Gyges on the ship, like stick it on the mast or something, and turn the whole darn ship invisible."

Victor said, "Might work. But the same objection as to number two applies. If Mavors has any cyclopes aboard, they might not be fooled by mere magic."

Colin said, "Even you have trouble seeing through this ring, Vicky-boy."

Victor nodded. "But I am young and new at this, Collie-boy. It might work, though, if Amelia floated this ship into the so-called fourth dimension at the same time, which might confuse cyclopean detection powers."

Black ships astern slightly closer. Black ships ahead very much closer, eating up the miles.

I said, "Idea number four: Vanity zaps them with her power, so that those ships are not sailing through dream-waters, but suddenly find themselves traveling at the speed of sound in wooden ships in the waters of Earth. Momentum kicks in. They wreck."

Vanity said, "I cannot do that without having it happen to us. We'd have to slow down to Earth-speed first. I mean, I can do it, I think I can do it, because there is a boundary around the railing of each ship. But I do not think I can do it unevenly. That's why Grendel's mom could not turn off Colin's power. Hey—you know what I just thought? Phaeacian powers must be something you can learn, or get, because people like Boggin and Echidna have them— Oops! Damn." Vanity jumped as if a bug had stung her.

Echidna could hear when her name was spoken, as Vanity had just reminded Colin.

Victor said dryly to a chagrined Vanity, "I thought we agreed to call her 'the fishmonger.' "

I said, "Okay, troops, I am open to suggestions. For one thing, how are we being tracked? Why did Mavors pick this moment in time to come get us?"

As soon as I had asked the question, phrased in that way, the answer came to me. I threw back my head and laughed and laughed, and the others looked at me as if I had lost my mind.

I put my hands overhead. "Victory is ours! Any of the ideas we attempt will work. All we have to do is make it look as if we are even half-serious. In fact, if we just point the prow of the ship between two of those black pyramids and make a break for it, with a little curving and dodging, I think you will find that the black ships will be strangely incompetent. For some reason they will fall behind."

Victor looked at me, puzzled. "Why in the world are you saying that, Amelia?"

"I could be wrong, and if I am wrong, we will all be captured again, have our memories erased, and get turned back into unhappy children. Maybe Vanity and I will end up as Boggin's sex toys, and Colin will have to marry the wrinkled old Mrs. Wren. So what do we have to lose? Vanity, set your course! Full speed ahead! Ramming speed! Just ignore the enemy. I am sure they will go away if we just don't pay them any mind!"

Colin said, "She's gone nuts. I vote we vote her out and put in a leader who is more on the non-nuts side of the nuts/non-nuts spectrum."

I pointed a finger at him: "You are still going to stand court-martial for your disobedience of a direct order, mister! So don't you give me any lip."

Victor was smart. I saw his eyes twinkle, and he snorted. "No. The leader is right. Vanity, just steer between them. They will part and let us pass." He looked at me: "Assuming they have not suffered a change in policy in the meanwhile."

I spread my hands. "I admit it is a risk. I am making an assumption."

Vanity raised her hand. "Ooh! Me next! My question! What assumption? What the heck are you two talking about?"

Quentin was standing with his head cocked to one side, as if listening to a whisper that no one else could hear. He had one hand on his staff, which was set firmly against the deck to help brace him, and the other hand was cupped in front of him. Perhaps he was reading the lines of his own palm.

Quentin said, "I think fate just altered. I would have to do a more detailed reading to get a clear result. Something just happened." He looked up at me, and looked rather impressed and rather surprised. "How did you do that?"

Vanity said, "Do what? What is going on? Is today just official Everybody-Picks-on-Vanity day?"

I said to Quentin, "A magician never reveals her secrets!"

Colin said, "This isn't funny! You're all going mad as March bunnies! And someone is going to tell me what is going on! I have a right to know!"

I stood up, giving Colin a cold and haughty look: "No! No you don't! You have a right to obey orders, which you never do, even though the rest of us do! It is damn hard to be leader, and I don't like it, and I am tired of you trying to make my job harder! So you don't get to know! And stop calling for votes and stop undercutting my authority, or I actually will take a riding crop to your butt and I will enjoy it and you won't!"

Colin stepped back, amazed by my outburst.

Vanity raised her hand. "Don't I get to know? I promise to be good. Oh, pul-eese! You've got to tell me what's going on!"

I said, "Well, okay. But you were disobedient, too. You should have run away and left me when I told you to. Come here."

I leaned and whispered in her ear.

Vanity actually giggled. "Oh, that is so obvious! Oh, that is funny, isn't it?"

Colin said, "What? What?"

I said, "Today is hereby declared official Everybody-Picks-on-Colin day! The Dark Mistress has spoken!"

Colin muttered, "And this is different from every other day how, again, exactly?"

4.

Twenty minutes later, with the dawn sun appearing on the horizon ahead, we heard a shrill horn-call pass from ship to ship, and banners rose in signal on the huge battle barges on the horizon astern of us. The speeding black ships curveted and turned port and starboard, leaving trails of foam hissing in the waters, like the palm-tree decorations in an Egyptian temple, parallel lines suddenly spreading and curving left and right.

The forces of Mavors fell astern and were lost.

I spread my hands and said, "Ta-da!"

Colin got down on one knee. "Please tell me. This is torture."

I said, "Maybe I want to torture you, little boy! The Catwoman brooks no defiance from her henchmen! The torture will continue until you learn how to hench when it is henching time!"

He clasped his hands in prayer: "Okay, okay. I'll be good, up until the moment you are no longer leader. Then I am going to find some excuse, I swear to God, to do a Boggin on you. An opportunity will come. I know it. You'll create one. But I am sorry I disobeyed, I won't do it again; I will be good! May I never see you half-naked again if I am forsworn of this oath! Please tell me what the hell just happened?"

I paused a moment, glaring down at him.

Well, he had chucked an Atlantis guy overboard for me, after making him praise me. That was worth something.

Besides, I wasn't sure what "do a Boggin" meant, but it did not sound decent, so I was inclined to avoid the matter.

"Fine," I said, "the Dark Mistress is appeased. For now. What happened is this. Grendel's mom really was about to kill me at one point. The curse of Mavors went off. Instead of sending one vulture, he sent his whole fleet. Since they had Atlantis people with them, the same paradigm Vanity has, they arrived in a few minutes. But Lamia was not here. False alarm. Mavors is the guy who told Boggin to let us escape, so he could follow us and trap Lamia when she came to kill us. Remember? Mavors had to let us go; we still are the only bait he can use to lure out Lamia, and whoever sent her."

Colin got to his feet and brushed off his knees. "Great. So we are all still about to be killed. That makes me feel so much better."

Vanity pointed and yodeled, "Yoo hoo! Land! Land ho!"

Vanity pointed, and we saw the Golden Gate Bridge, rising, shining and splendid, from out of the waters of the San Francisco Bay. In the cherry light of the newly risen sun, tall buildings of steel and glass rose up behind it, a textured green at their feet. Climbing up the slopes beyond them rose, rank on rank like rectilinear cloud banks, a crumbled mosaic of white and pale gray squares, as red-tiled houses and buildings of stucco caught the glancing dawn-light. The hills rose up brown and tawny, like sleeping lions with bunched muscles.

I murmured, "I've never seen so many houses."

Colin said, "I guess that's why they call it a 'city.' Um—aren't we on the wrong side of the world? How did we get to the Pacific? That's not New York."

Vanity, her green eyes wide and innocent, said, "Sure it is—that's the Brooklyn Bridge right there. . . ."

Victor turned his head toward me. "What are your orders, Leader?"

I said, a hint of surprise in my voice, "But we made it. This is it. We can go off and do whatever we like. Get jobs, raise kids, fund a private space-venture to Mars. . . . Right? We won. Game over. Right?"

3

WITHIN SIGHT OF THE LAND OF FREEDOM

1.

All three boys exchanged glances, a look of mingled superiority and worry on their faces. A look that said, *Oh, come on. How come she doesn't get it? I guess she is more tired than we thought. . . .*

Vanity said, "Why don't you sit down, Amelia . . . ? You look a bit overwrought."

I sat down on the little bench of silver cushions in the stern of the ship.

Colin said, "If you want to appoint a second and third in command, Dark Mistress, you can take a break if you want. . . ."

I said, "No, no. I feel okay. I guess the game isn't nearly over. Lamia is still looking to kill us, and Boggin still has some method of finding me, I guess at any time he wants, and Mavors can find us any time our lives are imperiled. We have not escaped yet. The Olympians have let us out on a leash. It's a long leash, but it is still a leash, and we are not free until we get the collar off."

Victor said, "We also know from your experience with Sam the Drayman that the Olympians routinely erase memories and falsify evidence to hide their presence from the human beings, whom they regard as cattle. I suppose we can expect to see headlines in the news about the accidental sinking of the *Queen Elizabeth II* some time within the next few days. I am sorry about that. We already speculated that there may be a spell or 'fate' in place to prevent the humans from seeing evidence of people like us. If so, any use of our powers in front of human witnesses may trigger an alarm, just in the same way Mavors gets an alarm when we are threatened with death."

Quentin said, "This ship, the *Argent Nautilus,* also can be detected when she moves, or when Vanity calls for her."

Colin said, "Yep, but apparently—correct me if I am wrong on this, guys—apparently only Mestor or some Atlantans have a whatchamacallit—"

"Magic lodestone," provided Vanity.

"—magic lodestone to find the ship in motion. If Lamia had one, she'd have come to get us all by now, right? Mestor hasn't come for us, because Mavors told him to let us run around till Lamia showed up to kill us."

Quentin said to me, "Leader, our experience on the ocean liner shows that we endanger any human beings we are around. I suggest we just turn around and find some deserted island somewhere."

I looked at the beautiful, tall buildings, towers made by human hands, human minds, works of fine engineering. Built by free people, who explored and conquered the new world not so very long ago. People in a land where women owned property, carried guns, ran businesses, worked in laboratories, became astronauts. People like what I wanted to be like.

"Live like Robinson Crusoe? For how long?"

Quentin spread his hands. "Tell me what our long-term goals are."

I said, "Well, gosh, I assume we all have different goals. I want to be the first woman on Mars. Vanity wants to be a movie actress. Colin wants to get into my pants."

Colin actually looked embarrassed. "Hey!" he said. Then, to cover up his embarrassment, he tried to make a joke of it. "That was supposed to be a secret."

I was actually so puzzled by his reaction that I stared at him, looking into his inner nature, guessing what the lines of moral energy between us were supposed to mean, watching the little flickering ripples of usefulness travel on the sound waves he made with his voice, wondering what use those words were to him.

At a guess . . . ? He thought he had a chance with me. Before, it was all rude jokes because I was out of reach. Now I was coming within his reach, and it was serious. No more jokes.

Quentin said, "I want to solve the mystery of creation. Why did Saturn make the material universe? Why trap all the free and perfect spirits inside gross material bodies?" Quentin looked at Victor. "What about you, Victor?"

Victor gave the smallest of smiles. "I have an ongoing operational preference, rather than an end goal. I was raised in a prison, as a war hostage. War is illogical, wasteful. Wars become less frequent the more incentives rational beings have to cooperate rather than to compete. A free and peaceful commonwealth embracing all rational entities of this and every other universe, Cosmic and Chaotic, mortal and immortal, will deter wars.

"The primary requirement, however, is freedom: universal freedom. If there are other people out there, raised in imprisonment as I was, I have a duty to liberate them, for the same reason why I would have welcomed any outside liberator who would have attempted to free me. We were in the most pleasant prison imaginable. It was still unacceptable. The present condition of the universe is unacceptable. Anything I can do, large or small, along these lines, I will do. Other problems are secondary, and may resolve themselves once this primary problem is solved."

If Victor had said this in any other tone of voice besides his normal cold and methodical tone, I would have shrugged it off as a daydream. It would have been pompous.

But he said it so reasonably. *Anything I can do, large or small, along these lines, I will do.* Vanity was staring at Victor with sort of an awestruck hero-worship-type look in her eyes.

"Wow," said Vanity. "Pretty cool. You think it will work? Conquering all the universes?"

Victor put his hands in his pockets, shrugging a bit, and seemed relaxed and faintly amused in that nonchalant way he had about him now, which he never had had before. He did not look like a young god who had just declared war on the universe.

Victor said, "That depends on what you mean by 'work.' Miss Daw, for example, is as much a prisoner as we ever were. I know Colin hates her, but if I could, I would free her. I doubt the chance will present itself. Reality is complex. The most we can hope for in life is partial solutions. And even such partial solutions as that are temporary, and may require irritating compromises. That is why I defined my actions in terms of an operational process, not in terms of an end goal. There is no end. Nothing ever ends. We do what we can when we can. Factors beyond our control—" He made a gesture at the horizon and the sky, a gesture that seemed to encompass the material world, humanity, the stars, the fates, the actions and opinions of other people, all of external reality. "—factors beyond our control . . . we disregard."

He turned and looked at me.

I have not said what color his eyes are. They are hazel, a penetrating golden brown, like eyes that could look at anything, large or small, and would never be afraid: eyes that could see through all the lies and fears of everyone around him, and penetrate to the cold and certain truth; eyes that would never blink and look away, never hold shame, never be uncertain. Victor had beautiful eyes.

He turned and looked at me and said something, but I was not sure what he said, because I was looking at his eyes.

The words penetrated: "But for now, our goal is to escape from the Olympians, who are apparently still so confident about their ability to recapture us that they are letting us wander among the human beings, whom they rule and control. We must prove that confidence to be false, and defeat Olympos. What do we do, Leader?"

So it was back to that.

2.

Well, just because I had been railroaded into being leader didn't mean I had to do all the thinking for myself. I said, "The floor is open to suggestions. We have already heard from Quentin. Go to a deserted island. Colin . . . ?"

He was standing with his arms folded, frowning toward the city. He looked up, startled. Perhaps he had not been listening. "What? What is it?"

"We are looking for suggestions."

Colin pointed at the city and said, "Is that Hollywood?"

I said, "What? The city? That's San Francisco. Don't you ever look at maps?"

Quentin said softly, "You know he never looks at maps."

Vanity smiled broadly, and gave a little clap of her hands together, and said, "Hollywood is somewhere in this area, isn't it? This is California." She rolled her enormous green eyes at Colin. "He is thinking about his girlfriends. Those starlets he wrote letters to."

Colin said, "Boggin intercepted the replies. Who knows what they might have said? Anything from *get lost* to *let's do it in the road*. You can't blame a guy for wondering."

I said, "At the moment, we're wondering about what to do next. In effect, the question is, Where do we want to go to wait for Lamia to attack us?"

Colin said, "That's easy. We go home to Chaos. My dad, Morpheus, can protect us from Lamia, and from Boggin and Mavors, too."

Quentin looked both sad and stern. I could see he did not want to bring up his idea he had shared with Vanity, that none of us could go home. In fact, he looked so pained that I decided to spare him.

Vanity saw the same look and had the same thought, because she blurted out, "That will start the war between Cosmos and Chaos, and the material universe will get destroyed!"

Colin said, "So? What's so great about the material universe?"

I said under my breath, "It is where that nice stuff called 'matter' is, for one thing."

Colin did not hear. He continued, "How's this for a plan: We go home, I get my parents back, war starts, universe ends, good guys win and bad guys die, and we all live happily ever after. Roll credits."

Victor said, "This will sound unpopular, but I am afraid we cannot necessarily trust that our parents are on the right side. We have no evidence either way as to what they are like. We do not know who is in the right or wrong between Cosmos and Chaos. We ought not give loyalty or aid to any group until we know what they stand for."

I raised my hand in a commanding gesture. "The Dark Mistress hereby orders that we table this conversation for later. Mavors would not have let us go if he did not have a mechanism in place to prevent us from leaving the universe and going home. He let us go to act as bait for Lamia; he would not take the risk of triggering Ragnarok. So there must be something watching us, something that will swoop down and stop us if we get close to the gates at the edge of the world, or wherever you have to go to get out of the universe. Find out what the mechanism is and how to disarm it, or find out where the Gates at the End of Creation are, and who or what is guarding them, and then we'll talk about going home. Until then, let's talk about getting free and staying alive."

Victor said, "I would raise the same objection to talk of approaching one faction or another among the Olympians. Mulciber might help us escape Mavors, for example, and protect us from Lamia, but only if we promised to support his bid for the throne of Heaven. He also might simply imprison us and erase our memories. Or he might be the one who sent Lamia. The same is true of anyone else." To Vanity, he added, "Even the Phaeacians might start a war, or turn us back over to the Olympians, if we approached them. And we do not know who sent Lamia."

Quentin said, "But we are not perfectly ignorant. What about the three Olympians who were allied with Chaos? They are almost sure to be our friends: Dionysus, Athena, and Hermes. Or, to use the names they are using these days, Lord Anacreon, Lady Tritogenia, and Lord Trismegistus. They are all gods of wisdom and magic, mysticism. They have nothing to gain from the status quo. We could take precautions, make a careful approach."

Victor said, "My suggestion is to approach nobody, nobody, until we discover more information."

I said, "One suggestion for deserted island, one for back to Chaos and destroy the universe, one for find out more. Vanity? You are the only one who hasn't said anything yet."

Vanity said meekly, "Is going to Hollywood and becoming famous an allowed suggestion?"

I shrugged. "Why not? It is not any more unreasonable than the 'destroy the universe' suggestion. But it is going to be hard to stay hidden if you are posing for Sudsy-Fun Soap and for Shine-Rite Tooth Grease, appearing in rock videos and on billboards or something. And Quentin has a good point. I mean, let's suppose you are there eating brunch at the Brown Derby with Elizabeth Taylor and Cindy Crawford and Cecil B. DeMille, and a blood-drinking vampiress with no eyes comes in to kill you. See the problem?"

Vanity surprised me. She is smarter than she sometimes acts. Her response was, "This is not a problem of how to get free or stay safe. This is a problem of how to find out how they are finding us. Mavors expects Lamia to find us. How? Mavors expects to find out she has found us, and further expects to find out who is sending her. How? You said Grendel's mother followed some sort of trail or signal left by the wedding dress. Did Lamia put anything on Quentin or in his bloodstream that would enable her to track him down? Let's find out how they are finding us."

I smiled. "A capital suggestion! But you cannot sense Mavors being aware of us, can you?"

She said, "Boggin is aware of where you are. Right now. He knows."

It wasn't news to me; I had been expecting it. On the other hand, it did not make me happy, either.

Vanity said, "I felt the moment in time when Mavors became aware of you. It was when you were alone with Grendel's mother."

I said, "When I was threatened with death. The object his curse is meant to protect us against."

Quentin said softly, "Call it a decree. A declaration. The word 'curse' implies malice; the Olympians can decree any number of things."

Colin made a gargling sort of sigh, something like the sound of a man preparing to spit. "Come on! The Olympians have to have a weak spot!

There has got to be some limit to their power, something beyond their range."

I turned to him. "Like what?"

He said, "I don't know. But why didn't Mavors just 'decree' that the guy sending Lamia would write out a confession and then have a heart attack and die?"

Victor said, "The person who sent Lamia could also be an Olympian. They must be immune to each other's powers or, at least, able to resist."

Colin said, "Quentin detected that Mavors could manipulate fate, and make it so that his ships could outmaneuver us. Okay, fine. That's fine. He's the god of war; I guess one of his perks is to be able to dictate the outcome of sea combats. But apparently Boggin can't just decree that we'd all be good students and never give him any problems. Or else he would have done so. Maybe he's decreed we will always be caught each time we try to escape, but why not just decree that we won't even try in the first place? You see? You see what I mean? Is there a price they have to pay? A limit? Do they only get three tries?"

I said to Quentin, "Are there any myths or legends about people who escape from the fates the gods set for them?"

Quentin smiled and said, "No. No poet would dare write such a tale, would they?"

Vanity said, "Yes there is. Wagner's Ring Cycle. *Die Walküre* and those other operas. Siegfried and Tod, or whatever the names were. Remember? The fates decree that Ragnarok will destroy the universe and everyone in it, but Wotan finds that if he can create a man brave and free enough not to be bound by any destiny, Siegfried, that Siegfried can break the magic spear of Wotan with his magic sword Nothung, and he frees the girls from the magic circle of fire, but drinks a magic potion by mistake. . . ."

Colin said, "Isn't that the opera where everyone is stabbed and poisoned at the end, except the girl, who sings, jumps on a funeral pyre, has the roof fall on her, and the Rhine floods and sweeps the ashes away? Not exactly a happy ending."

Vanity said, "Two humans survive the death of all the gods, hiding in a beech tree. I thought that was the happy ending you were just wishing for. End of the universe. Roll credits."

I said, "Hold it. Dark Mistress hereby says we table the seminar on Wagner opera. The question raised by Colin is perfectly valid: What are the limits on Olympian fate-control, and how can we elude them? Vanity's question is equally valid, and I think it is brilliant. What are the limits on Olympian divination, and how do we hide from it? I am interpreting both of those as motions on the floor for the plan: go somewhere and find out. The question is, where? Who knows the stuff we need to know?"

Quentin said, "There are readings I could do. But I was not able to find a way to make them secure from eavesdropping."

" 'Star-dropping,' " murmured Colin.

Victor said, "We have as yet made no experiment as to the capacities of this ship, Vanity's ship, to carry us to places we cannot describe or name. Does it have a memory? A database of locations?"

Vanity said, "What happens if we say, 'Sail to the nearest person who can protect us from Lamia'? Will the ship go anywhere? Do we need to know the name of the person or the place where he is? Can we say, 'Sail us away outside of the range of the Olympian detection system'? 'Sail us beyond the range and reach of their spells'?"

Quentin said gently, "I hate to keep bringing this up, but even if we decide to go somewhere and take horoscopes or experiment with the *Argent Nautilus,* do we dare do it in any place where the humans live? It is going to be one or the other.

"Leader," Quentin continued, turning to me, "if we are willing to live among the humans, let us go now to shore, find an apartment we can rent or a kindhearted farmer who will take us in or something, and hide, and do our experiments and investigations in secret. There are big advantages to getting help from the humans. We could hire scientists or detectives. We could get hot running water and cooked meals.

"If we are not willing to risk living among the humans, then let us turn this boat around now and seek some deserted place on this world or in another, and do our experiments where no human will see. But that issue we must decide now, before we decide anything else. Do we land here, and drag our boat ashore? Or do we sail away to a lonely wasteland? It is your decision, Amelia."

3.

I sat for a time on the bench, one arm on the back and my cheek on my arm, looking back across the stern. The sun rose higher, burning off the mist of dawn, and the level beams of cherry light grew more yellow, bright, vertical, and strong. The mosaic of white and gray, steel and glass, grew more clear and particular as details emerged from the departing gloom. I saw the tiny sparks, red and green by turns, of streetlamps; I saw a surprising number (considering the hour) of cars crawling the roads, the bridge, the highways, made, by the distance, into a caterpillar of many-colored metal scales. I saw motion at the marina and docks, ships of many shapes and sizes, trailing white foam in their wakes, busy in the early morning waters.

I thought it was only a matter of time before the shore patrol or coast guard or whatever they called it in America would come by and demand to know what we were doing in an ancient Greek pentaconter off the coast of California.

And still I sat and watched the city, and still my friends stood nearby, silently or speaking but softly, awaiting my decision.

I had never seen a sight so glorious, it seemed to me, as the light growing strong across that city, as if some sunken island were rising to the surface of a sea of twilight shadows and, as the little rivulets and pools of reddish gloom departed, displaying proud and tall her alabaster towers, arrayed in the strong young light, with lesser buildings and well-made homes gathered like retainers about their knees.

If you have known cities or lived in them, or if you think only of their flaws, their crowded sleeplessness or crimes, I cannot explain the romance or beauty of what I saw to you. Perhaps a shepherd from some houseless hill-country, peopled by a dull-eyed and simple folk, whose only roads are muddy goat-paths, if he has spent restless nightwatches dreaming of a better life, and yearns to see and to know the arts and letters, the men of renown, artists and engineers touched by genius, women of grace, refined and fair, of civilized existence, perhaps that shepherd, when he at last, after long months of trudging ever-wider roads, comes by morning light to see the wide walls of Babylon looming above the colossal statues of the Ishtar gate, or he beholds by dawn the seven hills of Rome above the flowing Tiber, the aqueducts of Hadrian and the baths of Caracalla, and his rustic jaw drops because all words leave him, to that shepherd I could explain what seeing San Francisco by the light of a new day meant, at that moment, to Amelia Armstrong Windrose.

It meant all the things I would never have, all the life I would never lead.

I said heavily, "Deserted island."

No smiles greeted my decision. Neither Colin nor Vanity was too happy about leaving civilization; Quentin nodded, but was not pleased; Victor had his usual self-controlled expression.

I said, "Once there, we can perform certain experiments, such as seeing if

Gyges' ring can make us invisible to other systems being used to track us. We can have Quentin take more readings from the stars and from the invisible people who live in the middle air. Victor can go through his blood library; Colin can try to learn music."

"Bleh," commented Colin. Then he said to Quentin, "Gimme the magic ring back, Big Q. I feel the need to disappear."

"Vanity can experiment with her green stone and discover what her capacities are. I can take up knitting or bird-watching or something. So wave bye-bye to the lights of the big city, people; we are going to go somewhere where there is nothing but sand, sand-fleas, sandpipers, and sand-crabs."

A moment of gloom hung over the group.

Vanity brightened up. "What about sandwiches?"

I blinked. Vanity sometimes acts the way she acts. "What witches?"

"I mean, we have to eat, don't we? We have to go ashore to get food! And supplies! And do some shopping! How much money is left?"

"Um . . . You have the envelope, don't you?" I asked Vanity.

"So I do! So I do! Well . . . ? It's not going to kill the humans if we just go ashore for a few hours, is it?"

"Well . . ."

I looked out over the water at the gleaming, brilliant city, the engineering wonder of the Golden Gate Bridge. I thought about hot running water. We had just been in a sea-fight, right? And I had missed the chance to shop in Paris, right?

"Well, okay," I said, finding myself beginning to smile, "but only until the noon high tide!"

Quentin said, "Leader, are you sure that this is wise . . . ?"

"Oh, come on!" I said, pouting. "I haven't even had a chance to spend a single pound-note of that money!"

4

THE CREATURES OF PROMETHEUS

1.

We smuggled ourselves into the country.

Quentin and I were carried over by Colin first. We were standing in a little spot of greenery called Corona Heights Park, between Haight-Ashbury and Twin Peaks. Across the grass, I could see a little museum, austere and white. Across the street (which fell in dizzying straight steps toward the sea), I could see another park, shining with green trees, surrounded by houses and buildings with sharply peaked roofs of black slate, the ones nearer us carved with ornate gables and fluted columns. I had been expecting to see everything in California made of white plaster and red tile, Spanish architecture. The buildings near us had a Norwegian extravagance to them.

Across the other way, we had a perfectly breathtaking view of the metropolis; we stood on a tall hill overlooking the buildings, and only the tallest buildings (made blue by the distance) were level with us.

The air smelled differently than it did in England. It was warmer. A little bit, not much.

I said to Quentin, "Won't you get in trouble? Sneaking into a country?"

Quentin said, "Any other country, yes. Not this one."

"I thought you had to obey all the rules anyone makes, or else your spirit-friends turn on you."

"Some rules carry more weight than others. The invitation on the base of the Statue of Liberty—and I assure you that I am a huddled mass right now, yearning to breathe free, and I certainly am tired, poor, and homeless, not to mention tempest-tossed—that invitation opens the ward and acts as consent to permit me into the country. My friends regard that statue as a tribute to the reigning goddess here, no matter what the human lawmakers say or do. She is a symbol, and her name is Mother of Exiles. The spirit world pays more heed to symbols than to mere words. They would have to knock Liberty's arm off, or douse the torch, in order to revoke that invitation."

I hugged myself. "It is colder than I thought here."

Quentin raised his hand and waved at some joggers bouncing by, little electronic gizmos in their ears. One of the girls waved back. Apparently his sweeping black robes and five-foot warlock wand did not seem odd or out of place here. Did I mention we were not far away from Haight-Ashbury?

There was an invisible stirring in the air near us, the grass shivered and blew, and I suddenly became aware of a giant black bird carrying Vanity and Victor in its talons. Quentin pointed his wand at the bird, spoke a word in Latin, and Colin was there. All three sort of tumbled to the ground. Well, not exactly all three; Victor caught Vanity. All one tumbled to the ground.

"Ouch," mentioned Colin. "Warn me next time." He fiddled with the ring on his finger to make sure the collet was pointing outward. The ring had been on his talon claw a moment before, which should have been his foot. He had also not been dressed and had enjoyed a different mass. I guess his paradigm just did not worry about details like that.

2.

First order of business was changing money. We spent an hour or so sightseeing, watching trolley cars go by, that sort of thing, waiting for the banks to open.

Finally, we went into one. The metal detectors at the door decided not to go off when Victor entered, even though he was wearing forty pounds of chain mail under his long white jacket. Guess how that happened . . . ?

The bank was enormous, bright with streamlined columns of gold, and a floor of shining marble. There was an art deco statue of Atlas shouldering his globe in the center. A golden figure with a torch streamed across a high upper panel above the glassed-in counter. A repeating design of wheels with wings sprouting from their hubs ran to the figure's left and right. The place looked like a temple, but more grand.

And it was convenient. We did not have to show any paperwork or visas; the clerk at the exchange desk looked up the current exchange rates, explained there was a fee, took our British pound-notes, and gave us Yankee greenbacks. *Voilà.*

I noticed, as the people waited in line, one underclass type, a poorly dressed day laborer from the look of him, who got waited on when his turn came. The clerks did not move to the more nicely dressed gentlemen first. That is not the way it happens in British shops. It was also hard to tell a person's class by how he dressed. The Americans all dressed pretty much the same. Even the bank clerks did not wear neckties. It was all so Bohemian and informal. I overheard one clerk calling his manager—a woman, mind you—by her Christian name, rather than by her family name. Small wonder they call this the New World.

It was not until we were outside again that I noticed one drawback. We were standing on the sidewalk, near a hot-dog vendor. I said to Vanity, "Can you buy me some breakfast? I've never had a real Chicago chili dog."

"This isn't Chicago!" she said.

"The sign says—"

"Oh, Amelia, that's just *advertising*. . . . Where is your money?"

"In the fourth dimension. I stepped in the bathroom at the bank and folded the envelope into my wings."

Vanity said, "Why put your money where you can't get it?"

"Isn't America full of footpads and crime bosses? That's what the telly shows."

Colin broke in, "Let me take care of it."

Colin bought me a hot dog with his money. It was loaded with so much chili and a yellow syrup pretending to be cheese that the bun would not close. He mock-solemnly got down on one knee and held up the little paper container it came in, a knight presenting the head of an enemy to his lady.

It was as drippy as the head of an enemy. The thing was greasy and disgusting, and I should have been disgusted. It was wonderful. I wolfed the sloppy thing down in huge and very unladylike bites, enjoying the sensation of being an American girl.

"Thank you, Colin," I said, daubing my lips with a napkin. I should have just wiped my mouth on my sleeve, I suppose.

He said, "You shall have to satisfy some hunger of mine in return, Dark Mistress. You see, I have this hot dog of my own which needs—"

Quentin (thanks be to Gabriel) interrupted the oncoming filthy double entendre by saying, "I was sure at any minute we were going to be arrested. In the bank. Did you notice the decorations? No one saw them?"

I said, "Atlas. Prometheus. Winged wheels."

Quentin said, "That place was a fane of usury, where they make gold, not out of base metal, but out of nothing. There was a power there. I was sure that armed men would come swarming out of the back rooms at any moment. This is Mulciber's place; this is the world of Mulciber, an ugly world of gold and iron."

I said, "They seemed friendly enough." Friendlier than English clerks would have been, I thought.

Quentin said darkly, "Talos also had a friendly smile."

Colin said, "Who . . . ?"

I said, "Well, lady and gentlemen, I suggest we make a list of what we need and a list of what we want, and go shopping."

3.

We bought first what any self-respecting group of adventurers chased by ancient pagan gods and blood-sucking vampiresses would buy: cell phones.

The Americans make radio-telephones small enough to fit in one's palm, feather-light, which can be programmed to listen to your spoken commands and dial numbers for you; record, store, and forward messages; and probably walk the dog and change the baby. Only someone who has never held such a thing in hand before can appreciate the marvel of it. Buck Rogers himself would have been goggle-eyed.

4.

Originally, we meant to stay for only a short time. Only until high tide, no longer. But there was no point in leaving America while we were still hungry, and so we decided to spend a limited amount of money eating. And there was no point in eating in some dull burger joint when we could visit a first-class restaurant, not for our last civilized meal. And there was no point in fine dining without wearing the nice clothes Vanity had bought in Paris, and the boys dressed up in their formal suit and tie. Vanity wore a peach evening dress, flattering to her figure, with a strand of pearls dripping down her cleavage. I wore that little black outfit with stockings and pumps, silver earrings, and a matching silvery choker. We looked like grown-ups.

We squabbled like children. After much debate, we finally decided on a restaurant called Gary Danko, which the guide we'd bought listed as number one in the local area.

Lovely place, all polished wood floors gleaming like gold, dimmed lights over cozy white tables, wood-slatted windows casting striped shadows from the setting sun across the silverware and linen. The fragrance of roses and of wine hung in the air. I suppose it was a small restaurant, compared with some, but to me it looked enormous.

They never starved us at the Academy, and they had staff to wait on us at meals, which I suppose is unusual, so you would think we'd be used to dining. But the difference here was that we got to choose our own food.

What food it was! It was served on little white dishes, looking almost too beautiful to eat. (I recommend the guinea hen breast and rillettes, though the lobster salad—I ate some off Vanity's plate—was quite tasty, too.) They served twenty types of cheeses from a cart, each one better than the last.

Imagine being able to eat as much as you'd like, without Mrs. Wren or Dr. Fell telling you no. Freedom cannot be good for the figure. Are Americans fatter than Cubans because they're free?

I remember making some comment along these lines to the group.

Quentin looked glum and shook his head. "Unleashing the appetites is not freedom, but another type of slavery. Freedom in the absence of virtue will destroy a country as quickly as any tyranny."

Victor said, "Virtue imposed from without is not virtue at all, but merely prudence. A man who avoids lying merely because a law tells him to tell the truth will avoid telling the truth as soon as the law tells him to lie."

Quentin said, "The whole universe is built on a hierarchic principle, spirits being made of finer substances than gross matter, quintessence being finer than aether. A democracy flattens differences between men, and too soon they lose the distinction between better and worse, noble and base, good and evil. Have you seen what they call art here, compared to what we studied in school? These people need a queen. To bow to a crowned sovereign would teach them respect for great and ancient things, so that when, after death, they met things greater and more ancient than mere man, they would be ready."

Victor, who cared nothing one way or the other for art, said, "I believe in the principle of atomism: let each individual stand or fall on his own. The ancient things we are running from have done nothing to convince me the Americans, or anyone else, should bow to them."

I said, "Speaking of gross matter, what do you think, Colin?"

He raised his wineglass. "When Ireland gets the atom bomb, we'll see how well Q-man's 'hierarchic principle of the universe' holds out! Down with crowned head, on Earth, in Heaven, or in Hell!"

Vanity said, "You're not really Irish, you know."

Colin said, "So what? I like 'em. Oscar Wilde, W. B. Yeats."

"Do you know anything about Yeats?"

Colin looked pompous and offended. He jarred the wineglass down on the table. "Do I indeed, the colleen, she asks? And me a true son of the Old Sod? Faith! Hear this:

When you are old and gray and full of sleep,
And nodding by the fire, take down this book,
And slowly read, and dream of the soft look
Your eyes had once, and of their shadows deep;

How many loved your moments of glad grace,
And loved your beauty with love false or true;
But one man loved the pilgrim soul in you,
And loved the sorrows of your changing face.

And bending down beside the glowing bars
Murmur, a little sadly, how Love fled
And paced upon the mountains overhead
And hid his face amid a crowd of stars.

Vanity was taken aback. "That's a beautiful poem."

"To be sure, and it is!" declared Colin, lifting his wineglass again to his lips with relish. "I don't know what the first two stanzas are on about, but I've always wanted a crown of stars like the one Love hides his face in on the mountain. I assume he meant Cupid atop Olympos. Wonder how he knew Cupid was crowned King after Terminus fell? Quentin, can you summon up his ghost to ask him?"

Quentin nodded, and mentioned some of the disgusting things he'd have to get or to do to perform the necromancy.

Victor said, "The poem said 'crowd,' not 'crown.'"

Colin shrugged. "Miss Daw told me once that you can interpret a poem how you like, so I interpret that Yeats's pen slipped when he wrote that last line. I'm sure he meant to say 'crown.'"

I said, "And what do you think of America?"

Colin nodded at me. "I am suspicious of anything you like, Amelia, just on principle; but on the other hand, everyone says California girls are hot, young, wet, and eager, so the place cannot be all bad."

Vanity commented: "Ah! The echoes from the shallow well! Colin, I would call you a boor, except I know some boors who are quite nicer than you. She was asking what you thought of their system of government."

Colin spread his hands. "What? I've walked into a bank and ate in a restaurant. I haven't seen a race riot or a public hanging since I've been here, so I guess their system of government is holding up for this afternoon. What kind of question is that, anyway? That's all theory. Democracy or tyranny or communism or capitalism. It's all something someone made up in his head. It's not real. The reality is that people will do whatever they want to do, and make up some excuse later why they did. Political economics is a list of excuses to use."

I said, "Well, God bless America, I say. These people are the freest on Earth."

Colin picked up his fork and jabbed it in my direction. "Which means they are the freest pigs in the sty. And the Olympians are the swineherds. It does not matter what these people do or do not do. The bloody gods and goddesses are running the show here. The freedom you see around you is a façade, a false face. If you care about freedom for Americans or Englishmen or Irishmen (the finest race on Earth, let me just say), then you have to declare war against Heaven and Hell, against wind and wave and fire, and every other place the old gods dwell."

Victor said calmly, "I do not disagree with what you say, Colin, but let us see to securing our own freedom first."

We all toasted that remark.

It was based on that conversation that I started to wonder—if the human world were a false face, what lay under the mask?

Why were the gods in hiding, if men were their cattle?

5.

My cash was still trapped in my fourth-dimensional pocket, but I had no chance to go to the ladies' room and rotate it into being. Colin, with grand and solemn drama, swept up the bill when the waiter brought it, and he left a healthy tip, bankrupting himself for a gesture.

"Now you have to put out," he said to me with his crooked smile. "It's tradition."

Insults bubbled up to my lips (a natural process brought on by exposure to Colin). Victor spoke before I did, though, saying in the cool, remote voice, "I believe the American tradition, in cases where the gentleman propositions a lady after paying for her meal with money she secured for him, is to take him out back and drub him. Quentin, would you care to join me?"

To my surprise, little Quentin did step up to Colin and grab him by one arm, while Victor grabbed the other.

"Hey!" shouted Colin. Heads turned at the shout. Patrons of the restaurant murmured in alarm.

I said, "The Dark Mistress is amused by the circus of gladiators, but this is not the place! If you boys can peer through the cloud of manly testosterone you're emitting, note the approach of the maître d'hôtel! Don't do anything that will make them call the police!"

Victor nodded at Quentin, and in a trice, they had Colin hoisted up to their shoulders (lopsidedly, since Victor is taller than Quentin) and were singing, "He's a jolly good fellow! So say all of us!"

The patrons, relieved, smiled and turned back to their meals. One or two even clapped.

The maître d' approached anyway. "What is the meaning of this?"

I said, "Well . . . we're British."

He blinked, but the answer seemed to satisfy him. Victor and Quentin staggered out under their load, who waved and smiled at the other patrons, especially the ladies. Once outside in the parking lot, away from other eyes, the two unceremoniously dumped him to the pavement.

"Ow!" Colin stood and tried to rub both his bum and his head at the same time, which had collided loudly with the pavement, also at the same time.

Vanity uttered a moan of disappointment. "There is a Dumpster not five steps away! You could have at least tossed him in the trash!"

6.

By that time it was dark, and there was really no point in setting off into the sea at night, rather than wait till morning. And a comfortable bed in a hotel with room service and cable television was preferable to sleeping aboard the ship, right? And we did not have to save our money, since we were about to travel to some uncharted island, right? So why not rent the penthouse suite?

All were pleased with that decision, but less pleased when I announced, once we were alone in the room, the girls were taking one room and the boys were bunking in the other. Vanity scowled and wondered aloud when I had gotten so prissy in my old age.

I said sternly, "It is a matter of maintaining unit discipline, troops! Vanity, you will have to do your snogging with Quentin in the daytime, with no extramarital temptations to put added stress on this group. We were properly brought up little gods and goddesses, all except for Colin, and I see no reason to descend into lusty barbarism merely because we are in America."

That got me boos and catcalls (one catcall), but there were only two rooms in the suite, and I was not going to bunk with Victor and Colin.

Vanity said, "You sound like Boggin. This is out of your jurisdiction, Leader! What we do with our time off is not your business."

I shrugged and said, "Elect Colin leader if you like, but while I am Dark Mistress of the Merry Wee Titans of Chaos, we are going to maintain our dignity and decorum. Makes the boys fight harder."

Well, it was put to a vote of confidence immediately. Vanity voted against me, but could not bring herself to vote for Colin, so she voted for Quentin; Victor and Quentin supported me. I voted for Victor. Colin voted for himself, of course.

Quentin caught my eye and gave me a nod of approval. Quentin was no more likely to offend the sacrament of marriage than Grendel Glum had been. Humans might have some option about which laws to obey and which to ignore, but I don't think monsters and warlocks do.

"A clear and overwhelming plurality," I sighed. "That's it, people: While in America, we act like Puritans. It's tradition."

Vanity, at this point, asked if we could depart America as soon as possible. She started pointing out the advantages of camping out on some deserted island, and saying how our limited funds had been used for extraordinary extravagances lately.

"A quick trip to the all-night sporting-goods store, to pick up a few needed supplies," Vanity said, "and then we should be on our way."

Colin nodded somberly and said, "By 'needed supplies,' you mean birth control, right?"

That was too much for Quentin, who did not want to see his beloved called a harlot. He muttered a curse under his breath and made a small gesture with his walking stick. Of course, when Quentin mutters a curse, it works: Colin hopped as if stung by a bee, yowling in pain and clutching his bum.

Yes, there was an all-night sporting-goods store in San Francisco. The store's loudspeakers were vibrating with energetic dance tunes, and the clerks working there were bright-eyed and hyperactive, no doubt as a side effect. They even had a little elevator just for the sports shoes to ride. What a country! The cash that Victor and Vanity still carried was enough to cover the costs of tents and tarps and sleeping bags made of shiny space-age materials I had never heard tell of. Quentin paid for the cooking gear, knives, a hatchet, and an axe. Victor invested twenty dollars in a *Boy Scout Handbook* and a U.S. Army *Survival Manual.*

Vanity called her ship to her, and we all flew over to the deck, either levitating magnetically, or by warping space-time to deflect gravity, or by uttering a charm to the unseen spirits of the middle air, or by jumping off the docks with a scream that turned in midscream into the shrill of a hawk. Vanity rode on my back amid wings made of flame-colored music-energy.

Of course she would have preferred Quentin to carry her in his arms, but the nervous shyness of his familiar spirits made that unlikely. She complained while we flew that she could have found a shortcut through a phone-booth door or something directly to the deck. Then she said I was too close to the water, and then that I was too high, yak, yak, yak. Backbone driver!

Through the dark clouds above the nocturnal sea, I saw the red planet, Mars, winking at me like a distant light above the far horizon, mysterious, untrod by man, and I wondered how high I could fly. These are questions every young aviatrix asks herself: How far, how high, how fast, under what weather conditions?

We lit on the deck with a swirl of gravitic rainbows, or levitated silently as if riding an invisible elevator, or stepped down from the shadows in the night air, or pretended to be a bird until tickled and kissed by Vanity and me back into being human. Jerk.

We stowed the gear in convenient cabins under the deck that Vanity found (or created) for us. The boys waited above impatiently while Vanity and I changed. I am sure they rolled their eyes and made boyish comments, but still, I was not going to go sailing in an evening dress. I put on a very sensible dark sweater, dark blue jacket, white slacks, deck shoes. And no reason not to accessorize, since Vanity had bought me a cute little necklace of fine gold in Paris. And no reason not to brush my hair, since it did not make sense for me to have my hair amess if I were dressed nicely, did it?

Back up on deck, Victor seemed not to notice how I was dressed. Second jerk.

But I looked all captainy and official. "Miss Fair!" I called out in my best Bligh voice. "You may weigh anchor and set our destination. Some fine deserted island, empty of men or gods, where we may tarry for a while in peace!"

Vanity raised her hands and closed her eyes, and intoned in a theatrical voice: "*Argent Nautilus,* beloved ship, vessel white to carry us to freedom! Find me an uninhabited island!"

The Silvery Ship raised no sail. Silently, with no hand at the tiller, we sped away under the stars.

UNTASTED WATERS AND UNTRODDEN SANDS

1.

I suppose this has happened to everyone: It is easy enough to say to a magic boat, *Find me an uninhabited island,* but the first place we made landfall was a rock less than an acre wide, half-submerged at high tide, covered with ice at low tide. There were some tough-looking birds, their feathers gray as lead, who had built their nests among the frost-coated rocks. Nothing else grew on the rock but lichen and clinging green seaweed.

We were all shivering in the gray and snowy air, except for Victor, who did not notice cold.

"Vanity!" I said through chattering teeth. "Whose idiot idea was this? I told you to find some deserted tropical island!"

Vanity stamped her boot against the deck. "You did not! I said just what you said! A deserted island!"

Colin and Quentin were both looking at me. Oops. First lesson about being a leader. If it goes wrong on your watch, it is your fault. I could have given a different order, been more specific, said something else. Bossing is like an unwritten contract: The men obey your dumb orders without question, and in return you don't give any dumb orders. You use your brain. You make the plan. You're in charge.

"At ease, Miss Fair!" I barked out. "We'll say no more about it. Tell the vessel to find someplace warmer! In the tropics! Double time!"

Vanity squinted at me. Her red hair was being tossed about by the cold wind, and her lips were blue. "What does 'at ease' mean?"

"It means you don't have to stand at attention."

"I wasn't standing at attention."

"Good. Because you don't have to! Tell the *Nautilus* to find an island currently empty of man or god, spirit or spy devices, in a warmer clime, someplace large enough to pitch a tent. Someplace with grass and trees. Now, step lively, spit spot!"

"What does 'spit spot' mean?" Vanity asked.

Colin said, "It means Amelia thinks she's Mary Poppins now. Quick, send this boat to someplace warm, or she'll have us clean the nursery while she sings."

2.

It is easy enough to say to a magic boat, *Find me a warm and uninhabited island,* but if you forgot to say, *with a safe anchorage,* then you might end up having to fly to shore at night. There was no opening in the reef, no safe passage. Well, I suppose a deserted island has to be deserted for a reason.

The necessity gave an excuse to be cunning: We sent the boat on her way, with instructions to visit the islands of Micronesia in alphabetical order, to lead any magic watching her away from us.

Beneath a midnight sky, in our various flying forms, we circled the island once and twice before landing. Victor said loudly through the night wind that he detected no electrical signals of motors, telephones, radios. Vanity (who was riding my back again) said she sensed no one looking. I gave the order to land.

Descending, I smelled green, growing things and heard the dry rustling of broad leaves. Funny, the leaves sounded different here than they do in Wales: like huge fans whispering.

But, ah! The warmth of the tropics! Why in the world would anyone live anywhere else? The land of endless summertime.

Victor had levitated down nearby. I heard him trampling through hissing grass blades toward me, and saw the dull blue beam from his metallic third eye. Against the stars and palm trees, his silhouette looked like that of a miniature lighthouse.

"Any idea where we are, Mr. Triumph?" I said, setting Vanity on her feet and refolding myself into human form. I felt sand and soil under my shoes, and long grass or ferns tickling my knees.

"About four hundred British nautical miles northwest of Tahiti, Leader," he said. "That is a rough guess based on star positions. I will need time to correlate and make adjustments to my internal instrumentation before I can interpret global positioning satellite signals correctly." A wry note crept into his voice. "My paradigm does not allow me to invent new sense impressions without knowing how they work."

Quentin spoke in the gloom, making me jump. I had not heard him walk up. "Leader, my friends tell me there are houses or huts, some place that lacked a lares or a lemur, not far from here."

I felt a sense of disappointment. No matter how far I traveled, I was still in the middle of the map, not at the edge. Always someone here before me. I said, "Vanity, I thought this island was deserted?"

Vanity said crossly, "Leaderwoman, you asked Silver to find a *deserted* island, not an undiscovered one. There is no one here *now*."

I was irked. "Are you sure your boat knows what she is doing?"

To answer, Vanity suddenly emitted a shrill, bloodcurdling scream.

"Lux fiat!" shouted Quentin, and a corona of flame appeared around his head. He had his walking stick raised high, shivering with eldritch power, his cloak billowing around him in a wind that was touching nothing but him. Victor rose slightly into the air, and tiny hissing dots of matter fled from his azure-flaming eye in all directions about us. I could not see them, but their internal nature was watchful and dangerous: some sort of prepared nanomachine package.

I did not flinch, of course, because I saw the utility and the inner nature of her scream. It was not a scream of fear or pain.

Colin stumbled into view at that moment and wrestled the bag hoodwinking him off his head. As leader, I bestowed on him the privilege of riding with Quentin, because Vanity and I were not going to do any naughtiness to restore him to lusty boy form. Colin scrambled on the ground for a moment, looking no doubt for a rock or stick to use as a club, but all he came up with was a handful of grass and fern. The bouquet of grass did not make a very good bludgeon, but his anger and shock made it burst into flame, which was pretty impressive, considering. The hairs of his head stirred and stood up, and the veins stood out on his neck as he screeched his war cry. "WINDROSE!"

(I assume it was his war cry. He was standing only two feet from me, so I doubt he was calling for me.)

Vanity was making a little pirouette in the grass. "See?" she said brightly. "No one heard me. No one is in earshot, Leaderess. Deserted. *Argent Nautilus* did exactly as told."

Colin threw the burning twigs from his hand with a scowl. "Scared the piss out of me, Red! You owe me a pair of new silk boxers. And that is the last time I fly through the air with Quentin."

Darkness gathered itself up around Quentin as silently as a black silk handkerchief when he whispered the word to end his spell, and banished whatever fallen angel had lent him a blazing crown.

I said, "Let's find dry ground and make camp. We can look at the empty huts in the morning: groping into them at night is not a good idea."

No one moved. Victor said slowly, "I suppose we should look for higher ground, if we want it dry."

Did I mention that none of us were Boy Scouts? We had never been camping. We had never been anywhere on our own. So: take four young Titans and a young Phaeacian princess, set them in the middle of dark tropic scrub at night, and have them try to find a campsite. It was midnight, so those of us who get tired (everyone but Victor) were tired, and it was dark and tangled underfoot, so those of us who get cross (everyone but Victor) were cross. Everything we stumbled into seemed to have thorns and every patch that did not have thicket was flinty and hard, a rubble of rocks no sleeping bag could sit on. The ground was furthermore cut in places with some sort of drainage ditches or furrows, which threatened to stub toes, twist ankles, or break legs in the dark, and more than once we stepped in slime that Victor told us calmly was guano.

"At least," he said, "I assume it's guano. I can detect oxalic, uric, carbonic, and phosphoric acids, as well as earth salts and impurities."

"What's guano?" asked Colin.

"Bat crap," said Victor.

"Bat crap!" yodeled Colin, as loud as if he were helping Vanity check to see if anyone was in earshot. By some dull throb of feminine intuition, I was sure the phrase would turn into Colin's curse of choice over the next few days, and we'd be hearing a lot of it.

"Hold up, troops," I said in an exhausted voice. "Let's head toward the · sound of the shore. Maybe we can find some nice, soft, sandy beach to make a tent."

"Pitch a tent," Vanity said. "You make a bed."

I was carrying all the gear, of course, in a large fold of my fourth-dimensional energy-wings, with the gravity world-lines all bent away, so that, for me, it was feather-light. When we found the sand, there was a shimmer of reddish light as I pulled the knapsacks and newly bought tents, tarps, and bedrolls into this three-space. I had it blue-side red at first, so all the lettering or trademarks on the fabric were mirror-reversed. I guess I was tired. I rotated the mass of it out of the hyperplane and back into it, and carefully flattened out the crinkles, so that everything was oriented right.

Well, we could not pound tent stakes into the sand, so I made the executive decision that we could sleep under the stars on a warm night just in our sleeping bags.

How soft the sand was. I nodded off, congratulating myself on my decision.

I dreamed I was back with Grendel Glum at the bottom of the sea. Waking up half-drowned, with a sodden sleeping bag twisted like heavy concrete about your ankles, in the darkness before dawn is not pleasant, nor is having half your gear carried off by the tide. We were all muddy with sand by the time we recovered what we could recover and retreated to the rocks above the high-tide line.

You see, I could tell you the fluxions Newton used to calculate the pull of the moon on the tides. We had done them in math class. But I did not know what any seven-year-old who went backpacking with her father might know: Don't pitch camp below the tide line.

I lost the vote of confidence before breakfast.

Vanity cooked a splendid breakfast with some of what we salvaged from our foodstuff, and she managed to get a fire started with just one match, like a real Girl Guide, and when we were done debating and voting, she was in charge.

Her first decree was to name the place Vanity Island.

I got KP.

SIX SCORE LEAGUES NORTHWEST
OF PARADISE

1.

We explored the island in about, I dunno, fifteen minutes that first morning, some of us still dripping from our saltwater dunking when the high tide tried to carry off our rucksacks. There was something cute about an island that you can explore on foot in a quarter hour.

At sunup, a flock of seabirds took to the air from a nesting place atop the big rock in the middle of the island. We followed the raucous noise through the coconut palms to the nesting grounds, at its highest point maybe twenty-five feet above sea level. The birds screamed at us, but did not seem afraid. Too few generations of them exposed to guns, I suppose.

Colin aided their education by bringing one down out of the air with a rock and came trotting back with the feathery corpse dangling proudly in his fist. "It'll taste like chicken!" he assured us. He looked around doubtfully. "Who here knows how to pluck and dress a bird, eh?"

Vanity set about looking for eggs to steal; I thought it was the wrong time of year, but no doubt she wanted to cook up a superb lunch to maintain her stranglehold on absolute power.

Meanwhile Victor, in his chain-mail shirt, levitated about thirty feet into the air, above the palm tree crowns, to get a commanding view of the island. I joined him in midair (obviously not because I needed elevation to see over objects).

Vanity Island was long and narrow, maybe three miles long and half a mile wide, a rough dagger of land with no springs or other freshwater sources. To my special senses the ring of reef all around the island was black with utter uselessness, with an interior nature that was coarse, crooked, treacherous. To the north, the reef extended nearly half a mile.

There were small lagoons filled with brackish water, and the sides carved by heavy tools: These were the remnant of some old excavation. Also black with uselessness.

I decided my race must be city folk. No matter how pretty nature's wild might seem to the human eye, every object in a cityscape is man-made and shines with human purposes, human uses.

We discovered a ditch of mud overgrown with weeds, marked by the stumps of man-made posts. This formed the remains of a road or tramway running from a grove of coconut trees near the middle of the island down to the westernmost jut of the island. We followed the ditch to what seemed the ruins of a plantation. We could see the square discolorations, mounds of collapsed timber and tin overgrown with weed, grass, and fern, where there had been houses or barracks. The ground here was overrun with brilliant flowers and edible plants whose ancestors had long ago escaped from decorative window boxes and vegetable gardens. Some of the flowers were European and had killed off the native flora.

Some of the weird bulbs dangling in heavy clusters from the trees shone brightly in my utility sense. They were useful to us. I looked inside the green husk and saw a golden oblong I had only seen carved in fruit dishes before. It took me a moment to figure out that these plants growing everywhere were papayas: We were not going to starve.

There was one place where the builders had poured concrete for a foundation: a blank square of gray surrounded by ferns and palm trees, empty except for the whitish stain where lead pipes had rusted to nothing.

I saw a spot beneath the ground where the texture was different, and, more out of curiosity than anything else, I moved into the "red" direction, pushed my way through the heavy medium of hyperspace, and stepped past the ground without moving through it. The interior volume of the earth was like a flat wall next to me. Embedded in it was a buried rubbish heap. I gathered the mass in my tendrils, picked it up (or, should I say, picked it "blue" since it was moving in a direction neither up nor down, left nor right), and hauled it up a few feet (and now I do mean "up") to clear the surface of the soil, and pushed it redward into three-space.

It was rubbish. Victor and Quentin actually poked with some interest through the find, coming up with a rusted tin box, cigarette butts, a slender notebook. The interior papers had long ago turned to mulch, but the waxy leather cover was still intact. The notebook cover read MANGAREVAN EXPEDI-

TION, BISHOP MUSEUM, OCTOBER 1934. Also in the trove was dirt-caked remains of a stemwinder pocket watch. The round leaf of the timepiece was intact. Its inner face had been etched with the legend USS ANNAPOLIS MCMVI.

"Well!" said Vanity. "They're not coming back anytime soon. We have the place to ourselves!"

Vanity outlined her three-step program: Step one, we were all to help build a serviceable campsite; step two, we were all to experiment with our newfound powers and abilities, making nightly reports on progress; step three, we had to be ready in three weeks for what Vanity called a final exam. When pressed, she gave no hint what she meant by a final exam, but she smiled a pretty smile.

"First step of step one!" she announced. "Amelia will help us all live like civilized boys and girls."

"Help how?" I asked suspiciously.

"Guess who I've picked to dig the latrine?"

2.

Vanity divided all our chores into campwork and homework. Yes, we still had homework. Who says you get to leave it behind when you graduate?

My basic camp chore for the next two weeks, aside from dishwashing, was lumberjack. (Lumberjackess? Lumberjane?) Anyway, was chopping down trees. So, yes, I got the axe. I mean, I got to use the axe. I did it for maybe one, two hours a day in the mornings before it got really hot. Vanity used the excuse that I was the only one who could distort gravity to make certain the tree toppled in a safe direction. I thought it was a really unfair reason to give me the chore. I mean, it made perfect sense, so, as far as I was concerned, it was really unfair.

What did we need wood for? Practically everything. Firewood for heat and light, to save our limited supply of butane. A lean-to to act as a windbreak. A wooden foundation to pitch our two tents on, to keep us above the soggy, rocky, guano-stained soil. An A-frame to hold our tarp. A screen for the latrine, and guess who ended up doing most of the digging?

The excuse was that I could distort gravity to make the soil light, and see through the ground to avoid rocks and roots. So unfair.

To make matters worse, Colin came by during the afternoon when I was knee-deep in soil to watch me dig. It was hot in the tropics, so I was wearing my yellow one-piece bathing suit, and had my hair tied back to keep it out of the way. I was all sweaty and looked horrible, but Colin would stand in the shade leaning against a tree, chewing on the end of a fern and making unhelpful suggestions, and staring carefully at my bum whenever I bent over the shovel, giving me the wolf-eye like I was Miss Island or something. Jerk.

And I was mad at Victor. Why wasn't he coming by to stare at my legs while I dug? I slammed the shovel hard into the ground. Victor was a jerk, too. All boys are jerks.

In practically no time, we soon had a clean and serviceable campsite, with two tents, a suspended tarp that formed sort of a larger but unwalled tent, a windbreak, a fire pit with a tripod for the kettle, a laid-in firewood supply, a latrine, a Victor-built magic still for extracting fresh water from salt water, a laundry, and a place we called the "fishmarket," where our experiments, both successful and unsuccessful, in gutting and cleaning fish and shellfish we caught were performed.

We had brought nails, but the ones we had bought were too small (how were we to know?), and they bent into question-mark shapes when hammered into hard wood. So the camp furniture was clumsily lashed together with twine, at least until Victor discovered how to secrete some sort of resin or glue from his glands in a fashion I can only call disgusting.

Not bad for five kids raised in a mansion their whole lives, with servants and staff and jailers to wait on them.

It was ours.

3.

Oh, the nights! Campfire tales! Marshmallow toasts! Sort of. We toasted chunks of papaya instead, since our marshmallows floated away.

The times when I did not mind having chopped so much wood were when we made blazing bonfires in our nicely stone-paved fire pit. Crawling red and black logs of palmwood would send up a blaze, crackling with sap, and sparks would fly up like jeweled insects toward the whispering canopy. Between these leafy Venetian blinds, stars winked.

We would report on daily progress, those who made any, or talk about our dreams and our fears, or crack jokes, or make fun of each other.

Victor's reports were usually terse: He spent his afternoons underwater offshore, trying to build or, rather, grow a particle accelerator out of a coral bed into which he'd designed cells like those in an electric eel. He would be speaking one moment about peroxisomes and sphingolipids, alleles and

demes, and the next about RF cavity resonators, Cockcroft-Walton generators or voltage multipliers, or plasma wakefield acceleration.

Quentin's reports were even more incomprehensible: He had covered the
concrete floor of the abandoned cabin with chalk and paint, and each night
he interviewed a different creature, and at report times, he could produce
lists of the various felonies and enormities they could commit, "at the behest
of the operator," or the liberal arts they could teach. He ended every report
with a plea to Vanity to go back to civilization for a day, so he could reference
books on goetics, or silver and tin to forge talismans, materials to build a
proper anthanor.

It was like living on an island with Nikola Tesla and Johann Faust.

Vanity, being the captain of the group, did not give reports, but she had
found a geologically impossible series of caves to the south of the island,
erected different laws of nature in each, and was trying to tinker slowly with
them. She ordered us to avoid the spot. The caves grew prone to odd noises
and earth tremors, but Vanity did not quit. Being buried alive simply held no
terror for her. "What are the odds the rock will be solid, and not have a hidden door?" she asked dismissively.

Colin refused to give reports. He would talk smugly about how his paradigm ". . . had no research, no astrology, no physics, no demonology. Focus
my emotions, they come to a point, and everything I'm trying to do just
clicks into place. I'm a point-and-click interface! User-friendly!"

"Music!" Vanity would say. "You should be practicing music! It's the key
to your powers!"

"Gah! Music is my worst class."

"How can you tell," I chimed in sweetly, "among so many contenders for
the honor, Colin?"

"I still haven't done my Mozart paper for Miss . . . Jesus nailed up a tree!
I'm never going to have to do that paper. Not ever. No symphony in E-flat.
No Baroque period, no Classical, no Romantic. I don't have any worst class
anymore. Or a best class! I don't have any class at all!"

So he stood, with his eyes illuminated by the beatific vision of Life without School. His eyes were blind with happiness, and his mouth hung open in
a smile.

I opened my mouth to make the obvious joke, but closed it again. He was
just too happy.

4.

On the third night, Vanity told me to take up my old office of Keeper of the Tales, and lead the group in the Telling once more: those dim fragments of memory we recalled from before our capture. The night became solemn. We each stood up before the fire and took our turns speaking.

It was strange, strange to hear those old words spoken, now, by young men and women, which had once been spoken only by children. Vanity's gold and silver dogs; Victor in space, making a worm out of falling rain; Quentin seeing a giant in the ice; Colin, urged on by his brothers, stealing a wolf pelt from the roofpole of his father's lodge, which held up the North Star. And me, remembering a pool like a globe larger than universes, in which the stars and worlds swam; and one small world was dark, a tiny world where time, death, and entropy were sovereign.

We spoke the words; we vowed not to forget. We promised each other we would escape and find our families again, our folk who loved us.

Colin said, "And we have not done it yet. We are still in prison. This world is not of our making."

Victor said, "I am not sure it is of their making, either. The Olympians seized control from an older being: Saturn, Father Time. He made this place. And what he seized to remake is a fragment of a larger, Uranian universe, a large volume, more disorganized."

"Disorganized, or free?" I asked.

Quentin said softly, "I think I understand my story now."

We all turned to look at him. He sat with his back to the fire, so that his face was a mass of shadow, and red light beat against his shoulders and back. "Certain things were explained to me by mighty spirits, Principalities, Dominions, and Potentates from places lower than Heaven. The chamber I remember in my father's house, the one filled with statues and chessmen, was my father's wardrobe. What looked like chessmen to me were figurines of human beings, who are naturally much smaller than my people. Those are bodies the Fallen can wear.

"The harp in his lap was the kantele, made of the bones of the leviathan and strung with the hair of fallen angels, who in grief and pride sheared their locks, as the ambrosial fragrance lingering there caused them the pain of memory.

"My father is Väinämöinen, who was an old man before he was born, spending seven hundred and thirty years in his mother's womb. The Greeks called him Proteus, the First, the Old Man of the Sea. The blind old women I remember are my three mothers, the Graeae, the Gray Sisters, white-haired hags from birth. They had but one eye and one tooth between them, which they had to pass back and forth: Only one at a time could see, or could chew."

He paused and wiped his eyes, perhaps in weariness, perhaps to brush away a tear. "I was supposed to help them. My mothers, I mean. To lead one around by the hand, when it wasn't her turn to use the eye; to moisten bread in wine for another to gnaw, when it wasn't her turn to use the tooth. My mothers were not godlike beings, not Titans, but cripples. Handicapped, I mean."

Victor said, "Did they also share one, um . . . I mean, how were you born from three women? Physically, how was it done?"

Quentin scowled. "I assume I was born in sections and joined. Plato speaks of the three parts of the soul: the reason, the passions, the appetites. Certainly I feel always as if my conscience, my body, and my spirit are at odds, born of different mothers, as if I am pulled on a rack between opposites. I thought every man felt this way, like a fallen creature who dimly remembers he should be better."

Victor said, "I don't feel the way Quentin describes. One conforms one's actions to logic. There are no other alternatives."

Colin belched loudly, and said, "I don't feel that way, either. Should be better? If anything, I feel like I should be worse. You know, a drunk or something. A guy who gets in fights. To live up to my Irish heritage."

I said, "That is such a stereotype!"

He shrugged. "I'm allowed, that I am. They're my people, after all. Faith and begorra!"

"But you're not really Irish. You've never set foot in Ireland."

"Lassie," he said expansively, "put a stout pint o' bitter in me good right hand, and a stout stick in me left, and put an orange Ulsterman before me, stout or not, and by Saint Patty, you'll see what a good son of Eire I am, and how many heads I can break, drunk or sober."

Vanity said, "None of you are Irish or Welsh or English or anything. Even I am not British. I'm Greek or Albanian or something. From Corcyra. You are not human beings."

Quentin said with quiet emphasis, "We are indeed human beings. We are merely not *Homo sapiens*. *Homo sapiens* is a species, something into which one is born. Humanity one chooses. Men who choose inhumanity are merely upright beasts."

Vanity changed the subject. "I am curious why we have not been able to get our real, original memories back. I used to be a princess: I saved Odysseus, according to Homer. I'm like the only woman in the whole dumb poem who is nice to anyone! I'm . . ." Her face grew blank.

"What is it?" asked Quentin, worried.

". . . I'm responsible. In *The Odyssey,* at the end, the island of Corcyra: It's blockaded. A stone mountain fills the harbor, and the ships are cut off from reaching the human world ever again. Neptune, the sea-god, punishes the Phaeacians for having helped Odysseus. But they didn't help him. I did. According to the poem, I mean. I destroyed the Phaeacians. Is that—is that why they sent me away? Is that why my mother and father sent me off to be a hostage, to be put in prison? And such a cruel prison! Aristotle said I married and had a baby. My own baby! If a woman has a baby, she can't really forget him, right?"

Vanity's voice (it was hard to make out expressions in the firelight) held such a note of pain that a moment of silence passed.

She broke the silence: "Quentin, can you get your Mafia friends, your imps or whatever they are, to find out more about us? How do we get our original selves back? Colin, or anyone else, if you have an idea, an experiment you can try, a messenger from another world you can contact, your Fearless Leader authorizes the attempt."

Quentin said, "I am curious myself. Was I sent into this world as a penance? What did I do to deserve it?" He shook his head.

5.

I spent more than one afternoon looking into Victor's nervous system, trying to find and stimulate monads, or set the meaningless ripples of atoms in motion that would stimulate his buried memories.

Quentin worked his astronomical calculations and walked in dreams with fantastic beings who appeared in the forms of raven-headed men, or mighty kings mounted on dromedaries and holding vipers.

Colin patiently wove himself a hammock and spent his afternoons in it, going on a dream-quest, or so he said, to find the lost dreams of our former lives.

Each night before the campfire, we shared what results we could.

6.

Colin, one night, said he had remembered some things, including something of Quentin's and Vanity's.

"I talked to my brother Phantasmos tonight. He said that this world I'm trapped in is a dream, just a bigger and nastier one than most, because it is the one dream that says no other dreams are real. That is why men forget dreams on waking here—to preserve the illusion. Saturn was originally one of us, a Dream-Lord of Cimmeria, the world without sunlight, but he found a way to deceive the night sky, and separate Uranus and Gaea. The stars used to walk freely on Earth, back when Earth and Heaven were merely two equal dreams, and there was no solid matter to hinder mankind, or to make them greedy for material things.

"The divorce of Heaven and Earth changed all that. The only way for the stars to reach Earth now was a one-way dive: a falling star. They cannot get back up again. This is the cool part: I know what part of Quentin's tale means. Listen up, Big Q. Those silver mountains where the stars fall down, that is a real place, a landing zone, sort of, for bearded comets and spirits from the astral heavens to touch down and enter the material world. Some fell through pride or because they lusted after the daughters of mankind, but others came down willingly, even though they can't go back. That big giant in your dream is Ouranos, the eldest primal god: the father of Cosmos and Chaos both. The little dwarves chipping him out of the ice, Phantasmos said were Hours and Days, wearing away at the chains Father Time put on Eternity. Time itself will end when Eternity breaks free and rises up as lord of all this world again.

"And, Vanity, my brother knew you, too. Those dogs of silver and gold at your house are real, and so are the walking tripods that cook food of their own accord. These are robots or golems, living metal creatures made by Hephaestus, who—guess what?—is that same big ugly guy Amelia met who tried to hire her. Lord Talbot, who owns the estate where we were raised. My brother knows your people because the Phaeacians helped the Sons of Morpheus, the Lords of the Dark.

" 'Your people are smugglers,' my brother said. I am hoping he means, you know, good smugglers, lovable rogues like the Scarecrow of Romney Marsh, or Han Solo or something, not just drug-runners."

7.

Vanity asked Colin, "What did they smuggle? My people, I mean?"

Colin poked the fire with a stick, throwing up a spray of sparks, and in the sudden light I saw his eyes dancing. "I don't know what they smuggled in from other worlds, but from my home, from dreamland, they smuggled dreams. That's what my brother told me. I don't know what it means. He said a time had come, in ancient days, when all the dreams of man had died, and men bowed and sacrificed to unworthy gods, lecherous and cruel. Odysseus spied on the paths through the realm of shadows and found the empty kingdom of Lord Dis was not the final place to which men's souls fled—there was an Elysium beyond—and so the Phaeacians help him smuggle the truth back to mankind. The myth of Er, the tales of Zoroaster, legends hinting that this material world is but a dismal dream from which we wake to brightest sunlight—Socrates knew the truth of it, which is why he scoffs at Homer."

Vanity, for some reason not clear to me, looked guiltily at Quentin, and then asked Colin, "Did he say anything else? About Odysseus, I mean. Did your brother Phantasmos say anything else about Odysseus?"

"In my land, in Cimmeria, he is regarded as a great hero. He was much further traveled than he let on. He sailed to the foot of Mount Purgatory in the South Pole, which is this mountain so tall that tresses of the trees of the Earthly Paradise atop it scrape the bottom of the turning dome of Heaven, and starlight is tangled in their leaves and twigs. Odysseus sailed beyond the sunset, and he would not let the gods tell him no. So, buck up, Red." And then he turned to me, and said, "Your kind of guy, too, Amelia. You know, to boldly go where no man has gone before."

And he threw out his chest, and said,

> . . . Come, my friends.
> 'Tis not too late to seek a newer world.
> Push off, and sitting well in order smite
> The sounding furrows: for my purpose holds
> To sail beyond the sunset, and the baths
> Of all the western stars, until I die.

We all clapped for him, and I clapped loudest of all. (Gee. Sometimes I could almost like Colin, you know? If he weren't such a jackass.)

8.

One night it was Victor's turn.

Victor said, "I remember the name of my teacher: It was Ormenus."

"I remember walking on an island barren of all life. All around me were yellow clouds: poison gas or molecular dissembler engines, Styx-water mixed with sulfur. It was war: The Olympians were driving us out of our homes, and we were leaving nothing alive behind.

"Almost nothing. There were only two, an old woman and a young, of our race we left. Maleco and Dexithea were their names. The Olympians favored them, as they were the first to erect statues to the gods. We walked away across the dead soil, without any word of farewell, regret, or blame. They stood and watched us depart as we walked into the sea.

"My people are stoic and dispassionate; they act without anger but kill without mercy. They do not regard life as a sacred thing, since it is merely a complex mechanism made of atoms in motion. But we do have duties, and one of the duties, the one my teacher placed within my long-term memory, was that the strong protect the weak. Otherwise, we would be destroyed by creatures stronger than we, our creators. Any living machinery we create, we also must encode this same thought-mechanism into them, so that the thought is passed though the generations like a virus.

"Another thought-chain Amelia found and stimulated in me is this: I remember a necklace I helped forge for someone named Harmonia. It was shaped like an amphisbaena, a two-headed snake, and the two mouths clasped ornaments of jasper and moonstone. Each gem, each molecule, even each atom, contained parts of the code of prior ages of the Earth, earlier evolutionary stages of the cosmos, reflected in miniature.

"Built into the scales and patterns of the necklace were energy-bundles related to earlier strata of evolution, including the primal atom-shapes adapted to the conditions of the early universe. The necklace was a history: but a cyclic history, for one head eats and consumes the other, without ending and without beginning.

"The cosmos undergoes periodic universal conflagrations, a concentration of matter that compresses, builds up heat, and destroys sun, moon, stars, void, earth, ocean—everything. This is the meaning of the jasper stone, which is ruddy. After the conflagration consumes all, the universe is empty again. This is the meaning of the moonstone, which is clear.

"The ashes consist of atoms falling in straight lines through the void.

Some atoms contain a swerve or variation which causes them to collide. The collisions, happening with increasing frequency as immense time passes, sort the atoms (who are attracted and repelled from each other in different ways) into their various elements and molecules. Certain molecules are more complex, and form self-replicating chains of elements, and they make more like themselves out of the falling atoms. Complex enough self-replicating mechanisms seem to be self-aware, because the actions of internal mechanism, their nervous systems, retain shapes or impressions of previous events. I can show you the math if anyone is interested.

"As befits a mechanical cosmos, the early creatures were mechanisms of survival, like insects, without emotion. Those that had maladaptive survival behaviors did not survive and did not pass on the molecular programming of their behaviors to their next generation.

"I remember being taught that Saturn was one of us. But the swerve, the unexpected motion of certain of his brain atoms, broke his programming. He is a mutant. He used his cryptognosis to find a new method of controlling created life-mechanisms. He gave them illusions, passions, and emotions. He divorced their internal reality from strict empirical reality. They were no longer insects or living robots, but birds, mammals, man. Our form of life was superceded. There was war. We were driven into the void. Saturn invented false thoughts, lies, false hopes. This gave his creatures some extra incentives to survive that we did not possess."

Victor stood in the darkness, frowning at the fire. "Maybe he invented love. You can see why I am not so certain that our people are the good guys.

"We must have independent confirmation before we proceed. To be independent, we must be free of interference. To be free, we must gain strength. This time on the island is nothing but a brief respite between battles. A breather."

And I said, "A holiday."

He smiled at me, one of his rare smiles. "A holiday, if you like."

"Have a papaya chunk. I burned it just for you."

He came, and lay down beside me, where I was sitting cross-legged by the fire, and he put his head in my lap and ate the "marshmallow" out of my hands. "Ah, such a good cook you are, Amelia. You'll make someone a fine wife someday."

I cannot tell you how many times I replayed that scene in my mind, wondering if he meant what I think he meant.

If we fell into enemy hands again, they would take that memory from me, the firelight, Victor, his golden hair on my bare leg, his green eyes filled, for once, with warmth and humor. A man of duty, and a man of honor: a man without fear.

9.

One night not long after that, while I was asleep, I saw Colin walking toward me in the moonlight. He was dressed in black, and he wore a coronet, and his face was the face of a many-antlered stag and not that of a man. In that odd way that dreams have, it did not seem abnormal.

He drew a colored light out from his pouch. "My father gave me presents. Look what I found for you, Amelia. It was yours once, and I found it. A lost dream."

I never quite saw the thing in his hand. Perhaps it was like a wafer, and I ate it; or perhaps it was like a syrup, and I drank it; but most likely it was like a goblet of perfumed vapor, and I dipped my head to the rim of the cup and breathed the dream into me.

10.

I saw Myriagon.

It was my home. I saw the thousand-sided towers reaching through the myriad dimensions, golden with the layers of time-energy, windows shining with reflected thought-progressions like many-faceted crystals. I saw the highways made of nine directions of contemplation and four modes of existence, reaching down-up past folds in space to the Uttermost Singularity, that mysterious source of all-ness, brighter than a sun, whose infinitely recurving rays shone from the gravity-spires and polished mind-forms and hyperspheric domes of Myriagon, glittering on memory-images, or glancing trails of fire across the ten thousand layered sides of many-dimensional oceans held in tiny grails and falling teardrops.

The symphony fountains bubbled with fractal spaces and fractional dimensions, and strolling figures would pause, gemlike subuniverses in their hands, and draw the living waters into their vest-pocket dimensions, where each person kept spare bodies folded, useful laws of nature like colored webs of string. I saw grandees leaning on staffs made out of micro-time, to allow them to walk sideways across probabilities, and poets fingering instruments made of macro-time, to allow them to play the years, and send months and seasons like flowers over the heads of smiling demoiselles.

Between the towers were gardens made of folded origami shapes of virtue, crystallized forms of the morality energy, resplendent, wondrous, but much more glorious than the simple strands and webs of reciprocity I saw here.

I knew that the virtue gardens of my father were grander and wilder than those known elsewhere, for he had located that tiny spot of darkness Saturn made, and he saw the sorrowing of souls trapped in there, and he had vowed a great vow of compassion.

But none who walks into one of those virtue gardens returns unchanged, nor can the changes be known beforehand. The moral obligations affect and are affected by the observer.

In the dream, I emerged from my father's virtue garden, stern and frightened, and took a single step to activate a soul-path that hung to one side of me. The specialized cluster of hyperspatial bubbles wherein both my private chambers, and my childhood memories, dwelt were linked by this soul-path to a distant spot where a time-mirror hung. Its glass showed me images, not merely of linear future and past, but planes of probability, volumes of potential, hypervolumes of rationality. One image in the mirror of time shifted from being an alternative version of me to become my sister, the sweet Lampetia.

In the hands of Lampetia the Bright was a silver shepherd's crook, made of solidified time-energy taken from a logic tree. Her hair was disheveled, and her face was weary with tears shed for me. Behind her was a field of thought, and behind the field, the outer spaces and earlier time-segments of Myriagon: In this darkness, the simpler and older creatures of Myriagon rose up, roaring and lamenting.

Lampetia said, "Despite our father's pleas, O Phaethusa, do not look into the dark world; do not go into the tiny cosmos of crooked Saturn."

"I must," I said, or seemed to say in the dream. "The awkward primordial beings whom we displaced as rulers here, the original inhabitants, recall Saturn's great crime, and know how many living beings he trapped within the linear collapse of entropy, when cosmos was created. Shall all their suffering be in vain?"

"Why you, beloved Phaethusa? Why not me? The theft of those spirits, loyal to the Bright One, which Saturn in mirth calls the cattle of the sun, was as much my fault as yours, for we both crept into the Garden of Virtue and saw the moral obligations leading from our perfections into the lapsed worlds of Saturn."

I said, "I am more suited to go. There in the distance is the ocean of moral obligations. Here are the positive and negative values of each monad-atom. You may check my calculations."

She said, "Sister, a world where time flows in one direction only is a world where sins cannot be undone before their commission, and effect cannot precede cause! It is a world of terror, where sorrow is absolute, and death comes to all. How can you hope to return to us?"

I said, "Even now, another version of me meets with Father in the shining hall of all-knowing, where the energy of omniscience has been compressed into the mirrored substances on which his twenty-dimensional throne-world sits. That version was, is, and always shall be recently returned from the horrid capture I must suffer, if those who suffer more than I are to be saved. From that point of view, all this has been accomplished; all the horror is a distant memory."

"From that point of view!" she exclaimed. "Have you forgotten that, from that point of view, you will be trapped, and all this glory be forgotten: From that frame of reference, years and centuries must pass, and you must crawl, one second per second from past to future. You cannot imagine what the dark world is like: No! You cannot limit your imagination enough to imagine the limits."

I reached out with my own crosier, which was of gold, and took a box of folded eternity from a shelf in my chambers to bring it into this scene, where it retroactively had always been. From within the box, I drew out a garment of time, ten thousand years woven into a shining dress, delicate as dew, bright as the rosy dawn.

"Here!" I said. "Ten subjective millennia I will interpose between 'now' and the point at which I must depart. Join me in my frame of reference, and to us it will seem a century of centuries before my captivity begins. Do not weep. How can any sorrow be here, in a world where infinity, morality, eternity, are known and understood, and the light of the Primal Singularity illumes the segmented spaces of Myriagon, and the Hours wait on the King our father as his handmaidens?"

She said, "One of those Hours is already selected as your escort whose soft hands will lead you down the funnel of moral-energy and across the event horizon of the Inner Dimensions. Saturn himself will have been overthrown by the time you pass within the plenum of the enemy!"

I saw her take thoughts from her inner nature, and I saw the way she manipulated space to create a fold, or lapse. She did it right in front of me. It was the basic geometry of how to use the fourth dimension to lapse the third.

In large enough volumes, such a thing could create a universe. She was doing on a small scale what Saturn had done on a vast, unparalleled scale. His universe was merely a lapse, a space-warp, a singularity surrounded by an event horizon. My father, all of us, we were the people who were older and above that singularity: the prelapsarians.

The twist of space was shining like a jewel in her hand, and yet it was made of memory-substance, not matter.

"Take this parting gift from me," her soft voice cooed, "which I give to our ancient foes, the dark and horrent Lord of Dream. Morpheus will bring to you this dream, and emplace within your frame of reference, selecting a point in the time-stream when your consciousness might be reached."

"What is it?"

"Hope! Hope I give you! Once you are free of your captors, the greater things you are destined to accomplish will be made real. Were it not for Man, nobler souls than any the demiurge could have made (Saturn did but capture and demean them) all Myriagon would rise as one to oppose your downfall. The primal beings, more crude and more ancient than the bright children of your father, who dwelt in this place before us, hang thick as clouds about the tiny, dim spot of the material world, ready to close with it and crack it open like a seed, should any word of you come forth: Phlegon our bold cousin will prepare the Thousand-Dimensional Object!

"Remember that from our point of view, those of us who love you, you have already escaped and been welcomed with rejoicing arms back to us: Happiness and freedom are inevitable. Any world path you select will lead you back to us; your task is merely to find the shortest. Let this thought buoy you while you labor in that world where despair is absolute: Your first duty is escape. Accomplish that."

I woke with tears in my eyes.

I rolled over and shook Vanity awake. "I volunteered! I volunteered for this!"

Her hair was mussed with sleep, and her eyes half-closed. "Mm? Why are you crying, Amelia?"

"Because I'm an idiot!" I sobbed, "I volunteered! I could have stayed home!"

WORK AND DAYS

1.

Swimming time! My way of mixing business with pleasure was to follow Victor's example and perform my experiments underwater. Morning, noon, or evening, it was always a good time to swim.

I could hold my breath longer than a three-dimensional person (hint: a volume is only a cross-section of a hypervolume), and even when I dove deep, the pressure was less than the crushing oily thickness of hyperspace.

I did not have a book to read in my dreams, or a new body to build. But I could see how quickly I could switch my body sidewise into the fourth dimension, or rotate another aspect of my complex origami-folded body here and there into the environment, or find how far the curvature of local space would let me reach a limb. (From beneath the waterline, I could pluck a coconut from a tree ashore.)

And so I dove.

Not only was the water relaxing to swim in, but I could float on my back under a sky wider and bluer than any sky of England, and practice coordinating my internal energy signals: turning my senses on and off in different combinations, getting information bundles to take bypaths through hyperspace, or bouncing photons off the interiors of closed boxes, trying to pick up the usefulness and interior nature of distant islands, things like that. I had at least seven extra senses, not to mention internal kinesthetics. I looked at things.

The reef was colored more brightly than anything in the whole British Isles. I come from a gray place, after all, all drabs and duns. Here was something as strange as I had ever dreamed in youth of seeing; this was indeed the island beyond the horizon. Tropical fish as colorful as flowers would dart by, shining in the green sunlight, or all the red-gold worms of the reef would poke their heads at once back in their bone-crusted homes, so that the whole coral breathed white and pink. Segmented armored invertebrates would scuttle in the slow-motion underwater murk, stiff as knights, or insect-things with delicate eyes would peer from gem-hued rocks or cast-off shells, furtively imitating the beauty around them, camouflaged, in the midst of weird beauties of the undersea, moving from war to war. Jellies as lacy as a lady's parasol drifted by, in the same lazy warmth where I was drifting. It was the sum of all delight.

Or not quite all. You see, we'd reached a place where someone had been before. We were not at the edge of the map, not yet. Amelia Earhart would not have been content. Neil Armstrong would have won no fame for discovering Vanity Island.

I wanted to plant the Union Jack on some spot no Englishwoman had ever stepped before.

I wanted Mars.

2.

When I wasn't performing my own experiments, I would go by to watch Victor. His experimentation area was a little ways offshore in ninety-five fathoms of water. He said he wanted the water to dampen out any escaped high-energy particles, and for coolant mass.

His underwater skin was a thick, almost metallic, bluish hide, with goggle-eyes and extra horns and antennae for picking up microwaves and radioactivity.

(He still looked handsome to me. I could still see his unchanged internal nature. There were many advantages of possessing a multidimensional girlfriend, if only you would notice them, Victor!)

He would just anchor himself, motionless, near his gigantic coral-grown tube-shaped mechanism, which lay stretched along the seabed like a whale made of armor. No bubbles left his body; he had built some sort of exchange filters between his lungs to circulate carbon dioxide back into oxygen. Only the azure ray from his brow would dart here and there. His tools, varying in size from invisible clusters of artificial molecules to metallic caterpillar-shaped manipulators with as many arms as a Swiss Army knife, swam around him, and drilled, and bit, and severed, and jointed, and glued, and started chemical chain reactions. Around him there were always flares of burning substances, kilns and molecular sieves where he made new substances, little underwater volcanoes that sent columns of steam rushing surfaceward. The fish avoided the place.

The inside of the giant tubelike mechanism was clear enough to me: an amazing labyrinth of geometrical shapes, lines of lenses, carbon fiberoptics, energy cells, alternating layers of cathodes and anodes, rings of electromagnets, shells of lead and ribs of titanium-hard ceramic, lumps of heavy water held in special bladders, webs of controlling and sensory tissue, crystals like a million snowflakes interlocked into a dazzling complexity.

"What is it?" I finally asked him.

"My new body," he said. "If it works out. Or rather, a model of the instructions needed to make it. Get behind that lead shielding."

A mouth like a vise opened in the forward part of the structure, and a set of metallic lens-shapes clicked into place in the aperture. A line of white-hot steam erupted in the midst of the waters, joining the lenses with a distant sunken wreck Victor was using for target practice. I was momentarily blinded by the shock wave. When I could see again, I noticed the wreck had been cut in half, and an undersea mountain five miles farther beyond now had a neat hole drilled into it, large as the entrance to a coal mine, from which bubbling steam and mud poured.

He sent off a set of magnetic signals, which one of my higher senses could interpret. "Amelia, you are throwing off my results. When you are around, I cannot accelerate particles faster than that velocity you arbitrarily designate as the speed of light. Instead the energy required for the acceleration simply increases. My beam focus is distorted."

I could not answer him on his own wavelength, but I could dip a tendril-tip from the fourth dimension into his ear to carry sounds. "You are not taking into account that the accelerated particles increase in mass as they approach light speed."

"Illogical. Nothing comes from nothing; how could the particles be picking up mass without picking up additional substance? No, your paradigm is overwriting my results. I should be able to focus a beam more tightly, and use the different velocities of light-atoms so that the reflections of the faster-moving light-atoms will attract and correct the paths of the slower-moving light-atoms."

"Light doesn't come in atoms," I explained. "It is a wave-particle, which, to outside observers, all seem to travel at the same speed in a vacuum. It—"

"Please, Amelia," he interrupted. "You are throwing off my results. We are short on time."

He was right. I turned and sped off in a rush of accelerated water. Our final exam was only a week away.

I am sure I was not crying. It's stupid to cry. Besides, the water would have hidden it.

3.

The three weeks were nearly done. My reports at night were even more incomprehensible than Victor's or Quentin's. Simply, no one could follow what I was saying. They could not imagine a hypercube, or follow the math used to describe one. I was tired of Vanity and the boys giving me funny looks: I had to try experiments whose results they would understand. Something plain. Something clear.

Once I tried playing with the fishes. I reached into their governing monads, the point of nonbeing where their material and mental states overlapped, and tried to give them more free will. Free will is always good, right?

Five days later, the last Saturday before Vanity's dreaded exam, came a strange night. A school of my fishes levitated out of the water, glowing with unearthly fire all over their scales, and the coral growths they drifted across turned into bubbles of some substance harder than jade.

Colin was on watch; we woke to the sound of him screaming in panic. Rushing out of the tent stark naked (who uses a nightshirt in the tropics?), I was in time to see a line of twelve bloated sea-forms, glowing like fireflies, bobbing toward us through the trees, their little mouths opening and shutting.

Quentin tapped on the ground with his staff, and words like slithering snakes shivered from his mouth. A dark thing it was not good to look at too closely reached out from behind the trees and began snatching up the little fire-fishes, one by one.

Victor said, "Leader, should we keep them for study?"

Vanity, crouched in the tent flap, said in a shaky voice, "The world, the universe, is not paying attention to them right. They're not . . . right. I think the laws of nature don't like them. Kill them."

Victor waved his hand. Nails bent awry during early, unsuccessful experiments in carpentry, Victor had not thrown away. Now they came out of a neatly labeled pouch on his belt, flew through the air at twice the speed of sound. The shrapnel splashed fishy guts across the trees, where they glittered with unnatural gemlike fire, dripping against gravity.

He also picked up a dropcloth and draped it over my shoulders, and wrapped it around me, very gently.

Colin, for once, had not been staring at me. He was watching the little fiery silver shapes dissolve. "We can deform reality, can't we?"

I nodded. "Yeah. We're dangerous people."

Victor said, "Good. Maybe if we are dangerous enough, we can kill the enemy, and stay alive. Leader, do you want me to gather those fish? As a food supply?"

Vanity shivered, and shook her head. "We're not eating those. Amelia, was that your handiwork?"

I nodded. "Yes, ma'am. I increased the inclination of the latitude of action. I was trying to splay the number of possible futures to give them more free will."

"Colin, since it was Amelia's paradigm, you're on burial detail. Quentin, if Colin needs to be inspired with how to keep the dead fish . . . normal . . . you know, not enough free will to move around as icky corpses or something, can you inspire him? Do you have a spell for keeping fish, um, fishy?"

Quentin bowed, touching his forelock. "Yes, Leader. I can tell him the true name of the first salmon."

To me she said quietly, "Keep the trick in mind to use against an enemy weapon or something. But don't be rash, Amelia. Work with Colin if things get out of hand."

(Work with Colin? Colin, the walking bag of sperm? No, ma'am, thank you, ma'am.)

Vanity added, "And, Amelia . . ."

"Yes, Leader?"

Loud enough for the others to hear, she said, "This episode will not go on your permanent record, but our final exam is in three days. I am hoping for better results than this! Please keep that in mind, Miss Windrose."

Something clear. Something plain.

That was when I decided to see how high I could fly. Oh, yes.

Oh, yes indeed. I waited till no one was around.

4.

Dawn. The layabouts were still asleep. The air was crisp and the morning sea breeze was still cool. I stood on trampled ferns, and the scent of bruised grasses mingled with the ever-present smell of coconut palms.

I pulled on my leather flying jacket and donned my lucky aviatrix cap, buckled the chin strap, adjusted the goggles over my eyes. And the long white scarf: We mustn't forget the scarf! A lady pilot is practically naked without it.

I bent the world-lines to minimize gravity. I rotated my wings into Earth's three-space, so that fans of shining blue-white light seemed to be to the right and left of me. Little glints and highlights shone from the leaves around me, and I could feel the tickling warmth of higher-dimensional reflections on my cheeks.

And, then, a deep breath, bend the legs, and a little jump in the air. Up, up, and away.

The greedy Earth with its mindless, massive pull held me no longer.

The palm trees' crowns were below my toes, a feathery green lawn that soon dwindled to the toy garden a child might make with moss in a shoebox. The island was a streak of green and brown lost in a wide empty waste of water, blue and gray, crawling with ripples of white: Then it was a pebble; then it was a speck. The sheer space, the wild wideness of the ocean, was exhilarating, almost frightening.

But I was heading for an ocean wider and emptier far.

The thin white plumes of the clouds were below me now, a dazzle of white that seemed to rest on the indigo bosom of the ocean. The air had a width to it, a whiteness, I had not seen before. There was nothing around; the nearest island to us was still behind the visible horizon, even at this height.

I did not head straight up, as that was not the easiest way to gain altitude. I picked a spot above the horizon, bent the energies of gravity and timespace around me, and soared.

As I rose through ever-higher strata of atmosphere, I had to keep adjusting the contours in my fourth-dimensional body. This was a delicate balance of several factors.

For thrust, I was swimming in the heavier medium of four-space, being carried along by supermassive particles in that parallel continuum. The flows of heaver-than-matter substance in the fourth dimension were not even. From time to time I sensed (shining with utility) favorable currents in the thick medium, things like updrafts. I could sail up these not-quite-thermals with my blue-shining wing surfaces no three-dimensional wing could reach, and ride the current upward. When I reached the top of the not-thermal, I had to start pumping wings again. To get the best speed, I had to flatten and fold as much of my many-dimensional body as I could into the "plane" of the Earth's continuum, but I had to keep enough wing in four-space to grip the medium. This increased my drag.

For lift, I was not shooting rockets out of my boots or anything like that. I attempted the thing I had seen my sister Lampetia do in the dream: forming a lapse in space.

The resistance of the earthly gravity made folding space impossible at first. Then I discovered if I attempted a lapse on a submicroscopic level, where the position of particles of known mass was uncertain in any case, even the nearby mass of the Earth did not bother to hinder the effect.

You cannot really call it "falling up." It was a series of perspective adjustments taking place more rapidly than the acceleration due to gravity: My frame of reference was moving upward more quickly than I was falling downward within my frame of reference.

Imagine the space like a bit of paper. I fall down nine meters per second per second: I fold ten meters of the paper and introduce an uncertainty as to my location, and move up one inch across the fold. I snap the paper open, and find myself ten meters up: net gain of a meter.

In reality the effect was too small to see, a million times per square inch in continuous ripples down my body as I soared aloft. I could see little nets of light and dark shimmering down my limbs, as my submicroscopic-size, submicrosecond-long space warps were deflecting photons from their straightline paths. Even in the air, I looked like a swimmer in the water.

Spacelapsing is not so tiring as it sounds, and I was in good shape. It was like long-distance running. I was glad I put in all the hours at the gym at school: Whoever says athletics are unladylike—come, sir, and try to catch me in midair!

5.

I thought it would be cold this high, but the faster-than-sound friction of the ascent was heating my cap and jacket. I had to keep rotating several bodies (actually, three-dimensional cross-sections of one body) into and out of the three-space to give the skin of one body a moment in hyperspace to cool down before plunging it back into the screaming hurricane of air. (For obvious reasons, four-dimensional objects lose heat more slowly than three, but I found a heat-dispelling geometry.)

I could see the utility shining from my velocity. Too dim. Not useful. I was not achieving the speed I wanted.

I tried a new technique: finding the monads or controlling principles of the incoming air molecules. I granted them free will and asked them nicely not to buffet me. Oh, and while they were at it, could they form a cloud of breathable atmosphere at a temperature and pressure comfortable for me around my face? Thanks, and you are all darlings, little molecules.

This was a luxury, I admit. I had a dolphin-shaped fourth-dimensional body I could use in hyperspace that did not need to breathe. I could have used it, I suppose. But what girl does not like the feel of wind in her face? And my human face needed oxygen, so I asked the air molecules, and they did not seem to mind providing for me.

Of course, little things with free will could choose whether to be grateful, and some did not. But the statistical majority of them did as I suggested and did as their neighbors were doing, and there seemed to be a general drop of the amount of free will as peer pressure brought the halo of breathable air into conformity. My own little pressure suit without the suit. But it is the nonconformists who pull the stunts.

The air around my head flared up with strange light, and I saw I was leaving a contrail of multicolored smoke and swirls of glitter behind me. Some of the air molecules, granted their freedom, were deciding to turn into light or diamonds or notes of music or Cherenkov radiation. I had a tail like the aurora borealis shining behind.

But my speed increased, and the friction dropped. I also noticed that the thickness of hyperspace fell off much more quickly than the air pressure dropped. The difference between an inverse-square and an inverse-cube law, I suppose.

Higher and higher. Vast, so vast, this wide world: at fifty-five thousand meters, eight hundred kilometers of ocean were in one glance beneath my feet. It might have been a floor of rippled bluish marble, only inches from my pointed toes. Below, the sea was dark purple, its color made bluish by the intervening masses of air. The horizon was curved, and seemed to have a glowing blue swath of light following its bow. And above! Above the sky was black, the freedom of unobstructed outer space. I could see the dim, untwinkling lights of brighter stars, the colored points of planets.

Here, only my earthly eyes were useful. I could not pick up the internal natures of the distant worlds and suns, and their utility to me was nothing, so

far out of reach; I could sense no controlling principles, no degrees of variation or freedom, no bonds of moral obligations. Whatever dwelt among the
stars had nothing to do with earthly concerns. I wonder if you will understand me if I said, staring at the indifference of the cold heavens, that I never
felt less religious than in that moment, but staring at their majesty, the
grandeur, I never felt more. Cruel Saturn's created world was worthy of awe.

Lapsing space was easier this far from the Earth. The friction of hyperspace had dropped nearly to nothing, so that I could put more of my fourth-
dimensional limbs into the act, grab wider sections of the fabric of space,
and bend them more pliantly.

The air was too thin, and I was ready to attempt speeds more immense
than an atmosphere would permit. I was about to assume a shape something
more like a dolphin made of light: It was a cross-section of mine I suspected
might be spaceworthy. Vacuum and hard radiation form an environment
more welcoming than hyperspace, and my body could adapt.

A bright light below my feet and to the left pulled at my attention. I rotated back to my earthly form, which has the best eyesight, and pulled in my
extra energy-fans, so that I was little more than a girl in a brown jacket and
goggles, in free fall, weightless. My scarf fluttered overhead.

I was seeing a glitter of the moral strands that tied me to some object below. In a moment, it became visible: a streamlined shape of golden metal, its
blunt head reddish with friction, an aura of heat around it. With my upper
senses, I could tell it was propelling itself upward by manipulating magnetic
energy, powered by some sort of controlled hydrogen-fusion reaction taking
place in the chest cavity. There was a trail of expelled metallic motes behind
it: Where cosmic rays or other high-speed particles had disturbed the body
on a cellular level, it had ejected the damaged tissue.

And I saw its inner nature: powerful, masculine, rational, slightly worried,
slightly impatient. Victor Triumph.

We matched velocities, and the golden humanoid shape directed a beam
of radio-energy in my direction. Like all forms of communication, I can read
the internal nature and intention of the message, even if I cannot pick up the
radio blips in which it is coded.

"Amelia, this was gross negligence on your part. Your contrail is leaking
exotic particles that don't exist in nature, some of them radioactive and
highly visible. You may have given away our position. Come back down to
Earth. We are going to have to sneak back to the island by a circuitous route.
Vanity is going to have to arrange some sort of punishment."

6.

I would have been more in a mood to be chastised by Leader Vanity if I hadn't reported to her just as she was posing nude for little Quentin. Quentin had dug up some white mud that, with Victor's help (and of course I noticed that no one can get anything done without Victor's help, the man who should really have been in charge this whole time) had been transmogrified via molecular engines into a serviceable fine clay. Quentin had no kiln other than a corner of concrete with some parts of a stone wall still standing, but he had Victor to come by and superheat his clay figurines into porcelain.

So there she was, kneeling with her hands up in her hair, elbows up and back arched, not exactly the pose of the Venus de Milo, and here was Quentin, wearing little more than shorts and a smock, all covered with clay, scraping with a sharpened wooden spoon at the five-foot-tall mass of white clay he had heaped up before him. To one side was a bucket of water in which a rolled-up shirt was soaking, an impromptu sponge.

There were other figurines sitting in the shade of a tarp along a section of broken wall, about a dozen, and all were small: a seagull, a mouse, a fish, a snake, all perfectly realistic and glazed white. The face and shoulders only just now emerging from the clay mass did look remarkably like Vanity. Professional-level work. It was a skill I never would have suspected in Quentin.

She saw me, and must have seen the dubious look on my face, for she stood and, with more dignity than I have seen her use before, excused Quentin. That's right; she told him to go and he just nodded his head, like a little bow, and went away without a word.

Now she wrapped herself in a white towel, and with her pinkish-red complexion, under the tropic daylight, even in the striped shade of the palms, she looked flushed and hot and too freckled. I suppose the equatorial clime did not agree with her. Certainly her look was disagreeable.

"Well, Miss Windrose?" she said, just as if she were a headmistress or something, not a girl younger and shorter than me wrapped in a towel.

"I was just doing as ordered, Leader."

"Breaking orders, you mean! Do you want to get us captured? Do you want to get us killed? No one goes off alone. That's the rule. All of you chaoticists have a weakness, a power you cannot stop. Suppose Echidn— I mean, suppose the fishmonger had just glanced up at you, just a glance, while you were flying off at Mach twenty-four! You would have just fallen to

Earth and died! You weren't even wearing a parachute! Then your family, your kingdom, your creatures, whatever the heck they are, the fourth-dimensional people, attack the universe and destroy everything! Is that what you want?"

"Leader, don't be silly," I said sharply. "We don't even have a parachute. Besides, at that speed, the reentry heat would have killed me much quicker. . . . Say, did I actually achieve Mach twenty-four?" That was below escape velocity, but it was above orbital velocity, at least for some altitudes.

"Victor measured it and yes it was fast and don't change the subject. What's your excuse?"

"Do I need an excuse, Vanity?" I said back. Well, maybe I raised my voice a little. It was hot here, and I wasn't wearing a nice cool towel, but a heavy leather jacket, jodhpurs, gloves, scarf, and leather cap. "Do I need an excuse? You've been pushing me to try out my powers, to experiment, and now you're barking mad because I did what you said! You're snapping at me because I might have attracted spies, but did you say anything to Victor when he blew a hole in an undersea mountain with a death ray? You give one order and then directly contradict it, and you make these stupid work schedules, except Quentin never seems to have work to do: When is the last time he chopped down a tree?"

"Mr. Nemo," she said in a voice so icy that it hardly sounded like Vanity, "has successfully discovered how to emerge from his body and assume an insubstantial form. This could prove to be quite useful to our little company. Last night, he entered the body of the fish he made from clay, and animated it, and he swam quite naturally and freely in the sea. He has discovered the secret of how his people, the Fallen, make new shapes for themselves. In the meanwhile, you have discovered how to moon around after Victor and take leisurely swims in your bathing suit."

"At least I wear a bathing suit," I said with a snort. Okay, maybe I rolled my eyes a bit.

"That comment was quite a bit out of line, Miss Windrose, and you will apologize for it immediately." I swear she sounded just like Boggin when she said that. No emotion at all. Not "you shall apologize," like a demand, but "you will," like a predicted certainty.

No, not like Boggin. Like Nausicaa, a princess from a Bronze Age Greek culture of supernatural beings.

If I had been leader, and she'd caught me nude, I would have tried to make a joke out of it. I would have handled it better. I would have . . .

But I was not leader. Right or wrong, I had to support the group. So I apologized. "Sorry, Leader. Please forgive me, Leader."

"Apology accepted," she said curtly. "Let us say no more about it."

"How did you get to be leader, anyhow?" I burst out. That kind of surprised me. If you had asked, I would not have said I felt any resentment. But no eyeball can see its own interior; no mind can know its own buried thoughts.

"You were there. I cooked breakfast."

"That's so . . . so . . . chauvinist! It is such a stereotype! The girl cooking breakfast. Victor's a better cook than you! Victor's better at everything."

She crinkled her little freckled nose. "Is that what this is about? You think I am upstaging Victor? Listen, Amelia. The boys were all disorganized after our first campsite floated away. They needed something reassuring, domestic, orderly. I had to bring order to the chaos. I got things going, had firewood brought, found a clean pan. I notice when people are paying attention, what they are looking at. I notice details. I knew which foods each boy liked because I remembered what he had picked out in the stops during our supply run. Victor's a better cook, but he didn't think of feeding the depressed and disorganized troops.

"Once I did that, I had to organize the schedule for training. I had to decide," she said gravely. "There was no one to ask. On the one hand, there is a chance that any use of our powers can be detected by means we can only guess. Oracular owls or orbital spy-rays or periscopes from dimensions even you don't have a number for. On the other hand, we have to get stronger. We have to get smarter. We have to figure out what it is we can do that makes them so afraid of us. That means everyone works on schedule, including tree chopping to break up the monotony of experiments. Tell me: Did you enjoy getting back to them, after all that mindless work? Yes? So that's how I got to be leader. That is what leaders do.

"Speaking of what leaders do, I have good news and bad news. Bad news: I still have to assign you some sort of punishment detail, to keep order in the ranks. The good news is that we can throw you a birthday party after."

"What? No one knows when my birthday is."

"No one knows when baby Jesus was born, but there is a date all picked out for Christmas, isn't there? As leader, I can assign a date. Your birthday is the day after next. Then, the next bit of good news: the final exam!"

"Leader, what is going to be on the final? I mean, the reason why I got in trouble flying off . . . Well, you should tell us what we should be preparing for, right?"

"For the final, we are going to be sneaking back into civilization. Colin needs a piano or something. He should be practicing music. Quentin needs all sorts of supplies, everything from tarot cards to real clay. We need to replace missing mess gear."

"That doesn't seem that hard." I remember a distinct feeling of disappointment.

Now she smiled, and her eyes twinkled, and she knelt down again beside me to speak in a low voice. It is the kind of voice you use when you are telling a secret, whether there is anyone around or not. "We are going to see if we can help your old friend Sam. The drayman who gave you a lift."

Less than thirty-six hours later, after an afternoon of punishment chores I do not want to remember, and the most charming birthday I do not want to forget, we five were aboard the *Argent Nautilus,* in a fogbound Irish Sea, rolling and pitching in the choppy waves, and the smothering cold was leaving droplets on our thick woolen sea-coats.

Sam had mentioned to me that he had a nephew in an institution with a mental disease. I had once, half-jokingly, offered to grant him a wish. He wished for a cure.

Now we would see what we could do.

8

PALLID HOUNDS A-HUNTING

1.

This trip, we had bought supplies with more forethought. We had drifted off the coast of the Isle of Man. Quentin had passed across the waves as silently as a shadow, to approach Castletown, on the south of the island. He returned with the sweaters and jackets and caps we wore, and a heavy backpack filled with chow. We were still low on some things, but he had restocked our larder. There was no piano to buy for Colin on the Isle of Man.

"The severed head of Bran has not seen us yet," said Quentin as he stepped out of the shadows and down to the deck. "The Isle of Man is not part of the United Kingdom, merely a possession of the Crown. I saw the shivering ghosts of Vikings, still hungry for blood, but no sigils of Arthur, no ravens loyal to the spells of Elizabeth the First. Officially, I did not step foot on the soil Bran protects. Now, since we are coming on a mission of mercy, perhaps, even when we do, he will not inform the gods of our coming. Perhaps." He gave Vanity a look of doubt, but said no more. Very Victor-like.

A few hours later, after midnight, we had crossed the rough North Sea and were approaching the opposite coast. Quentin, on the bow, summoned friends of his from below the waters, while we all huddled in the stern, trying not to overhear the sinister whispers. But that worked, or something did, and the fog thickened as we crept silently into the mouth of the river Wear, with the lights of Sunderland above us. A short way up the river were the ancient stone bridges and modern iron shipyards of Durham.

Quentin hissed when we passed the peninsula where Durham Cathedral rose up against the foggy lights of the city. He announced that certain of his "covenants" would not operate here, since the bone of Saint Cuthbert scared his allies away.

Edgestow is just north of Stockton-on-Tees, not far from Durham. We disembarked and sent the *Argent Nautilus* away to lead Mestor's needle somewhere else, and we spent most of the night tramping down roads, or occasionally crossing fields and climbing over walls and hedgerows. (Yes, hedgerows, just the kind you think they don't make in England anymore, but this was the Northwest.)

It was a bitter January night, and the snow lay wet and thick on the ground, trampled into mud by the roads. The stars were hidden, but the moon rode veiled between tattered streamers of cold clouds.

Between my higher senses, Quentin's divining rod, Colin's hunches, and Victor's tapping into the global-positioning satellites, without trouble we found the tiny institution just before dawn.

We were all behind a snowy hedge, dressed in our thick blue coats and white turtlenecks, looking like a bunch of fishermen. Sneaky fishermen. The boys and Vanity were peering suspiciously down at an empty, snowy road—which looked sickly and yellow beneath the unflickering streetlamps—at the ugly cubical building of glass and concrete beyond.

We could see the ancient buttresses and Gothic spires of some ancient buildings on our side of the street. Perhaps the mental ward had originally been associated with the medical college here; at least, the solemn beautiful architecture of the ancient buildings looked like a campus to me, and I know what a campus looks like.

Orange light pollution lit the sky in one direction, and there was a dim noise of traffic elsewhere, but there was nothing in our immediate environment but those college buildings, an empty field we'd cut across, a white graveyard to one side, and beyond it, a chapel wearing a wimple of snow.

I should mention there was a smaller graveyard at the crossroads, not on the chapel grounds. Quentin, following a croaking raven and carrying an entrenching tool, went off to do his spooky business there, while we shivered in the cold, waiting. Warlocks are something like doctors, I guess. No matter how much you like them personally, there is quite a bit of nasty mess involved in their line of work.

By the time Quentin got back, Vanity was casing the joint through the snowy twigs of the hedge, and listening to Colin and Victor give her completely contradictory advice about a plan of attack. Vanity asked us all to report on what we could see.

I was standing farther from the hedge, two paces down the slope. I did not bother to turn my head in the direction of the modern building.

Now was my chance to show my time on the island had not been all wasted. I took my glass globe out of my pocket, unfolded it into a hypersphere. In that thick light, I could examine the immediate fourth-dimensional environment. A trick I'd learned allowed me to send the light down one of my limbs (a part of my body that looked like a strand of music) to shine it against distant objects. Down that same strand, I reached a cluster of sense-receptors.

The three-dimensional building was laid out before me like a blueprint. To my fourth-dimensional eyes, it looked flat. I could see internal natures, utility, monads, all that 4-D stuff. But now, I could agitate the photons in the area, give just enough of them free will to ask them to carry information back to my eyes, so that the number of nonconformist photons who went giggling off as rainbows was relatively small. In effect, I had just made the dimensional periscope Vanity mentioned earlier. Into any one of the squares of the rooms or corridors, I could dip a photon-freeing note of energy and get a 3-D picture of what was in there, too.

I reported my findings. "He's alone. Sleeping on a cot in a cell. Window has steel netting across it, and the door is locked. I can see wires on the main doors into the wing, but no security cameras or anything like that. The alarms back on campus were more sophisticated. There is one guy on guard duty, two floors down, and he is sleeping in his chair."

Vanity said, "Can you confirm that this is the right guy?"

To them, it must have looked like I merely reached my hand up into the air and had it bend strangely, turn red, vanish, and reappear. In my hand was a clipboard. I had merely picked it up with a gleaming whiplike tendril, pulled it "blue" an inch or two, and then pushed it "red" into the hand of my three-dimensional cross-section. One hundred yards in three-space, slightly longer than that in four-space, I could reach with some straining.

"Mortimer Finklestein," I read off the top sheet. "List of the stuff they are doping him with. What he eats, when he cra—uh, goes potty. Hunh. Here is the diagnosis and history. He was out hunting in Teesdale. Wandered off by himself. When his friends found him, he had the mind of a five-year-old."

Colin said, "I thought hunting was illegal now. No more toffs trampling through other people's gardens, you know, killing innocent foxes."

I checked the date. "This was years ago, back when Englishmen still had rights. He was in the estuary below Middlesbrough, hunting small game birds, which were every one as guilty as sin, I'm sure. Anyway, the diagnosis here is of a trauma to the diencephalic-mesencephalic core—anyone know what that means?"

"It's part of an auto," Colin offered.

"It's part of his head," Quentin said. "Cephalic is from the Latin for 'head.'"

"The chart mentions severe cognitive impairment. And something happened to his Ommaya and Gennarelli. No, wait, that's the name of the scale he was tested against." I breathed a sigh. "Leader, I'm sorry. I've studied grammar, logic, rhetoric, as well as astronomy, music, arithmetic, and geometry, but I cannot read a medical chart. This is written in another language only remotely related to the Queen's English. At a guess? Mortimer here went into the marsh and came out stupid. They think he fell and hit his head."

We had discussed the plans for this exhaustively during the boat ride. Vanity stepped down toward the road, found a manhole cover, which, at Victor's gesture, flew open silently. She descended a ladder to where, not by coincidence, she "found" a large underground river. She called her boat. Then she scampered back up the ladder.

She said, "We have our escape route, and our getaway boat coming. Amelia, is it obvious?"

I had to say, "Sort of. To me it looks like this big tube filled with river water just dipped out of the parallel plane where the dreamlands are and intersected the Earth continuum. I dunno. There are other fourth-dimensional topography features here, stuff from the cathedral and old Roman ruins, other old roads through hyperspace, hidden groves of trees at right angles to normal space. Druid stuff, I guess. Someone like you was really active here, years ago. Your river might pass unnoticed if a siren walks by, but it's not exactly hidden, either."

Vanity frowned. "In that case, let me keep the secret-passage-making to a minimum. We go in the front way. Victor, your turn."

He walked across the snowy road and we followed him.

I noticed invisible forces leaving his body and reaching up to nearby lampposts. "Victor!" I whispered. "Are you knocking out the cameras? I think those are just for traffic, not part of the hospital. You know, to catch jaywalkers and stuff. They're innocent."

Victor said darkly, "Cameras like that are always put up by men like Boggin. I am sure whoever put them up told his students they were for their own good, too, using the same jolly tones our Boggin uses."

At the front door, Victor manipulated the lock mechanism and the wires I described to him. The door clicked open. Quentin brought out from beneath his cloak a severed human hand dipped in wax, and he carefully lit each of the fingers on fire. Holding it before him, he strode down the corridors. He stood with his eerie candle between us and the main desk where the guard was sleeping, and the smoke from the candles reached like tentacles toward the guard's face. We all made noise as we crept past him, but somehow, the guard did not wake.

The elevators were locked down at night. Rather than asking us to trace wires and locks and fiddle with the unfamiliar controls, Vanity gave Colin the high sign. Colin grinned a wicked grin, stepping forward. He grew at least two inches, and his muscles swelled and thickened on his frame, until his coat buttons and seams were straining. Then, like some abominable snowman, he just plunged his bare hands into the steel doors and tore them from their tracks.

Victor had him tear one metal door in half, which made such a noise that it should have set the entire ward screaming, but Quentin's candle protected us, or something did. Colin thrust the broken door into the empty elevator shaft, and we all stepped on it, and Victor levitated us up to the third floor.

This time, before Colin could show off, I reached into the locking mechanism and removed the little iron pins through the untouched surface of the door, and the doors could be slid aside without further ado.

The corridor was a drab olive hue, thick-shadowed in the light of a single night-bulb held in a cage of wires on the ceiling. Vanity started looking at the room numbers painted on the wall, but I just took her elbow and pointed.

And here was our next locked door in an evening of locked doors.

I whispered, "There are five of us, and five ways to open this door. Who does the honor, Leader?"

Vanity whispered back, "How do you figure five?"

"Fourth dimension, magnetic powers, magic, brute strength. And you can open a locked door, too. I mean, you don't know for sure the lock is engaged, do you? No one knows what is inside a wall."

She shook her head. "I can only find a secret passage if there might be one. Here there is nothing I can work with: Too much attention has already been paid to these walls."

But Quentin said, "Leader! We cannot open this door."

"Why not?" she said. "Are you worried about the rules here? We're already breaking and entering."

He shook his head. "I don't know why, but I see the signs. This door is forbidden."

Vanity looked at me and I looked at the threads of moral energy in the place. "He's right," I said. "But I don't see anything like that on the other doors. Why is this door different? I wonder if we should abort."

Vanity said, "We can go in without touching the door."

Victor said, "To get in without touching the door requires we break in through an adjoining wall, the outside window, the ceiling, or the floor."

Vanity said, "Amelia, if you would . . . ?"

"Gladly, Leader."

I have no idea what it looked like to them. I asked them to close their eyes anyway. I stood with one foot in the corridor and one foot in the room, with my leg going "over" the wall in the red direction, without touching it. I picked up Vanity first, and ballet-lifted her from right to left, and I made sure there were no wrinkles or rotations when I flattened their paper-doll bodies back into the flat square that formed the room.

When it came Victor's turn, I balked. "Leader, I think it might be bad for him. He is kind of thinner than you people are in the fourth dimension. I don't want to hurt him."

Quentin said, "He can go through the door. It won't see him."

Blue light dazzled from Victor's head, and the lock clicked of its own accord, and he walked through. The azure light fell into the small, grim room and snuffed out Quentin's candle.

The man, Mortimer, stirred on the white metal-framed bed, opened his eyes, and sat up.

"Who're you?" His eyes were as blue and empty as a summer sky. Innocent. A child's eyes.

A dart of light left Victor's metallic third eye and flicked into the man's face. His eyelids drooped, and he lay back down, snoring before he hit the thin yellow pillow.

Vanity said, "What was that?"

Victor closed the door behind him. "Narcolepsy. I stimulated the pons area of the brain and activated his sleep cycle."

Vanity looked a little miffed that Victor had acted without waiting for orders, but she didn't say anything aside from, "Can you fix him?"

"Let me look." And the azure beam played over the young man's face for many minutes. "Leader, I have been instructed, programmed, in a science called cryptognosis, which involves the manipulation of the nervous system on a fine structural level. There is nothing physically wrong with his brain. If it is a spell, anything from Quentin's paradigm, I should have been unable to undo it."

Vanity said, "Should have been?"

Victor said, "The proper stimulation sequences are occurring, but the synapses in certain brain areas will not fire. I can detect the microvoltage changes on the dendrites, which should trigger corresponding actions in the axons, but nothing happens. There are no proteins that would attenuate the signals in operation."

"Amelia, report."

I said, "Something is lowering the utility, the usefulness of his brain cells to him. I see moral connections running into the past and future. There is a confusion of time-energy. There is something, some awareness, which is in the future, that reacts to changes in Mr. Finklestein here. Its interior nature is watchful and stern, but it has no free will. Its moral stance, um, changed, when Victor negated all the magic in the patient. I don't know what I am looking at. It could be natural. It could be artificial."

"Can you do your monad thing?"

I reached into the man's nervous system and straightened what I could. "Leader, I don't see a change. It is like it is something he's doing to himself, maybe? If he's not really hurt, could it be hypnosis? He has free will; he is just not using it."

Quentin said, "This sounds like it is up my alley, Leader. An enchantment, something that bound his will. Maybe he ran into a bad elf in the swamp? I suggest we retire to the graveyard across the street and let me try something. I know the formulae to summon and command the Great King and President called Zagam. He will appear at first in the form of a bull with gryphon's wings. He has the power to make fools witty. I need but a drop of blood from the patient."

I reached into a cabinet one floor down and several yards up the corridor. Quentin looked startled when my hand turned red and vanished and reappeared. "Sterile lancet?" I offered. "This is a hospital, you know."

Vanity unbuttoned her sea-coat and pulled her necklace out from her sweater. She was sweating. It had been cool outside, but the air in this small dun room was hot and close. "Let me see if I can get a more magical set of laws of nature working here, to help you out."

"You know," I said doubtfully, "if we mess up something here, it could be bad. I mean, we're trying to do neurosurgery on this guy without anyone's permission, and . . ."

No one was listening. They were all staring at Vanity's bosom. I mean, it is large and round and nicely shaped, but . . .

Oh. There was a face in the middle of the green stone around her neck. That was what the boys were staring at.

Vanity said, "Who are you?"

A fair soft voice seemed to have spoken, although it did not speak. It was like we were remembering words, not hearing words. A queenly face in the dim depth of the green stone had answered wordlessly: "Andromeda am I, the queen of Ethiopia's daughter, prideful Cassiopeia. In all the devastated lands from Philistia to Lebanon, none save the fairest could be found to sate the monster, and so to pay my mother's guilt, with modest piety, uncomplaining, with daughterish obedience, I chained myself to the sacrificial searock, to save the human lands from horrid Typhon's brood." Her eyes turned toward Victor as she spoke this. "Great Perseus me succored, who slew Medusa, cousin of the Graeae." Now she looked at Quentin. "And after life and death, Olympian Lord Terminus, All-highest, he who guards the boundary stone, opened the boundaries of starry night for me, had my figure placed within the heavens, a guide to mariners. The Phaeacians befriended my folk in times past, the mariners of Phoenicia and Tyre. I watch your silver ships even as Bran watches Cassiterides, the island of Tin. Ask of me, Daughter of Arete."

"Can you make the room here hold the laws of nature that will let Quentin cast his magic?"

The woman's voice hung in our memories, as if she had spoken: "There is no magic, only mysteries explained, and mysteries unexplained."

Quentin muttered, "See? As I've always said."

Vanity seemed at a loss. "Well—can you help us some other way?"

"I will bestow what grace is mine to give, for any demoiselle who suffers chains is mine, and any savior who breaks those chains, and you are both at once, Phaeacian. The young man is chained, but he is not one of mine: On your oath to harm him not, I will perform."

We all agreed.

In our memories, we heard her words: "Phobetor, Nightmare-prince, this room is yours: I gift it you."

The room did not change shape, nor did the moonlight falling in through the grille of the window darken, but something like that should have happened, because a strange dreamlike sensation crept over me, a sense that I could not move, or that the objects around me were alive, silently chuckling, merely holding into the familiar shapes of floor and bed out of a watchful malice.

Colin said, "Hey. I can see his dreams. He is dreaming right now."

Vanity said, "Colin, Amelia is freaking out. I think your dreamworld is bad for her. Can you do something?"

He pulled his eyes away from the figure on the bed. "Um. Like what, Red Leader?"

The man on the bed opened his eyes. It was horrible, like looking at a zombie. His mouth was open, and his voice came out, but I did not see any tongue or teeth. The lips did not move. It was like the real Mortimer was crouched below the bed, speaking up through a tube shoved through the back of a corpse. Nothing *looked* wrong, but it was horrible for the same reason dreams are horrible, when you dream about an empty white room with an empty wooden chair in it, and cannot remember why that terrifies you.

Colin was holding me by the shoulders, and Victor was standing behind me with his arm around my waist. Funny. I didn't remember them reaching for me.

"Amelia," said Colin. "Calm down. You have nothing to be afraid of. By the authority vested in me as a Prince of Chaos, son of Morpheus, I invite you into my realm, um, this whole room, the land on which it stands and the sky above, and all the rights, rents, and privileges appertaining thereto. There. Did anything happen?"

I said in a calm, slow voice: "His eyes are open. He's talking. Can't you hear him?"

"Amelia, stop screaming. Um." Colin shrugged. "Leader, what's going on?"

Vanity spoke up, "Ask her what the voice said."

I said, "I can hear you, Vanity. Mortimer is talking. He says he saw her bathing. The girl was naked. It was freezing winter, and the snow was on the sedge and swamp-grass, but she laughed and sported in the pool like it was a bath. Her dogs were blind, no eyes in the sockets, and white and pale as death. She set her dogs on him."

Colin said, "She's right. That is what I am seeing inside his head. There is a girl, maybe fourteen, fifteen. Athletic build, sort of Jewish-looking, olive-skinned, with her hair all pinned up. Huh. That's funny. She just turned and looked at me."

Vanity said, "Someone is watching us."

Colin said, "She's whistling for her dogs. How can she be doing that? This is something in his dream."

I spoke. My words sounded odd to me. "He is dreaming a real thing."

"Actaeon," said Quentin. "I told you about him before. His own hounds turn on him. I guess in the modern version, his brain cells turn on him. Leader, we had best start the retreat!"

Colin reached forward and touched the figure on the bed. Suddenly, the dream sensations left me. The man's eyes were closed again; his mouth was relaxed. Colin spoke in a voice of solemn command: "I release you from your nightmare. Be whole! I release you from the curse of the goddess! Wake! OH, BAT CRAP! She's coming! Don't any of you see her! She's coming with her dogs! Leader, whaddya wanna do?"

Vanity said in a voice that squeaked with panic, "Can any of you see anything?"

Victor said, "I think only Colin's laws of nature are working now."

Vanity clutched at her stone. "Okay. I can—"

I shouted, "Leader, no! Wait! I can see her, too. She is approaching through the dream-realm, a plane parallel to the plane of earth. But the world-paths curve away from this room. I don't think she can get into the room, not while you are maintaining a boundary with your green stone."

The moon shining in through the window changed suddenly, and an olive-skinned girl stood outside, looking in. She was dressed in a brief white tunic, leather leggings, and a forearm-guard on her right arm. In that hand, she held a bow that was as silver and lustrous as the moon. Atop her tightly bunned and netted hair, she wore a coronet shaped like a crescent. With her other hand, she was fishing an arrow from her ivory quiver. Her eyes were the color of moonlight, and eerie, and cold. Her internal nature was fierce and clean and young, untouched by any man.

"Chaotic creatures, dressed like humans, and standing in a house!" she said, and her voice was like a crystal goblet chiming. It was more regal than pretty, but it was the kind of voice that could say things like *off with their heads* or *throw them to the snakes* without any hint of pity or doubt. From the shape of her legs and her general trim, I could tell she'd be good at the hundred-meter dash. Her shoulders were broad and sinewy for a girl, the muscles sculpted from endlessly pulling a bowstring.

Victor raised his hand. "Miss, don't shoot! We're the hostages from Chaos. If we die, the war between Cosmos and Chaos starts again."

She rolled her silvery blind-seeming eyes in mirth. "You give commands to me, little boar piglet, little wolf cub? Your kind is my prey: I hunt you for sport. Cunning it is of you vile creatures to pretend to be the babies Father gave to Boreas. But the wise North Wind would never let the real hostages of Chaos escape his sight, would he? My Big Brother would know, for he sees everything, and Mavors would know, too. I will cut out your tongue for that lie, unhearted dragon-boy, and cook it for soup. You others I will stuff. Release your hostage!"

Vanity was standing there, her mouth open, her face blank with fear. I knew that look. I had seen it on her when she was called on in class, on days when we hadn't studied the lesson. Out of ideas.

I saw the morality webs fletch and twitch. "She means you, Leader. She thinks we've captured you."

I could see the dogs through the walls. They were coming out of the moon-lit clouds, silvery white, as if made of cloud-stuff, solidifying as they ran through the air. Blind things with red ears. Their internal nature was deadly and cold: These were things from Hell. Everyone heard them baying.

The queenly teenager said to me, "You have spoken out of turn, Un-known One. For that affront, I demand the sacrifice of life and limb and everything. Do you deny me?"

Quentin said quickly, "Don't answer! It is a trap. What are your orders, Leader?"

But the young goddess now turned her fierce gaze to Quentin. "A Fallen creature from the Pit? My! What craft your body has! I almost took you for a man, instead of one of mine. Every hair, every internal organ, is fitted in place. That is a masterpiece of sculpture. You even did the little veins and nerves. Well! Enough! Invite me into the wards, little magician—or else, by your silence, deny my right to step anywhere my hounds can track."

Colin said to Vanity. "Leader! I think I can take her. Just say the word." With a clang of ear-ringing noise, he broke the metal strut off the foot of the bed and hefted it as a bludgeon. It would have impressed a mortal.

The Huntress drew back her head: Her eyes were as cold and inhuman as arctic stars. "You think to lay hands on me, the Virgin, inviolate, divine, and sacred? This world, this human earth, this dirty spot within heavenly sphere, it is overwhelmed by all the bloodshed and pollutions of men, their stinking lusts, their cities a-drip with oil, their battlefields with carrion. Who told the Phaeacian to smuggle you into the world, sons of Chaos, dream things, Tar-tarians, soulless wights? Who discovered our weakness to you? Who told you of the madness of my adulterous Father, who did not slay the orphans of Chaos, those four children you impersonate? Was it Lady Cyprian? Was it the Whore of Heaven? Was it she? Who else is the enemy of purity? Who else hates the clean wilderness, the sacred chastity? Answer! Answer in the name of the untainted and fierce hatred only untouched maidens know!"

I saw the morality strands begin to wind around Quentin. "Leader! Have Andromeda shut off all magic! Quick!"

Vanity clutched at her stone. Green light throbbed through her fingers. The tendrils I could see were still issuing from the bow of the goddess, the substance of enchantment, reaching here and there, but they could not enter the room. On the other side of the locked door, a pack of hounds material- ized suddenly in the moonlight. Also in the bed cells to the left and right of us, in the adjacent rooms.

"Leader, I can see where the dog packs are! We're surrounded!"

Quentin bowed and said to the goddess, "Diane Artemis, mighty Potnia Theron, Mistress of the Wild, who is called also Courotrophos the Nour- isher, Locheia and Agrotora, Healer and Huntress, Shining One, Born of Leto! We have not forgotten your names nor ever held your shrine in dis- honor! We proffer you no disrespect, and deeply do we genuflect to you, sovereign goddess, White Lady, Maiden of Heaven! We do not disobey the wise commands of any god or goddess, we do not meddle with sacred things, but in preserving the world, we do your will and do not oppose it. . . ."

"Phoebe," she said, waving her bow in the air as if to clear away cobwebs. "I am Lady Phoebe now. Call me that. Cunning, you are! How can you be disobeying me, without triggering the demands of fate?"

Victor said to Quentin, "Don't answer. Tell the enemy nothing. Leader, orders?"

Quentin said, "Lady Phoebe." Then he shrugged and smiled, and said to Victor. "Sorry, but that was worded as a direct command. . . ."

I said, "Leader, listen to me! I can see what is going on. The laws of nature in the room—"

Vanity looked like she was about to break down. "Amelia is now second in command. Do what she says."

Oops.

All eyes turned toward me, including the penetrating, silver-white eyes of the girl hanging in midair outside the window.

She smiled a truly chilling smile, as cold as the far side of the moon. "Come out, come out, prelapsarian. I part my hounds and give you a running start: You look swift. Your ham is firm and thigh is sleek. Am I not generous? Otherwise you are surrounded."

I said, "Colin, Andromeda gave you this room and you gave it to me, right? In the eyes of the law, how far down, or how far up, do the bound- aries go?"

Quentin answered, "To the core of the Earth, and up to infinity."

The moment he said that, the uncertainty collapsed, and I saw, like a forcefield, the lines flush with the square floor of the room. Four walls of light dwindling to a vanishing point far underfoot, and reaching upward

like a slowly expanding cone overhead. The moral energy lines were gathered around it, trying to get in, but they could not cross the boundary. My
property.

Colin grunted. "What he said. Leader, let me rip her head off, huhn?"

Victor said, "Leader, your orders?"

"Everyone hold hands," I said.

Lady Phoebe was right. I was fast.

2.

I pulled the suddenly weightless team "past" the ceiling, the attic, and the
roof tiles without disturbing them. I was still directly above the room, still
within the cone of my legal property, and accelerating straight up. Zero to
Mach four in thirty seconds.

Victor slid through without much problem, though it did kill him, until I
tilted his monad back in place and the mechanical processes of his life
started again. The fact that Colin had been able to make his deadly dream-
environment friendly to me made me think I could do the same for Victor.
(In hindsight, Colin should have been the one impossible to pull into the
fourth dimension, but maybe he can turn off his anti-Amelia-ness somehow.
Maybe he was inspired to pass through the roof.)

I was two miles up, going Mach ten, before the dogs of cloud closed in on
me. The blind, narrow-headed greyhounds were horrible to look at, and their
teeth were like icicles. But they hung to every side of me, running straight up
as I soared, some leaping ahead, baying and barking, some falling behind. I
ignited the atmosphere around me to form a multicolored aura of free-willed
air to protect my friends, and Vanity made a quick pass with her green stone
to give us laws of nature favorable to our attempt.

She must have done something clever, because the dogs still could not
close with us, but our other abilities were permitted. Victor was turning to
gold, his flesh peeling away in grotesque strips so that a harder integument
underneath could take its place. A darkness gathered around Quentin, and
he seemed to burn with black fire, but the acceleration was not hurting him,
and his speed was as great as mine, or Victor's.

Colin was hanging on for dear life. No, sorry, he was grinning like a devil,
with one arm clenching my waist, and one arm around Vanity. He was slipping slowly downward, so his nose was somewhere pressed into my bosom,

and Vanity was being likewise crushed up against his lusty self. Jerk. But he must have been inspired, or something, because the friction and acceleration were not even mussing his hair.

Underfoot, I heard Lady Phoebe wind her hunting horn, a long, chilling note.

At that noise, Victor pointed a finger, and an invisible beam punched a clean hole though the skull and breast of two of the clamoring dogs at his heels, passed through the clouds below, and left a circle in the cloudbank as neat as a mechanical punch might make. The Huntress must have been directly below. The horn-note squawked and died.

Victor sent a radio beam toward me, a silent commutation that ignored the hurricane of wind noise all around us. "She is doing magic. I can hold some of it back, but she has millions of ergs of electromagnetic life-forms, many more than Quentin commands."

Up. Straight up. There was nowhere else to go. I could not go right or left. If I went into the fourth dimension, I would be going much slower, and I could also see her dog things were partly in my paradigm: They were flickering in and out of the moonlight of earthland and dreamland freely. If I left three-dimensional space entirely, they might get me.

The goddess was coming. She was not so fast as I was, not so fast as her own dogs, but I could see the winding strands of energy reaching into the past and future. I was gripped with the sick, sudden certainty that, in the same way that Mavors the Warrior could not be defeated in melee, Phoebe the Huntress could not lose her prey.

Cloud. The dogs had the internal nature of clouds. They were made out of cloud. An atmospheric phenomenon.

I could not reach escape velocity. Orbital velocity is a different thing. But . . .

The air should have been too thin for speech, or life, at this altitude, but the free air blanketing us, and Vanity's imposition of more Aristotelian laws of nature that did not worry about concepts like friction and air pressure, allowed us to talk.

I put my mouth to Vanity's ear and shouted. "Call your ship!"

She yelled back, "It's a ship, not a plane!"

"Call your ship! That's an order!"

"There is no water up here!" she said in a voice of misery.

The dark world was underfoot. The pattern of city lights followed the coastlines of England and, across the channel, Normandy. A curving red line

of fire defined the distant dawn to the east. To either side was thin stratosphere. And still the pale, blind dogs chased us. And overhead . . .

The shadowy form of Quentin pointed with an ebon finger. "I see a river,"
he said. By some trick of his, the words were clear and close within our ears,
despite the raging noise of our terrible acceleration.

Vanity's eyes followed where he pointed. There, mystical, wondrous, were
the million gem-gleaming stars of the Milky Way, a stream of light.

Silhouetted against the jeweled splendor of the Milky Way was the slender
silhouette of a Greek trireme. The solemn eyes painted on the prow were
looking at us.

I said, "She has to match velocities with us, because we need to remain
geosynchronous above the room. The dogs will have a chance to attack when
we board. Um, everyone, if my bubble of free-willed air around us breaks
when we cross to the ship, you'll get an attack of flatulence. Let it out,
Chaucer-like, if you know what I mean, or else your internal organs might
get damaged. Colin! I am counting on you to kill and slay and maim like
Cuchulainn, or one of those heroes from your ridiculous Irish epics. Once
we board, Vanity looks for a secret compartment that is airtight; Colin and I
saw her find a trapdoor leading into a hold, so maybe she can find a pressurized cabin. And then, um, and then . . ."

Quentin said, "Where can we go that the goddess will not follow? She
will pursue us to the ends of the Earth."

The word came to my lips without effort. "Mars!" I breathed. "The Red
Planet!"

I gave Colin a kiss on the top of his head. "Kill the dogs for me, Colin, and
we'll go put the first footprints on the planet Mars!"

When we engaged, Colin ripped the jawbone out of the first monster
hound his hands found, and he beat the others to pulp with it, and gore was
sprayed in slowly falling crescents of mist across the upper atmosphere.

THE RED PLANET

1.

During those frantic moments when we had to cross several yards of high stratosphere to the hull of the ship, I think Victor actually killed more dogs, because they disintegrated into cloud when his azure beam lanced through them. But Colin fought like a demon, laughing. His skin was dark and hot as blood suffused it, and the hair on his head stood up like the arched back of a witch's cat.

Yes, it was in midair, in the troposphere, and yes, Colin should have simply fallen to his death, like a parachutist with no chute, and should have suffered frostbite and decompression, but no, his paradigm did not work that way. He was inspired to slaughter the dogs. He went berserk.

2.

Vanity sought and "found" an airlock leading into a space below the hull, a wooden torpedo-shape, reinforced with iron ribs, pierced by small, round portholes above and below. It looked like the type of submersible Jules Verne would have developed. The upper deck and the mast could fold themselves into the dream-dimension (I don't know what that process looked like to anyone but me), and the whole ship, now a spindle-shaped cylinder of ivory, silver, and wood, darted like a slender fish through the troposphere.

She still had a ram on her prow, painted eyes to either side. There were no lifting surfaces, or ailerons, no source of thrust in the spacegoing aspect of the ship, any more than there had been sail or steering board in the seagoing version.

"Who built this ship?" I remember asking Vanity in wonder and awe. It was the perfect vessel to explore the universe in.

Vanity fiddled with her glowing green necklace until she found and established a set of laws of nature amenable to our needs. Aristotle thought the air was a transparency that conveyed the potential for light to the eye, made of a continuous substance. No molecules, no partial pressures, none of the Pascalian air-has-weight stuff.

And no oxygen–carbon dioxide cycles, not in a universe with only four elements. We did not worry about the air going stale, because that was not something that happened in the particular paradigm of the universe that currently obtained within the hull of our craft.

3.

The ship flew at the speed of dreams, and climbed to an altitude Victor announced was two hundred miles high. We were in low Earth orbit. All sign of pursuit was gone.

My heart soared higher than any mere two hundred miles. Outer space was at my fingertips! Orbit is halfway to anywhere.

The sensation of being in a falling elevator made Quentin puke. He was quick-witted enough to throw his cloak before his face and catch the mess before it formed a cloud, but the stinking drench was as disgusting as you might imagine. Ask someone who has small children what it's like. Now picture that floating in three dimensions.

Other business was put on hold until Vanity found a set of laws of nature in her green stone that would allow for some gravity. Aristotelian physics had drawbacks: The ship, made of noncelestial substance, did not move in the divine circular motions natural to the crystal spheres of Aristotle's concentric heavens, but instead started to plunge back toward Earth, where her natural motion inclined it—and since she was a heavier object, she fell faster.

We could not maintain orbit with Aristotle's physics: He did not believe in inertia, in centrifugal and centripetal forces. Vanity found something more Newtonian. Victor imparted a spin to the ship, magnetically adding angular momentum to the metal joists and bolts. The sunlight, unhampered by any atmosphere, shot blinding rays through the portholes, first above and then below, as if a lamp, unendurably brilliant, were being spun on the chain just outside our windows.

I found the easiest way to converse was to lie on my back between two port-holes, looking "up" at Vanity and the boys, who were stuck to the walls of the cylinder. It was like those rapidly spinning barrels you see in rides at the fair.

Vanity resigned. "I am a peacetime leader, really, and I don't think my administration is that good in time of war. I mean, I could feel her staring at me, you know? Staring like she was picking out which wallpaper would look good on the spot in her house where she would nail my skinned pelt." Vanity shivered.

I could tell from the looks on the boys' faces that Colin thought Vanity was being a sissy; Quentin was more forgiving. He said, "The Lady Phoebe may have known a weakness associated with the Phaeacian ability to feel that 'being watched' sensation. It is a sense impression of some sort. Why couldn't it be dazzled or deafened?"

Victor had put his prosthetic face back on, but his expression, as usual, was composed and dispassionate. "In any case, we must decide our next course of action. We have no reason to believe the Huntress cannot follow us up out of the atmosphere. She is a moon goddess, after all."

I said, "Mars! Who here wants to go to Mars? We'll be famous!"

Victor said, "Well, for one thing, people trying to hide should not be famous."

"If the gods are so secretive, they might not be willing to strike out against famous people, right?" I pointed out.

Colin said sarcastically, "Yeah, look at how well things turned out for famous guys like Agamemnon and Ajax and Oedipus and Icarus . . ."

I said, "Listen! We're free for the first time in our lives, and now is our chance to spread our wings, to test our strength against the odds, to attempt bold things, to sail beyond the sunset!" Colin grinned at that.

I looked at Quentin and said, "To learn things never learned, to step where none have stepped, to fly higher than even the princes of the Middle Air."

And to Victor I said, "Even if she follows us up out of the atmosphere, then Phoebe might not be able to achieve escape velocity. If she cannot, then the whole solar system, the whole universe, is ours! What will we care then about the gods? What is Olympos but one small mountain on one small world?"

The motion was carried, and I found myself in the leadership position once again.

4.

As they say, the devil is in the details. We need an Aristotelian paradigm in order to keep our air from going stale, but Aristotle did not allow for the Newtonian orbital mechanics we need to reach another planet.

We discussed whether we could merely turn one cabinet, or a small area of deck, into an Aristotelian vest-pocket cosmos, and pump our carbon dioxide into it, and pump out fresh air, without having that cabinet be pulled to Earth by its natural motion. Vanity, based on the results of her research back on the island, seemed to think having two nonharmonious laws of nature right next to each other might cause problems. Colin was urging Vanity to use her stone to summon up something more primitive, pre-Ptolemaic. His argument was that Stone Age shamans did not worry about or know how the sky-people breathed or moved. No one wanted to take Victor up on his offer to grow specially designed algae in our lungs that would allow us to breathe oxygen and carbon dioxide indifferently.

"Don't expeditions like this usually involve, you know, more planning . . . ?" asked Vanity. "Like NASA and getting food and space suits and all sorts of stuff? We have the knapsacks of gear lashed to the deck, which is in a vacuum right now, I should mention."

Victor said, "I thought there were launch windows controlling the timing of space shots?"

I was bubbling with enthusiasm. "Sure, Victor, there would be, if we were dealing with the rocket equation, and if conserving fuel were our main concern. In such a case, the most efficient method would be to begin from low Earth orbit, achieve a six-point-six kilometers per second delta-V, to put us into a Hohmann transfer ellipse, where its perihelion is tangential to Earth's orbit and its aphelion at Mars! In such a case, the next available launch date would be July ninth of this year, when Mars is past its closest approach by forty-five degrees, and the orbit out would take about two hundred fifty-nine days! After four hundred and fifty-five days on Mars, the planets would be in a good relative position, and we could make a second burn of seven point two kilometers per second! Let me show you how these figures are derived! First, remember that Kepler's third law states that for all objects orbiting the sun, the square of the orbital period is inversely proportional to the cube of the semi-major axis . . ."

Colin, who was pinned to the curved ceiling above me, groaned. "Bat crap! She's talking in equations again! You've memorized the acceleration requirements for a Mars shot? Girl, you have thought about this entirely too much."

I said impatiently, "What else was there to think about, back when we were trapped in the orphanage, but how to get off the planet?"

"Wait, wait," said Quentin, who was halfway up the wall to my left. "Amelia, I mean, um, Leader, were you proposing we sail to Mars in a wooden boat for eight and a half months?"

Colin said, "And we don't have a bathroom aboard."

"Head," I said. "Aboard a ship, it's called a 'head.' "

"Fine, we don't have one."

Victor said, "I assume we can use our special powers to overcome the need for oxygen at sea-level pressure, or do without food or water. But what about radiation from solar activity? The walls of this vessel are made of wood. I should not even mention the fuel supply, except: Vanity, what does this ship use for fuel, anyhow? What makes it go?"

Vanity was lying with both hands behind her red curls, one leg bent, the other crossed over it, so she could bounce her foot idly in the air. It was the kind of posture one would assume for watching clouds passing by, but in this case she was looking up (her "up," my "down") at her friends. "I dunno. The ship goes where I tell her. I did not think she could fly into space."

Quentin said, "If the vessel is moved by a spirit, there may be limitations on where the spirit has leave to go. Is it lawful for a Phaeacian ship to sail beyond the circles of the Earth? The laws of magic may differ in the superlunary realms."

Colin said, "I am not living in a coffin one hundred twenty feet long and twelve feet wide for eight months. And then how long on Mars to wait for the planets to move back to the right positions?"

I said, "No, no, no! That figure was for a fuel-flightpath efficient orbit. We are supernatural creatures in a supernatural boat. We can cheat. If the *Nautilus* can achieve and maintain a one-g acceleration throughout the trip, it should only take about two days."

Victor said, "Actually, Leader, we don't know if this ship can even achieve escape velocity."

"Then that will be the first thing to test!" I declared.

Victor said, "Very good, Leader. How do we measure our velocity?"

I said, "We don't. We measure acceleration. Vanity, ask your ship to maintain an acceleration equal to one gravity as measured at sea level on Earth. Victor, can you measure the fall of an object in seconds per second? You go up on deck, get a tin cup or something out of the knapsacks, and we drop it from the bow to the stern."

Colin looked to the stern. "If this works, that will be the floor, right? We'll be stuck at the bottom of a wooden well, which is six feet in radius, for two days with no bathroom . . . 'scuse me, Leader, no head. Where are you and Vanity going to take showers? I want to watch you scrub each other's backs with sudsy soap in zero-g."

I said, "Maybe we can take a shortcut and be there in a few minutes!"

Vanity closed her eyes and asked her boat for a path to the planet Mars. Nothing of any particular import happened. She opened her eyes and said, "I cannot find a secret passage through a wall if there is no wall. It's all empty nothingness up here. Also, I think my power is at least a bit like yours: a place someone has looked before is already 'fixed.' You know what I mean? It's taken, established, claimed. I can convince the world there might be a shortcut in some place no one has ever looked before; I cannot do that in a night sky the whole planet of astronomers look at every day, er, night. Unless you can bend the fourth dimension for me, Amelia?"

Which I could not think of how to do just at that moment. Her ship was much bigger in the fourth dimension than in three, and I could not see how I could move the vessel at all, as it was attached to a complex and huge struc- ture of space-warps and energy-obligations. I could throw things past the walls, but I could not move the ship herself. As far as my race was concerned, the ship was anchored in one spot. I could make the ship heavier or lighter, but I could not add momentum to her. Go figure.

I tried to tell Vanity how big her ship was, but she covered her ears and warned me not to look at the ship too closely, or else I would kill off any chance of finding other secret doors in the hull.

So I said, "We have to go through outer space, just like any other astro- nauts, then."

Quentin shook his head. "Which might prove impossible, Leader. Are X-rays and gamma rays and cosmic rays from the sun sterilizing us right now?"

It was not impossible, but we spent longer getting the vessel ready for the trip than the trip itself took.

5.

The Huntress did not overtake us. We took up a middle-distance orbit about one thousand miles above the Earth and set to work.

First, Vanity found the laws of nature from what must have been an ancient Greek atomist theory, something like what Lucretius or Democritus imagined. These laws did not have the problems with Aristotelian natural motions pulling us toward the Earth, but the "atomies" were made of essential airy bits, not something that broke down into oxygen-nitrogen. Vanity found she could apply them to the interior of the cylinder and leave the outside Newtonian, so mass and acceleration and all those laws of motion acted normally.

Second, Quentin worked his astrology, using just the tables he carried in his head, which was good enough to tell us that Mars was in opposition, at its closest approach to Earth. He did not know the distance of Mars at closest approach, but I did: 56 million kilometers. The equation for a Brachistochrone curve was simple to solve using calculus of variations.

(I always thought Leibniz's solution to Bernoulli's problem was more elegant than Newton's. But I am British, so I say Newton invented the calculus, and we'll invade the damn foreigners who say otherwise. Soon as we get another Wellington.)

Quentin and Colin, working together, managed to cast a whopper of a spell. Hours were spent drawing pentagrams and circles, inscribed minutely with Latin, all across the curving inner walls of our ship. Colin knelt down and handed me the gold ring of Gyges, making several rude suggestions that earned him KP. During the experiment, I wore the ring with the collet turned in, so the manifestation would not see me, and I had to carry Vanity in my arms so that she was invisible, too. Victor scoffed at the notion that one of Quentin's "imaginary friends" could see him—and he was right, and it did not.

A creature named Saburac, "a Marquis mighty, great and strong" (as Quentin called him), appeared in the midst of smoke and fumes that filled our cramped living space, and this apparition took the form of an Elizabethan soldier in breastplate and helm, armed at all points, with the head of the lion, riding a horse as white as bone. He roared with scornful laughter when Quentin commanded him to build a tower, filled and furnished with victuals, arms, and armor, in the void of space, but Colin threatened him, and the monster called him "Prince Phobetor," and bowed. (Which surprised me, because Colin's paradigm was trumped by Quentin's. I guess not every creature from Quentin's paradigm trumped Colin, though.)

"Mine office also be to afflict men for many days with wounds and sores, rotten and full of worms," the lion-headed knight announced. Colin was interested in the possibilities here, but by that time, Quentin had banished the entity to its tasks. A tower made of great gray stones, tumbling hugely in the zero-g, was beginning to fall to pieces off our port bow. I had seen the tower cross over from the parallel plane of Earth's dreamland, but to the others, the tower must have seemed to appear from nowhere.

Of course, we really did not need a tower. We needed the metals and other elements, or, I should say, Victor did. He assumed his faceless, gold-skinned spaceworthy form and pulled himself across the vacuum on magnetic beams. In the wreckage of the tower were iron and steel, carbon and water, and so on.

The food the creature conjured from nothing was not harmed by exposure to vacuum and radiation: If anything, it was safer than normal. Radiation kills germs.

It was salt pork and hardtack, with a barrel of apples and a barrel of limes: soldiers' food from the days when soldiers manned towers. The water barrels made it intact, being watertight. Vanity was surprised the water did not freeze in the cold of outer space, and I tried to explain to her how a thermos bottle worked.

The Marquis had also thoughtfully supplied the tower with strands of cable, useful for any number of things in wartime, but they shattered like glass after exposure to vacuum. Colin wanted to keep the culverins and bombards, but Victor melted them down with molecular engines. He let Colin keep a harquebus, along with a forked stick to rest it on.

The Marquis was thorough. There were drums and trumpets and other military odds and ends. The prize of the collection, and something I slid through the fourth dimension and swept across the vacuum to recover myself, was the standard: It was the Union Jack. I also kept a spear to fly it from.

Victor manipulated the elements, absorbing mass from the walls and armory of the tower, and grew new forms of life in his stomach, which he vomited out after gestation. I like Victor a lot, as we all know, but sometimes I wonder about kissing him, you know?

He created metallic plant-mollusk creatures that looked like green clams. They adhered to the outer surface of Vanity's ship, perfectly happy in the airlessness, and multiplied until, at the end of five days, they covered every square inch. Victor said they were iron-based life-forms that could absorb and block dangerous radiation, and protect us from the reentry heat of the Martian atmosphere. Vanity doubted the laws of nature inside the ship would allow for radiation, but Quentin thought that Lucretius-theory might permit small, fast-moving atomies of fire-essence to exist, so I ruled in favor of Victor.

The portholes were occluded by clams, which bothered everyone but Victor (who doesn't get bothered) and me (who doesn't need portholes). Victor and Quentin designed a light source that looked like a basin of burning water, which also fed oxygen and hydrogen into the little air-atomies. Vanity had to green-stone the basin so that its rim formed another boundary for yet a third set of laws of nature.

There was enough lumber left over from the wreckage of the tower to build two crude platforms, one above the other, amidships, to divide our cylinder into three chambers. Victor glued the lumber together with a resin he secreted from an orifice that, shall we say, made the vomiting up of green clams look in contrast like a wholesome process.

This timber was too bulky to fit in our Jules Verne–style brass airlock, so my job was to reach through the walls and pull the lumber inside. The tower came with a chamber pot, and I volunteered to empty it overboard, which I could do without touching the hull. When the ship was under thrust, the stern became floor. With our lamp hanging in the bow, the third chamber was dark and private enough, even with all the light leaking through the crudely glued floorboards, to serve as the head.

Victor broke the remaining pieces of the tower into small bits, too small to survive reentry heat and reach the ground in lumps, once their orbit decayed.

And yes, the ship could maintain one-g for two days.

We spent the time telling each other ghost stories. Quentin's were the best.

6.

The fourth world out from Sol swelled in my vision, red as rust, lifeless as a skull, and capped with dry ice at the poles. It was beautiful.

7.

You are wondering how the Dark Mistress prevented her troops from going stir-crazy when locked in a large coffin for nine days. Well, keep in mind our background: We were used to confinement, to boring assignments, to grueling schoolwork.

So everyone checked my figures. The motivation was simple: You flunk the math problem, the ship misses the target, we all die.

We did trigonometry and calculus. Victor magnetically opened his layer of clams so we could clear a porthole and take measurements of the planets with binoculars and homemade sextants. We did our figuring on slide rules. You heard me: good old-fashioned slipsticks, those things everyone says are dead as a dodo. They are easy to make with two sticks, or even two pieces of paper laid side by side. Try making an electronic adding machine with what you have in your knapsack. Victor had the log tables memorized, and several of the Dukes, Great Kings, and Presidents of the Middle Air that Quentin could call up teach liberal arts and useful sciences, including mathematics.

An abacus is pretty easy to make, too, if you have a Telchine boy who can sculpt materials to fine-machine standards with his brain. Vanity and I contributed pearl necklaces and beaded bracelets to the project.

Four days of playing with numbers, and you can get pretty quick with an abacus.

I also staggered the watches, so that not everyone was awake at the same time. It was the only privacy we had, to have some time when the guy who is getting on your nerves is asleep. And yes, Colin did talk after lights out, and Victor did tell him to shut up. Just like in school.

We celebrated at the skew-turn point. One minute of zero gravity, while we howled like monkeys and bounced off the walls, doing fast somersaults and slow cartwheels. Vanity's hair was like a puffball surrounding her head; I was blinded by a blond cloud. Note to female cosmonauts: Short hair is in fashion.

Then the *Nautilus* was running prow-backwards, and decelerating toward Mars.

8.

The ship did seem to have some arbitrary limitations. She could drive through space, but not fly through the air.

Propelled how, by the way? I could see lines of energy reaching from the vessel into the complexities of higher dimensions, and see the rippling activity in the strange dreamlands surrounding Mars, but I could not figure out how the ship moved. But I saw the utility dimming dangerously toward uselessness, and I knew she could not land under her own power.

So we cheated on the landing again. I simply bent the world-lines radiating from the center of Mars away from the vessel. The ship, aerodynamic as a falling log, was lapsed into a feather-slow fall by me, while we were still high enough in the thin Martian atmosphere that four-space was pliant; then she was magnetically levitated down by Victor the rest of the way.

Victor, with his brain, had read the location of the most-recent lander from various computer sites before we left Earth. He was confident that he could restore power to the cameras, and the antennae, and send a signal back to Earth. He was not confident that any receiving stations were operating on Earth, space-exploration budgets being what they were, but I wanted to have a go nonetheless. So we fell through the sky in that direction.

Where to set down? Quentin had prepared one of our three chambers with his hexagons and pentagrams, and he burned a candle and summoned up one of his allies. Our procedure was the same as before: I used the ring of Gyges to hide us from the entity, and Victor did not. This one looked like a lion carrying a viper in its paw, and riding the back of a coal-black steed, but Quentin tricked it into assuming human form, and then it was dressed like a Dominican friar.

The black friar gestured with his viper. "Mine office is to make waters rough with stones. As Moses with his rod, so I. Soil of sullen red, yield up thy ancient waters!"

Through the uncovered portholes, we saw, two hundred yards below our hull, one of the dry riverbeds of Mars, which had not known water for three billion years, now bubbled white and crimson with muddy and torrential floods.

The ship that landed on the single living waterway of Mars was shaped like a trireme again, not a torpedo, when Victor and I emerged onto the upper deck. We did not have pressure suits with us, and our attempts to construct them from materials aboard, or from materials taken from the dreamlands, did not thrill and amaze the others to the point of trusting their lives to them.

Colin was particularly peeved at this, and he begged Quentin to summon up some spirit from the vasty deep that could inspire him to survive the sub-artic, low-pressure, high-ultraviolet conditions. Quentin leafed through his translated notes of his grimoire, and said he had barons who could command ninety-nine legions, and discover the virtues of birds and precious stones, but there was nothing about radiation poisoning.

I said, "Sorry, Colin, you are just going to have to play Collins."

"Who is Collins?"

"The first man not on the moon," I said.

"Maybe I could just step outside for a minute and take the damage, and heal myself?" Colin suggested.

I said, "The air is thinner than the top of Mount Everest, there is no free oxygen in it to breathe, and the temperature is between minus eighty and minus one hundred and ten!"

"Fahrenheit or Celsius?"

"I am English!" I said. "Do you think I would use the continental system invented by Jacobins?"

Quentin inquired in a soft voice, "Wasn't Fahrenheit a German?"

Vanity said, "We did our estimates of the Mars positions in kilometers."

"Well, I may be English, but I am also an astronaut! So there!" I retorted triumphantly.

Colin said, "Leader, that does not make any sense."

So they were left belowdecks. I was carrying Colin's boot, which I had promised to push into the soil and return to him, so he could at least boast later his bootprint had been left in the rust-red soil of this dead, outer world. I looked something more like a winged centaur made of solidified energy than I did a girl, and an aura of blue light surrounded my head and shoulders as I kept a one-molecule-thin layer of hyperspatial substance between me and the Martian air. In my human arms I carried the Union Jack, furled on a spearshaft.

Victor looked like a faceless gold statue, with arms and legs little more than streamlined tubes marring the symmetry of his bulletlike space-body. He did not walk. His legs were one solid fused mass, their internal consistency hardened into a many-textured bonelike growth. But he could move himself by balancing positive and negative energy flows, and manipulated the environment with particles finer and surer than hands.

The waters of the canal were already turning the color of old blood and forming lumpy rose-gray ice. (Yes, I know it was a dry riverbed, filled via magic, but no girl explorer worth her salt is going to call a streambed on Mars anything but a canal.) Vapor was also pouring up from the orange waters, which might have been sublimation because the air temperature was so low. Red frost had collected at the waterline of our ship.

The windy shoreline, and the dead rocks and fine sands of the cracked surface, gave off a high-pitched wail. This shrilling wavered and rose and fell, like a woman of Arabia lamenting at a funeral: a nerve-racking noise. There was no smell I could smell. The horizon seemed strangely close. The sun was a dim smudge, smaller than seen from Earth, but the sky was rose, crimson, and pale orange in concentric bands centered on the sun, like a dust storm seen in the distance. The zenith was a chilly deep indigo, strange to see.

I spent some minutes looking for Phobos and Deimos, but they were not the luminous hurling moons of Barsoom that John Carter had promised me. Perhaps that dim spot there, like a Sputnik? The senses of my race are just not that good for picking out astronomical objects, which have no moral entanglements or immediate utility.

We set off, flying and levitating, toward the calculated location of the Mars lander. I wanted to unfurl my Union Jack where someone could see it. I had had over a week to shift through the candidates for the first words spoken on Mars. "That's one small step for a woman, one giant leap for mankind," still seemed best. "God save the Queen!" had a nice ring to it, too. Traditional. What had Roald Amundsen said when he planted a flag at the South Pole? You'd think they'd teach children important facts like that in school.

Victor and I soared through the thin atmosphere. Supersonic dust particles bounced from his gold integument, leaving streaks, or were turned aside by my extradimensional aura.

As I said, Victor knew the longitude and latitude of the lander; our latitude we knew from measuring the rise and fall of northern stars. But we did not know our longitude. (Obviously Polaris is not the North Star, not here, nor were any of the stars I used to watch from my window—obvious, yet it was still strange.) Once we reached the correct latitude, we started searching west, hoping to come across the site. Soon Victor detected metallic pings, consistent with the expected radar-contour of the lander we sought.

Here we saw a slight circular depression, about half a mile wide, like a crater from an ancient meteor, weathered by years of sandstorms. Rocks of red, red-gray, rose, and dirty gray littered the ground; streamers of orange dust tiger-striped the pebbles and the permafrost of dry ice. In the middle of the depression was the lander. It looked like a circular coffee table, about four feet across, on which some coffee drinkers had left squares of white and black metal, stubby cylinders, hoops of foil-covered steel, hourglasses of dun ceramic, radio dishes, a camera on a tall mast, and a telescoping arm on a gimbal. To the left and right of the coffee table were expanded fans shaped like glassy black stop signs. Hemispheres and cones of orange and black huddled underneath the coffee table, visible between the leg struts. The legs were tipped with wide pads, as one might see on the heel of a crutch. It was kind of surprising how crude the machine looked, all wrapped in tinfoil. It was sitting in the middle of a radiating flower of scorch marks made by its landing rockets.

Victor radioed me. "The UHF antenna is active. These signals reach to an orbiter package, no farther."

I said, "There must be a stronger broadcaster on the satellite. Let's land in front of the camera and hoist the Union Jack."

When we passed over the rim of the crater, suddenly the air got very thick and very warm. It was like running facefirst into a hot towel. The lander shimmered like a heat mirage and vanished.

At that same moment, the fourth dimension collapsed around me, and I forgot what it looked like. I was only a yard or so off the cold rocky soil. I landed heavily, however, taken by surprise when my 3-D girl-body winked into reality around me. In addition to my lucky aviatrix cap and long scarf, my three-dimensional cross-section was wearing my riding boots, jodhpurs, and leather coat, which provided enough padding that I was not injured as I fell.

On hands and knees, I looked up as Victor clanged heavily to the ground also, a statue without expression or motion, and did not get up. Dead? I hoped not.

I looked up. Before me, where the lander had been, on a throne made of crudely hewn slabs of the rust-streaked black rock, was a soldier in the panoply of a Greek hoplite. His breastplate and helm were coppery bronze, and his cloak was bloodred, as was the horsehair plume nodding above. A round shield painted with a gorgon face rested against his knee, and a slender lance was in his hand. Anachronistically, his arms and legs were covered in fatigues of red and brown and black camouflage patterns. Both katana and Mauser broom-handle pistol dangled from his web-belt in holster and sheath.

Beaten again. Oh, I did not mind being a prisoner—heck, I was used to that by now. I had lost another race. Someone got to Mars before me.

"You will plant no flags on the soil of my world," Lord Mavors said. Behind him was a banner standing: a black field with a red circle, from which a single arrow pointed to the upper right.

Behind and above Mavors, I could see a flickering discontinuity, like the ripples on the surface of a lake. On this side was breathable earthlike air; on the other side, the thin subarctic atmosphere of Mars. I guessed I was seeing the refraction from the change in density of the medium: the boundary between two sets of natural law. The film was stretched like a drumhead over the half-mile-wide crater valley.

Before I could get up, Mavors tipped his lance, and the blade touched me lightly on the shoulder, not two inches from my naked cheek.

He said, "It takes about four pounds per inch of pressure for a blade to penetrate the skin. Once the skin is broken, no other internal organs—all of which are necessary for life, or useful—offer any real resistance. Only bone. A man skilled with a spear, of course, knows to avoid bone."

So there I knelt before his crude throne on all fours, looking up at him. The Union Jack had spun from my hand as I collapsed, and I could see it, an impromptu parachute, unrolled in midair over Mavors' head.

He moved his eyes, but no other part of him, and glanced up. The rippling fabric of red, white, and blue, bold with the cross of Saint Andrew and Saint George, seemed to be caught or suspended in the surface tension of the air boundary separating the crater bowl from the thin Martian air above. Now it began to sink in the slight Martian gravity, and started to fall, pulled down by the weight of its pikeshaft.

Mavors said, "Boreas, don't let her banner touch the soil."

There was another eye-wrenching distortion, like a heat shimmer, and I could see Headmaster Boggin standing beside the throne. He was wearing a flowing garment like a tunic, but backless to allow for his wide red wings, and his unbound tresses of fine rose red brushed his shoulders. Only the breadth of those shoulders and the thickness of his chest saved his appearance from girlishness. His shins and feet were bare, and I saw the green stone, jade-hued like Vanity's, winking on his toe.

With a whirl of wings, he jumped into the air and caught the falling flag before it touched down. He landed and bowed to Mavors, and returned to his spot by the side of the throne.

"Why did you do that?" I asked Mavors.

He raised an eyebrow and glanced at Boggin, whose expression was mild and unreadable. Maybe most people on their hands and knees in the dirt before him did not ask curt questions. Looking back to me, Mavors said, "I did not want your colors to touch the soil."

"Then you are a man of honor," I said.

"No farther than is practical," he allowed, with a slight inclination of his head. By this he meant that dirtying my banner would have (in his eyes) obligated me to fight until I died.

I drew in a shivering breath. "And so you will understand why I must stand up, even if you kill me for it."

Did I mention that I was scared? The hair inside my cap was lank with sweat, and my jacket felt close. Even my scarf was strangling me. The knowledge that he had vowed to protect us children did not seem like a very solid comfort when I was looking in his eyes, and trying to find the strength in my knees.

I expected the eyes of a murderer, pitiless and cold. Instead, his eyes were old with sorrow, wise and ancient as winter. They were the eyes of a veteran, weary of war, but still iron-hard. He wanted to go home, put down his red-hot sword, throw his heavy helm aside, and lay his head in the lap of the glancing-eyed love-goddess.

And I was the obstacle in his way.

He let me get to my feet alive. That was something, at least.

Mavors spoke. "Your presence on my dead, war-slain world is unexpected. I can make no sense of it. Why come here?"

I just shrugged, and said nothing. If he didn't understand, it wasn't my place to explain it to him.

Boggin leaned and whispered, "Highness, if I may mention, the young lady is of the blood of Helion, not to mention, ah, Oceanos and Tethys, lords of the endless waste. Our universe must seem a small place to her, three cramped dimensions, a mere fifteen billion light-years across. The girl suffers from claustrophobia."

Mavors waved him away. To me, he said, "I am not asking why you came to see me; I am asking why you are absent from your post without my leave. These were not your orders."

"Wh—? I mean, I beg your pardon, sir? Orders?"

"You and yours went to ground on an island. You knew, at least from the moment you saw my fleet part to let you pass, that you were meant to serve as bait for Lamia, and whoever is behind her. Obviously I meant you to draw her out; for that reason I let you go. By going, you acknowledged. You were impressed into my service as of that moment. But if you will not perform, I have no reason not to gather you back in."

"Are you making a bargain with me? We can be free as long as we act as bait for Lamia?"

"Bargain?" The tiniest hint of a frown darkened Mavors' features. "My bastard half brother Mulciber bargains. I do not bargain. A sovereign imposes duties. What sort of nation could stand, were every man a shopkeeper, like Mulciber?"

"That greatest nation in war and peace, in the arts and sciences, in laws and in letters, the world has ever known!" I said hotly. "Great Britain is a nation of shopkeepers, and the foe who mocked her with those words was laid low."

Mavors raised an eyebrow and glanced once more at Boggin. Boggin was still holding the Union Jack, idly puffing to make the colors stream: He could make a breeze stiff enough to lift the flag without even distending his cheeks. When he felt Mavors' eyes upon him, he casually put the standard behind his back.

With a rustling shrug of his red wings, he said in a confidential tone, "Your father Lord Terminus gave me the latitude, that is to say, the discretion to choose in which nation to raise the children, ah, the monsters, Highness. Your stern cities of Rome and Sparta had both known days of ascendancy, that is glorious days, um, at one time, historically speaking, of that we need harbor no doubt, but I have always had a weakness, as one might expect, for the colder and paler peoples of the North."

Mavors made a slight, dismissive gesture with his hand. "Even the mortals know the north wind favors England, since the storm whelmed the Armada of Spain. I am merely surprised a Chaos-daughter could be raised to learn so noble a passion. Too many mock homeland-love."

Boggin smirked and bowed low again.

Mavors turned back to me. "Your loyalty does you credit, woman of Britain, especially since you are not Saxon, not Norman, not any blood of theirs. You are wise enough to know that the British Isles will not survive once the supporting globe is shattered to asteroids."

"What do you mean?"

"I mean your orders are these: Return to your atoll and carry on as normal. It is serviceable to my needs, remote from human habitation or any sunken city of the sea-elves. I have positioned troop-bearing ships around the island, below and above, and ranged my cannon and orbital emplacements. My forces are hidden by the same deception technique Boggin used to place the image of the Mars lander here. Even the many senses of your people, Phaethusa, cannot penetrate such Hecatean counterfeits. Your venture above the orbit of the moon, and your downfall once more to Earth cannot fail to attract the enemy's attention. You need take no heed for your safety: Once battle erupts, the environment is in my realm, and under my authority. Over other things, I have less control, but the outcome of battles is mine. If you fall, you will be avenged, which is all that any man can ask. Is there any part of these orders you do not understand?"

My eye fell on the golden body, still motionless on the ground next to me. "What happened to Victor? Is he dead?"

Boggin spoke up: "Members of his race, they are not so, ah, friable or, immaterial, there is a perfect word, not so *immaterial* as to die when their life processes are interrupted. Mr. Triumph is in what we might call a halted condition. He can be restarted without harm to him." To Mavors, he bowed once more, saying, "Dread Prince of ultralunar Heaven, if I might be so bold, the young lady might be, ah, less prone to distraction, not to mention more, what is the word, pliant? Ah, more attentive to Your Highness's words if the burden of worrying about her fallen comrade were, ah, lessened? Ameliorated? Sated? Perhaps if your guest were permitted to view the, ah, mechanisms . . ."

Mavors said, "Carry on."

The green stone on Boggin's toe winked and shimmered, and my upper senses turned back on. My fourth-dimensional limbs, the parts of my body made of light and music and various shades of emotion and energy, were still numb, but I was no longer blind.

I could see Victor's internal workings were undamaged. A simple twist of his monad would have restored him to action, but the manipulator I used to do that was numb.

I also saw, shining with utility, something hidden in Boggin's belt pouch. The usefulness to me was almost blinding.

It was a note. Addressed to me. Folded up, crumbled into a ball, stuck in the bowl of his clay pipe. Right out in plain sight where I could not fail to see it.

Reading the note, I said, "Mavors—excuse me, Lord Mavors—I do have a question. Lady Phoebe, the moon-goddess, your royal sister—"

"Half sister!" he said sharply.

"—ah, half sister, she was on our trail when we fled the Earth. Am I correct in assuming she is to hunts as you are to battles? If she overtakes us . . ."

Mavors nodded briefly. Now he waved his spear in the air. "Hear me, O Furies! I decree, by my authority as God of Battles and Lord of Men, that the flight of the children of Chaos from Earth, and their doings there, were part of my battle with Lamia. No foxhunt can cross a battlefield. Luna is the lowest of heavens, and the martial heavens, fifth of the Spheres, is ulterior and superior to it."

He did it right in front of me. I saw him change fate. It was complex, and I did not understand what I was seeing, but I saw it.

9.

It was as if the reddish strands of moral energy binding me to what fate had been decreed by Lady Phoebe were parted by the sweep of that spear. Something in the future, an entity, perhaps, or a process, shifted its attention. The internal nature of objects changed slightly but definitely, losing free will in one vector of possibilities and gaining it back again in another.

Mavors ordered Boggin to return my flag to me, which he did. Then Mavors spoke one last time, "To any who challenge my sovereignty, I will answer with a weapon, thus." And he threw the lance into the rust-colored soil at his feet, splitting a rock in half with a noise like a gunshot. The lance stuck fast and stood quivering.

This time, I saw how Boggin made himself and Mavors disappear. They had not been in the crater any more than the Mars lander had been. It was a Phaeacian technique. It looked to me like a tube of force running from this spot, up out of the continuum, through the dreamlands, and back into the continuum at another spot, their real location. The three-dimensional energies, such as light waves, as well as fourth-dimensional media, by which I perceived such things as internal natures, utilities, monads, and moral obligations, were all swept from one spot to another through the Phaeacian shortcut. Presumably, they could be manipulated, dreamed into new shapes, while they passed through the dreamlands, before being deposited here, in a spot where the laws of nature had been changed to allow for this type of illusion. The photons were not emerging from trapdoors, but from subatomic areas of uncertainty in the base vacuum of space itself.

Magnetic waves had been present, too. Something from Victor's paradigm had allowed these three-dimensional light images to manipulate my flagpole and Mavors' spear in coordination with the actions of their hands. I had not seen how the wind and air had been manipulated, but it was not hard to guess that Boreas might have fine control over such things, fine enough to make the sound waves of a spoken voice. Since I could detect no clue, perhaps Colin's paradigm was involved? Hard to say.

And also, somehow, the Phaeacian ability to detect attention must have been tied into an ability to deflect attention: The clues that would have warned me that the lander was not below as we flew down toward it had been hypnotically thrust aside in my brain.

The moment I woke up Victor, I knew why they had to knock him out. He called it cryptognosis. He said he had detected the interference in my perception system the moment we crossed the boundary into the special laws of nature obtaining in the crater basin. He had been silenced before he could speak. He was immune to illusions woven by magic.

10.

I attuned my senses to a distant spot, during that moment while I had the chance. The place where Boggin and Mavors had truly been standing was atop Mons Olympos, the tallest mountain in the solar system.

And it was not a barren waste: Mavors had a camp there. A camp? A city. I saw endless arsenals and munitions factories half-buried beneath the rock and crag of the mountain, manned by shark-toothed snake-skinned Laestry-gonians. Poking up through the bedrock and casting long shadows across the landscape of snow and rust loomed launching towers, magnetic rails, and missile emplacements large enough to shoot down the tiny moons, cyclo-pean, huge and dark, beneath the dusty pink sky. The Laestrygonians man-ning these skyscraper-size guns wore no pressure suits on the surface: Perhaps they were the original inhabitants of Mars.

Out from this fortress-city ran corridors into the fourth dimension, short-cuts through space exactly the type Vanity had been unable to make.

I could see the distant points to where these corridors led: I saw strange cathedrals made of glass beneath black skies that rained sulfuric acid; I saw a soaring fortress, slim as an upraised sword, towering over a cratered gray land where stars burned to either side of a pitiless sun. At the end of one cor-ridor made of darkened air, I saw a space station made of carven wood, its hull overgrown with metal trees and leaves of purest silver, hanging above cold, swirled methane-snowstorms of a gas giant surrounded by broken and scattered rings.

Venus, Luna, Neptune. Of course, I knew these places at a glance. Had I not seen a hundred artists' renditions, had I not pored over *Voyager* photo-graphs, hadn't I dreamt of nothing else my whole life? These were the un-claimed worlds into whose alien soils I had meant one day to plant the Union Jack.

Someone had beaten me to it. All these planets were explored.

I saw ships plying these space routes. I saw the gilled men of Atlantis, brothers to Mestor, in shining black scale-mail, wearing neither helmets nor gauntlets, hanging weightlessly by tethers from long cylindrical vehicles of open grillework, vessels poised in the airless, interplanetary void. Atlanteans were amphibious, not just to water, but to outer space as well. A pang of envy went through me. No need to carry heavy life support if you were a race born for space.

Some of the vessels were heavily armed, and crewed by Laestrygonians. These had the circle-and-arrow emblem of Mars painted on their hulls. The

Atlantean ships were bronze or cerulean blue, and bore the emblem of the trident.

11.

The trip back across the cold red landscape of Mars at dusk was bleak and melancholy.

The ship was trapped in the ice, and Victor circled it slowly, bathing the waters in infrared and microwave radiation until she floated on a very small, steaming lake of dirty red water.

I turned and looked over the globe of the Fourth World from Sol, a blasted desert that had known life a million years ago, perhaps—or never. It had been so easy for us to get here. An impromptu expedition, a bit of skylarking.

I was thinking of those poor humans, trapped on their world. Not unless they expended their utmost, cleverly used the technology at their command, could they match what we had accomplished in a fortnight, and then only with months and years of genius devoted and treasure expended, and with the toil, and sweat, and courage of multitudes.

They had the ability now. Why hadn't they come? Why hadn't someone planted a flag to defy the grim black banner of Ares?

Were they content to remain trapped? I would not believe that of anyone.

12.

Not until we were back aboard the *Argent Nautilus,* and I had Vanity check me for bugging devices and Quentin for divination spells, did I tell them what had happened.

"They were too scared to meet me face-to-face. It was an elaborate illusion, and Boggin messed it up for me, showed me how it was being done."

Colin said, "I hope he is not on our side. That would make me barf."

I said, "He is not on our side. But he is not on Mavors' side either. Mavors cast a spell, a decree, a fate on me. Imposed a moral obligation. On all of us. Boggin had a note in his pocket, telling me where to go to have it nullified."

"Where are we going, Leader?" asked Quentin.

I smiled at Vanity. "Hollywood!"

Her face lit up.

LOVE'S PROPER HUE

1.

The reentry heat killed Victor's green metal clams, and his mood was grim as he spent an hour stripping them from the hull, because he felt responsible for life he had created. Vanity was pleased because her ship was silver-white again, and the painted eyes uncovered. I was pleased because the clams, alive or dead, had been able to act like ablative tiles and had prevented our wooden ship from going up like kindling.

Quentin seemed, not glad exactly, but relieved, that they were dead. "We don't need to worry about what happens when you introduce a self-replicating nonorganic life-form into terrestrial ecology," he murmured to me. I think he felt about Victor's mechanistic view of the world the way I felt about Colin's passion-driven mysticism. He liked Victor, but did not like Victor's universe.

2.

Our splashdown point was in the Pacific, off the coast of Oregon. There are three assumptions I was operating on:

First, I assumed all sorts of air-traffic controllers, military radar stations, satellites from NASA and Red China, high-flying spy-planes, aircraft carriers, speedboats, and Polynesians in canoes saw us: They all wondered about the falling Greek trireme shining green and white and silver, miraculously unburned by reentry heat.

Second, I assumed the Olympian gods, no friends of mankind, erased records and memories and people as needed to make the happening into an Orwellian unhappening, the people into nonpersons.

Third, I assumed the Olympians followed the boat as it sailed leisurely toward Vanity Island. We, of course, winged our way in a menagerie of shapes to Catalina Island, and then to Los Angeles.

A cold north wind blew us past the coast until we saw below the hurrying clouds, the city lights, crawling lines of red traffic, a glitter of signs, a solemn glow from empty offices.

Boggin's letter had been written in his backwards-slanting, wide-looped style:

> *My dear Miss Windrose,*
> *If you have not overlooked the evident usefulness to your party*
> *of this note, and if my assumption is sound that you do not wish*
> *to be burdened by fates more than is natural, then you may take*
> *it as given that Lord Mavors has overstepped his authority in*
> *the matter of arranging your current dangerous circumstances.*
> *Nonetheless, being an Olympian, he can decree fate to his*
> *wishes, including his wish to involve boys and girls of tender*
> *years in affairs best left to professional military men.*
>
> *Matters being as they are, I am confident that you would*
> *care to explore any avenue that might promise solution to this*
> *conundrum. There is but one god who can overrule even the*
> *war-god, even in matters of war. For obvious reasons, he is a*
> *fellow of cautious retiring temperament, so take care not to*
> *startle him upon your approach.*
>
> *I have sent my regards ahead of you, that he awaits your*
> *coming.*

Below this, an address and a name.

The name was Valentine Archer.

The address turned out to be a swank club on Santa Monica Boulevard.

3.

It was night as we approached, which, I suppose, is the proper time to approach a Hollywood nightclub. (If they are open during the day, are they called dayclubs?) A line of limousines, like shining black jewels, threaded its way past the fountains, with here and there a red sports car for contrast.

Some were magnificently dressed: The men were in black tie and tails, the women in flimsy silks of sable or scarlet, or clinging short dresses of peach hue, which left their arms and long legs bare to the cool night air; the ladies had gems at their wrists and throats, or winking in their hair. Others looked like day laborers, longshoremen, or criminals, with tattered dungarees, wild dreadlocks, caps on backwards, T-shirts with tails untucked. I stared in fascination at one smiling woman whose teeth had been studded with diamonds.

There was an honest-to-goodness red carpet leading from the curb to the tall glass doors. The walls beyond were green and lit with olive lights, giving the building an unearthly look, and atop the central tower was, I kid you not, a giant-size Robin Hood hat, complete with five yards of feather.

The garish neon sign spelled out ARCHER'S BULL'S-EYE. In smaller letters beneath: THE PLACE TO SCORE.

We had circled the block once and twice, trying to get a view from all angles, but other buildings, including a discotheque and a restaurant, blocked approach from the rear. Now we joined the line. The scent of perfume from many bodies hung in the air, and the tang of cigarette smoke, along with the endless mutter of traffic from the street, and the dimly heard banging of the music from the club. When the wind blew, droplets from the fountains fell among us, refreshing.

Colin nudged me. "Hey! There she is! I wrote her a letter. Why is there another guy with her? I thought I was supposed to have mind-control powers or something. What's the point of mind control if your girls date other guys? What's up with that?"

Vanity said, "She's not your girl because you wrote her a love letter."

Colin muttered, "If I had mind-control powers, she would be!"

Quentin said mildly, "I've seen that guy on TV. Funny, I thought he was done with computers."

I started to look "past" the walls of the building, but Vanity hissed, "Stop!"

"What?" I said.

"Your eyes turn red when you do that, and they seem to be, sort of, further away than your head is."

"Well . . ."

Colin said, "I'll handle it."

Without another word, he jumped over the velvet rope separating one part of the line from another. He was speaking to a young woman with long chestnut hair that brushed her hips. Her hair was longer than her dress, which almost did not make it all the way from her armpits to the top of her legs. Whatever he said, he was making her laugh, and I noticed he touched her bare shoulder when he spoke.

He was wearing her sunglasses when he returned and, without a word, he passed them to me.

"I could have just closed my eyes, you know," I said crossly. "I can see through my lids."

"Gross," opined Vanity.

In a higher dimension, where no mortals could see, I opened my hypersphere and jarred it to set it ringing. The concentric pressure waves of not-light radiated out in four directions, filling hypervolumes rather than volumes. In the sudden gleam, I looked.

"The buildings are interconnected. Two dance floors with lights and lasers. A bar. Basement rooms contain refrigerators, wine cellars. There are offices on the top floor."

"Can you see through lead? Look for a safe," suggested Colin.

"Are you an idiot? I am looking over the sides of things. It doesn't matter what they're made of."

"Anyone look like a god?" Colin asked. "They have ichor inside 'em instead of blood."

Victor said, "Leader, I just noticed the electromagnetic aura concentrated here dropped. The signatures are consistent with the standing-wave phenomena Quentin manipulates. Magic."

"Dropped, meaning . . . ?"

"Something just went away, or reduced output. Doesn't look like a threat."

I winced and bit my lip. In the higher plane, I folded my hypersphere back into a disk, feeling foolish. "Boggin warned me to be cautious. I might have scared Archer away. If he sees in the fourth dimension, he just saw a spotlight passing over his house here, or if he has a Phaeacian . . . Vanity, is anyone looking at us?"

Vanity was signing an autograph for a young man who mistook her for Lindsay Lohan. He was trying to wheedle her phone number from her when Quentin stepped between the two, letting his walking stick rap threateningly near the boy's feet and allowing her to disengage.

Vanity said, "Amelia, that is the dumbest question since the question mark was invented in 500 A.D. Every man here is looking at us, comparing us to his date, and every date is sizing us up, too. And the boys are staring, wishing they were men. So, yes, a lot of people are looking." She turned and waved at several tall men in tuxedoes, who were smiling toward her. Over her shoulder, she said, "If there is a sniper on the roof, I can't tell, not in a crowd."

Then we were at the front of the line. The doorman was dressed in Lincoln green, with a peaked cap on his head and a clipboard in his hand. The Merry Man effect was jarred by his sunglasses and hearing aid, which made him look like a Secret Service agent from a movie.

"Names?"

"Amelia Windrose, how do you do?" "Vanity Fair." "Victor Invictus Triumph, sir." "Call me Nemo." "Randy Johnson Willie Joystick, but friends call me Dick."

He looked up. "Vanity Fair? Like the magazine?"

Vanity smiled brightly. "They named a magazine after me? This is a wonderful country!"

The expression in his eyes was hidden. "You kids make those names up?"

Quentin said, "Actually, we did. The North Wind sent us. We're here to see Archer."

The guy looked back down at his checklist. "I'm sorry, your names, made up or not, are not on my list. The Bull's-Eye Club is invitation only. Next!"

Vanity said, "But we have an invitation! Boreas said he sent word ahead." "Next!"

I said in my best Headmaster Boggin voice, "See here, young man! We are here to see Mr. Archer, and we have no intention of leaving without seeing him!"

The two guys behind us (one of whom had a ring both in his nostril and in his lip) started to shoulder forward, but Victor stood in the way. They made the mistake of deciding to manhandle him, grabbing at his shoulder and elbow. There was a loud snap of noise and a smell of ozone, and the two men jumped back, yowling and swearing.

Colin turned toward them, gritting his teeth, and his hair started to stand up, and his face to grow dark. Quentin tapped his walking stick on the ground, and a dark shadow began to stream from his feet and swell across the sidewalk and up the building.

"Troops!" I said sharply. "Stand down! The Dark Mistress has not given the word yet!"

This drew some hoots and murmurs from the crowd around us. We were suddenly the center of attention.

The guy with the rings in his nose and lip said, "Hey! He's got a stun gun! He shocked us! I'm calling the cops!"

A voice from the crowd called out, "The cops'll just kick your ass, man. This is L.A."

I did not see the fast-moving molecular packages leave Victor's body and enter the nervous systems of the two men behind us, but I noticed the sudden snarl of moral forces in the area as the angry young men behind us suddenly looked sleepy and forgetful.

To Victor I hissed, "I said stand down! Or you'll see a court-martial, I swear to you, Victor Triumph!"

"Yes, Leader," said Victor.

The Merry Man with the clipboard asked me carefully, "Did he just call you 'Leader'?"

At that moment, another man came over, stepping briskly. I assume from the way the Merry Man wordlessly deferred to him that he was a member of the staff, or maybe he just got out of the way because the guy was huge and heavily armed.

Could be a basketball player, if he wasn't already a linebacker. Heavy black boots, heavy black denim pants, heavy black leather jacket. Black on black on black. You get the picture. Every inch of the black leather jacket had a shining metal ring sewn to it, so he rang and glittered as he walked. Clipped among his rings were Japanese throwing stars, looking like harmless ornaments, lost in the glitter. The handle of a Bowie knife protruded from a sheath in his boot, a second was at his hip, a third up his sleeve. In his hand he carried not a spear (as I first had thought) but a harpoon with a sharpened steel togglehead and, incredibly, a loop of cable running through it, with the other end of the cord wrapping his spear hand.

He might have been a member of a biker gang. A really, really nasty biker gang. A biker gang of Eskimos, I should say, who harpooned seals between riots.

Oh, and he was handsome, in a rough way. Very rough. His face looked like something carved by rough hatchet blows out of a pine stump. His hair was done up in short gelled spikes, a look that went out of fashion in England after the defeat of the Picts. He had wide, high cheeks, blunt jaw, his mouth a single cruel slash beneath a proud nose, eyes like a wolf's eye beneath a wide overhanging brow, the forehead of a king or a philosopher: a warrior-king, though, or a Nietzschean philosopher. A scar ran from the corner of his eye across the muscles of his cheek, to where the deep lines formed brackets around his stern mouth. It was a big, ugly scar, but, somehow, it made his face look more striking, not less. I was sure he had gotten it at Heidelberg.

The crowd quieted down when he strode up. "May I help you?" he said in a tone that left no question that no help could possibly be forthcoming.

I said, "We are here to see Mr. Archer on a matter of very important, um, importance." (Boy, I could have said that better.)

Colin helped me. Sort of. Not. He chimed in, "Tell your boss that the world could be destroyed if he dicks around with us."

Tall, Dark, Scarred, and Handsome gave him a thoughtful look. "So . . . you can, um, destroy the world, issat right? Cute trick."

Colin grinned like an idiot. "Yeah, but we can only do it once."

He said, "Listen, kids. You know what my job here is?"

Vanity looked at his huge harpoon. She said gaily, "Let me guess. You seek the White Whale?"

She was doing that Vanity-thing she does with her eyelashes and bestowing the sweetest smile on him, so even his grim face softened, and he smiled back. "No, miss. I'm Mr. Nice Guy. I am here to see that the people who are invited into the club here have a nice time. Now you are blocking the line, and all of Mr. Archer's guests behind you might not have a nice time because of it. So I gotta make it right, okay?"

I thought this meant he was going to burn us to cinders with laser beams shooting from his eyes or something, but no. Instead, he led us a few steps to one side, and the Merry Man proceeded with the glittering people in line behind us. We were standing beside the doors, and long thin leaves from potted plants were poking me in the back.

"Now, your names are not on the list, are they?" said the huge man.

Quentin said quietly, "May we have your name, sir? Mr. Archer will be displeased if we are hindered, I assure you."

"I am Terro— ah, Terrance. Terrance, um, Miles. And Mr. Archer is my brother."

Quentin said, "If he's your brother, why isn't your last name—?"

"Stage name."

I said, "Listen. This is important. Do you know the world is run by pagan gods?"

"I know L.A. is, that's for sure. And one of the gods of L.A. says that no one gets in the Bull's-Eye Club unless they're properly dressed. We have a dress code."

I watched a couple go by. The man had glasses shaped like the number

2008, with an eye peering through each zero. His date was wearing see-through plastic pants.

"What about them?"

Tall and Dark said, "They're on the list. Dress code does not apply to Mr. Archer's special guests."

Victor said, "Leader, why don't we simply leave a cell phone number? Archer can call us, once he gets Boggin's message."

Before I could answer, Tall and Dark said, "Listen, you seem like nice kids. You go away and come back dressed properly, you can come in."

I said, "Then we can see Mr. Archer?"

A shrug. "Maybe he'll see you, maybe not. He's not here right now, but he might be back tonight."

Vanity said to me, "Amelia, my nice outfits are on the boat. And where are the boys going to get tuxedoes at this hour? We don't have that much money left, after all."

Tall and Dark said, "Kids, if you are not the kind of folk who can afford expensive suits with your pocket money, you're not getting into this club."

Vanity's face was flushed with anger. She stamped her foot and demanded, "What? Is there a tailor open at this hour?"

Her rosy-red features and low-cut blouse, well, they attracted his attention, and his craggy face softened once again with a smile. "Look, like I said, I'm Mr. Nice Guy. I stop fights, see? We like to have good-looking girls in the club. Here."

He took a card out of his pocket, leaned his harpoon against the wall, took out a ballpoint pen, and scribbled on the back. He proffered the card to Vanity. "Go to this address. Tuxedo shop, dresses, that sort of thing. Up-scale, very nice. They keep late hours. Show the manager my card, and he'll fix you up, give you ten percent off. He owes me a favor. And meanwhile, you there, Little Miss Blond Girl." He offered me the pen and a blank card. "Write a message. Any crazy thing you like, gods blowing up the world, whatever. I'll put it on Mr. Archer's desk. I can't guarantee he'll read it, I can't guarantee he'll believe it, but write what you like. Don't bother putting down your phone number. He never makes calls. Hates phones. Likes to talk to people face-to-face, you know?"

I knelt down to use the pavement for a desk. I forget what I wrote: something about how Boggin sent us, we were not from Mavors or Mulciber, but we have urgent business to discuss. I was kind of coy about saying too much, but I wanted to drop names so he'd know we were not humeys. Wolves, not cattle.

Then the huge guy politely escorted us to the curb, smiled, ignored whatever else we said, and stomped back to the club, his ring mail glittering and chiming at every footstep.

Vanity, staring at the broad back retreating said, "Why was he carrying a harpoon?"

Quentin said, "Because that was—"

Without warning, Vanity jumped into Quentin's arms and landed a big, wet, sloppy kiss on his lips. After a moment or two, Colin said, "Are you guys going to come up for air?"

I slapped myself on the neck. "Damn these mosquitoes." Then I said, "Let's go to this tux shop, whatever it is." And I began marching down the sidewalk. Vanity and Quentin broke their hold and followed.

After a short bit, we turned a corner, and Vanity said softly, "All clear."

Colin said to Vanity, "Red, if I am about to say something stupid, would you kiss me, too?"

Quentin said, "Down, hormone boy, down!"

Vanity smiled sweetly. "Each time you are about to say something stupid? Well, I'd have no time for anything else!"

I looked at Vanity, "If we are now in the clear . . . ?" She nodded.

To the group: "First, in the future, let the Leader do the talking. That was just disgraceful! Everyone jaw-jawing at once. If I had been the bouncer, I would have had us all arrested." I drew a deep breath and gave them all the basilisk eye. No one decided to talk back to me, not then.

To Quentin: "And what were you about to say, Quentin?"

"Deimos. That was Deimos, son of Mavors. Terror is his other name. *Miles* is just a word for 'soldier.' He stops fights because he is the god who causes one side to panic and rout, so that spearmen can cut them down from behind as they flee." Quentin breathed a sigh and wiped his brow. "He is not Mr. Nice Guy. Really. Not. Did none of you recognize him?"

Vanity said, "Why a harpoon?"

Quentin said, "Not sure. Maybe as a symbol? Terror, once it strikes, leaves its hook in your heart, and slowly pulls you in. Even the hugest creatures on earth cannot escape."

Victor said, "What now, Leader? I suggest we break into the club and wait for Mr. Archer to return—assuming he is actually gone."

I said, "Why would Mavors' son help us against his father?"

Quentin said, "Greek gods don't love their dads. Saturn castrated his father and ate his son, or tried to, and he, in turn, threw him into Tartarus." Quentin shivered again. "I have no love for the White Christ, but at least the God of Jerusalem was adored by his son."

Victor said sardonically, "Who adored the son enough in return to have him tortured to death for crimes he did not commit."

I said, "We are shelving the theology discussion. Advice on a course of action? We have one vote for break in and surprise him."

Colin licked his lower lip and said in a thoughtful tone, "That big guy? I think I can take him. Let's break in."

I had sudden insight into male psychology. My theory: Guys are idiots. Keep this theory in mind. It explains the phenomena while assuming no unnecessary agents.

Vanity said in exasperation, "Beggars can't be break-in-ers! We're trying to get ourselves free from Mavors' curse. If we disobey his direct order, then it's a Quentin thing again, right? Like poor Mr. Finklestein looking at Phoebe bathing. So we are coming to this guy for help." She turned to Quentin. "Deimos is really Archer, right? There are not two gods running around in L.A."

Quentin did not answer her, but said, "Leader, I cannot trespass, or break rules like that, or else my Art will endanger me."

I said, "If you were wearing a tux, could you break in? Think about the words Deimos said. He invited you back in, if you were dressed right. He did not say anything about going in through the front door."

Victor said, "So what's the plan?"

I said, "Let's go shopping! You know, I have not spent a single dime of my money yet, and I think I need a new dress."

4.

"Upscale" he called it. The place was huge. Glittering aisles of goods were piled deep as the rooms of gold the Aztecs gathered to ransom Montezuma. Fabrics, jewelry, more shoes than an elfish cobbler's shop. Sporting goods for sale in the back of the store. (I made a mental note to buy myself a shooting iron. I was in America, after all.) Electronics. Televisions. Musical instruments. Everything.

The store was strangely deserted—or, not so strange, considering the late hour—but the manager came hurrying down the empty aisles when the five of us entered the front door.

He smiled and inclined his head when we showed him the card Deimos had given us. "Gentlemen's apparel is on the second floor. . . ." He gestured toward the grand-ballroom-style staircase leading up to a sort of elevated courtyard surrounded by several departments or shops on the right. "Women's evening wear, yes? On the left . . ." A twin of the first staircase led up to an area the size of a small town, but one where an impatient sorcerer turned every inhabitant into a dressmaker. There was no balcony or bridge between the two departments: To cross from one to the other required descending one grand staircase, crossing the wealth-crowded aisles of the main salon, and ascending another.

Victor said, "Leader, I am not sure we should split up."

Colin said, "He's right, I mean, you girls might need help tucking your mammary glands into brassieres or something."

Vanity took me by the elbow. "We don't want to miss Archer; besides, this is still within screaming distance. And how fast can Victor fly? Mach twenty-two or something?"

I said, "Just stay alert. Go get your tuxes." But for some reason, Vanity and I started giggling as we tripped up the stairway to the palace of luxury atop. Here were mannequins in poses of grace, and acres of soft fabric hanging from padded hangers.

Vanity whispered: "The money! It is still folded up in your fourth dimension."

But there was a clerk watching. The young lady walked across the shimmering marble floor toward us, the only other person in sight, and it was not the time to pull my energy-shining wings down into this plenum.

5.

A man in purple pulled open the door of my little dressing room. Of course, the way this world works, it was just at the moment when I was wearing nothing but bra and panties, and I was bent over, pulling my toes out of a collapsed skirt.

I should explain how he sneaked up on me: I was not looking. Hyperspace in this area was dark, and I would have had to ring my sphere, sending not-light out in all directions, to keep an eye on what was happening around me, and I was wary of showing a light, not knowing if there were eyes like my eye watching. So, surprise!

I kept a cool head. I straightened like a diver jumping, and jumped a direction at right angles of all directions, neither right nor left, forward nor back, up nor down. My arm should have simply moved "past" his fingers, but instead he kept his grip. He was like Colin, at least a bit, a creature of passion.

But he did not shut off my powers; perhaps he could not. Instead I reared up into the fourth dimension, and he, keeping his grip, was lifted partway out of the "plane" of Earth's continuum. His feet were still in Earthly space, but his upper body was curled into the fourth dimension. To me his body looked like a streamer of bark peeling off a tree.

He had some thickness in the fourth dimension, not so much as Miss Daw and her body, which looked like a wheel of eyes within a wheel of eyes, but there was something feathered with strands of music, serpentine, with scales of alternating gravity and levity rippling down the solids that formed the surface of his snakelike body.

But he was not full, not like I was. I sensed his fourth dimensional extensions were of limited utility; their internal nature was artificial rather than natural. I was looking at some sort of living armor: a thing he wore, not a thing he was.

I screamed then: a loud, sustained, ear-piercing scream. In theory, I should have merely shouted, or struggled in grim silence, as a boy would do. Well, this was no time for theory. I needed help, and it was automatic anyway. Think of this as Nature's siren.

"Hush, Princess!" came the sharp command, which he flicked to me on a strand carrying an essence of meaning.

"The boys are coming!"

"Not unless they can hear sound waves in a volume skewed to the continuum, they aren't. Now, hush, or I'll make your true love a man with a jackass's head."

He moved his feet and pushed me in the "blue" direction, so that I landed in the changing room one or two over from where I had been. He was straddling me, pinning me down. He did not look like a snake in three-dimensional cross-section, but like a winged boy, and his vast purple plumes filled the cabinet above and to either side. He was dressed in gold-trimmed purple robes, and on his thick, dark, ambrosia-dripping curls of hair, he wore a diadem of woven poppies and red roses, thorns and all. Slung over one shoulder was a Turkish bow of rosy wood, shaped like a woman's upper lip. At his other shoulder was a quiver of ivory, in which arrows fletched with peacock feathers rattled.

He was strong, and very handsome, and he smelled good. What is wrong with having evil people be ugly guys with wormy features, eh? How come all the Greek gods look like, well, like Greek gods? It seemed unfair.

"You saw me naked," I said. "I get to turn you into a stag now, and have your dogs rend you."

He looked down at my cleavage. I was wearing a lacy black bra. And I started to blush. I am convinced it was a blush of rage, but it was so unfair.

"You're dressed in love's proper hue," he said dryly. "It is fitting. Besides, I've seen women with less on at the beach." But he stood up and—if I were in a good mood, I'd call what he did helping me to my feet. In a bad mood, I'd call it hauling me to my feet. With his bulky purple wings filling the changing closet, he was standing much too close. "You wanted to see me," he said.

I looked at this youngish fellow. "Are you Mr. Archer?"

"I'm the archer," he agreed.

"Who are you? Apollo?"

"Pshaw! Mightier than Apollo," said Archer with a quirk of his lips. "Ask Hyacinth about that. Apollo rules during the day; I rule day and night. *Omnia vincit amor!* All things I conquer. Even Death is not as strong."

I said doubtfully, "You mean the Rich One? I saw him—didn't see him, actually—once. Hades? Lord Dis, you call him?"

He nodded, and smiled at some pleasing memory. "We were in the library, arguing, and he claimed he was stronger than I, despite that he was blind. I lifted up the Great Weapon and shot, just as he donned his dread helm and vanished, and I had no more sight of him than he of me. The curtains billowed and the candles blew, so for a time I thought he had escaped my shot, for (as well we know) the Great Weapon often goes astray, but the next day he outraged the Maiden as she gathered flowers in the fields of Enna, and carried her down through sunless crevasses into the House of Woe, so I knew my bolt struck home."

"Death is blind?"

Archer nodded. "As Justice is: He makes no distinctions, plays no favorites." Now the boy took me by my naked shoulders and lowered his face toward mine. I thought he was about to kiss me, but instead he merely looked deeply in my eyes.

"You are in my realm as well," he said. "There is a boy you love, who steps across the threshold into manhood. I can grant your wish. But you must ask it, and be in my debt."

"Wait! When you said you could make my true love have the head of an ass, did you mean you were going to change Victor, or that you would change me?"

He said, "Is that your boon? Is that what Boreas sent you all this way to pray from my court?"

"Your . . . your court?"

"Know you not who We are, little daughter of Chaos? We are Cosmos it-self. The throne is Our own, granted by the Three Goddesses, confirmed by the Fates. Our Royal Person is no less than the Imperator of Heaven."

"Do you have—I don't mean to seem rude or anything, but—do you have a badge or anything?"

"A what?"

"A letter signed by your mother, or a driver's license, or something to prove you are the Emperor of Heaven? A golden stick, a fancy chair, a shiny hat?"

"I have the Great Weapon. Do you want to fall in love with a goat?"

Goat? I already had enough trouble with Colin. So I said, "Okay. You are the Cosmic Emperor and King of All Gods. Let's posit that. And you are talking to me, naked in a closet, because . . . Why?"

"I've never had a boring conversation with a girl in her lacy things. But once she puts on clothes and opens her mouth, then . . ."

I favored him with a withering look. "It's the 'in the closet' part I was wondering about. You are afraid to talk to five children in a group, aren't you? You are not really an emperor of anything, are you?"

"Well, that depends. I was pitched off the throne by my uncles, but I never formally abdicated. My realm is shrunken somewhat, so only my brothers Fear and Dread keep faith with me. My sister Trouble is with me, too, sort of, but she's almost more trouble than she's worth. Well, it's not much, but it is something." He shrugged. "Every leader has some setbacks from time to time. So? We are the sovereign power that rules the ordered universe. You have a petition to ask. Ask."

"Can I ask for peace between Cosmos and Chaos?"

"Petitions for peace can only be granted by both parties in contention, not by one. But I am pleased, very pleased, that you thought to ask for that before you asked for life or freedom. Lord Terminus had you raised together, as Earthly children, and instructed in the histories and arts of man. Have you never wondered why?"

"I have wondered," I admitted.

"Boreas told me the reason."

"You trust him?"

"Indeed. But I don't like him. Likeable and trustworthy are not the same thing, are they? But Boreas, even after Terminus died, kept faith with the orders he was given, kept his promises. Which is why I trust him now, that cold bastard, and I let him know where I was, despite the people hunting me—"

The door swung open. There was Vanity, wearing a sheer peach evening dress with the tags at the neckline. "I thought I heard voices. Who the heck are you? Leader, is someone molesting you again? I swear you give off a scent that attracts perverts."

Archer, startled, let go of me and straightened up slightly. Then he swung his gaze back toward me, but the moment he took his eyes from me, the wall behind me gave way, and I had fallen through a trapdoor that snapped silently shut behind me. I was in a little crawl space that ran behind the dressing rooms.

Smoothly done. I had no idea Vanity was so smooth. I was in a crawl space: so I crawled.

Archer said, "Where'd she go?"

Vanity was saying, "You're Cupid, aren't you? The one who lost the throne?"

"I know exactly where is it, Lady Nausicaa." Through the wall, I could see him smile an ingratiating smile and place his hand on his heart. "It is merely that armed warriors stand between me and it."

Vanity did not smile back, which was rare for her. Instead she said in a businesslike tone, "Boggin says you can overrule Mavors. Is that true?"

"The matter is complex. Each god has certain terrain that is his own, a realm where his will rules fate. But if events occur where two influences overlap, there is considerable controversy, restrained, to a degree, by precedents long ago established, and to a degree the conflict is restrained by a gentlemen's agreement among ourselves to avoid an open fate-war."

"Mavors ordered Amelia to lead the five of us back to an island where we would be attacked by Lamia, a blood-drinking vampiress, who wants to kill us as the quickest way to break the truce between Cosmos and Chaos. Can you stop this decree?"

This was the Vanity from Vanity Island: the leader-woman, sharp and concise. I admit I used to think of her as silly. But silly was not the same as happy.

And anyone can afford to be silly when she is a prisoner, or a child, not in control of her own life, making no decisions that matter to anyone. That is what she used to be. Helpless and therefore silly. Me, too, I guess.

Through the walls, I saw Archer, with a rustle of his wide wings, step from the closet and advance toward Vanity. "Indeed I can halt the decree of the war-god, sending young girls in love to war, for you are in my realm, not his. But will I? Love is a fickle thing. Why should I grant this petition? Have any of you vowed fealty to me?" He looked left and right again. I could sense some sort of pressure wave coming from his fourth-dimensional armor, and sweeping back and forth to the "red" and "blue" of me. Again, his extensions into the fourth dimension were artificial, not part of his nervous system. I don't think his senses could interpret what he saw very clearly. He could not just look through walls. If I stayed flat in three dimensions, his radar (or whatever it was) did not see me.

"Where is your leader? Helion's daughter, the shepherdess? Boreas told me she was the one who was in charge of your merry band. The smart one, he called her."

Well, the so-called smart one at that moment did not want him to know how Vanity had gotten me out of the room; nor was I eager to continue the conversation in my underthings. Nude and blushing is not the way to talk to a love-god. I noticed that Vanity was not being distracted by asides as I had been.

Following the shortcut Vanity made for me, I found myself back in my little dressing room.

Even though Vanity was holding up her end of the conversation just fine, if Boggin told Archer I was the leader, he would not negotiate with her. Since I did not want him to deduce how I'd gotten out of his grip, and since I wanted to get dressed, I decided it was time to let him see me again.

I found an easy way to get dressed on the quick was merely to pluck my shed clothes up into the fourth dimension, scrunch my three-dimensional cross-section into a point inside my outfit, and rotate it so that the point expanded outward suddenly. I had my left arm in my right sleeve and vice versa, but it was quicker to twist dimensions in a half circle than it was to take the clothes off and put them back on again. I left the evening gown on the hanger: I was dressed in my flying leathers, with track shoes on my feet and my lucky cap on my head.

So I pushed open the door and stepped out. "Here I am, Mr. Archer! I need to know something about you before we close the deal."

He nodded briefly. "You need only know whether I have the power to do as you ask. I do."

Vanity spoke up. "If you are so powerful, why'd you lose the throne?"

He gave her a cryptic, sidelong glance. "That is sort of a personal question, Princess. Ask a historian."

I said, "We need to know the situation. You say you are powerful enough to overrule Mavors, but if he is the war-god, can't he win any battle with you? With anyone? Come to think of it, why didn't he take the throne by force when Terminus died? I'm asking the wrong question. Not how you got pushed off the throne, but how you ever got on it? How did you inherit Heaven?"

Archer smiled that type of smile I've seen on Boggin's face when he hears a clever question from Colin. Smiling at the unexpected. "I was deposed because of my power, not despite it."

"What does that mean?" Vanity asked, her hand on her hips, her green eyes glinting.

He paused to smile at her, perhaps gathering bitter memories in his head. "When Lord Terminus fell beneath Typhon, the secret of the lightning bolt was lost. Lady Tritogenia can wield the Bolt of Heaven, but even she knows not how to make it; they say the cyclopes of Mulciber can make it, but he cannot use it in battle; and the God of Battles, Mavors, who knows the outcome of war, knows that only the Lightning can drive Chaos away. You see? With our Great King dead, our only defense against Chaos is to hide behind you children. But there is a weapon greater than the greatest weapon of Heaven; even the gods bow to it."

He looked back and forth at Vanity and me, expectant, smug.

I said, "The Great Weapon."

6.

He nodded, and one hand touched the pink curves of his Turkish bow with unconscious pride. "Indeed. The Great Weapon. How could Chaos resist, if I had all the queens of the underworld, of dreamland and outer void fall in love with the world? What can quiet the hatred of all enemies, but love, beautiful love?"

I shuddered at the thought of my mother, or the beautiful Lady Nepenthe, Colin's mother, whom I had once seen in a dream, in this man's arms.

He must have guessed my thought, for he looked at me and said sharply, "Not like that! I am a happily married man, little girl. I meant to have the enemies of this world fall in love with the world, with Gaea herself, her mountains and rushing streams, majestic forests of green, somber artic seas of blue, and deserts all encrimsoned with the many colors of a flame: and overhead the ordered spheres of heaven with their gemlike stars remote, the planets wheeling like falcons in their cycles and epicycles. Who, seeing the Cosmos, would not fall in love?"

"What went wrong?" I asked.

He spread his hands. "My mother told me that people do not always treat the ones they love so well. She thought it was madness."

Vanity said, "Your mother is Lady Cyprian? Aphrodite, Venus? Why does she get a vote? I thought you were the Emperor of Cosmos?"

"Ah, but even Monarchy is based on the willingness of the Led to be led. You see, three goddesses crowned me: Lady Tritogenia the Wise, also called Athena, who controls the Thunderbolt and the starry hosts of heaven; the Lady Cyprian, who bestows the love of the people; and the Great Queen Basilissa, called Hera, who grants the Mandate of Heaven, and decrees Sovereignty itself. Only the head those three sovereign goddesses anoint, the martial maiden, the beloved, and the mother of gods and man, can sustain the oak-leaf crown.

"Do you know the meaning of the old history?" Archer continued. "King Terminus was a parricide; his hands were polluted with his father's blood. Only these three could wash the stains away: wisdom, and love, and the law. The Great Queen of Heaven is also the High Lady of Forgiveness, and Grandfather Terminus repaid her kindness by giving her ever more adulteries to forgive."

He seemed lost in thought for a moment, frowning.

"So these three goddesses picked you?" I said softly.

"I was the compromise candidate. The Great Queen was my grandmother, and Lady Cyprian was my mother, and Lady Tritogenia was as afraid of me as all intellectuals should be. (Merlin and Solomon can tell you how well the wise and learned can withstand the foolishness of love!) Mavors did not want to war on his own son, and Mulciber did not dare earn the hate of his wife, my mother. And everyone thought I was a foolish boy, young and weak and easily led.

"But my flaw was not that I was weak. As I said, I was too strong. Do you see? They were afraid to follow the love-god to war with Chaos. And when the Goddess of Love herself, the Lady Cyprian, said no . . . well, let us say that she is considerably older and greater than any of us know. She was found floating on a seashell in the Western Sea, surrounded by singing Graces, and she may be older than Chaos or Old Night."

I said, "Is that why Mavors is not in charge of everything? He needs the three goddesses to coronate him?"

He nodded. "Partly why. Who wants War to rule the universe, rather than Love? My father Mavors is a strange man. I think he hates himself. He rejoices in the glory and virtue of war, but he hates the carnage, the madness, the tears, the bloody business of it, the lies. So many lies. He is basically an honest fellow, in his own way, and he doesn't like how enemies use spies and traitors; kings lie to men; men lie to their wives; and wives tell their children how brave their fathers are; cowards get medals and real heroes die un-marked; and bards lie about it all. He is not a happy man, my father, except when he's with Mother.

"And Father can never be with her, lawfully, unless he gains the throne and changes the laws. If he becomes the Lord of Sovereignty, no longer merely the Lord of War, he can bind his heavy red sword in olive branches and retire from his bloody work, spend his days at home with the prettiest wife in Heaven. What veteran wants more than that?"

Archer shrugged and seemed a little sad. "In any case, Mavors does not dare rule a Cosmos torn with bloody civil war, not with Chaos encamped in strength outside our crystal walls. It might be different if Father had the un-ambiguous support of Mother. But my mother, the Cyprian, merely looks at him through her long lashes and smiles and does not leave her crook-backed soot-streaked husband—but neither does she leave the rough and handsome war-god to his loneliness.

"So every eye is on Mavors now, now that he has imprudently risked the Children of Chaos to winkle out the traitors among us. If he finds the hidden foe whose hand guides Lamia to her sick crimes, the Great Queen, Mavors' mother, will support him, so she has said, and we all believe his lover, the Cyprian, will also, once a firm excuse allows her. Even his enemy, Tritogenia, the war-goddess, who hates him, cannot withhold her grace from a victor crowned by fate. If the Three Goddesses give him the auspices, Lord Pela-gaeus the Earthshaker will withdraw his claim, and even Lord Dis may with-draw his threat to give the throne of brightest heaven to the sad girl-queen of darkest hell.

"Is the moral of my little story clear? Mavors, utterly unsuited to the task, must win the love of those he seeks to lead. He, who could conquer Heaven by fighting, will not be fit to rule in Heaven, unless he can conquer it without fighting. Letting you five run free until his prey starts from the brush is his way of proving to his peers that he is a master of policy and craft, not of bloodshed only. He has to prove he can cooperate with Mul-ciber and outthink the conspiracy that threatens us all. He has to prove he is as cunning and cold as old Boreas, or else old Boreas will not serve him loyally.

"So much is riding on this episode, but he should not have crossed me. I am his son. My wars are fought in the heart, and my battlefields are more ter-rible than his! Do you doubt me, that I can overcome his curse, and free you from his command? Look at the orderly Cosmos around you! What power guides the planets in their courses? What keeps the stars in place? What keeps the Earth firm on her center, and the polestar on his axle? Look, and answer! Is not love stronger than war? If you agree, vow fealty to me!"

7.

I was impressed, in that I did not think Archer was exaggerating, but I reminded myself that Boreas had sent me here, and so this might be merely another and larger trap. I wanted to talk to Victor.

I said, "Sir, I cannot answer you quickly, or you will think me flippant. And I will need to consult with my crew before we make any deals."

At that moment, I heard Quentin's voice in my ear, clear and close as Jiminy Cricket. *"Leader, Victor says he has built up sufficient potential to discharge a one hundred and twenty-megavolt X-ray laser into Archer's skull. If you want us to attack, extend your middle finger toward him. If not, touch your nose."*

I rubbed my nose. How unladylike. I wish they had come up with a better signal system. I was glad (for once) that the boys had decided to spy on us while we changed: I assume Colin was behind this.

Of course, had I been a good leader, I would have set this all up ahead of time, signals and all.

Archer's eyes narrowed. If he had sense impressions like mine, which could detect the nature and use of objects and events, he might have seen my nose glow just now, and might know what it meant.

Quentin, in my ear, whispered, *"Leader, we sign our death warrants if we back one faction over another, in a civil war where we don't know the identities, issues, or the strengths of the sides. We cannot agree to those terms. You have to find another common ground."*

Archer said carefully, "I think you have consulted with your crew sufficiently, Lady Phaethusa of Myriagon. Your choices are clear, but narrow."

I nodded, agreeing with what both Archer and Quentin said.

Now that it was time to talk seriously, a sense of dread surprised me. Suddenly my mouth felt dry. I think I kept licking my lips, because Archer kept staring at them.

I drew a breath and straightened my spine. I reminded myself that I was not a schoolgirl talking to a teacher: I was an independent and equal player in some terrible game of war, with the lives of my four friends, and many more lives than that, depending on what I said next.

Okay. It was no harder than walking a tightrope over a pit, was it?

I said, "I am not sure any of us can swear fealty to you. I mean, no offense, but we cannot really afford to take sides in your civil cold war, cold civil war, whatever. We'd just get crushed. Used, then crushed. Because why would you trust us, once we were no longer necessary?"

He said smoothly, "You must weigh the comparative dangers. Mavors' curse will drive you into this island, where you will serve as bait for his ambuscade, if I do nothing. If we come to an agreement, and you support my claim to kingship, there is a danger I will not keep faith. Which danger seems more immediate, likelier, deadlier?"

No harder than walking a tightrope over a pit. A deep pit. Filled with sharks. Radioactive sharks.

I said, "But surely, milord . . ."

"You're demoting me. I'm a 'Your Imperial Majesty.' "

I nodded. I was not going to quibble with touchy gods over titles. "But surely, Your Imperial Majesty, you have a similar choice. You must weigh the dangers, how likely they are, how severe they are, of your several possible courses of action. If you do not help us, Mavors drives us to the island, where we may die, precipitating a war the Olympians cannot afford to fight right now. Or if we do not die, and Mavors is successful, he is covered with glory, not you, and some who waver now might cleave to him—am I guessing wrong here?—when the real fight starts over the throne. If Mavors saves us, we might have to keep helping him, simply because he is trying to kill someone who is trying to kill us, isn't he? The question is whether there is any advantage for you, in this course."

Archer's eye twinkled, and he smiled a charming, charming smile. "No, milady, the question is what you are offering me . . ."

"If I'm really a princess, isn't that 'Your Highness' also, Your Imperial Majesty?"

He nodded gracefully. "Your Highness. The question is, if I help Your Highness, what's in it for me? Royalty is not so different from piracy. We both have some reason to cooperate on a venture, and we must agree on the division of loot."

Radioactive sharks with charming smiles.

Think, Amelia, think. You read all those books. What would Odysseus do? Dress up like a beggar, and then shoot everyone. No help there. What would Achilles do? Go sulk in his tent. Nope. Aeneas? Sacrifice a cow or something. Boy, these old heroes are really not useful as role models. Who were my other heroes? Margaret Thatcher? Attack Argentina. No time to go wobbly.

Good advice, I guess. And what would Headmaster Boggin do? He was no hero of mine, and yet he was a master of intrigue . . .

. . . one who apparently kept his promises and followed orders even when his master was dead. And if I had actually volunteered for this mission, what promises had I made to my mother and father back home? Why was I here? What were my orders?

No matter what I had sworn back home, my duty now was to escape. Every prisoner's duty was escape. It is what we all swore back when we were children. Freedom was the goal. A freedom we could keep.

The deep pit suddenly did not look so deep. And sharks can be handled if you keep your wits about you.

I said, "Here is what is in it for you, sir. You override and undo the fate Mavors decreed, so that we are not caught each time we are in danger. We are not obligated to go act as bait for Lamia, or to cooperate with any war plans of Mavors. You decree that what law Lord Terminus made to keep us captive is null and void. Can you do that?"

He nodded. "And?"

"And we agree in return to vow that we will not, deliberately or negligently, endanger the Cosmos or threaten mankind. The moment we put man or man's universe in current and obvious danger, we are forsworn, and you, and only you, can find us again. In other words, we keep our liberty because the reason for keeping us prisoner no longer applies. Then you are the one who is in a position to save the world; the other gods and goddesses will have to come to you to find out where we are."

He said, "This would prevent you from returning to Chaos, would it not?"

I said, "Probably, but not necessarily. This oath would prevent us from returning for so long as such an act would endanger the universe. Anything might happen. Chaos could make peace with Cosmos. The horse could learn how to sing. Anything."

"And why do I want four dangerous little chaoticists running around my universe in the first place? If I let Mavors have his way, you'll get swept up in his battle, and, once on the battlefield, he can make sure you're captured again, unless he is wounded or killed."

I licked my lips, and picked each word carefully. I had messed up negotiating with ap Cymru, and had messed up talking with Mavors. Time to make good.

"Because as long as we are free, we have a good reason to see you get back on the throne again, don't we? We won't swear any oath. We don't know you well enough for that. But, whether we like it or not, if someone else achieved the throne of Olympos, someone other than you, the King of the Cosmos would no longer have a reason to allow us our liberty. It will be in our best interest, in our enlightened self-interest, to see that you get your way. And, for all you know, this deal might be the first of a beautiful relationship. You treat us well now; we have reason to treat you well next time. You let Mavors win this round, there is no next time."

He pursed his lips. "Is that your best offer?"

I gave him a coy look sidelong, through half-lowered eyelashes, but did not answer the question. There are some questions it is better not to answer.

He took his rose-hued bow in hand and shrugged, and spread his wings, so that the purple plumage stretched out for yards to each side of him, brushing the dresses hanging there. "I could use the Great Weapon."

Archer paused to let that sink in, and then he said with soft danger in his voice, "Lord Terminus, for all his power and might, could not escape my darts, nor pull the barbed heads free of his enflamed heart. Ask Io, ask Europa, ask Leto."

I was suddenly certain he could do it. Take away what I felt for Victor, just like that. Make me fall in love with Colin, or Quentin. Or Grendel Glum, for that matter. All the warmth, all the special, hidden thoughts I had, all my plans: They could be turned to dust with a pluck of the string.

Something more precious than life itself, and it could be lost.

Now is not the time to go wobbly.

I said, "Controlling someone's mind is generally not a good foundation for a long-term, working relationship of mutual trust. Besides, if you make me fall in love with you, I'll try to change you. So, you have the Great Weapon. You can threaten me with a nasty crush. But is that your best offer? Mavors can threaten me with bloodshed, death, and ruin."

Archer laughed and put the heel of the bow on the tiles, and leaned on it. "Okay. Let's make a best offer. I have limits on what I can decree, as all gods do. But I have the authority to prevent other gods from decreeing your capture. That is not the same as decreeing your freedom. You understand? I cannot be seen helping you. If you can make it, on your own, into a position where no one is chasing you, well and good: My oath will allow you to keep the freedom you earn. But you must earn it, and I cannot give it. I cannot deflect Lamia or the other vampires from your trail, because they are creatures no one loves or can love."

I said, "What about Boggin being able to trace me?"

He answered as I thought he would, "Even could I, I would not free you of your debt to him. That was the price he asked for selling me the chance of meeting you.”

“But you have the power to free us from Mavors’ curse?”

“Mavors is beholden, most shamefully, to my mother, Lady Cyprian, and his decrees I can undo, even in matters of war, for Love conquers War, and the Imperial Seal is still mine, and my bow is greater than his bloodthirsty spear. No more can I do.”

I made myself wait, despite the bubbling sense of triumph rising inside me, and I made myself pause and look thoughtful, and I am sure I fooled nobody, because I am the world’s worst actress.

With as much dignity as I could muster, I said to Vanity, “Go get the boys. We are going to exchange oaths with Mr. Archer.”

8.

While she was gone, he and I stood, awkwardly saying nothing for a moment. At least it was awkward for me. Guys do not usually feel a need to talk, because maybe they aren’t curious about what people are up to, or their brains are built wrong, or something, and getting them to open up is like pulling teeth.

“I’m curious,” I said. “Um, Mr. Imperial Majestic—”

“Let us not stand on ceremony,” he said, leaning on his Turkish-style bow. “Just call me ‘Handsome,’ that’ll do.”

“Your Handsomeness, I was just curious about—”

“You want me to make someone love you? Who, Boggin? Wouldn’t make him any nicer. He’d still be your enemy, except now he’d lust after you, too. Or maybe, should I say, more? And him a married man. Hmph.”

“No!” I said, my face hot. I could feel my ears blushing hot, even in places where I thought ears did not have capillaries. “I was going to ask about, about . . . something else . . . an unrelated topic.”

“What topic?”

I groped for one. “The Norse gods! Odin and Thor. Are they around? And, and, I dunno, Aztec gods and stuff?”

“They’re around, some of them. Some of them are us, called by other names in Germany, and some are homegrown. They call Uranus by the name of Ymir, and claim Hermes, Vili, and Ve killed him, not Saturn, the liars. A lot of the Norse guys were wiped out during our last war with Chaos. Jormungander was like your friend Victor, and Fenrir was like your friend Colin.

Surtur is a first cousin to Quentin Nemo on his mothers' side. You folks do a lot of damage when you cooperate.

"Whom else did you ask about? The ten thousand gods of Japan are real, and we've had a fruitful relationship with Amaterasu-ō-mi-kami and her folk for years. The Aztec gods are mostly wiped out by the gods of Iberia, Cario-ciecus and his crew. Never heard of them? Iberian. They were close enough relations to absorb, and we could steal their honors. I am glad they were around long enough to deal with the New World gods, because the Aztecs were a nasty, filthy bunch. You wouldn't want to meet them."

"Why do you hide from the humans?"

"We need the worship. If they saw us as we were, they'd hate us."

"But they don't worship you, not the pagan gods, not anymore."

"My mom and dad are Lust and Violence. You telling me human beings don't worship them? We're in L.A.! Race riots and Hollywood. Men don't worship what they think they do, no matter what they say."

"You don't hide from other creatures. Cyclopes and Laestrygonians and mermaids and stuff."

He smiled a strange little smile. "Humans are different from other created creatures. Prometheus used something he stole from Lord Terminus and kindled a fire in the human souls. An inextinguishable flame. Indestructible. We don't know what it is. Lord Terminus did not know what Prometheus did, but he was scared silly. He ordered the Titan tormented, to get the information, but Prometheus spat in his eye and prophesied betrayal and death for Grandfather Terminus. The King of Heaven would be overthrown by his son, even as he overthrew his father, and his father overthrew his grandfather. A family tradition. No more than that did he say." Archer shivered slightly, and drew his purple wings close about himself, as if cold. "If you find out who is trying to kill you, you'll find out who sent Typhon of Chaos to kill Heaven's Great King."

I said in a hollow voice, "Prometheus foretold that men would overthrow you, as you overthrew the Titans, and the Titans overthrew the Uranians. That's what he did, isn't it?"

Archer shook off the mood and smiled again. "This was not what we came here to discuss. You had quite another question, did you not?"

"Well," I said, "if, as part of our bargain, if I also asked, I mean, can you make it so my boyfriend, um—"

He laughed. "Now you see why everybody hates me, and wanted me off the throne. I've got the one thing everyone, gods and men alike, thinks he wants, but nobody ever really wants it once he gets it. The first answer to your question is no. I have come around to the opinion that messing up the lives of mortals, and driving them to poetry, or madness, or suicide, is not as funny as it once was.

"You see, I'm a married man these days. Psyche is her name, and she went to Hell and back for me.

"So I believe in true love, now, and my Soul tells me there is a greater love in the universe, a Timelessness beyond time, a supernal Eternity. A Forevermore. I'm a changed man. I'm still cruel, but I don't enjoy it as much.

"The second answer is, you picked the wrong boyfriend. He's the Lost One, isn't he? The Telchine? Your people, the Nameless Ones, can reach into Telchine skulls and rewire them. You could make him love you with no help from me—and the fact you can do that, just by itself, whether I use the Great Weapon or not, will kill your relationship."

I said, "I would never . . . never do anything . . . like that! It would be cheating!"

He grinned his charming grin and shrugged his feathery shrug. "Women are supposed to domesticate men. List the countries where they treat women like dirt, and then list the crude, warlike, and brutal countries. Same list, yes? So you sweet little dears cannot help your sweet little selves. You have to try to change men. Remember your sister, Circe? Women are like that in reverse. Turn pigs into human beings. But a man you can control is not really a man, is he? He's a boychild, not a paterfamilias."

By then Vanity and the boys were approaching, so there was no more time for talk.

THE SURPRISE

1.

I wish I could remember whose idea it was to split up in the shop after Archer left. It must have been mine, because I was the leader. I guess I am responsible for the decision, no matter whose idea it was.

After seeing the boys all dressed up and handsome in their tuxes, the leader made the unilateral decision that we really ought to visit the club down the street anyway.

I said to them, "The same problem exists now as before. As long as we are being hunted, we endanger humans by being near them. So we'll have to search for some spot remoter than the planet Mars. Promixa Centauri might be nice!"

That was greeted by a choir of moans and groans. The troops were not eager for another long trip in an ancient Greek spaceship.

"But this is a victory, troops!" I said over the noise of dissent. "Sort of. The authority of Mavors is overruled. We're not out of the woods yet, but now getting out of the woods is possible. Archer was not willing to stop other fates already in motion, but no new ones will be set against us. If we ever, by our own efforts, get free from the gods, they cannot now simply decree that we'll be caught again. In other words, we still have to find some way to sever the bond between me and Boggin, or deceive Mestor's needle, but once that is done, Phoebe or someone else will not and cannot just predestine us to be found again. The game is still on, but now the playing field is level.

"So how about one last night of celebration before we leave? We're all dressed up, or, at least Vanity is"—I had not even tried on the dress I picked out—"so who wants to go dancing?"

The reaction to that was more enthused.

We had none of us left the store yet. I had gotten the money out from the fourth dimension where it had rested for so long, and everyone but me was all decked out in his finest, with old clothes balled up in shopping bags.

And all seemed amenable to a last night out on the town. Vanity and I still had one or two things to buy. Because who knew when we would get the chance again?

But since sensible people (girls) like to, you know, actually look at what we are buying and actually make informed decisions, it was driving certain not-so-sensible people (boys) slowly crazy, especially since they were standing around in tuxedoes I hadn't paid for yet.

So Colin and Victor wandered off to look at something else, or maybe I ordered them to find a clerk and find out where the checkout was. I don't remember. It just seemed natural at the time. Quentin went with them.

We were going back into the dress department when Vanity's cell phone played the theme from the *William Tell* overture in electronic cricket chirps. That is what phones do in America instead of ringing.

Vanity was giggling, and her emerald eyes were dancing with light, and her cheeks turned ever-so-pink (her light complexion lends itself quite easily to blushing) and she was holding the little gizmo-phone in both hands, so that she could cover her mouth with her fingers to hide the giddy smile. . . .

Okay, I am not an idiot. It was not Victor or Colin calling her, see?

Vanity, blushing red as a beet, snapped shut the little phone and, looking only at my chin or ear, said she had something else she had to do right now, and did I mind? She could put in a call to Victor and Colin, and have them come here from wherever part of this vast store into which they had wandered, so I would not be left alone.

"I need to go look at something over by the jewelry counter," she said.

My first thought, of course, was that Quentin was going to pick out a wedding ring. When else do men look at jewelry? But maybe she just wanted him aside to herself for a little snogging practice.

I did not want to be left alone, but, just at that moment, I saw something shining so brightly, so useful, even through the intervening walls and floors, that I knew I had to get it.

That little voice people are supposed to hear when they are in deep need of common sense spoke now in my ear. It told me to go back and get Victor and

Colin, because I should not be alone. This shop filled up most of a long city block. It was bigger than Abertwyi village. The fact that Archer could walk up to me in the dressing room showed that across the shop was too far away.

I did not tell my little common sense voice to shut up—I would never do that—but I told it to talk a little quieter. Just a little. Only for a minute.

Because at that very moment, I was looking out across a wide countryside of modern musical instruments. There, bright beneath the neon lights, alone in an almost empty store, I saw it.

There it was, perfect and perfectly tasteless.

It was a guitar. An American guitar. Just like the ones the rock stars use, all those loud and unkempt boys Colin had watched so avidly on the telly during our crossing on the *Queen Elizabeth II*.

It was black and sleek and metallic and shiny, and had a weird-looking triangular sound-box instead of the normal hourglass shape. It looked like an alien rocket ship poised for takeoff.

My eye fell on that guitar, and I fell in love with it. I had to have it, to get it for Colin, and it had to be a surprise.

My thought: Colin didn't hate music. He only hated *good* music. Classical music, Brahms and Bach and Beethoven. Music in four voices, point and counterpoint, grace notes and floating glissandos.

Ah, but rock and roll was a different matter, wasn't it? Drumming backbeat, screaming guitar, banshee-shrieks of sound, all mangled and compressed together into thundering avalanches of pure noise! It had Colin written all over it. It was perfect for him. Perfect!

2.

So I went off alone. The clerk, or maybe he was the manager, was a bent, balding man with a sunburned scalp and white puffs for eyebrows. He unlocked the display case and took the guitar out and showed it to me. "What type of amplifier does your friend have?"

"How do you know I am not buying it for myself?"

He smiled a bit into his mustache, and nodded and looked shy, but did not answer the question. Maybe I was holding it in a way that showed I knew nothing about guitars.

The price he asked was more than I wanted to spend. On the other hand, we were about to leave civilization forever, and the money would be of no earthly use to me hereafter.

I was not very good at haggling, higgling, or chaffering, but I admitted it was a gift for a friend, and that I did not have very much money.

He could probably see that my upbringing had burdened me with ideas of polite behavior and ladylike refinement that, I am sure, have no place among the brash businesswomen of America. The old man cut the price, just a bit, perhaps as a reward for the fact that I at least tried to get into the dickering spirit.

I could not afford any cords or amplifiers; the thing was worthless without them, but I had a vague notion that Victor could cobble something together.

I bought the thing anyway. The final thought that weakened my resolve to hold out for a reasonable price was this: Everything we bought on the cruise ship, either Victor or Vanity had bought (since they had been holding the envelope at that time), and I was not present during the Paris shopping spree. Come to think of it, hadn't Colin picked up the tab when we ate out our last night ashore? And Quentin bought the coats and stuff from the Isle of Man? I had not spent a single pound-note of the money yet.

So the bad news was that it was expensive. The good news was that I had just enough.

3.

It must have happened the moment he rang up the cash register and handed me the receipt.

I was riding back up to the ground-floor level on an empty escalator, the sleek black guitar in its case in one hand, my purse in the other, into which I was still (with one or two fingers not being used) trying to stuff the folded bills of my change while, at the same time, performing the not-quite-topologically-impossible act of trying to stuff the slender purse into the rather voluminous pocket of my leather jacket . . . when my radio phone chirruped the opening to the "Moonlight" sonata in electronic cricket-beeps.

Okay. Enough was enough. Granted, I was in a store, and there might have been security cameras, but, on the other hand, no one was around me at that moment. No one was looking.

I stepped "past" the surface of the escalator and found myself in a little maintenance or machinery room in an unpainted section of the store customers are not supposed to see. There was a loading dock off to my left and a bare concrete corridor off to my right.

Now I reached "down" into the flat plane of three-space with a number of limbs made of motes of light, like tendrils of music, if music were made of solid energy-forms.

One group of motes diverted the mass-relationship leading from the guitar to the center of the Earth, to make it lighter in my hand; a second group folded my stray bills and slid them "past" the surface of my purse into its interior; and a third group superimposed the purse on the interior of my pocket. To me, it looked much like putting a paper cutout of a purse inside a pocket-shaped line drawn on a plane. Since the purse actually (now that I could see it from more than 180 degrees at once) looked too large to fit through the mouth of the pocket, I would have to use the same means to get it out again, or resort to knifing open the pocket seams.

A fourth group of motes reached "into" my pants pocket and tilted the switch-hook of my phone into the fourth dimension, so that it popped "up." The mere fact that the lid of the phone was shut no longer engaged the OFF button. In effect, this took the cell phone off the hook without actually opening it.

A fifth group of motes folded the tiny area of time-space around my pants pocket to hold it against my ear.

I am not sure what this might have looked like to outside three-dimensional observers. Maybe they would have seen me bend at the waist at an impossible angle to put my ear to my hip. Maybe they would have seen or heard sound waves being teleported out of my pocket through a wormhole directly into my ear.

A manipulation set up a second distance-negating space-fold between my mouth and the cell phone's cunningly made little mouthpiece.

Maybe an outside observer would have seen me twisted like a Möbius pretzel to have my mouth and ear both pressed up against the same convex surface in a way spherical heads cannot. I prefer to think they would have seen a second wormhole opening between my head and my pocket, without any gross distortions. After all, the limited three-dimensional light would have followed the space-time curve as if it were flat, right? Outside observers surely would have seen a pretty girl with little firefly glints in a complex halo around her head. Hope so, anyway. Multidimensional continuum control is a fine superpower—there is none better—but no girl wants a paradigm she cannot use without looking icky.

Vanity's voice came over the phone speaker: "Amelia! Amelia! Oh, God, please answer!"

"I'm here."

"Something just saw you. Something powerful and terrible. Then another group of somethings joined in. There is a crowd looking at you."

I looked left and right. Bare walls. Loading dock with empty trucks. Behind me was a space filled with a diesel engine, calmly purring. I ran the few yards, down a set of metal stairs, and eased open a rear door leading to the loading bay. Outside was a short alley leading to a nighttime street, neon-lit. There were people on it, couples walking, perhaps headed to the club just down the way. No one stopping to turn and look toward the store.

I opened up eyes in the fourth dimension. There was a blaze of utility from the music section of the store overhead, but now I saw it was not useful to me or Colin; the supply of instruments was very useful to someone else.

That same light sent out a streamer of moral obligation like a spiderweb. I traced the strands.

One bundle went toward Deimos, who was sitting in a glassed-in office high above a dancing floor of many dazzling lights. He had his harpoon in his hand, facing the direction of the store, as if the intervening walls and buildings were no barrier to his dread weapon. The threads there ran from him to Archer, who was on the street between the store and the club. Deimos was acting as a sniper, a friendly one, ready to strike down anyone who threatened his brother. Had he been watching the whole exchange between me and Archer? Probably not, or Vanity would have sensed his eyesight. No—something had startled him into a warlike stance, a warning that his oath to protect his brother was about to be challenged.

I saw a second bundle leaving him and leading back to me. He had made a promise to me to show my card to Archer. It was a dim connection, but enough that Deimos could sense a threat to me as well. If I were killed, he could not keep his promise.

I am lucky Deimos had made that promise, because I could see through his tangle of moral connections something I could not see radiating from myself.

A final bundle had reached down from a point immensely remote in space, right to my position, glowing, shivering, and crawling with motes and flickers of communication-purpose. It was as if the line was shouting to someone, HERE! SHE IS HERE!

"Damn!" I breathed.

12

WIVES OF THE PSYCHOPOMP

1.

"Do you see anyone?" asked Vanity over the phone.

"The money. I spent the money. . . ."

I could dimly hear, in the background, Quentin's voice saying, "It's ap Cymru. Amelia's in debt to him now. That's why they gave her such an absurd amount of money. The obligation was not actual before, because she herself never spent it. Tell her to throw away whatever it is she just bought. . . ."

Vanity: "Did you hear Quentin?"

"Yes." I tossed the sleek black guitar into a Dumpster filled with packing material. And immediately: "Didn't work," I said. The obligation lines continued to lead to me, not to it. Oh well. I picked up the guitar again. No reason to throw away a perfectly good guitar.

I said to Vanity: "Which floor are you on?"

Vanity said: "I am not in the store anymore. I led the boys into a secret elevator behind the jewelry department when I felt someone find you. I am hoping it will lead down to a sewer or—Listen! Get to the docks, get to the shore. Or to the nearest body of water. I am ordering my ship to go find you."

"I—"

Vanity shouted over the tiny phone speaker: "Do not dare tell me you are going to lead them away! What if we get attacked by Dr. Fell and you are not there? What if Mrs. Wren attacks you, and it is something Quentin could save you from by saying the name of a fish? We are all in danger if you are in danger! Don't you dare run off on us or be brave, or so help me God, I will never forgive you, Amelia Armstrong Windrose!"

Quentin, in the background, softly: "Colin can find her. She still owes him a favor."

2.

I should have run back into the store, but the fact that streamers of obligation-energy were reaching from Deimos to this area frightened me irrationally. This store was part of a trap. Vanity was not in it, anyway.

I ran from the alley to the street. It was bright and crowded for a nighttime street, and the night air was warm.

People were staring at me, so I slowed down to a brisk trot. Just a lady in a leather jacket and cap, out for a walk with her space-age guitar! Everything is normal!

As I continued to walk, I noticed that everything did look normal. Whatever alarm I had just set off, it might be weeks or years before ap Cymru answered. Maybe I was safe for now.

I pulled the phone from my pocket and held it up to my ear. "Vanity! I'm in the main street in front of the shop. There are people all around me, humans. If we're right about the gods, they will not show themselves in front of a crowd. I am making my way West on . . ."

That was when I noticed the phone was dead. There was no click of disconnection, no hum of the power shutting off, just . . . silence.

"Vanity? Hello . . . ?"

All the bright, noisy cars moving from light to light along the street now slowed and halted. Radio music banging from the nearer cars squawked and stopped.

The pedestrians, wherever they were, beneath the neon signs at the bus stops, in the middle of the crosswalk, on the sidewalks, fell, or slumped, or keeled over.

Blackness rushed across the cityscape as lights from the building across the way went out. The streetlamps turned dark. A thousand teeny tiny machine noises, radios, the hissing of the portable popcorn popper of a late-night street vendor, the whirr of distant automatic doors opening and closing, the hum from refrigerators, elevators, other motors . . . all muttered and fell into a deep, tomblike hush.

The clock on the bell tower of the bank across the street from my position emitted one last peal, and then stopped, its second hand frozen. The electronic sign turned all white as all the bulbs lit up, and then went black.

I felt a pressure in the sleep centers of my brain, activity in my pons attempting to trigger narcolepsy, changes in my medulla oblongata trying to switch my brain-wave pattern from alpha-beta consciousness to delta-wave dream state.

If my brain continued to obey the laws of nature, I would have to sleep, and immediately.

I jumped into another dimension.

3.

I was through and "past" the stone surface of the building in front of me in a moment. I saw the cubicles and interior spaces of the building, the pipes beneath the street, the interstices between the walls, all laid out like a flat blueprint. I saw the various textures of internal natures: greedy billboards, generous water pipes, frowning walls, ambitious electrical generators, patient power lines.

At this point I was some nine hundred feet above the street, and about forty feet or so in the "blue" direction of overspace, not so far away from the plane of Earth's home continuum that I could not see it, albeit everything was now made soft and mysterious by a haze of blue, a Doppler shift created by the curving metric.

Through the blue haze, I could see other planes of other continua around me, to my left and right, up and down, before me, behind me, and blue and red of me. Only then did I notice what was odd about this four-space. Unlike the street level, it was lit. It was much brighter here than the analogous four-space "above" England. I was seeing farther than I ever had before.

I looked "above" and "behind" me for the source of the light.

The light (actually, volumes of an energy for which we have no name) was coming from (issuing in concentric hyperspheres) a curving bubble or blister in a nearby continuum. This continuum was in a plane parallel to Earth's continuum. It lay about a hundred yards in the "blue" direction, and had formed this reddish blister on its hypersurface, which was swelling and shimmering. The sight reminded me of a steel door being melted, as if the metal were expanding and about to explode outward. . . .

The sight made me feel, despite that I was in the freedom of hyperspace, claustrophobic.

In that gushing light, I could see that the hyperspace was swarming with traffic. In seventeen different time-space pockets, with the watery corridors before and behind them pinched shut, were great fleets of floating mountains of black metal, deck upon deck and turret upon turret bristling with deck-guns, bombards, and cannons. We had seen these lumbering battle barges on the horizon when Mavors had allowed us to escape. Their flags showed the circle-and-spear emblem of Mars. Laestragonians.

Not far from these barges, patrolling the time-space corridors, were slim black ships, pentaconters and triremes, skipping across the curving interdimensional waters like bolts shot from crossbows. These black ships flew banners displaying a trident. Atlanteans.

Hanging in little time-space pockets of their own were huge machines shaped like suits of armor, half a mile or more from crown to spurs. The hulls of the machines were blazing with silver and gold, brightly enameled and decorated with delicate bas-relief. Spears or war-hammers the size of aircraft carriers rested at the sides of the metal warlords. I gazed "past" their armored hulls at their interior clockworks, engines, amplifiers, linkages; I saw alchemical hearts of white fire burning in glass vessels. I saw pistons the size of the Empire State Building. Tubes charged with atomic energy, like veins from the heart of the sun, ran down the core of each suit, from shoulder to heel.

The massive visors of the machines were being cranked open. Their lantern-eyes were being lit by attendants, who stood on ladders clamped to the cheek-plates, and reached carefully upward with long poles tipped with fire. Their symbol was a crane in flight. Mulciber's people.

4.

I was used to hyperspace being empty, my own private playground. Here it was seething with a hornet's nest of ships and men and armaments, the crossroads of hundreds of pathways through time-space. A port city for the traffic of the gods. And it was under guard. Archer's place had been in one of the few dark corners of this multidimensional edifice.

And we had been skipping along in the middle of it. Shopping.

I had let one of the members of my squad leave me alone, to go off and play smooch-face with another member. . . .

Where, in all this mess and splendor and commotion of hyperspace, was Vanity?

5.

I followed a group of morality strands, my obligations to the group, with my eye. . . .

There! I saw the *Argent Nautilus,* with Vanity at the prow, sailing down one sharply curving tube (although, to her, I assume, the space looked flat and open) about twenty-five feet below the surface of the street beneath the streets of Los Angeles, and about twenty meters in the dream-plane. Looking for me . . . ?

I tilted my wings and swam through the thick medium of hyperspace, moving toward Vanity and the *Argent Nautilus.* She was about a quarter mile away from me, no farther, but the hyperspatial distances here were longer because of the positive curve of the plane: It would take me twice as long to cover the distance here that I could have covered on foot, had I dipped back into Earth's home dimension. I was still afraid of the sleep effect rippling through the city, and wanted to stay above (or should I say a-blue) of it.

I drew closer slowly. Victor and Quentin were standing on deck next to her, and Vanity (who, no doubt, felt my gaze on her) was trying to point in my direction. It was not a direction she could turn. Victor and Quentin turned their eyes left and right, but I was not left or right of them. They looked up and down, but I was not above or below them.

I shouted, but they did not seem to hear me. Where was Colin?

I redoubled my speed. With wings and tail and hands and feet, I clawed and waded, sloshed and swam and flew toward my friends.

6.

There came a flash. A group of morality strands looping widely from the near distance running to me now lit up and glittered.

That blister bulging out from the dream-plane, I now saw, was the source of the sleep-spell sweeping over Los Angeles. Morality radiated in concentric waves from it, somehow obligating the men and machines, clocks and electric circuits of Earth to slumber.

The internal nature of the obligation I could see: It affected everyone who used telephones, telegraphs, cars, other means of transport. Anyone who hired a lawyer, who made money, who trafficked with merchants. Anyone who told a lie. They all owed something to . . . whom?

Whoever was behind this spell. An Olympian calling in a debt.

Into the middle of the effect, the strands that drew my gaze led. In the epicenter of that blister, deep in the dreamworld, was a small bubble of stable reality where the laws of Earth were mimicked.

There, I saw a black mountainside surrounded by clouds of twilight red. Here on a shelf of rock, a score of columns stood in a circle, a temple with no roof.

On the altar-stone, kneeling, back straight, head down, buttocks on her heels, was a feminine figure wearing a red kimono. Her hair was black and straight, shining like India ink. The red silk fabric was decorated with images of butterflies and bats, blank-faced cherubs presenting lilies to tiny skeletons. In a semicircle before her on the stone there gleamed a strand of crystal marbles, arranged in pairs. In one hand she held a knife, in the other an ivory drinking horn.

To her left stood the girl-form of ap Cymru: dark-haired and dark-eyed Laverna, goddess of fraud. She was wearing a skintight black sheath of fabric and carrying a snake in either hand. One was lashing its tail in the air; the other was twining her wrist, a living bracelet.

Laverna's lips moved. My sense that detected inner meanings of things told me what their words meant to convey, even though I did not hear them: *Try again. If she is not asleep, then she is fleeing. We must come at them one at a time. . . .*

There was a third woman, standing to the other side. She was dressed in a folded garb of many pockets and pleated layers of cloth, intricate, with sea motifs of green and blue. Her hair was red as new blood. She wore a long veil of aquamarine. I saw only her eyes, which were emeralds sparkling with light.

The words from the woman in white were: *No need. She looks at me now. I feel the pressure of her gaze. She is outside of the plane of Earth, and alone. Another of my kind is also watching her—the Princess Nausicaa. The two are apart.*

When the woman in the red kimono raised her head and her loose hair parted, I saw it was Lamia. I saw the raw and empty red sockets where her eyes had been. I knew now what the marbles in the semicircle before her were: disembodied eyes.

The marbles twinkled and turned toward me.

Lamia—*I see her. I see them both.*

Laverna said—*Begin!*

Lamia upended the drinking horn. A splash of blood struck the stone before her. She threw back her head, mouth wide. I heard no scream, yet still I sensed the meaning of what was said: *Wives of the Psychopomp, I release thee: All ye fair captives who sold white bodies and dark souls to the lust of Trismegistus for promises of escape from Hell, I put aside your chains: Let slip thy leash, and run thee down my prey!*

The red-haired woman raised her hand, saying, *Guardian of Dreams! I call upon our ancient covenant. I open the gate, I break the boundaries, I let pass my Lord's many wives into the daylight world: I let pass the laws of dreams as well.*

A green stone, a twin to the one I had seen on Boggin's toe, glimmered in her palm like a star made of poison.

(I noticed then, too late . . . far too late . . . that the glinting strands whose flash had attracted my attention were running from Laverna to me to the guitar I still held. My debt to ap Cymru.)

The blister from the dream-plane expanded, grew brighter, and intersected the plane of Earth. The blister erupted. There was an explosion, then darkness.

The heavy medium of hyperspace shook with the concussion. A force violent beyond all description sent me tumbling end over end.

7.

An automatic reflex had made me turn headfirst into the wave, and to "yank in" the various red and blue limbs and wings of my hyperbody. I folded myself into a three-dimensional shape (to narrow my 4-D cross-section to nothing) and let the concussion flow over me. It helped—I was not broken in half—but I still was thrown.

I did not lose consciousness, but my senses spun. I remember dazed images of useful tubes through hyperspace, used by the Atlantean ships, being blown and twisted by the explosion, and darkening to uselessness.

I remember seeing the hidden half-mile-tall giants of Mulciber's army being scattered hither and yon throughout four-space. The blister itself, the source of the light, erupted into Earth's plane, depositing armies of dream-women into the sleeping metropolis and blowing aside the normal laws of nature of Earth in the Los Angeles area—I saw the internal nature of all objects flutter violently with the new impositions—become dreamlike, charged with magic.

The echoes of the fading light failed, and it was suddenly as dark here as it had ever been in hyperspace above England. Remember England, where I had gotten lost less than an inch or two away from the plane of Earth? Here, I was at least fifty yards away, and had been blown farther still, and tumbled. I did not know at what angle my present three-body might be relative to Earth's space-time.

8.

So I floundered for another long minute or so in the gloom and gluey thickness of hyperspace. Then I gathered my wits, glad no one was around to see me panicking.

I looked for morality strands. There were two pairs, of different internal natures. One set was glittering with how useful it was to Lamia. I selected the other set and chased it.

I saw disconnected clouds of bluish light, like nebulae in a sky without stars. When I passed through one such cloud, I saw an image of Earth's home dimension, with the expanding blister of the dreamworld still touching it and intersecting. Was this a current image, and the cloud a medium to carry the image to me? Or perhaps I was passing through patches of slowly traveling light that were tumbling like shards of a broken mirror through the vast gloom of hyperspace, debris from the explosion.

Whatever they were, when I passed through the first cloud, I saw it light up with usefulness to someone or something.

There was a glint of shimmering music-energy ahead of me. I saw two of them advancing toward me through the gloom, wheel within wheel and circle within circle, with eyes of fire on the rim of every wheel. They were made of a substance higher and finer than matter, and extended into upper and lower dimensions. The wheels orbiting them, if they passed through the "plane" of three-space, would be perceived not as a single perfect whole, but as a succession of mathematically distinct notes and tones, distributed across time from beginning to end. Music, in other words. These were creatures of living song, with strands of destiny-force extending futureward and pastward from their blazing, beautiful eyes.

Sirens. These were the race of Miss Daw. The sirens were coming for me, glittering and shining, wheels within wheels of slow, grand, solemn force, awful as the motions of the starry spheres. . . .

Without a word, they attacked.

SIRENS

1.

Harmoniously the sirens sang out loudly, one voice clear and high, the other dulcet and soft and low. I saw it as a wave of advancing energy, and concussion of force rippling through the medium of hyperspace, flattening everything in its path into three dimensions, then two, then one, then zero. It was a force of utter annihilation.

The force expanded in spheres and hyperspheres, filling the area. It was broad and wide and high, and also filled the spaces to the blue and red directions of me.

There was no direction to turn. Except . . .

I was still carrying the talisman of Chaos. With a wingtip, I opened my hypersphere and folded it into its fifth-dimensional form. My sphere lit up with a potent energy-echo, sending a shock wave into each direction, including two new directions at right angles to all others, showing me the dark, grainy beingness of the fifth dimension. *You will never be without light again . . .*

I could see that new, strange direction: I moved there.

The substance of five-space was so thick as to make the cores of neutron stars seem like vacuum by contrast. I could press, or seep, my now five-dimensional body into the gray solid wall and push it out of shape: a quarter inch, maybe, maybe an eighth of an inch in the direction I now called "strangeward."

But a three-dimensional cube one eighth of an inch above a flat plane where an angry square sends out a flat knife of all-destructive energy is safe. The knife misses. The target is in another dimension, infinitely out of reach.

And this was all-destructive energy. This was not something meant to stun or trap me. I could hear the interior reality of the four-dimensional expanding hypersphere of deadly music as it passed by an eighth of an inch "beneath" me. ("Beneath" a better word than "antistrangeward.")

My five-dimensional senses opened up. Once more, I had adapted to this new, intensely pressurized, endlessly black dimension. Once more, I could hear three new conditions or sensations: being, relation, and extension.

The neutronium medium of five-space rang like a dull bell. I heard messages made of relational "sets" or "frames" being passed back and forth through this area of over-reality:

Your wife, Parthenope, speaks: Lord Husband, I detect the interior nature of the shadow of the target, Phaethusa. She is nearby, at right angles to our present theme.

Your wife, Leucosia, speaks: There is another force in this area. We detect the chaoticists: Titan shadows, larger than universes, fall across all the themes of the overworld. They are far away, but still we hear the echo of their dread music.

Parthenope speaks: My Lord Husband, send aid quickly, or the prey is escaped!

A much louder gong-note, rasping as if to shatter all the lower dimensions, vibrated through the area. At first I thought it was an answer, perhaps from the Lord Husband these two sirens sang to—but no. The character of its existence was different. The sirens were real, and my fifth-level senses told me they partook of reality. The voice came from somewhere beyond reality, neither below nor above it, but somehow, simply, starkly other—

Phaethusa, daughter of Neaera, it is I, Thrinax, your half brother, son of Rhode, consort of bright Helios. I am sent from Myriagon, from the golden towers of infinity, because I once entered Saturn's submicroscopic world, when I overthrew the Telchine, our helpless enemies, and broke their power.

A weapon of light is mine. Insubstantial, its stroke cannot be parried. A breastplate of seven virtues encircles me. Impalpable, it cannot be pierced. I am the warlord of our realm of endless crystalline peace. The time-restrictions of the Saturnine singularity do not permit you to draw memories of me from the aeon-filaments where I dwell into that tiny coffin of a universe now restricting you.

I waited aeons, but have bent the years so that, to me, it was but an hour; and the name of the Hour, your father's servant girl, when we should meet, was told to me. All, all has been done so that you may answer.

Was it talking to me? I tried to form words in this strange relational-set language. I had an organ for producing a frame: "Help me! They are going to kill me!"

Helios is cognizant, on several levels, of the threat. You are too small, at present, for us to reach. The entire sidereal universe of Saturn is no more than a black spot on a slide in the library of Helios. However, the infinite can save the finite in a way you cannot understand.

"What can you do?"

We stand ready to avenge you.

"What?"

The puzzlement of a world of perfect immortality, perfect evil, confounds our mathematicians. Hence, the final solution is prepared, an absolute crime. I summon Phlegon! He progresses through eighteen millions of collapsed relational sets!

A solemn gong-note rang through the neutronium, and a wailing clamor of horns and drumbeats—or something my brain interpreted as horns and drums. It was an astonishing noise, something louder than the whole universe.

A second voice emerged from that clamor and spoke in existential sets that threatened to crack the neutron substance around me: WE HAVE TOLERATED THE AFFRONT OF SATURN FOR NINE UNCOUNTABLE INFINITIES OF TIME. ADVANCE THE THOUSAND-DIMENSIONAL OBJECT! AT PHAETHUSA'S WORD, WE INITIATE THE RETALIATORY ANNIHILATION!

Trinax called out to me, and now his signal sounded dim and remote: *Daughter of Helios and Neaera! Speak if you wish us to slay and murder all of time and space, and all things great and small within it. The Green Energy Smiths are alert—the Thousand-Dimensional Object is in a state of readiness.*

The gong-note sounded again, and all the lesser dimensions shook.

2.

The siren Parthenope signaled to her sister, using an energy-weft that smote my ears as a normal voice: "Leucosia, our prey is now being observed by the horrors of the Namelessness, the creatures of Myriagon. Now, at last, we can kill her when and where they can witness the crime, and see our songs stained red with her virgin blood. At last! This weary playacting, pretending that she could escape us, chasing her until she called them, at last is ended."

The two sirens unfolded themselves into the fifth dimension from the fourth, growing into solidity around me. I could not tell the distance, but my sense-impressions heard echoes from their existential patterns very nearby. They had not been unable to reach me.

Parthenope said wearily, "Slay her with a diminished fifth, my sister, and be done with it, that the world may die, and we be at rest."

But Leucosia answered, "Sister, something is amiss. My lance is pointed at her heart, but I dare not strike. Observe the colors of the moral warp. What is wrong?"

Parthenope whispered in awe: "Madness! She has gone insane! She will not strike back, even if we kill her for it."

"Tell her we will despoil her naked corpse in public after the murder and will vaunt and caper, merely to taunt her weeping mother."

"Phaethusa! Can you not hear our words?"

I gritted my teeth and said nothing. For one thing, to deflect the neutron medium of five-space even one-eighth inch out of its normal rest-state required immense energy. I am sure my three-dimensional girl-body would have been sweating and shaking by now.

For another, I damn well was not going to die to please them.

And, bloody hell, I was the heroine here, wasn't I? The human race, all those planets, the sun and moon and stars, time and space—all the beautiful things Archer talked about—it was not going to be wiped out because of me. Not while I was leader. Not on my watch. No sir. No.

3.

Thrinax: *Phaethusa's silence passes verdict on the world of Saturn. Arrest the Thousand-Dimensional Object! I see countless strands of ethical and entropic energy stream from my garments into the blank spot of Saturn's dead world, but one returns bright as silver, untarnished. Phaethusa would forgive her slayers. She was raised as human, thinks as a human, and yet she reached the conclusion Helios foresaw, even in a world where moral facts cannot be seen, only imagined. The universe is proved. Spare it.*

A new voice spoke, a feminine voice, but not human-sounding, as if a harp of fine crystal were playing: *Lampetia, save for Phaethusa, youngest daughter of the Bright One, addresses my brothers. In my glass I see the universe of Saturn is now within our debt, and by the foolish rules that Cosmos uses, this means Captain Thrinax wins another victory, to us instantaneous, even if, to her, many weary aeons of suffering must pass.*

Indeed, the weapon of light, stronger than any weapons of the material world: a weapon not in his hand, but in a girl's heart. The mercy of bright

Phaethusa is mightier than the Scythe of Time, more far-reaching than the Thunderbolt of Jove.

I admit I was wondering what good this would do me, when a second woman's voice, this one sounding much more lively, and more human, spoke. *Sister, I am Circe, Enchantress, daughter of Helios the Bright and lovely Neaera the Dark of the Moon. I alone of our folk have dwelt for a time within Saturn's realm, and studied its lore. The tiniest part of the debt the Cosmos now owes you I use to transform you to a new shape.*

All transformations are by knowledge: Knowledge changes you into something other than you are. For this purpose you were incarnated. Receive now the secret of how to escape the Olympian power of destiny control. . . .

At that same moment, a hurried group of messages passed back and forth between Leucosia and Parthenope. They screamed.

One was a shriek of fear. "She must be slain before she drinks this knowledge!"

But the other was a victory scream. "Too late! They are too late! Phaethusa dies this moment! The maenads are here!"

4.

"Leucosia—the other wives have arrived, dangerous to us. Abandon this paradigm. Change, now, dancing sister, our notes to flatter shape, and call this strangeness of high space down into the beauty of the world—a beauty which will not perish with Phaethusa's death, as our Lord Husband planned."

An answer came: "Parthenope, let other hands now slay the maiden of Chaos: Let another lance, less reluctant than my own, pierce her soft, white breast and rend asunder all her loveliness. I do not kill for pleasure, but to work the old world's fall, that I may one day rejoice with golden voice in the new world, phoenixlike, our Master promises shall rise! We must away."

Before Circe could utter another word, before the secret was spoken, the world collapsed. It was like what Mr. Glum had done to me. Reality snapped, and I was in another scene.

There was no transition, no logic to it. I had been there; now I was here.

I was a girl. Sunlight was falling on me. I lay on the grass. Around me rose tall trees, bright with greenery and dappled light. A breeze made the leafy masses shimmer with a rustling noise.

5.

Another noise came from the near distance. Women, many women, shrieked and screamed and sang: *"Ite Bacchai! Ite Bacchai! Ite Bacchai!"*

I saw a pine tree tremble from root to crown, and sway, and topple grandly.

A woman stood there. She wore a tattered toga, and the torn strips fluttered like strange wings around her. Around her waist was wound a zone of ivy; her breasts were scratched and exposed, as if she had been nursing wild beasts. A wreath of ivy rode aslant her wild and disordered hair, and curlicues of green vine twined through her straggling curls. In one hand she held a slender wand, wound with grapevine, topped with a pinecone.

With her other hand, a hand as slim and delicate as my own, she plucked a second pine tree up by the roots with an easy gesture, and tossed it lightly aside. The tree was a hundred yards high. She let fly several tons of lumber, as if the weight were nothing to her.

Her mad eyes, dancing with odd dreams, lit upon me. She tilted her head to one side, almost shyly, and smiled a smile of happiness. She pointed the wand at me. "Yoo-hoo! Sisters! Here she is, here she is, here she is! Alone, alone, all on her own!"

A second maiden, a girl perhaps fifteen years old or less, stepped into view behind her. Her dress was as torn as the first girl's had been, and her anadem was made of rose thorns and belladonna. She also held a wand tipped with a pinecone, but in her other hand she held a little baby, upside down by the foot. I did not see the baby moving; I thought it might be dead.

This second girl sang out: "Fall upon her, wild maenads! Tear and bite and rip and slay! The daughter of the Daystar-Titan shall be our raw pork!"

I saw blood was coming out of her mouth. I wondered if she had bitten her tongue.

I have heard a crowd scream before, at a rugby match Headmaster Boggin took us all to once, a treat for doing particularly well that semester. The crowd there was men and boys, and their voices were deep, and their roar, when they roared, was like an ocean noise. There were women in the audience that day, but I doubt if they had screamed with such bloodlust and abandon as the men.

Now I heard a noise not unlike the roar that rang when the final winning score was made, and the crowd of men had screamed in joy. Except this noise was an octave or two higher. I had never heard so many high-pitched voices scream at once.

In horror movies, girls scream only when they are terrified, not to terrify. Of course, in horror movies, the buxom blondes are usually not breaking rocks in two with their feet, knocking trees aside with their hands.

A throng of girls, all of them young and shapely, some in torn dresses, some in panther or leopard skins, some nude, some running upright, some running (hips impossibly high) on all fours like beasts, some bounding from tree to tree like frogs, now came through the forest like an avalanche. The noise of timber falling was like the noise of the end of the world.

Did I mention that I was running away at this point?

14

MAENADS

1.

By pure lucky mishap, I had not had time to don the evening gown I had entered the store to buy. Instead I was in my lightest pair of sneakers, the running shoes Vanity had bought me in Paris. I would have hated to try to run, leaping bushes and rocks, dodging around trees, wearing heels. Also, I was wearing blue jeans like a proper American girl. Thank God for blue jeans.

Ululating, shrieking, screaming, the maenads tumbled and thundered and flew through the trees after me.

There was no one giving orders. Had they merely sent two teams of runners to my right and left, they could have surrounded me. But no: The mob just all came in the straight line toward what they saw, trampling each other.

But they were so strong and so fleet of foot, they really did not need a plan. Every moment as I ran, they cut the distance between us in half.

A one-hundred-yard length of pine tree came crashing like a battering ram through the air behind me, flung like a javelin. I ducked and swerved in time, and saw the wall of bark, yard upon yard of it, sailing by, a few feet from my face, wrinkled black texture of the bark whistling and whispering.

Some drunken girl had thrown a tree. At me. Thrown a tree. You would think, once I found out I lived in a world ruled by pagan gods, that not much would surprise me. I staggered and gawped at the sight of a mast-tall tower of living wood, dirt clods still clinging to its many roots, slipping past my face.

The stagger saved my life. A boulder the size of a car hissed past me to the other side, flung like a baseball, and shattered against the ground with a sound like a bomb igniting, sending rock chips flying. *Pow.* If I had not stopped to stare, I would have been right about there right about now.

A shrill yell like a flock of falcons screeching rent the air. They thought it was cute to throw rocks and trees. Now they all wanted to do it.

I stopped short and turned, and saw, like a herd of whales jumping all at once, arching, fifty huge and ponderous cylinders of wood toppling grandly, hugely, unstoppably, crashing down through the air toward me.

Two of the airborne trees had shrieking maenads clinging to them: One was yodeling like a cowgirl, happy to the last; the other was covered in blood and tried to leap clear of the branches as the tree toppled. Apparently these women did not pause to find out who or what was in the things they threw, or who or what was in the way.

I sprinted toward the area that seemed most clear of landing lumber-yards, the part of the forest with the most trees and other obstructions to slow the immense rain. Only one or two rocks were rocketed my way—there simply were not that many boulders for the shrieking women to pull up.

The trees all fell, uprooting other trees, quaking and crashing, and the earth cried out in pain and shook. I ran toward the thickest part of the dust cloud, which now expanded, gale-winged, out from the toppling wreckage of the broken forest.

I was blind for a moment and ran with my best sprinter's speed. These maenads were all stronger than me, and faster, too, but they could not hit what they could not see.

When I came clear of the dust cloud, the trees were thicker than before. Only a handful of the maenads had me in direct sight, and one of them was sitting down to cry, because there was dust in her eyes.

Into the thicket. Breath short. Lungs burning from dust. Left, right, left again. Double back. Leap a fallen trunk. Graceful leap, good form. Still too close behind me. Heard trunk behind me snap in half. Less graceful form. Dodge right. Broken half of fallen trunk smashes trees and bushes to my left.

Suddenly, ravine. Two sharp cliffs, with a trickle of water at the bottom. Thornbushes and trees on the far side, no place to land. Trees on far side splintered and broken, fallout from maenad-fury earlier?

Think I can make it. Too late to stop anyway.

Up. Good takeoff.

Air.

Oops. Not going to make it. Oh shit oh shit oh shit.

Catch the cliff edge right at breast level. Ow, ow, ow. Hands claw at thorns. Thornbush in midair with me, roots trailing clods of dirt. Traitor.

Maenad flies by overhead, turns head to stare curiously at me. Very strong. Makes the leap with ease, lands on broken splinters of branches, impaled, dies. Her limbs jerk and thrash. Can't stop dancing, frenzy, even when dead.

Splash.

Pain. Darkness. Water.

2.

I am not a bad swimmer. I assumed the pursuit would look downstream for me. Staying underwater, I struggled against the current. Maybe that was a stupid idea. Maybe I should have gone with the current, tried to get as far away as possible.

When I had to break the water, I struggled again toward shore. For a moment, I did not know where I was. I thought I was swimming through the medium of hyperspace again. When I clutched, dripping and battered, the hard rocks of the shore, I stared about myself stupidly, wondering why everything seemed so small and flat, why my vision was stopped by the surfaces of objects.

Yells and ululations behind me. I dragged my legs out of the water, looked over my shoulder. Several hundred yards downstream from my position, I saw the motion and silhouettes of maenads on the cliff opposite me. Two of them jumped lithely across the chasm to my side of the bank, rags and vine-wrapped hair a-flutter. Others jumped, or were pushed, into the stream. Some hit the stream; some hit rocks. Girlish yells of joy rose up when that happened. Sick, sick, sick.

I saw this horrid scene with misery and pain clouding my eyes. A few hundred yards. Is that all the farther I had swum? It had seemed like hours I had been in the river. How long had it been? A few minutes?

They were coming.

I examined the bank on my side of the river. There was a cleft, a spot where the cliff was low and broken, and a tumble of rocks was heaped just below it.

I made it to the top of the cliff with surprising speed, considering my aches and pains. The maenads yelled and yodeled when they saw me in motion, and one ill-aimed tree fell across the rock face above me, wedged solid. It provided me a quick impromptu ladder to the top.

At the top, I saw a break in the trees, a meadow sloping away to my left. A line of electrical power poles ran down the middle of the open area.

I wondered if I was on Earth. The writing on the transformer boxes was English. This could still be in America, perhaps even in Northern California.

I thought: a straight sprint down the meadow, with no obstructions, while the maenads jump the river and swarm up the cliff. Gives me some distance. Downhill; slope will block the view. When they lose sight of me, vault into the forest, hide. Good plan? Good plan.

My feet felt light as I sped across the grass, transformer towers buzzing and muttering above me. Too light? Maybe the hallucination that I had been in four-space while I was swimming had been half-true. Maybe I could just get out of range of the Glum-effect the maenads were radiating.

Oh, I know Mr. Glum had not suffered from any range limits when he was wishing me into a three-dimensional girl-shape. And I know the blood-lust of the intoxicated bacchants was no doubt as fierce and powerful as Mr. Glum's lust-lust. But I had to have a reason to hope. Even an irrational reason.

So down the slope at my best speed, and then, after a glance over my shoulder to confirm that the shoulder of the slope was blocking the maenad view (They were in the riverbed, I guessed. No lookouts in the trees. No leader, remember?) I took off into the brush.

The trees grew thick, and then thin again. With unexpected suddenness, I broke out on a little trail or deer-path.

There were two women on horseback, dressed in skintight films of black metallic substance. They wore futuristic-looking helmets of black ceramic fiber, and the ponytails of their hair were pulled through holes in the rear of each helmet, giving them a pseudo-Roman look. They both had identical weapon belts with cartridges slung low across their rounded hips, holstered pistols tied to their left thighs, slim knife sheaths tied to their right.

Both women were young, trim, athletic, attractive. Both had expressionless expressions, eyes without passion or compassion. They held riding crops in hand.

For a moment, I was confused about what I was seeing. Two bathing-beauties in skintight catsuits, carrying whips? It sounded like one of Colin's earlier wishes had come true.

Neither wore makeup. The only ornament I saw was a gem, the size and shape of a crystal marble, riding atop the black helmet of the warrior-babe on the right.

I skidded to a halt.

The horses turned narrow heads to look at me. Each horse had a metallic blue orb, like a third eye, shimmering and throbbing in the center of its forehead. A cyclopes-eye.

With the precision of machines, the two beauties dropped their reins; each one tucked her riding crop away, drew a streamlined glittering rifle from a holster built into her saddle and shouldered the weapon, and took aim.

At me.

3.

The one on the left spoke in a soft, unemotional tone: "Leader! Target identification?"

For a moment, I thought she was talking to me.

The one on the right measured me with cold eyes. Her voice was also soft and cool: "The Phaeacian. Use the anti-psychic shell, medium charge."

There was a double click as both women chambered a round.

At the same time I shouted, "Wait—! Don't shoot!" another voice, Lamia's voice, issued from the crystal marble (which had swiveled in its socket to look at me) the leader wore on her helmet. This voice said, "Wait—! Hold your fire! That's not—"

The women must have been confused, and thought that only I was speaking. Had I been silent, they would have heard, and no doubt obeyed, the command not to fire.

I did not hear any noise from the weapons. A dull vibration passed through my body as I was flung back by the force of the shots against a tree by the side of the path. My head lolled, wildly twisted more than 180 degrees backwards against my spine. With my remaining eye, the last sight I saw was the bloody stump of my arm, flying up, hanging in midair, surrounded by red droplets and white bone fragments.

Strange that I did not hear anything.

4.

Sister, it was for this purpose you were sent into the hells of time: the indebtedness of your murder triggers now my spell. With my moly wand I transform you from this shape to a new shape that unlocks the messages buried by the dreamlord Morpheus into your hidden soul, and imprinted by Argyron of the Telchine into your nervous system. You will hear this only during a moment between life, when you are not properly in the Cosmos, and free, if only at that moment, from the meddling of fate, surrounded by silence far from the endless noise of crystal heavens turning.

Saturn built his world out of the raw materials of Chaos. The destiny-binding power of the Olympians can thus be factored into four component powers.

I listened with great interest as Circe taught me. Memories of a science I never knew blossomed in my brain.

5.

From overspace, I sensed the internal nature of the bullets that had blown that cross-section of my body into bloody rags. They contained a powerful field that sharply reduced the utility of matter, rotating the meaning-axis of material things toward zero.

It negated psychics, rendering matter useless to the paradigm used by Colin, which was also, according to our theory, one half of the same paradigm used by Vanity.

It negated what the maenads had done to me.

Please don't misunderstand me. It hurt. It really hurt. Usually hydrostatic shock will kill any human struck with bullets of heavy caliber. A human body does not contain enough volume to disperse the kinetic energy of the impact.

But that body down there was merely a cross-section of mine. Merely one surface. And not my only surface, either, and not my largest surface.

My true mass, calculating all the volumes of all my possible cross-sections, greatly exceeds what could be packed into a mere three-dimensional body.

No matter how much damage they did to that body, it was only harming one surface. Imagine a very painful skin wound. Even if your outermost layer of one patch of skin were entirely burned, ripped away, and destroyed, it would not destroy your body, reach any important organs, or do any real damage.

It really hurt. It hurt like the dickens.

And it made me mad.

6.

The Amazon leader on the right—I could see from her internal information that her name was Antiope—was saying aloud, "Target destroyed. Request confirmation. . . ."

Lamia was shouting, "Not Nausicaa! That one is not Nausicaa! Shoot her with the anti-siren shell! Shoot, shoot, shoot!"

The interior workings of the rifles were fascinating. There were four separate magazines with four separate types of ammunition. There were four thumb-switches to select which magazine was active. As the round was chambered, a magnetic impulse accelerated it from the barrel. These devices were not "rifles" at all, but rail guns.

One bullet was silver, and wrapped with webs of moral energy. One was charged with a monad-rotating vortex. Fascinating. One contained a charge of the matter-utility-negating energy—this is the one I had felt. The final one was the 3-D cross-section of twenty-one strands of 4-D dimension-compressing musical wave fronts. This was the one the ladies had chambered.

The power supply came from something that looked like a miniature cyclopes eye embedded in the stock. Buttons along the barrel controlled a microcomputer that fed commands to this hidden eye. There were packages of material set in the stock, and the beams from the eye could be focused to pass through one or more of them, altering their contents; and there was a chambering section to load the altered contents into a magazine of empty shells, which could then be chambered by working a lever above the trigger. Thus, in addition to the four main types of shells, these weapons could fire any number of possible nanite-packages to produce a very wide range of effects, limited only by the skill of the weapon programmer.

When I twisted the controlling monad of the power supply, and then granted the mechanisms free will, the guns did not know what to do. Of course, since the silly things had been (until this very moment) only made of groups of mindless atoms organized without final causes or moral purposes, once free, they had no unity to hold them together. One barrel blew bubbles; the other smacked its lips and started warbling Bing Crosby tunes. The bullets trickled out of the no-longer barrels and dropped limply to the grass.

So glad Vanity suggested that idea.

Negating the controlling monad of these robotlike women robbed them of purpose and made them, also, drop limply to the grass.

The horses were also artificial constructs, made with a very advanced form of biotechnology, perhaps constructed one molecule at a time. Instead of protein, their bodies were made of something more like fiberglass, layered with Kevlar. The bones were some sort of flexible living ceramic.

The steeds were smart, fast, tireless, and strong. And brave. And well-trained. (Or should I say "well-programmed"?) Just the kind of steed every girl dreams about.

The horses, like the women, were also "flat" in the fourth-dimensional direction, not unlike Victor, or Dr. Fell.

I should mention that I moved my cross-section one-hundredth of an inch redward into the material plane.

Had I rotated my body further, I could have produced any number of other cross-sections: phoenix, centaur, deer, dolphin, squid, energy ball, seven notes of music, or any combination thereof. But I rotated my body as little as I could, to get a body as much like my destroyed body inserted into Earth's three-space as I could get. It would have taken a scientific instrument to detect the slight differences in measurements, volume, and bone structure from the destroyed body.

The destroyed body still hurt, so I folded it into a one-dimensional space so that the pain signals could not reach the rest of my nervous system.

Oh, and I should mention my clothes vanished.

Nude again. The story of my life.

I guess I should also mention that the horses attacked me. Their cyclopean-eyes glittered and flared with strange energies. Deadly chemicals, magnetic discharges, nanotechnology packets, nerve toxins, incendiaries, and so on and so forth blasted the trees behind me and blew wide craters into the ground.

It was really quite impressive. Really.

Then I made the horses stand on their heads.

It was fun. Really.

AMAZONS

1.

Lamia reacted quickly.

I saw, approaching from the fourth dimension, shining with orb within orb of death music, Parthenope and Leucosia.

I "ducked." I folded my body into a tightly three-dimensional shape. The guitar and the hypersphere manifested themselves: I had been carrying this stuff in four-space. I folded the hypersphere from a globe to a circle to a line, which I stuck into my billfold. I slung the guitar into the saddlebags of the biotech horse. My horse. I picked the prettier one.

Parthenope passed by, about one hundred yards underground, twenty yards or so "above" me in the blue direction. She was making a quick scan, simply looking for something popping up or dropping down out of the hyperplane. She did not see me. I was flat, like a soldier hugging the terrain.

2.

Lamia was still shouting orders to the Amazons over her little crystal eyeball when Hippolyta (at my instruction) crushed it to pieces beneath her boot heel.

Antiope was quite shapely in her birthday suit. I sort of wish Colin had been here to see it. She helped me on with the black metal-cloth catsuit and tucked my hair into her helmet. My suit. It took me less than a minute to wiggle into it.

My clothes, including the jacket Vanity had just bought for me, I bundled up and stuffed into a saddlebag.

During that minute, I saw two squirrels, a brace of rabbits, and several flocks of birds streaming out of the trees to my left. A fox ran alongside the squirrels without molesting them. The rabbit paused to thrum his hind paw against the dirt, giving off the drumming warning-signal of his kind. All the birds were shrieking with alarm.

I had heard about animals acting this way when they ran from forest fires. The noise and smoke and commotion coming through the wood was louder than any forest fire, and toppling trees groaned and creaked, wood snapped with reports like rifle shots, scores of trees smote the ground like thunder, and the cloud of dust approaching rose higher and ever higher.

Leucosia swam past, circles within circles of eyes blazing "beneath" us in the blue direction, only six inches or so below the world-plane, but scores of yards above the treetops and to our left.

Time to saddle up. I let Antiope keep the sidearm, which had bullets similar to the four types of shells carried in the rifle. My rifle. I gave her two extra magazines of the anti-psychic shells.

I figured that if those were the shells designed to work against Colin, they would work against the maenads.

It should have been the most terrible turning point in my life, the darkest moral quandary. Instead, it was thoughtless, almost automatic. You see, it never occurred to me that the maenads were real people, that they had souls or preferences or families or anything. I just thought they were crazed monsters. Without a qualm, I ordered my two Amazon-puppets to advance through the little stand of trees separating the deer-path from the clearing where the line of electrical towers stood, and open fire upon the maenads when they crossed the open grass. Number two cyclopes-horse I sent with them, so he could start fires, create explosives, turn the air into neurotoxins, do nasty things.

I did not tell the two Amazons to fight until they died, but I did not program them with any orders to retreat either. So I guess I sent them to their deaths. One of them was stark naked, and armed only with a pistol.

I did not feel bad about it at the time. Despite all of Quentin's warnings, despite that I had been brought up as a civilized and thoughtful girl . . . I just sent them off.

I rode in the other direction.

The three-eyed steeds were fast.

3.

Not fast enough. I had ridden the few tame ponies at the Academy, of course, but they were not horses like this. Everything about the artificial beast was different: its gait, its contours, its movements. I was not riding; I was clinging desperately to its back, with my hair blown back by the hurricane of its speed. The super-steed was barreling down the deer-path at the kind of clip one expects from a motorcycle, and the noise, dust, and shrieks of the maenads, undiminished, were rising through the trees behind me. After half a minute of flight, I had come only about half a mile down the path, when the deer-path opened suddenly into a little glade carpeted with knee-high marshy grass.

A troop of horsewomen were there, maybe a dozen young beauties in black catsuits and helmets, charging toward me at immense speed. The warrior-women were bent low over the necks of their steeds, their hips higher than their ponytail-shaking heads, their spines more or less parallel with the grass over which they flew.

Each rider was skilled. As each Amazonian steed jarred and thundered wetly across the whipping grass, each Amazonian rider absorbed the shocks with smooth, quick motions of her long legs, so that her prone black form seemed to float, moving not an inch up or down.

As I fumbled, trying to rein in my horse and get its head turned around, there came a loud, clear female voice rising over the riders: a command to break off. With the precision of a machine, the cavalry troop wheeled left and right, avoiding me.

The horsewomen also drew, aimed, and fired their rifles as they wheeled, their aim not one whit disturbed by the maneuvers, leaps, and gyrations of their steeds.

Some of the Amazons, I saw, did not even try to fire in my direction. They merely pointed their barrels at the ground and shot the dimension-collapsing shells into the grass.

Again, ribbons of energy unfolded. These acted like flares. Hyperspace lit up with the dazzle of musical spheres, expanding and popping like bubbles. To the red and to the blue of me, I saw Leucosia and Parthenope, strange as flying saucers made of rings of eyes and deadly light, emerge from the gloom of hyperspace and push through the dimensions toward the dazzle.

My horse reared up—it was some implanted program or instinct—to catch a volley of gunfire meant for me in its armored fiberglass chest. Hammer blows struck my shoulder and leg on my left side as I was flung back off the saddle. My armor stiffened into metal immobility, ringing like a bell as the two shots ricocheted from the suddenly rigid surface.

Thunk. Then I was in the wet grass, watching my horse toppling backwards, its chest blown open by incendiary fire. I reached up with tendrils of hyperspace energy to deflect his momentum and weight so he did not fall on me. With a roaring scream, almost like the whistle of a bird, my steed fell beside where I lay, but did not crush me. I took cover behind the still-heaving body.

I was lashing out with my tendrils, trying to turn off as many monads of as many troopers as I could, as they fled. I negated the energy supplies of several rifles. Others I gave free will, and they became snakes of iron, hissing, or molten ribbons, lashing.

Then certain of the shells, still flaring and buzzing, lodged among my dying steed's rib cage, erupted, sending ribbons of overspatial energy into the red and blue directions of hyperspace.

I felt a ripple of pressure across my hypersurface; my tendrils were crushed back into three-space and lay prostrate.

I saw the shining wheels of Leucosia and Parthenope draw back from the convulsion of hyperenergies; but then my "eyes" above and below the world-plane were dazed by the space-collapsing overpressure. I lost sight of the sirens, but they were not far away.

However, this was not the irresistible pressure of one of Miss Daw's songs, nor was the pressure even, or intelligently applied. I was still able to force more substance into an unwounded tendril, wrap it around a nearby tree, negate my weight, and pull myself briefly in and out of hyperspace. I disappeared and reappeared in a tree one hundred yards away.

I was glad I did: Blue dazzle lanced from the cyclopes-eyes of the fleeing Amazonian superhorses (who ran with their heads turned backwards) and smote the body of my steed. Some chemical or electrical reaction broke open the cyclopes-eye in my steed; a ten-foot-in-diameter area exploded into an instant mass of sticky white flame.

This was while they were running away at sixty miles an hour. I would hate to be a normal person on the receiving end of any serious attack from them.

4.

Shrill screams and yells came in the near distance. I saw three or four trees flipping end-over-end through the blue sky above the tree line. The maenads were near, and getting nearer.

Nine or ten svelte figures in black catsuits lay prone on the wet grasses near the edge of the glade, motionless as dropped dolls. These were the Amazons I had knocked senseless when I swept all their controlling monads out of alignment. Only one of them was up; she was on her knees, weapon to her shoulder, and firing at her fleeing comrades—I had taken more time with the first Amazon I struck, and implanted an entelechy, a set of instructions, into her brain atoms. Unfortunately, now with two sirens in the area, I could not open up any energy-channels in hyperspace to pass any new instructions to my doll. Like a windup toy, she merely fired till her magazine was empty, and then she knelt, motionless, eyes blank, finger still depressing the trigger.

I wanted to send more instructions to her, but could not. I dearly wanted to wake up all ten Amazons and have a personal force of deadly attack dolls—but hyperspace was confused and rippling. The pressure was patchy: immense in some places, weak in others. I was getting intermediate visions from my higher senses, but it hurt to try to open my higher eyes, and my sense-impressions were uncertain and blurry.

One thing I did sense was a flare of usefulness. With a flicker of motion, I detected a little crystal marble, one of the eyes of Lamia, sail past through the trees, not far from my position. I could not see where the marble was with my eye—the leaves blocked my vision, and my sight was impeded by surfaces at the moment. But that eye was so useful, for a moment, to Lamia, that I was sure she had found me.

The pressure in hyperspace increased. Now I heard the sirens singing. My senses dimmed and went entirely blind.

I started scrambling down from branch to branch.

5.

Through a gap in the leaves, I saw a girl. To her lips was pressed a double-flute, and her cheeks were belled out. With her right hand (on one flute) she played a tripping melody; with her left (on the other flute), she fingered the harmony. The reed had a buzzing quality like a recorder.

She was dressed in a white toga of classical design, a very wide belt, and sandals with straps crisscrossing all the way up her calves to tie at the knee. Her hair was piled atop her head and held in place with golden pins. I could see her bare back, and saw two long scars running parallel to her spine, where her wings had been removed after she and her sisters lost their duel with the Muses.

I unslung my rifle (Did I mention I had been carrying Antiope's rifle all this time, and that its stock had been swinging against my butt and hip and leaving a bruise?), brought it to my shoulder, and took aim. I used the thumb button to chamber a dimension-flattening round.

I could not remember if you were supposed to close one eye or not when aiming, or whether you were supposed to hold your breath, or breathe naturally, or what. Where was I supposed to put my other hand? Closer to the trigger or farther down the barrel? Was it okay to rest the barrel on a tree branch to steady it?

Dammit. Why hadn't I learned anything useful in school?

In films, people just shoot, and if they are bad guys they miss and if they are good guys they hit.

In films, they also don't hesitate.

I hesitated. Every thought I should have thought about the Amazons I now thought about this unarmed woman. I thought about Quentin's warnings, about how killing someone would bring a curse down on us.

On the other hand, if I were dead, what did I care if I were cursed or not?

I thought: Some woman had to suffer labor to bring into being the life I am about to destroy. When she was a baby, this woman had gooed and smiled and cried and taken her first steps. She was not evil, not back then. There is some mother who loves her, out there, somewhere. Even Grendel Glum had a mother who missed him.

I decided to close one eye, rest on the tree branch, put my other hand farther down the barrel, hold my breath.

I thought: There are countless millions of babies on this planet alone, gooing and smiling and crying and taking first steps. This woman is part of the group setting out to kill all of them. What's sauce for the goose is sauce for the gander. Any jury in the world would call this self-defense. Curse away, curses. Sorry.

There was no muzzle-flash, and the only noise was a sharp, flat crack. The recoil knocked me backwards off the branch, so that I was hanging upside down by my knees, the rifle swinging like a pendulum at the end of a shoulder strap I was still clutching.

Her music stopped. Upside down and facing the wrong way, I did not see where my shot had flown. (Was I a murderess, or not?) But the multiple strands of music-energy erupted like a flare into hyperspace to the blue and red of me. The fact that I could see that happening at all seemed to indicate that I had wounded her, or at least startled her.

The pressure in hyperspace was starting to get patchy and clear up. There

was a second siren song, this one played on strings (maybe a lyre?) somewhere in the area, but it must have been farther away, because I was able to
wiggle a hyperlimb into the substance of four-space, negate some of my
weight by bending world-lines, and drop lightly to the ground.

Or, not so lightly. In middrop, reality hiccuped. I was just a girl. Some
maenad nearby must have done her Grendel-thing. I fell hard, and it hurt,
but nothing seemed broken. I wiggled across the leaves and took up my
fallen rifle.

The lyre-music got louder. The second siren was near and getting nearer.
The shrill screams and yells of the maenads rose up and drowned and
quenched the lyre-music.

A maenad came suddenly around the tree where I crouched. She had in
hand a fourteen-foot length of iron pole. It looked like an I-beam ripped
from the electrical transformer towers I had passed. She turned to face me:
Less than a dozen feet separated us. There were worms and serpents woven
in her hair. Adders raised their heads from her oozy locks and stared at me.

Her eyes were two pools of drugged insanity. She opened her mouth and
screamed like a peacock.

No moralizing or hesitating this time. I chambered an anti-psychic round,
brought up the weapon, and shot. She was leaping toward me, and she
caught the shell in her mouth. Her head exploded. Blood and brains flew
everywhere. Instead of being grossed out, or horrified, I laughed aloud.

6.

I am sorry I laughed. It makes me sound like some sort of sick, sick person.
But I thought I was about to die. I was sure of it. And I was relieved. I was
glad to be alive.

Her eyes, her eyes had frightened me so. Sometimes, at night, I can still
see them.

7.

More running through the trees.

I could hear the noise and earthquake-clamor of the advancing maenads to
my left and right, and yellow smoke and dust hung over the treetops.

Then, a break in the trees. There was a narrow strip of grass, and then a cliff. I could see the texture of the trees far below, like green cumulus clouds. There was a line cutting through the trees. A highway? In the distance, in the horizon, a gray smudge was gathered around a long line of blue haze. The sea? I did not see how that could be Los Angeles—the terrain looked too green and hilly. On the other hand, I did not know what the city looked like from the landward side. I did not even know what planet this was.

I saw a group of maenads break free of the tree line about a hundred yards, maybe two hundred, to the left of me.

I stood still, hoping they would see the uniform and conclude I was an Amazon. But they were not fooled. On they came.

One of them laughed and simply jumped off the cliff to her death. The others screamed like falcons and ran toward me. Trees behind me swayed and toppled, and hundred-feet-tall cylinders of timber began raining over the cliffside. My armor stiffened once or twice as splinters as long as my forearm, shooting through the air at the speed of sound, bounced off the high-tech Amazonian fabric.

It knocked me sliding off the cliff. Before I fell, the last thing I did was chamber and shoot an anti-psychic round into the cliff face half a yard away from me.

The recoil tore the rifle out of my hands. But since the energy-pulse from the shell negated, for a moment, whatever it was the maenads were doing to me to compress me, I merely reached out with a tendril and organized the world-path of the falling rifle so that it jumped immediately back into my hand.

On wings of silver and red shining stuff, I soared down the cliff face. Reality blinked, and I was a falling girl. I shot again. I was a soaring four-dimensional angel-thing. Blink again: 3-D girl again, falling. Shot again: 4-D angel. Blink: 3-D. Shot: 4-D. You get the picture.

Twenty yards up from an inviting patch of grass, and I was out of that particular type of ammo. I had given Antiope my spare clips, after all. Blink: 3-D again. The girl falls.

The armor, which stiffened on impact to protect against rifle shots, also stiffened on impact when I fell. This meant no absorbing any shock with my legs, no clever tumbling, no rolling—just a bad, bad fall.

There was a terrible stabbing pain in my leg when I tried to stand, and I could not stand. And this was no mere "surface" pain; I was no longer occupying a huge fourth-dimensional volume, with plenty of room to disperse shocks into. No, I was simply the little blond girl the maenads wanted me to be.

I suppose it should have been impossible to break a leg when encased in a perfectly rigid metal suit. But maybe one of the smart maenads had been inspired to believe I would break a leg when I fell. So here I was.

The maenads swarmed down the cliff like a troop of monkeys. One girl ran down the cliffside as if it were a flat surface, her personal gravity at right angles to the rest of the Earth.

Several of the girls flew. They did not fly like birds do; they did not move through the air like Victor levitating. No: They whirled through the air like autumn leaves in a gale, swirling high and low, pitching up and down, arms and legs spread wide, tangled hair-mops shedding grape-leaf.

The maenads landed around me like paratroopers. Some merely touched down like ballerinas stepping off an invisible carriage step. Some landed on their heads. One of them splattered into a wash of broken bones and wide-splashed blood, and gathered herself together, and stood up, laughing drunkenly. Several of them splattered and did not get up.

I shot and shot and shot and shot.

The other shells, meant to stop the other paradigms, did little or nothing to these girls. Maybe one fell down on her rump and started crying, maybe two. Most of them slapped the bullets away like annoying hornets. Or brushed away the bleeding wounds as if they were nothing, Colin-like.

They had wands and spears in hand, and more than one girl was still clutching a convenient tree or oblong slab of rock. Then they were in a circle around me, dancing and screaming and laughing, pounding me over and over, stabbing, bludgeoning, whipping. One girl on her hands and knees put her teeth to my arm and bit.

I was bruised, but was not hurt. Even the tree trunk smashing over and over against me merely drove my armor-stiffened body into the dirt, but did not crush me instantly into red paste.

But I was blacking out, and the girl biting my vambrace was reaching for the seam where my helmet met my neck. . . .

A column of fire fell down from heaven. It was a pillar, a turning inferno fifty yards high and six yards in diameter, surrounded by a whirlwind of smoke and ash. It landed in the midst of the dancing maenads and exploded. Long ropes and tendrils of flame surged out in each direction, taking up the half-naked girls and throwing them against the cliffside.

The maenads shrilled their horrid war cry and rushed into the fire, stabbing and swinging their spears and tree trunks. The column vomited fire across the spears and trees and ignited them.

Then the column shrank, grew brighter, stiffened, and exploded outward in each direction with mind-numbing violence. The flash dazzled me; the report deafened me. In the afterimage, I saw the silhouettes of women spinning end over end, against rolling clouds of red and black smoke shot through with tongues of fire.

Good thing Amazons built their armor to be fireproof. Or maybe the column of fire had done something particular to save me. Because when the swirling fires died down, there, in the midst of the smoking crater, surrounded by smoking ropes and helixes of dying flame, was Colin.

"You look good in that outfit, Dark Mistress," were the first words out of his mouth.

"Yeah, so do you," I whispered. He was in his classy black tuxedo, with a large gold ring shining on his finger. "Kind of hurt, here . . . ," I finished.

All the rapid healing the maenads had been doing must have peopled the area with a lot of healing energies, because all Colin did was lean down and kiss me on the thigh, and my leg was fixed. Once again, there was no transition, no logic to his power. One moment: broken leg, pain . . . the next: no pain.

Maenads scattered to each side of us were groaning and giggling and climbing to their feet, shaking ashes from long (utterly unburned) hair.

Colin put his arm around me, picked me up, hugging me tightly to his chest, and he kissed me fiercely on the lips. With his thumb, he turned the collet of his ring inward. Maenads blinked, their eyes blank, and began looking left and right, making little murmurs of annoyance and wonder. The fire and ash had made the maenads take their crazed eyes off us for an eyeblink, and that was all the ring of Gyges needed.

A swarm of black feathers erupted from Colin's back as ten-feet-wide hawk wings expanded into view. And then I was in the arms of a dark-winged angel in a tux, and we were flying away, skimming the trees.

Behind us, disappointed maenads whined and stamped their feet.

NYMPHS

1.

In the air, his arms around me, I spoke over the rush and whistle of the winds against his black wings. "Pillar of fire. How did you manage that?"

He shouted back, cheerfully. "I am a shape-changer. Why assume we are limited to organic shapes? Quentin told me the secret name of fire."

I said, "Where are the others?"

At that moment, I saw or imagined the rifle slung over my shoulder flicker and grow bright. It was hard to use my higher senses when I was enclosed in Colin's arms, but something in the rifle had just become very useful to some-one else.

Without pause, I shrugged my shoulder half an inch into the blue direc-tion and let the shoulder strap fall past and through my arm, grabbed the barrel with the other hand, and flung the mass away, amplifying the outward momentum—it was the quickest way I could think of to get the weapon as far away from us as quickly as possible.

The weapon had a computer inside it. Why not a radio link, a tracking de-vice, a coordinating circuit for the commanding officer to find missing squad members? Why not a self-destruct mechanism?

The weapon opened up like a flower of pale fire. In the middle of the ex-plosion hovered a blue eye, shedding concentric shells of crystal. Shrapnel ricocheted off my suddenly stiff armor. Blue light clung to Colin, flaming like cold napalm; he was falling, his face covered with blood.

I was weightless, with wind in my face. Colin's arms were no longer around me.

I rotated energy-wings into this continuum and negated gravity beneath me. Weightless again, but this time the wind was blowing the other direction, since I was soaring up instead of falling down. Where was Colin? I saw blue sky and white clouds rotating around me as I spun.

Energy from the higher dimension struck me, a ringing lance made of music. It cut my wings from my body and crushed my higher sense into numbness. I screamed and screamed.

The sirens had found me.

Weightless again. Wind from below. The green clouds of forest below jumped up eagerly toward me.

Colin, black wings folded around him, dropped like a thunderbolt out from the glare of the sun. One strong arm went around my waist. He cupped his dark wings, and the world spun slowly around me, and the forest receded.

Colin, his face black with wrath, reached up and the sky *folded* and *rippled* around his hand. I did not see, my eyes could not focus on, what it was he did next.

But then he had a woman in a Greek toga by one ankle. A lyre was falling from her wildly clawing hands. Colin contemptuously let go of the ankle and let her drop.

He did not say anything, did not pause to wonder about it. He just flung her away as if she were garbage.

With a long, hideous wail, she fell away from us, growing smaller and smaller. I closed my eyes and clutched Colin with both arms, burying my head in his chest.

"Are you hurt?" he said, masculine anger still throbbing in his voice.

"My wings are reduced . . . crushed . . . I don't know if I can fly. . . ."

"I'll carry you, Amelia."

"Are you hurt?"

"No. Red ink. But the magic ring just went kaput. I think we're visible. . . . Hey. What is that . . . ?"

Colin had changed course and was now spiraling down toward a wide round clearing in the middle of the forest.

Slabs of fitted stone formed the circular foundations of a ruined building. Grass grew in the cracks between the stones. Rusted stumps of pipe protracted up from an underground space in one or two places. There was a circle of toadstools, bright and gay with spots of yellow and purple, making an outer circle exactly concentric with the circular rim of the grassy stones.

In the very center of the circle of grassy stones, a sleek, black, rocket-ship-shaped guitar was visible, unharmed, unscratched.

This looked like the selfsame guitar that had been slung over the saddle of the Amazonian horse shot to pieces and blown to smithereens before my eyes. How could it have survived . . . ?

Who had brought it here?

Colin said, "What is that?"

I said, "I bought it for you. A guitar. It was meant to be a surprise."

He laughed an odd laugh, and folded his wings, swooping down.

"Colin, what the hell are you doing? Up! Go up! Get us out of here!"

"Oh, come on, Amelia. Don't be silly. What could be the matter? I want to see this guitar you bought for me."

I was looking right at his eyes when it happened. His pupils shrank, contracting in a moment to tiny pinpoints, as if he were staring into a blinding light.

"Colin! This is magic! I am ordering you, as the leader, I am ordering you to get us out of here!"

"Oh . . . now you're just being pushy. Please, Amelia. Don't be so paranoid. That guitar is mine, isn't it? It looks cool."

"Colin! Wake up! Listen to me, for the love of God!"

"I am awake, Amelia," he said in a voice of maddening calm. "I can hear you just fine."

"Away! Fly us away!"

"I am not just going to go off and leave a nice present you bought for me. I want to see it. It looks nice. Very nice. So very nice."

I slapped him across the face. He just smiled at me, placid, his eyes going all blank, his smile empty and idiotic.

His feet touched down, and he folded his wings. We were on the ground, in the center of the grass-grown circle of stones, in the center of the ring of toadstools.

Colin said in a sleepy voice, "Why did you slap me, Amelia? That wasn't very nice. All I wanted to do was . . ."

I looked in the higher dimensions. Rising up from the guitar were webs upon webs. They were all around us, strands and nets of magic. They were winding more and more tightly around Colin and me, glistening ruddily.

This was magic: Quentin's paradigm. It neither automatically trumped my paradigm, nor did mine automatically trump it. Was there something I could do?

I reached into the nearest cluster of moral imperatives and . . . twisted . . . something, curving the morality-strand back inward on itself to form an infinitely recurring loop.

In effect, I hoped to do to the woven web of moral obligations what I had done to the nanotech virus Dr. Fell had injected in me. I thought that if I gave the moral obligations free will, they might not be able to be used as an enchantment or as a snare.

For a moment, it seemed as if the webs might wake up and loosen us.

But then a slim and beautiful woman, dark-haired and ivory-skinned, stepped out from a tree, her footstep as soft and shy as a doe stepping. Her corona was a wreath of living leaves. Her gown was green.

2.

She did not come from behind the tree, but from inside it: For a moment, her form was a mist or invisible essence sliding between the substance of the bark. With her next quiet step, she was solid. I could see from her inner nature that she resided in a vessel, shaped like a woman, which was, at that moment, made for her, solidified out of thin air.

In one hand she held a slender wand of willow. She tapped it on the ground, saying, "Phobetor, Prince of Night, my gentle sweet, look to me. Look, and be enchanted by, Oenone."

His face turned toward her. His eyes were utterly blank at this point.

I saw the strand of morality twisting, shaking, tossing. I reached more deeply into the energy knot involved, trying to liberate the core of the incoming power before . . .

"Phobetor, you have slain Leucosia, our husband's wife, ending and therefore owing us a life. You now are owned by the nymphs of stream and tree. . . ."

Part of the strand began to uncurl. I shouted in triumph and alarm, calling out to Colin, begging him to wake up.

Colin stirred and blinked. A tone of confusion and anger rang in his voice: "Amelia! What is happening to me—? Can you—?"

The nymph said softly, "Arms of Phaethusa, you have slain our lord's wild lady, grim Chalcomede—why should your bloodstained hands undo our work, when hers are nerveless and forever still? Hands and arms! An equal balance must require that you do our lord's and not your lady's will."

My arms tingled and fell numb, not merely my human arms in this dimension, but the energy-tendrils I was using in the other world to try to unwind the spell snaring us.

My legs went numb as well. I collapsed heavily into Colin's arms. He turned and caught me. Colin's eyes were now bright and awake.

My voice was working. "Drop me. Stop her!"

The idiot dropped me. When I said "drop," of course, I had meant for him to lower me quickly but gently to the ground, not just to let my head bounce off the pavement. What a jerk.

And he ran at her, his arms already beginning to turn into flame.

She said, "Phobetor—I call you by your true name. Resume that shape you knew on Earth, mortal boy."

His true shape snapped back into place, fires extinguished. He stumbled and slowed.

The nymph smiled, and cooed in a voice like a dove: "Your magics desert you, mortal boy. No powers remain you to employ."

He said, "Ah . . . but I still have the memory of my mother to inspire me. Funny things, memories. Here. Look."

From somewhere, or perhaps from nowhere, Colin drew out his card. The little black playing card on which was sketched his father, Morpheus, and his unknown mother.

Colin held the little card up before him, at arm's length, and advanced toward the nymph. Her eyes focused on the card. Then, either sensing magic, or fearing some trap, she held up her hand to shield her eyes and turned her head away.

It was at that moment her eyes went blank. When she looked away from the card, not when she looked at it, her memory was interrupted.

To her it must have seemed as if Colin had teleported. One moment he was in the middle of the glade; now he was next to her.

She raised her wand and began to chant another curse. He put the card away, or made it disappear, and once again, her eyes went blank a moment.

That moment was enough. Colin closed the distance and now had his hands around her throat.

With brutal force, Colin struck her head against the bole of the tree. There was a sickening sound. When she slumped away from the point of impact, bloodstains trailed behind her hair. Whether she was stunned or dead, I could not see.

3.

Four comely women stepped from the boles of four trees in the circle around us. Each was more beautiful than the last, soft-eyed, soft-voiced, folds of emerald gowns falling and flowing around long legs and trim ankles.

Each was dark-haired, with skin as pale as parchment, eyebrows delicate dark streaks above eyes like glittering black amethysts, lips smiling red cupid's bows.

Each had a willow wand in her slim-wristed and well-shaped hand.

One pointed her wand at Colin, cooing in a voice mild yet clear as cool water: "Phobetor, I call you by your true name. Red blood drips from your woman-slaying hands and cries out for vengeance. How will you account for the death of Parthenope, the wounds of unloved Oenone? Those hands I, death-defying Cyane, now call upon to do our work; seize the girl, Phaethusa, rob her powers from her."

Colin raised his hand. Reality hiccuped. My higher senses were dead. I could no longer see the magic boiling around us; there was nothing I could do to interfere.

Another nymph spoke. Her voice was rippling music: "Heart and sense and soul, cruel Phobetor, you have devoted to ruthless murder. I, Apostate Ethemea the Proud, now make your eyes as blind as your black heart."

Colin, though blind, still tried to attack. He ran toward the sound of the girl, his arms windmilling and wild.

As he ran, the grass and leaves began to swirl around him, and the sun was blotted out by cloud. The air seemed to tremble; Colin's wrath was growing thick around him, becoming visible.

He was fast on his feet, and he seemed not to need his eyes to sense where the girl stood. He grabbed the nymph who cursed him by one arm. He threw her to the stones with a violent cry. I heard bones break.

A third nymph cooed: "Panic and wrath you unleash into the darkening air. Murderer, I, Lara, whose voice Lord Hermes grants me nevermore be stilled, bestow on you the calmness and grave-peace into which you have thrown the women you have killed."

The swirl of leaves dropped and died. The sun came out.

The fourth one said, "Such strength, oh muscles, oh nerves, you used against us, I, Sagaritis, hated of the dread goddesses, now take from you. I turn your limbs to stone."

Colin staggered and fell to his knees.

He was next to the guitar I had bought him. My higher senses were not working, but I am sure that black guitar was the center of a snake's nest of magical strands and ropes.

What had ever possessed me to buy that dumb thing in the first place? Maybe my wits had been dulled by magic and adverse fate. How can you beat a foe who can make you stupid?

The woman he had struck against the tree, the first one, rose to her feet, unhurt. There was no sign of blood on her. She said, "Your authority over dream, abnormal, abortive, unclean, do I, Oenone, reave from you, just recompense for wicked deeds both done and dreamt. Dark powers of Dreaming, begone. You cannot overmatch, dream-shadows, these gentle hands which once refused to heal the traitor Paris, and wove, instead of bridal veil, the silken noose to hang me from a yew-wood tree: Lord Trismegistus me uprooted from unsacred grave; me power over Darkness gave!"

She stepped daintily forward and tapped Colin's kneeling body with her wand. He cried out, a great, horrible, strangled cry, and fell prone.

I blinked. I saw something glittering in the trees above. It was lit up with usefulness.

My upper senses were coming back. I tried to look in the other dimensions aside from the normal three. I could not, not yet.

4.

In a moment or two, the nymphs might realize that, by turning off Colin's powers, they had turned off their ability to stop mine.

But none of them was looking toward me. The woman who had blinded him now rose up, broken bones healed and whole, unharmed, her coiffure and gown unmussed, unwrinkled, untorn. She tapped Colin's motionless, screaming body with her wand, saying, "Murderer, who had sent our sisters down into the eternal sleep of death, a lesser sleep I put on you. Move not, stir not, speak not, but wait in all helplessness, awaiting the knife stroke which shall sever your false throat."

Colin's screaming stopped. I could see his body, fallen along the grass-covered stones, facing away from me.

Suddenly, I could see through the surfaces of objects.

I saw, in the distance, "through" the trees, a rout of wild maenads were pelting down the slope, ululating. *"Ite Bacchai! Ite Bacchai!"*

And, downslope from us, not far from the highway, I saw the "flat"-seeming shapes of lithe and calm-faced women in black skintight armor, bent low over the manes of their artificial super-steeds, moving in a well-ordered column, silent and rapid. There were scouts ahead of the main column, and flanking riders left and right.

If only I could get my tendrils on one of their rifles, I could shoot maenads and nymphs alike with bullets designed to cripple their particular powers.

The distance was far, but was it too far? I pushed first one, then two energy-tendrils into four-space. And . . .

The nymph standing over Colin smote him a second time with her wand, saying, "Powers used for evil deeds, this recompense we nymphs demand of you—serve now Ethemea, not Phobetor, and all the powers of Phaethusa undo."

Stepping lightly over to me as she spoke, this nymph struck me in the face with the butt of her wand. It was shockingly painful. I tasted blood where my lip had been cut on my teeth.

And I was three-dimensional again. Crushing pain pressed in where once my higher limbs had been. I could no longer even imagine the other directions.

The nymph Ethemea looked down at me, not smiling, not frowning; she did not gloat, but neither did any trace of sympathy mar the perfect coolness of her gaze.

I was vermin to her. She looked like a farmwife looking at a rat in a trap, or some vixen that had been killing her chickens.

I lay there helpless, numb, motionless, waiting for death. I could still speak, but what would I have said?

5.

The voice of Lamia now issued from the crystal marble hovering overhead: "Slay the dream-prince instantly! Why do you delay? Pierce his flesh with pitiless steel knives!"

The nymph Ethemea turned away from me and said in a voice as soft as falling snow, "We have witnessed in this place what curses, what weaknesses, cling thick and black to any who offend the laws of gods and men."

One of the nymphs—the one who had robbed Colin of his power, and called herself Cyane—spoke next, saying, "The crime of murder would render us vulnerable to the curses of that chaoticist whom you have not yet caught, nor yet discovered: Eidotheia, whom we have cause to fear."

Lamia said, "Fear more to disobey! Take up your athames, and slay!"

A third nymph, Lara, said softly, "Lord Trismegistus, swift guide of souls to Hell, and father of lies, promised me freedom from the Path of Sighs, and swore my soul would not in that Dark House dwell, if only I would forget all honor, and worship his body with feigned love and true concupiscence. Him alone, my husband is, to him alone, fealty and obedience I owe. What cause have we to obey cruel Lamia, who rejoices in blood and woe?"

Lamia's voice said, "Fools, was I not dead as well, and did not Trismegistus steal my soul from destined torments waiting me in Hell, to be his concubine and unwilling mate? All this is being done at his bidding. Why do you hesitate?"

The nymph Sagaritis, the one who had paralyzed Colin, said, "He never bade us kill and slay, never bade us murders do; bloody deeds were not his way—who wills this deed; our Lord . . . or you?"

Lamia said, "I waste no further breath: Maenads are here, and far more tractable to my will. Let the glorious and gory deeds be done by them who are not so nice and so fastidious as you!"

The nymphs, smiling cryptically, inclined their heads and stepped smoothly to the left and right, making way.

The storm of noise and fury approached down the slope. With my unaided eyes, I saw, between the toppling tree boles, women in torn dresses, or panther skins, or nude, running in huge long-legged strides through the trees, ivy-wreathed spears and truncheons of iron in their slim hands.

Many of them struck the ground with their spearheads as they ran, and wine bubbled up from rents in the earth those massive blows made. Some of the women who ran on all fours tore the ground with their fingernails, pulling up rocks and boulders; gushes of white milk fountained up from the soil in those places. A rolling wash of muddy wine and dirty milk was rippling and tumbling down the slope with the women, staining their bare calves and thighs.

And I wondered where Mavors was, with all his troops: troops destined to rescue us when death loomed. And yet I knew: I had seen the explosion through time-space that had snarled the dream-paths his Atlanteans were using, and sent the ships and giants tumbling into confusion. Mavors was not coming.

I whispered. "Echidna. Come. Can you hear me? Please come."

Even though my voice had barely breathed that name, the nymph who had struck me, Ethemea, who was standing twelve or so feet away, turned and said in a voice like music: "The creatures of dream cannot hear, unhoused souls, save for what we, souls in vessels, care to have them hear."

I shouted to her: "The maenads want to kill us all, kill everything. They plan to have the world end. When I die, my father in Chaos, Helios, will destroy the material universe. The Olympians are fighting each other, and they can't stop what's coming. Do you want to live?"

She smiled an eerie smile. "My Lord husband, Trismegistus, is the Psychopomp. No matter what sins I do on Earth, when this Flesh is dead, the guide who leads souls to underworld will lead me to no other place but to his marriage bed."

I said, "Don't you understand? There won't be any Heaven or Hell, no Earth, no underworld, no nothing! Trismegistus will die, too!"

Ethemea smiled thinly. "Perhaps you overestimate the powers Chaos wields. Trismegistus knows your art as well as his own. Your death may not lead to the universal apocalypse you say. His plans are deep and subtle. . . . But, too late for any further talk! The maenads come to tear and slay."

I shouted, "But Parthenope said Trismegistus wanted to end the world! He must be lying to someone! Why not to you?"

But she had glided backwards, well out of way of the oncoming avalanche of maenads.

6.

An inch-high flood of milk and wine flowed into the area, pushing a tide-ripple of grass blades, dead leaves, and litter.

The maenads splashed forward, screaming and yodeling. I saw how the calm nymphs each drew a circle in the grass around them with their willow wands. As if those gestured circles had created towers of invulnerable glass, the maenad horde spilled left and right around each unruffled and mysteriously smiling nymph, and none of the wild women, despite the press and the confusion, approached within a yard of them. Even the ripple of dirty milk parted and went around them.

I was looking at Colin during that moment. Maybe I was screaming to him. I don't know. But the shrilly shouting bacchants were between him and the undisturbed nymphs, reaching toward him with long fingernails. He was closer to them than I was. He would be first.

There was an altercation suddenly. Perhaps two maenads both wanted to be the first to sink her fine white teeth into Colin. Perhaps it was just an accident.

One ran her sister through the stomach with her spear; the impaled girl ripped off the spear arm of her attacker and flung it high overhead, forming a momentary rainbow of blood.

Because I was looking right at him, I actually saw it happen. The square slab of grassy stone on which he lay spun upside down. Colin was dumped into a square hole. The reverse side of this slab was decorated with an identical plot of grass. The pattern of cracks on this side of the stone was the same as on the other side.

And there was a Colin, in his black tuxedo, lying in the same place. He had been stuck to the underside of the stone, and the rotation lifted him into position. The new Colin was lying in the same position and posture, more or less, that the old Colin had been.

The only thing that was different was that the guitar got dumped down the hole with the real Colin.

The two fighting maenads were trampled and stabbed by their impatient sisters. Beautiful, screaming women, faces flushed with wine, eyes stark with madness, now stabbed Colin's prone form. A score of spears transfixed his flesh.

Or tried to. The tuxedo jacket ripped beneath the impact of the ivy-wreathed spearheads, but a jarring report, the clang of metal against metal, sang in the air as the spearheads skittered from the body, or snapped in two.

In that same moment, a dozen more maenads, ignoring Colin, jumped clean over him and over the women savaging him, and fell upon me. I could raise no hand to defend myself; my voice was drowned in screams, my powers were . . .

On. My powers were on. I could see hyperspace.

I moved my body slightly and let the spears and truncheons fall "through" the space my body occupied without touching me.

I saw Colin rising to his feet. He did not stand up as a man does, by bending his legs and putting his weigh beneath: No, he merely rose up like a flag-pole being hauled erect. The bloody-nailed maenads fell backwards, wary, their faces pale with anger.

The spears had torn both fabric and flesh, revealing an integument of metallic gold beneath. His face was wounded, and the flesh of his cheeks hung limply from this white bony substance beneath: but Colin's eyes were calm with a terrible calm. He put his hands to the flesh of his face. There was a hiss of noise, and the plasticlike flesh of his cheeks once more hid the bone structure beneath.

I did not see what passed from Colin to the women, or how the molecular engines entered the maenad bloodstreams, but I saw the effect. The wild women sank to the ground. Weapons dropped from limp fingers, and the women, no longer maddened, smiled empty smiles at each other, heavily sedated.

"The dream-lord robs the bacchants of their dreams of hate!" called Oenone in a voice of mingled fear and wonder. "Unmake his charm, O sisters mine, ere it is too late!"

The five nymphs pointed their wands at Colin, who stood in his torn tuxedo, hands casually in his pockets. They called out secret names and words of power. Whatever the nymphs had been expecting to happen, did not happen. Colin did not even bother to smile.

At this same time, a hole opened in the ground directly below me. I did not fall into it, only because my weight was no longer distributed into Earth's time-space.

Far below, I saw a buried river, some huge sewer main with concrete banks. In the middle of the river, directly below me, was the *Argent Nautilus.*

Vanity rose up into view. She was wrapped in a chain-mail jerkin. Her expression was thoughtful. She levitated into a position above and somewhat behind Colin.

With a shrill noise of hate, the white-faced bacchants darted their spears at the hovering girl, or threw their metal truncheons. The metal objects slowed, and came to rest hanging in a circle in the air near her.

She made a gesture: And the spears and truncheons tilted left and right, points outward, forming the pattern of a pentagram in the air, with herself in the midmost. A final spear she took in hand, one that had pierced Colin's torn face. Vanity laid the spearshaft across her knee and strained. The wood snapped in two.

Vanity spoke, and a voice that was not hers came from her mouth: "The power of the bacchants breaks. This demonstration involves the moral principle of balance, or quid pro quo. The essential nature of the wounds just now inflicted, I admix to the humors released into the air by the blood thus spilled. A sympathetic and contagious connection is formed to those who made the wounds. Clearly this assault has dissolved the wards that might otherwise deflect the returning, or responsive counterinfluence. Any questions . . . ?"

Utter silence had fallen across the maenads.

The nymphs raised their willow wands. Oenone said, "This is a sorceress! Sisters! Chant the counterspell, and infuse the furious spirits once again into the maenads!"

Vanity waved her broken spearshaft negligently toward Oenone. "I call these maenads killers-of-trees, despoilers of the sacred forests where happy meliads and tree-nymphs dwell. The vengeance I set in motion defends the nymphic race. Any nymph who hinders me admits she wishes no defense; I therefore step inside her ward. Speak, if you consent. Otherwise, your silence is consent. I, Eidotheia, friend of homeless Menelaus, by virtue of the kind act by which I found the hero his home, here now complete my demonstration. Maenads! The true name of the father of salmons is *Gwion*."

The whole army of maenads simply toppled: They fell on their faces and began flopping and writhing like fish out of water. With arched backs and hands held to their sides, the maenads rolled and kicked and shuddered, mouths gaping. It would have been funny, had they not been choking to death in air.

The form of Vanity turned pale, her flesh becoming porcelain. Above her and behind her stood a shadow with the features of Quentin, which had become visible when he spoke his name. Apparently it was a part of spellweaving; the nymphs had been announcing their own names as well.

All five nymphs now raised their willow wands and pointed them toward Vanity's body hanging in midair. Leaves of many colors and flower petals swirled up from the ground and made dancing spirals around the nymphs, circling high and low.

Quentin now began to grow. Inky shadows, despite that it was day, were streaming in billows out of Vanity's chain mail, and the lengthening shadow swirled around her form without weight, like the hem of a long cloak in a high wind.

The eyes of the nymphs were glittering with fear. The shadowy image of Quentin's face was smiling introspectively: the smile of the Sphinx of Memphis. His eyes, black lids over ebony orbs, were partly closed.

At that same moment in time, the first two of the Amazon outriders came suddenly and swiftly into the glade, their steeds loping with silent speed across the grass.

Both riders, in one smooth motion, chambered a different type of round and shot.

I bent the world-path of the bullet aimed toward Quentin into the chest of Ethemea. Her magic failed as the silver bullet struck her; there was a flash of azure light in her gaping chest wound, and her soul did not survive the scuttling of the vessel she was occupying.

The other bullet struck Colin. Colin tilted slightly, and more flesh was shaken from his damaged face, but otherwise there was no result. For some reason, the anti-psychic shell had no effect whatsoever.

A third eye opened on Colin's forehead. Blue, metallic, glittering with dazzling power, it sent out a beam that played across the four remaining nymphs. Two of them screamed and tried to jump back into the trees from which they had come. But it seemed as if that pesky law of nature, which says that two solids cannot occupy the same space at the same time, was being enforced, for once. The girls slammed their heads against the tree boles, and sat down. One of them put her hands to her broken nose and started crying.

I reached out and turned the one Amazon's mechanical soul to "off."

A trapdoor opened in the grass beneath the hooves of the other Amazon rider. The Amazon, even as she was falling, shouldered her weapon and shot round after round below her.

I could see through the intervening ground that the Amazon was shooting as she fell. Shooting a second girl who looked like Vanity.

Or, rather, shooting *at* Vanity. The green stone around Vanity's neck was pulsing and swimming with power. I saw the shells, as they flew over the railing of the ship, enter the laws of nature whose internal natures were a bit more Aristotelian and a bit less Newtonian. For Aristotle, heavy objects fall faster than light ones, and kinetic energy simply is not one-half momentum times velocity. The bullets slowed down considerably.

According to Aristotle, the natural motion of fire was to rise, and move toward the divine fires in the crystal spheres beyond the moon. Vanity must have persuaded the bullets something to the effect that the rules about fire applied to them. The bullets flew wide overhead, slowing and tumbling, rising toward the ceiling like bubbles.

I reached out farther, to the other Amazon riders coming up the slope. They could not see me, because of the intervening trees and leaves. But I could see them. I began switching them "off" as quickly as my energy tendrils could snap across the intervening time-space.

It was taking too long. I would never get them all in time.

Plan B: I traced the lines of moral obligation between them to identify the leader. I reprogrammed her to call off the attack and sound the retreat.

The other Amazons obeyed without question. Away they went, riding swiftly and silently.

Darkness floated out from Quentin. It passed over the maenads; and where it had passed, they were transformed. Some turned into furry sleek shapes. For others, skins grew thick and turned to bark; hair rose up, elongating strangely, becoming leaves and drooping vines. Toes dug into the soil.

In a few moments, we stood within the silence of a forest more thick and lush than before. The uprooted trees were now replaced by pines and cedars. Ivy and grapevines crawled from branch to branch. Hot-eyed leopardesses and she-panthers stalked among the trees, snarling, but the shadow-version of Quentin spoke a word, and they became gentle.

We were alone with one sleeping Amazon (asleep on her horse, seated at attention), three hollow-eyed nymphs (standing), and one weeping nymph (seated on the ground).

7.

I said to the version of Colin, "They thought I was Vanity. When they shot me. The Amazons used the wrong shell. Was that because you all were—?"

Colin pulled off the prosthetic, which once had been his face, and straightened up. Nanotech machines, small as molecules, rippled through his flesh, uncompressing his bones and muscles, shortening and coloring hair.

The spine opened up with ugly popping noises as the body grew a foot taller. His shape was rearranged from a thickset and hairy wrestler's body to a longer, thinner, swimmer's form.

When the one-eyed insectoid thing put the prosthetic face back in place, the features were different. The seam around his chin and ears hissed and vanished.

Victor said, "Well, come now, Amelia. We are shape-changers, after all."

8.

Quentin's voice spoke out of the shadow overhead: "Be careful lowering my statue."

The chain-mail-wrapped life-size porcelain statue of Vanity sank to the ground. Quentin's voice said, "I particularly like the hands. They were the hardest part to get right. Look at how lifelike the fingers are!"

Eagle-winged Colin (in the torn tatters of a once-fine tuxedo) fluttered up from a secret trapdoor in the grass, with a struggling Amazon in his arms. The girl was very strong, and she struck and kicked with savage precision, her face was without fear, and she fought in complete silence.

Colin managed to gasp out: "Amelia! Please . . . ?"

Make that, two sleeping Amazons. I noticed Colin managed to squeeze the sleeping girl's breasts as he lowered her to the ground. Jerk.

He spent a moment straightening his broken bones, popping an eye back into place, and wiping away what turned out to be red ink. Okay, so maybe he thought he deserved to cop a feel from a soldier-girl who had mauled him pretty heavily. That still made him a jerk.

Colin folded back his wings, and they turned into a wide-shouldered black garment, shimmering with feathers, a knee-length tuniclike affair that left his arms and legs free. Neat trick when one needs to change clothes.

The guitar was strapped over his back. He took it by the neck and held it out. "Is this really for me?"

I will never understand myself. Instead of flinging myself into Victor's arms, and kissing and hugging him with sighs and sobs of glad relief, I flung myself at a very surprised Colin, pushing aside the stupid guitar and eagerly seeking out his lips.

Don't ask me to explain it. I can't explain it.

But I could see (since I could look every direction at once, even with my eyes closed) the puzzled frown beginning to form on the face of Victor, the sternly repressed gleam of pain in his eyes.

17

DOORS AND CORRIDORS UNSEEN

1.

Quentin, hovering still within the swirled darkness of shadow and power, said quietly but sternly to the nymphs, "Surrender, and swear not to attack any of the five of us again, in person or by proxy, in word or deed."

One of the nymphs, Lara, said quietly, "Do you threaten us, Lord of Chaos? We helpless women? Cruel Olympians impressed us to these evil deeds; we are enspelled by Trismegistus, the God of Magic, Father of Lies."

Quentin raised his shadowy hand, and dark flame seemed to cling to his fingers. He spoke a Word of Power, and the stones rang underfoot as if a gong had rung, moaning, echoing, and vibrating.

"Swear!" He said in a soft voice, deadly with menace, "Swear, or I, Eidotheia, put upon you a curse as swift and bloody as that which you conspired to put on us!"

Lara held up her hands. "Our hands are clean of blood!"

He said, "As are mine, if the Amazon shoots you through the brainpan. Amelia . . . ? If you will do the honors . . . ?"

Hey. Wasn't I supposed to be in charge? On the other hand, all I was doing right now was pressing my shaking body up to Colin's, so I guess a little insubordination among the ranks was to be expected.

I manipulated the atoms in the Amazon's brain. She chambered an antipsychic round and raised the weapon to her shoulder, aiming at Lara.

Lara said softly, "Shoot. I do not know fear."

The other nymphs looked at each other. The one with the broken nose,

Sagaritis, murmured, "The maenads are trapped, motionless and paralyzed, imprisoned in forms alien to their wild freedom, but forms natural and dear to us. What is the worst this child might do to us? Turn us into trees?"

Another nymph murmured, "What is death to us? The guide of the dead has vowed to guide our shades astray, and lead us to the light again, where we never can belong."

It was Victor who interrupted, saying coldly to Quentin: "Call Hades."

Vanity—the real Vanity, who had come up through one of the trapdoors in the clearing just at that moment—put her hands in front of her mouth, and screamed in utmost panic. "Don't say that name! He heard! He's coming!"

Her eyes were rolling and starting with fear: Her voice and limbs shook.

The nymphs, so defiant a moment before, threw themselves on their faces, groveling, begging, and crying. The change from self-possessed enchantresses to quaking shapes of utter panic was too quick to be believed.

The shadow of Quentin casually moved over to where Vanity was. She had elevated his empty body into place through her trapdoor of grass. He shrank and resumed his flesh and stood. He put out his hand and called: From among the trees came flying a length of white wood, his wand, and it fell lightly into his palm. I suppressed a giggle: He looked so like a stage magician in his tuxedo.

Only now did he deign to turn and notice the groveling, pleading forms of the lovely nymphs. Their tresses, once crowned with flowers, were now tangled in the trampled mud and wine of the grass.

Quentin raised his white wand, saying, "There is but one world where the Lord of Death has no reign, and but one people beyond the power of his laws, beyond the power of all laws! I am a Prince of Chaos, the realm where time, and space, and order are jarred and confounded together in roaring tumult—what is death to me?"

There was more screaming from the nymphs, calls of "Save me!" "I'll swear!" "Master, spare me!" while he spoke sharply at them, demanding their oaths.

It was confusing, but Quentin pointed his stick at them, one after another, and exacted the wording of the vows he wanted.

Quentin waved his wand over them and demanded them to be silent. With a little whimpering and weeping, the girls fell quiet.

Victor seemed pleased. The nymphs had not seen what I saw when he spoke. I had seen the inner nature of the words coming from his mouth. When Victor spoke the dread true name of the Lord of Hell, it was merely air-compression waves forming an arbitrary symbol. He could not say magic words. His voice would never call up gods, no matter what forbidden names he spoke.

I had also seen the utility shining from Vanity's playacted panic, and had seen the deceptive inner nature of her frantic words.

Unlike me, Vanity was a good actress.

And unlike Victor, Vanity could not restrain herself from a mild gloat. She smiled archly at the prone women, and she made a little curtsy-pantomime. "Thank you for swearing, ladies. Now, Leader, can we get out of here?"

She was not talking to me. It was Quentin who answered: "Victor, can you stun our ladies here with some paralysis beam? They cannot attack us again without breaking the law of oaths. I spare their lives."

A glance from my higher sense showed me the strands of moral obligation running between Victor, Vanity, and Quentin. I saw group loyalty, and an obligation to abide by the outcome of elections. I had not appointed a proper chain of command, so no one had been in charge while Colin and I were missing. They had elected Quentin leader.

Well, that was a bit of a relief, wasn't it?

Quentin gave the order to Victor, who focused a narrow beam from his eye and touched one nymph after another with it. Something in their nerve-transmission changed when he touched them, and buried commands in their brain stems triggered their narcoleptic reflexes.

Good thing they were already lying down.

2.

I shouted, "Something just happened! I saw the lines of moral order flicker and jump—"

Quentin said, "What's it mean?"

I said, "There was something—a duty. When the nymphs broke that duty, it suddenly became useful to someone or something."

Colin said, "Bugs. The nymphs were bugged."

"Or booby-trapped. We were supposed to win. We tripped a trap by stunning them." I said, "Leader—what do we do . . . ?" (I really enjoyed being able to say that to someone else.)

Quentin said, "Well . . . first, let's all get aboard the ship. Vanity can select a set of laws of nature that does not allow for . . ."

Colin was not listening to the leader. He was staring at me.

No, not at me. He was looking at the Amazon, who was still seated, glassy-eyed, on her steed about ten yards behind me.

Colin shouted, "Bugs! Hey! Remember the— She's got the damn rifle bugged, too— Look out!"

The rifle barrel was evidently mounted on gimbals, and evidently controlled via some sort of remote-camera arrangement. Even though the Amazon was not moving, and the stock was motionless in her hands, the barrel had lifted and rotated to cover us. When I say "us," I mean Colin and me. We two were standing, from the point of view of the gun, one behind the other, so that one bullet could pass through us both.

There was no time to scream or blink or move. Victor exploded and fell over, as the rifle and the super-steed and the poor, unconscious Amazon were consumed in an explosion of blue fire.

3.

Far, far too rapidly for me to act . . .

I saw the internal nature of the bullets loaded into the chamber. I could see it clearly, the inner workings of the rifle laid out as if spread on a diagram.

All four bullet-types could not be loaded and shot at once—I could see the stresses in the space-time where the mutually contradictory paradigms cancelled each other out.

But up to two could. The anti-psychic bullet for Colin and the space-collapsing shell for me, with a buckshot shell behind them both, to make sure we were peppered with pellets. The space-collapsing shell did not even need to strike me. It did not need to be in the same dimension I was in. All it had to do was ignite somewhere in the area.

Victor must have been experimenting with neurotransmitters. I saw the internal nature of something very rapid happen in his brain stem, as if thoughts were being transmitted from one section of his brain to another by faster-than-light particles, not by the snail-pace electrochemical charges across nerve cell surfaces. Of course, it was not faster-than-light to him. It was merely particles moving in excess of three million kilometers per second. In his paradigm, there was no upper limit to velocity.

The rifle, to be sure, operated on the same paradigm, and added extra charge to the rail gun to make the bullets come out faster. But the total energy in Victor's metal eye was evidently greater than that in the smaller metal eye hidden in the stock of the barrel.

In effect, the gun-core poured as much power as possible into the rail gun as quickly as possible, and Victor poured as much power into a magnetic beam he was using to collapse the gun barrel . . .

The bullets came out at 6 billion meters per second, roughly two hundred times the speed of light.

The particle beam radiating from Victor traveled at roughly 7.5 billion meters per second. The kinetic energy released as heat by the motion of those particles created a flash of flame brighter than the surface of a blue-white star. . . .

4.

It all happened at once.

Colin stepped in front of me, using that same impossible speed he had used before. He had his hand on my wrist, and did . . . something . . . to me.

The space-collapsing shell passed through me at faster-than-light speeds. In my paradigm, that meant it was outside of my frame of reference. It was traveling too quickly to affect or be affected by anything in my light-cone. Colin did something to the damn bullet so that it obeyed my paradigm. It turned into tachyons and vanished forever from our perceptual sets.

Victor had deflected the anti-psychic shell, so that the grapeshot merely bounced off Colin's armor of arrogant self-confidence. Impatiently he brushed away red ink that, to anyone else, would have been deadly wounds.

5.

All at once . . .

Quentin must have been warned by his friends that our hour of death had come. Before the rifle even fired, he waved the white wand in the air and whispered a command. A glowing circle of dancing firefly lights appeared around the glade, embracing all of us, and lesser lights of blue-green formed a star shape inside the circle. Latin words written in cursive trails of smoke wove themselves into existence around the group.

Quentin really has the coolest special effects of any of the five of us. I mean, the fourth dimension is big and impressive, and being able to shoot blue light out of one's face to make deadly molecular machines is very useful. Also, being able to find a secret door in any blank wall had a definite utility, and it was darn convenient to be able to wipe any wounds or scars away.

But little firefly sparks of gold and green and twilight blue, shining and dancing, inscribing cryptic Latin pentagrams on command? That was just too damn cool for words.

The rush of terrible flame roared up to the edge of the circle, and the solar plasma touched the teeny tiny fireflies of Quentin's demonstration and . . .

Something inside the expanding ball of atomic fire was screaming in fear. It called out in a horrid language made all of harshly aspirated consonants and cracking sibilants, and Quentin shouted back in the same language. Something inside the flame—or maybe it was the flame itself—whimpered. Imagine an elephant whimpering, or a *Tyrannosaurus rex*. Heck, for that matter, try to imagine something the size of the *Queen Elizabeth II* whimpering.

The fireball spread to either side of us and did us no hurt. As for the radiant heat energy . . .

6.

We did not even feel any heat.

This last was thanks to Vanity, I should mention. The laws of nature of Aristotle obtained inside the boundary made by Quentin's glowing ring, and Aristotle did not believe in radiant heat energy. If you dropped a cubic meter of the surface of the sun onto the Earth, instead of exploding, the supramudane substance, made of quintessence, would merely return by its natural motion to its divine place in the crystal spheres that govern heaven in cycles and epicycles. A rather friendly and human set of laws of nature, if you think about it.

So the blast of intolerable energy released by the collision of two faster-than-light streams of superenergy, when it passed over the circle of Quentin's ward . . . turned into a soft, silvery light, the light of divine things, shot through with shivering glints of gold. The ancient Greek notion of the Sun was that it was a holy thing, the source of life, a great and benevolent daemon, perhaps even a god.

The alchemical, life-creating rays of the sun passed over us and swept smoothly upward and vanished.

7.

We stood in a green circle in the middle of a vast flat plain of smoldering stumps. The maenads, in what shape they had been, were dead. My pet Amazon had been instantly incinerated.

The forest for half a mile in each direction was gone. Ash covered the smoking earth. There was no forest fire raging. Evidently all combustibles had been instantly reduced to their basic elements.

Over a mile in each direction were scattered clouds of black and rolling red, embers and flashes of dying flame, dying perhaps because they had been blown out by the overpressure of the faster-than-light explosion.

The line of tall hills, once hidden by towering green trees, was now clear to see. The forest still existed on the upper slopes, but not the lower. Instead, gathered at the foot of the hills, standing tall and ruined, the color and texture of burned matchsticks, glades of smoking and leafless trees leaned, tilting drunkenly away from us. The sheer violence of what had been done here, and by the discharge of a single sidearm, was staggering. I thought I saw clouds of steam nodding high over the river whose bed I had crossed earlier. I saw the melted wreckage of the high-tension power cables dripping in the distance, as all the trees between here and there had been turned to tall posts of leafless ash.

Everything that had been inside Quentin's ward was saved. Even the dry leaves resting on the grassy stones were untouched.

Almost everything. There was one dark spot in the green circle of grass and trees around us. Victor.

I stared in horror at the prone body of Victor. I looked inside Victor to see if he was alive or not. Life? I am not sure. I saw motions on an atomic level, sensed a burst of radio-energy . . .

8.

All our cell phones rang.

Vanity yanked hers to her ear. "Yes?"

I was staring at where Victor's motionless body lay headlong in a crater, steaming and smoking. The chain mail he wore was drooling little molten metal droplets across his skin. He must have done some modification to his skin, because it was not charring, not melting, not burned. There were no holes in him. His hair was intact.

His hair was like gold wire. It was not burned.

I said, my voice all hollow with surprise, "It's Victor. The phone is useful to him. . . ."

The voice over Vanity's cell phone said, "This is Victor. I've lost power to my hull . . ."

Colin blenched. "His . . . 'hull'? Did he say—?"

". . . certain of my nerves and muscles will take time to repair. Prop me up so that my eye is facing East. The signal controlling the gun came from—"

Vanity interrupted, "Leader! We're being watched!"

I said, "Leader! A hole is opening in space-time. It's the enemy Phaeacian."

I was looking at Quentin, and saw, about two miles behind him, a tower set with stained-glass windows, rising suddenly out of the ground like a piston. It was near the edge of the burned area. Trees and soil were carried upward on the roof of the tower as it rose, and nodded over the tower sides like the crown of a colossus.

A smaller tower, this one made of brown stone, with narrow archer slits instead of windows, rose up to one side of the first tower, throwing soil and rocks each way. Dirt, like black water, dribbled and trickled down its eaves.

A third tower, this one in the burned zone, reared aloft out of the earth, carrying a cluster of stumps and ash on its head. A fourth tower a hundred yards beyond reared up, but was caught in a tangle of shattered and smoldering tree trunks, and could only get half its windows above the ground.

Quentin's eyes were focused behind me: Awe and astonishment had robbed him of expression.

I turned. There were more towers behind me. At least two dozen, rearing up, taller than the burned trees around them.

And trapdoors were opening, some slowly, some quickly. Not one, not ten, but hundreds. I saw doors an acre wide, rising up, carrying huge segments of the landscape with them, lifting rocks and tree stumps. Deep in these vast doors could be seen the heads of staircases fit for giants, inset with ivory ramparts, five hundred yards wide. There were battlements and windows like gems being pulled up to the surface, carried by the posts that lifted up these titanic roofs.

And beyond these hundred doors, one vast door that ran from horizon to horizon made itself known.

The hills opened.

Imagine that all the mountains and hills that embraced a quarter of the horizon, as far to the north and south as could be seen without turning, were not hills at all, but the rooftops and turrets and tower-tops of a buried city:

and not merely a city, but also its suburbs, and a goodly section of the surrounding farms and villages.

Now imagine that all the million columns supporting the roofs and towers, halls, palaces, esplanades, and wintergardens of that underground countryside moved upward with one ponderous, silent, earthquake-potent thrust. Those roofs and tower-tops with all the countless tons of rock atop them, and all the wide acres of burned forest-tops crowning them, were all moved upward with untroubled, infinite strength.

That was what we saw.

Vast pillars of ivory and marble pushed the miles of hillside, rock and trees and stream and woods, birds' nests and salt lick and brush, earth and stone and steaming wreckage of forest stump, acre upon acre, upward. A hundred yards aloft, two hundred, more.

Upward and upward. The underside of the hollow hills gleamed with the reflections of that ceiling, like a firmament, of a world that shone up from underfoot.

We saw the tops of pillars the size of skyscrapers holding up a sky of stone. Light from beneath, bright as the sun, but colored like moonlight seen through rippling water, played back and forth across the underside of this pillar-upheld firmament.

Like jagged teeth in the wide gap between the lower brink and the upper hill-covered roof now held aloft, we saw the many fortresses and walls, overlooking wide passes between them. These passes were the heads of roads and highways leading down into that underground universe. Only the tops of the roads were visible to us, but the shape of the mighty slope down which they rolled could be detected from the contour of the pillars, minarets, and hanging gardens that overtopped them. The upper battlements of the chain of fortress walls fell lower the farther they were from the lip of the pit—or should I call it the boundary of the landscape—and the roadways were no doubt parallel to them.

There were pennants and battle flags hanging from every window and archer slit. Siege guns peered from over the fortress walls, and sixteen-inch guns, something that would grace the heaviest dreadnought afloat, looked down from pillboxes and fortified positions beyond.

And from this chasm, roaring and murmuring, came a noise of many voices calling out.

My ear heard only a roar of ocean noise. A higher sense detected an inner meaning: "Death! To the Orphans of Chaos! Death!"

It was the battle cry of Lamia.

Like a river breaking from a dam, endless lines of cavalry poured forth from the passes between the forts. Amazons on their swift steeds streamed with quiet haste down the slope.

All the central, metal eyes of all the steeds were lit, a thousand little winks and flashes of azure light, a constellation of blue stars approaching through the green trees and brown stumps, the columns of ash.

With them, less orderly, were maenads. What I had seen before had not been an army, or even a horde. Compared to this, the hundreds from which I had been running had been merely a flying squad, a detachment.

Song rose up from the battlements. Thousand-voices strong, the choir of music and magic rose like a rising sun from out of that inner, underground universe. Siren song.

A river of eerie green-gold sparks poured out from one of the taller towers in the landscape and reached across three miles of green forest, brown ash-land, and green forest again, to wrap a distant tower in an aura of supernatural fire. Arms of gold and emerald fire streamed from that tower in answer, and rushed like a wall of burning flame across miles of landscape to a third tower. The third tower ignited and threw a river of gold-green power to a fourth; a fourth to a fifth, this one made all from a single huge slab of quartz; and this fifth back to the fourth again.

A pentacle. With walls of gold-green flaming energy reaching across four miles of space, the towers drew a star-shape around us. No doubt hidden nymphs, not merely four or five, but countless scores and hundreds, were practicing their craft and beginning their demonstrations.

And the siege guns opened fire.

9.

I saw the muzzle flashes of the gigantic siege cannons and sixteen-inch guns firing before we heard any noise. I should not call them muzzle flashes. Energy discharges. These were not gunpowder cannons; they were rail guns. Heavy artillery based roughly on the same weapon design that the Amazons used as rifles. There was not going to be any noise, except the rush of one-ton shells breaking the sound barrier.

In that moment of eerie silence, as the shells were falling, but before they hit, Quentin shouted, *"Aboard! Now!"*

The first note of siren-music had robbed me of my extra dimensions, powers, and senses. Colin was going cross-eyed with shock and pain as the miles-

wide pentagram was being drawn around us, but, before the fifth tower finished drawing arms of fire from across the forest to its sister towers, Colin
had caught me up in his arms, and heaved Victor's immobile body upright,
and fell, dragging us, into the open trapdoor that Vanity was, even now,
jumping down through.

Quentin's powers were not yet turned off, as the Amazons and their
metal-eyed horses were still far away. A shadow came around him as his feet
silently left the soil, and the cloak seemed to reach out with ever-widening
wings, and that shadow reached out and touched all of us, lifted, pushed,
and we were all standing on the deck of the *Argent Nautilus*. Except for Victor, who fell over.

Quentin said, "Vanity! If you would please—"

The trapdoor overhead exploded with blue light as the first of the hundred shells landed. The roof of the tunnel above us was turned instantly to
plasma. The vacuum created by the firestorm sucked the river water up in a
white spray, where the heat was breaking the water molecules into their con-
stituent oxygen and hydrogen.

The concussion would have instantly destroyed us (or anything made of
that fragile substance we call "matter") had we still been in the normal laws
of Earth. As it was, the blue light showered over all of us. There was no visible change.

The *Argent Nautilus* dashed through the waters of the underground river
like a flung spear. . . .

10.

The stone walls to either side of us were blurs. The piston of holocaust-fire
that the pressure of the explosion was driving down the tunnel in both directions was traveling faster than the speed of sound, so there was no noise
coming from it. We were receding from it faster than its advance, so that the
ball of flame behind dwindled immediately to a flare, a spark, a twinkle.

Quentin was frowning at the white wand he held. It was nothing but a
stick now. He tossed it overboard.

Then he said, "I'm neutralized. Who has anything?"

The cell phone speaker was very dim: "I have sustained major damage.
High-priority nervous system functions are continuing at half-power. All
auxiliary systems are nonfunctional."

Colin: "I've been hexed. I'm out."

I said, "There were sirens. They may still be around us. My powers are gone."

Quentin smiled and threw himself on the one bench at the stern of the *Argent Nautilus*. "You are the only one who can help us now, Vanity."

Vanity's look of fear stiffened into a look of resolve. The confidence I had seen on the island, or when she saved me from Archer, was back. Nausicaa confidence. She said, "I won't let you down, Leader!"

She laid her hand on the silver rail. Immediately in the water before us, a door made of water, with hinges and staples made of translucent fluid, opened up, revealing a long slope, an unwalled tunnel made of air, which dropped down through the water.

Quentin said, "Er . . . Vanity? You are doing that, right? That's one of yours?"

The *Argent Nautilus* tilted on the brink of the doorway made of water, her stern high, her prow dipping low. . . .

We all screamed as the ship fell headlong, except Victor (of course), and Vanity, who laughed like a madwoman.

Vanity yodeled and hiccuped and said over the roar, "I think I am getting the hang of this."

Down we plunged, a barrel tipping over a waterfall.

18

DREAM STORM

1.

We fell down a long steep slide, down a shaft of naked air, past walls of un-supported rippling water. Overhead was a roof of water equally unsupported and impossible: an upside-down river.

The trapdoor made of rippling water fell shut behind us. The flames that still were shooting after us merely flew on by overhead, filling the stone tunnel we had just quit.

The light here came from the glimmering silver of the phosphorescent hull, and from the leaping and rippling light receding so rapidly behind us, a white-hot flame seen through a wall of boiling water.

The cell phone asked Colin for help. Colin rolled Victor's stiff body over on its back and, putting his shoulder to Victor's spine, levered him more or less upright.

The third eye opened, glittering azure.

The silver ship-glow and dwindling flame light was joined by the dim blue light from Victor's third eye, of course. Useful to have a built-in flashlamp, I suppose.

Colin said, "Leader! Victor wants to try turning your powers back on. He says he's only got enough power for one try. You want to stand over here, please?"

Quentin said, "In the middle of a battle is the best time to experiment with untested superpowers. Sure. Zap me. If I become incapacitated, Victor is second-in-command. Then Amelia, Vanity, Colin, in that order."

Colin muttered, "Hmph—! Fifth-in-command. Thanks a lot."

Quentin said back, "It's for all those nights you kept me awake with your chatter after lights-out. Ready when you are, Victor."

A streaming azure beam played across Quentin's face for a moment. His features were lit from below, throwing the shadow of his cheeks and nose across his forehead. The effect gave his face a sinister cast.

The beam turned cherry red, then saffron, which melted into a ray of purest gold. Now Quentin's features looked pure, ennobled with a solemn, living energy.

The shadow Quentin cast across the deck grew black as ink, solid-seeming, and streamed away from his feet, growing larger and darker as the beam of gold light played down across Quentin's chest, stomach, and legs. The beam twinkled for a moment at his feet, and the shadow swelled up along the speed-blurred watery walls of the tube of liquid through which we flew, and nodded high above us.

Then the shadow faded and vanished.

Vanity said, "Did it work?"

Quentin picked up a belaying pin and whispered a word to it. There was no visible effect, but suddenly I had goose bumps, and a sensation that some potent and inhuman will was regarding me.

Quentin, instead of answering, took a piece of chalk out of his pocket and uttered three words that clanged like iron. The chalk, of its own accord, flew across to where Colin stood, fell to the deck, and slid around him in a circle: once, twice, thrice.

Quentin knelt, tapped the belaying pin on the deck, pointed at Colin, uttered a command word in some language that hissed like fire in his mouth.

Quentin muttered to himself. Then he said, more loudly, "Therefore what humors and essences which once touched Phobetor, shall now and always shall be of him, be with him, be obedient to him. So mote it be. *Quod erat faciendum.*"

Colin's face and features ran like wax, and black smoke boiled around him. Vanity looked shocked, and I think I must have screamed.

A demon-prince stood there. His skull was long and narrow, like the face of a stag or fox, and instead of a tongue, flame was in his mouth. His eyes were green lamps. Antlers tipped with silver glints, made perhaps of bone or ice, branched up like a crown. His chest and torso were manlike, albeit much brawnier and wider-shouldered than any man. In one hand he held a mace of silver; in the other, an orb of crystal carved like a moon. Vast bat wings pebbled and patterned like the neck of a venomous snake rose up hugely from his back. He had shaggy goat-legs and narrow feet, ending in split hoofs sharp as razors. His male member was appropriately large and godlike. A scent like ambergris came from him.

"Oh, cool!" said the stag-headed demon-prince with his tongue of flame. Little electric sparks played around the fangs of his sudden smile.

2.

The horned and narrow head turned toward me, the greenish dots it wore in place of eyes dancing with unholy mirth. "Hey, flying squid-girl. You think your true shape is freaky? Check this out."

Quentin said, "Return to that form you wore on Earth, O Prince of Nightmares. . . ."

"Hold on a sec," said Phobetor in Colin's voice. "My senses are sharper in this form. I can feel trouble coming. I can feel the hate in the air. I can see . . . I can see dreams. . . ."

"Fix me," I said to him.

He did not respond. His eyes were focused on something I could not see. "Hey, Leader! There is a big dream-storm coming."

Quentin asked, "What is a dream-storm?"

"Hell if I know. Looks like a tidal wave about to break over us."

"Can you fix me?" I shouted at him. The idiot.

"Hold on, sweet cheeks. There are also some singing fish women in long-boats dreaming about stopping us. . . . Your sirens? They'd just smite you if I turned you back on. Wait. I think I can do something. . . ."

Vanity said, "Leader! Tell him to do something about the tidal wave! This ship sails in dream-waters!"

"Leader, what about me . . . ?" I asked. "Can't I get my powers back on . . . ?"

Quentin said, "Who else is in the boat?"

The demon Phobetor said in Colin's voice, "How the hell do I know? I cannot see the boat, I can only see the dreams of the women in it."

Quentin said, "I was not talking to you."

A chilling voice spoke out of midair. "Maenads who kill; dryads who will not; Amazons of iron will; sirens whose songs fill strange nonrealms of other-space, unimagined, unshaped worlds the creation hath forgot. Master, I break faith with thee, and cry woe! Your vengeance shall not fall on me, for thy doom rides in that bark also."

There was a rustling in the air, and Quentin's robes flew and flapped in a breeze that was not there. Then the hems of his garments fell, and the air was still.

"Great," muttered Quentin.

Phobetor said, "What the hell was that?"

"A rat deserting a sinking ship."

Vanity: "Are we in trouble?"

Quentin: "Big trouble."

3.

Phobetor: "Dream-storm looming up, Leader. Suggest we go below, or batten hatches, or something—"

"Leader!" I said loudly. "I saw the dream-plane earlier form a bubble or blister and explode into Earth's continuum. That may be the same effect that is happening now. A spell. Your paradigm."

Quentin said, "But I don't know how to stop an unknown influence—"

"Listen, Leader! Victor can stop it, I'll bet. If he can get fixed in time."

The cell phone said in a dim, tinny voice: "And get an energy supply of sufficient magnitude."

I said, "If you will tell Bambi-head here to turn my powers back on, maybe I can fix Victor, or at least see what's wrong. . . ."

"Do it," said Quentin to Phobetor.

The demon-prince rolled his fiery eyes. "Um, Leader, there are still sirens in the area—"

"Risk it."

Phobetor looked at me. The green sparks that served him for eyes shrank into smaller dots, contracting. "I—I am not sure what to do. How do I make her stupid paradigm turn on?"

Quentin spoke, his voice quiet and forceful: "Do you love her? Have faith in her. Put energy in her. Believe in her vision, even if you do not understand it. Become like glass, and let the feelings she inspires in you flow through you and enter her."

Vanity gave out a yelp of fear. "The waters! The waters!"

The spray coming off the bow of the ship suddenly turned black, and had streamers of flame and smoke rippling through it. The *Argent Nautilus* started bucking and pitching.

The tube of water down which we flew dissolved like smoke, growing rapidly larger and swooping away from us. Suddenly and impossibly, we were in the middle of a large lake, then in midocean. But it was a boiling ocean of blood-splattered India ink, not water. Icebergs topped with flame buckled and broke against ice-coated piles of lava, red stones with black crusts. Open pits of air and smoke gaped here and there in the surface of the waters like holes in Swiss cheese.

There were storm clouds above us, but the lightning was red, and the hailstones showering down on us were mingled with falling mud, snow, freezing rain, and drops of something acidic that stung and burned.

The dream-smooth flight of the *Argent Nautilus* ended when the ship, boards groaning, pitched up as if struck from beneath.

Our silver sails were streaked with long stains from the acid hail, browned with mud streaks, and Vanity was cowering under the bench, stung by burns in several places, tears in her eyes, determined not to cry. She had the glowing green stone in her hand and was trying to find some set of laws of nature that would allow us to survive the attack.

Quentin was clinging to the rail as the ship jumped and rolled.

Victor's body, not lashed down, was sliding across the deck. I ran and threw myself atop it, so that we were now both sliding toward the fragile silver railing. . . .

Crash. The railing held, though it bent out alarmingly. Victor's stone-hard body was between me and the rail, but I had burned my hand on some patch of his skin . . . his hull . . . which was still smoldering.

I shouted in pain. Okay, well maybe it was a scream. But that damn stuff *hurt.* Being pelted by acid-stinking hailstones did not help either.

What the hell was this stuff? An attack?

Over the noise of the storm-wrack, Quentin spoke to Vanity. His voice was very quiet, but some magic made each word clear, distinct, and legible. I do not think I was hearing it through my ears.

"Keep moving. Can you find a door out of this acid storm?"

Vanity shouted back, her voice dim and interrupted beneath the mindless roar of sky-rage: "Leader! We're becalmed! The ship cannot find any boundaries. There are no doors because there is no *here* and no *there* anywhere. . . ."

Although the deck kicked and bucked, Phobetor was not moved. He stood, hooves spread, mace glowing in one hand, his mouth lit with flame. His eyes were on me, his ears no doubt still filled with Quentin's question. *Do you love her?* The storm clouds roared above him, and red lightning flashed between the clouds of hail and streaming mud.

"By God, I do love her, and woe betide mortal or immortal who raises a hand against her. Dark Mistress, when I rule in Hell, you shall be my Queen!"

I waited for something to happen.

"Not working," I shouted back over the storm-wrack.

The wind just screamed at me. I wanted to scream back at it.

Phobetor said, "And, um, thanks for helping me with my homework. I mean, well, this is sort of embarrassing, but, we all know you're, um, brighter about math and stuff than I am, and well, I just wanted to say . . ."

And my vision came back. I was four-dimensional again, full, complete.

I am not sure what the moral of that little incident was. Honest thanks for small favors is stronger than true love?

4.

Light!

There was a blister, similar to the one I had seen previously, swelling out from the dream-plane parallel to Earth, shedding energy in each direction. I could see what was around us.

There were things moving in the light. The tumult from the previous explosion had left wreckage strewn across the dimensions: I saw Mulciber's giants, fallen, with technicians in long brown coats walking across helmet-tops, directing spider-machines at their repairs. I saw fleets and battle-barges of Mavors, thrown onto shoals and rocks, with lizard-faced Laestrygonians bailing and shouting orders to running sailors. I saw one group of Atlanteans in outer space, abandoning a tumbling space vessel, which glowed cherry red as its orbit decayed into the poisonous upper atmosphere of Venus. Atlanteans in black and silver armor dropped out of the airlock like pearls on a slightly curving string, one after another, and fell out and away from the dying ship.

The blister grew and changed from a cherry red to a blue white. Another explosion was no doubt only moments away. And there were smoky forces stirring and boiling in the depths of the dream-plane, tangled strands and webs of some titanic magic being readied.

And closer, much closer, I saw a flotilla of longboats, manned (if that is the term) by black-suited Amazons, cutting through the channel of a dream-canal. Each boat carried a complement of maenads and nymphs, while above and below, to the blue and to the red, cycles within cycles of sirens spun, deadly energy filling hyperspace for many yards in each direction.

And, only inches away . . .

"Oh my God! We are only about six inches away from Los Angeles! There is about to be an irruption from dream-space, and if we get caught in it . . . Vanity! Go that way! Tell the ship to go that way!"

Vanity, from beneath the bench, called out in misery, "I cannot see where your hand is. Your arm turns red and vanishes. I cannot push through this lava anyway! The ship is dying! She can't move!"

My upper senses told me that this place, this lake of tumult, was on the borderland, stuck halfway in the uncertainty between two dimensions. The storm here was caused by the breakdown of the local laws of nature, as confused bits and atoms of matter turned this way and that, not knowing which set of laws to obey. We were on the cusp, on the storm front, of some powerful effect issuing from the dream-realm, trying to render nature dreamlike and fluid, and an equally powerful effect coming from Earth, trying to restore the Earthly laws of nature: nice things like inertia, persistence of object, measurable time, linear cause-and-effect, atomic and elemental structures.

It was shining, shining. Useful to us? Or useful to someone trapping us? I started trying to trace the lines of cause-effect and time-purpose backwards. . . .

Mud had stained Quentin's robes, and hail and acid droplets had raised small welts on his head and hands. He spoke, and his voice vanished in the storm-roar, but his quiet voice appeared behind my ears, quiet but cross: "The mission! Remember the mission! Examine Victor and see if you can make repairs!"

Enough sightseeing. I turned to Victor.

5.

I looked inside Victor. He had been doing massive alterations to his internal organs. He had run tubes of nervous tissue down his spine and into his abdominal cavity, creating backup brains programmed to come online should his main brain be destroyed. Instead of a central heart, there were millions of photochemical bodies lining his now inert bloodstreams, making oxygen by photosynthesis out of carbon dioxide in the blood. The muscle tissues had a different texture and arrangement, and were supersaturated with additional blood capillaries coming from some sort of reduction-still in his lung cavities, which was making pure oxygen by breaking down excess bodily fluids. Nerves had been replaced by superconductors. There were electric eel cells lining certain limbs, linked in parallel, special analytical amplifiers built behind his eyes and ear cavities, extra joints and subcutaneous armored plates, chemical packages, groups of metallic crystals held in frictionless matrices of bone, energy cores, lubricant slurries, two additional parasympathetic nerve webs to carry and prioritize the extra sensory information. Radar bafflers. Repair microbes. Flares. He had done away with his digestive tract and replaced it with a series of molecular assembly-disassembly sieves.

"Oh my heavens," I breathed. He had turned himself into a killing machine. I am not going to mention what he did to defend against groin kicks.

Each atom and cluster of atoms in his body had a set of monads, linked in a preestablished harmony with his central, controlling monad. The explosion from the rifle had disorganized his monad hierarchy, as well as doing physical damage to his skin, muscles, and nerves. It had overloaded and burned out nerve ganglia that acted as circuit breakers, destroyed part of his magnetic control array, fused his power supply, lost mass as his skin was burned and flaked off.

Okay. Start with first things first. I reached out, found one monad that governed one part of a fused metallic crystal, straightened it. There. Now it was back in harmony with the upper-level monad that governed the whole microscopic crystal. With five or ten more twists like that, I could repair one nucleus of one damaged nerve cell.

"Leader," I said, "I am not sure what to do. There are monads controlling the matter in his body, but they have been put out of synchronization. I can fix one at a time, but there are millions of them. It would take me years even to affect part of them. And he also needs mass, and I am not sure where to get that from. He can't eat anymore. I don't think I can do this. I don't really understand what he's done to himself. Everything is all backwards. The matter is moving the consciousness, as if they are two separate substances. Everything has an internal nature, but nothing has an entelechy or an innate purpose. This isn't my paradigm—"

I suppose I sounded more nervous than I should have, because Phobetor shouted over the storm, his mouth fanged with flame, "Steady on, Blondie. If I can do you, you can do him."

I shouted back, "I don't know what to do. What do I do, Leader?"

Boy, I just really loved saying that to someone else.

6.

I was not the only one who loved saying it. Vanity was nearly in tears, asking Quentin what to do. She was screaming over the storm noise, "We're trapped here! My ship can't move! Whose chaos is this? Don't you guys rule this stuff?"

You guys. Huhn. File that one away to think about later.

The ship was now being tossed and slammed from side to side so violently that Quentin could not remain upright on deck. Phobetor had his arm around Quentin, and was walking across the tilting deck, supporting him, one snake-patterned wing held high to ward off falling pellets of ice, mud, and acid. Phobetor's hooves clung to the deck as if it were solid and calm, no matter at what crazy angle it jumped. With the flaming, lightning-lashed clouds behind him, and his long mane streaming, the antler-crowned demon-prince seemed, with every step, to grow larger and more solid.

As Phobetor supported Quentin past my position, Quentin's mild voice appeared inside my ear again, bypassing all the furious noise outside, "Where is the repair-creature made of blood? The one you gave life to? Is it in me, or does Victor still carry it?"

I understood his idea. The blood creature could carry out an operation on its own. If it could make repairs, I could concentrate on making more blood-creatures. They could even make each other, self-reproducing machines. I could fix the millions of damaged cells if I had millions of little helpers.

I took out my cell phone and explained my idea to Victor. The original molecular engine made by Dr. Fell, which I had turned into a living being, Victor could make inside his bone marrow with the molecular factories he now had there. He had the blueprints for the repair creature. I could start changing them into self-motivated things as soon as he made them.

Victor, his voice tiny over the cell phone, said, "It sounds like a bad idea, Amelia. If you give random programs to the atoms in my body, they will act randomly. I do not see the advantage."

"I am not talking about random! I am talking about giving them free will."

"Free will means random. The concepts are one and the same."

I opened my mouth to explain about self-organizing systems, such as evolution or free-market forces, which create purposeful action in concert, in spite of any separate purposes of the individual actors, but then I stopped. The concept was not in his paradigm. For him, logic was a mechanical thing, not an organic self-correcting dialogue. There was no Gödelian incompleteness in Victor's universe. It was all clean and sterile and perfect. Inanimate.

No creative initiative for the atoms in Victor's universe. No surprises.

Well, this was going to be a surprise. I reached out and down with an energy-tendril, and out and over with another. I located the living molecular creature inside Quentin's body, plucked it out of the middle of him, and rotated it across four-space (without crossing the intervening distance) to deposit it inside Victor. As I moved it, I passed the creature through a field of force spreading from my wings in the upper dimensions, which oriented it to its repair-purpose. I pointed it in the direction of Final Cause and gave it a little bit of thickness in that direction.

Into Victor it went—and it multiplied. Its essence spread to everything like it. I saw his bloodstream light up with entelechy. Suddenly it was not just a stream of atoms forming inanimate carbon molecules in his blood anymore. The atoms had a purpose. They existed for the sake of curing Victor. That was their final cause.

Aside from that, they were free; they could evolve, adapt, mutate, and modify themselves as they each individually saw fit. But to prevent any wild nonconformity, such as had bedeviled my fish back on the island, I established an identity-purpose, a set of conformities, so that any group of molecules that cooperated with another group for their mutual benefit would be advantaged in the competition over molecule-groups that just struck out on their own.

That was the theory. Activity started in his bloodstream and soon spread to all cells. Slow mutations started, then more rapid ones; I saw ten then one hundred monads get repaired. Then a thousand. Then ten thousand. It was working! It was going to work!

His skin started changing.

Meanwhile, Phobetor had carried Quentin (tucked under one huge and hairy arm) across the shaking, jumping deck (not shaking to Phobetor), swept by burning rain and hail (Phobetor ignored the weather), to where Vanity crouched under the bench. Phobetor spread one wing on high, like an impromptu umbrella, sheltering his two puny human-shaped comrades.

Quentin was trying to get a coherent report on the situation from Vanity. Why wasn't the ship moving?

Vanity said, "I can't open any new doors. There are no unseen places to look, no walls for doors to be in. There are no boundaries in this place!"

Phobetor said, over the storm noise, flame flicking on his tongue: "Leader, it sounds like this place was set here to trap us."

Meanwhile, Victor's skin changed color, becoming blotchy. Red, yellow, blue-black blotches chased each other across his integument. Why was that happening? Maybe I had given the creatures too much free latitude. They were supposed to fix things, not change things.

I drew back in alarm. The skin was hot to the touch.

Victor's flesh began to boil and bubble and fall off. His chest split open, and organs, struggling and fighting against each other, began to slide away in each direction across the deck. I saw hearts and lungs and livers growing tentacles and eyes and multiple tongues slipping and sliding around, throwing out thorns, growing shells, spitting poisons. His bones all curved into crooked shapes, and put out spines.

Oh my God, was it horrible. It was a nightmare. My Victor was melting.

I called out to Quentin for help. Called out? I screamed like a girl.

A girl who had just killed the man she loved.

7.

At that same instant, as if my scream had summoned it, the waters to each side of us suddenly exploded. Jets of water, or lava, or acid, or whatever that damnable stuff was, rose up before us, forming spouts or columns. The storm of flame and hail suddenly dwindled, falling silent.

In hyperspace, explosion. Darkness. The blister had ignited again. The scattered troops and navies of Mavors and Mulciber went whirling in knotted folds of space-time off into outer dimensional wilderness, and were gone.

The boiling masses under the keel of the *Argent Nautilus* were beginning to solidify, becoming like molasses, then like mud.

The ship ran aground. The deck tilted over forty-five degrees. The bow of the ship was crushed between rocks, rock grown suddenly solid and firm; the stern was jumping for a moment, bubbles of churning chaos-stuff surging and sloping up over the stern rail splattered the bench under which Vanity still hid. Then the stern waters iced over, slid to one side, dragging the keel with them. A horrid popping and cracking came from below, as if the keel had broken. The sloughs of liquid to the stern changed and started to grow muddy, thick.

Vanity sobbed as if she could feel the pain of the ship. The beautiful silver ship, so swift and graceful, now lay canted far over, her prow out of line with her stern, her hull scarred and scratched with acid stains, her once-proud sail now brown tatters. Her keel had been broken, her proud spine snapped.

A wave of flaming muck surged over Quentin, who made an impatient gesture. A gasp of fear or awe came from the boiling black syrup, and it politely parted to either side, splashed past to his left and right, and did not get a drop on him. The rest of the deck was washed under with a ripple of brownish slop.

The bent segment of railing supporting Victor gave way. I reached out and down with tendrils of energy, upper-dimensional songs made solid.

The wave of goo from the stern picked me up and tossed me roughly against the railing at the same time. Some of it got in my eyes. My skin was burned and frostbitten.

And I lost my grip on Victor. He is so thin in the fourth dimension, so paper-thin.

His dissolving body fell into the muck, which bubbled and became solid as the flopping and dripping body fell into it. It turned from mud then into rock. There was a green wash of color, and the rocks were coated with grass.

The columns and spouts of mud then changed. Their inner natures altered. With the suddenness and meaninglessness of a dream, they all turned into trees. The tall fountains grew bark and solidified; the explosion of lava and red spray at the top turned green, became leafy and cool, and began rustling.

And we were in another landscape, a fairy-forest, dreamlike, cool and soft. The one ugly thing in a grove of delicate cherry trees was the grounded, keel-broken boat, lying half on her side, half buried in rock and grass.

8.

I rotated another face into existence. It was quicker than wiping the hot goo out of the eyes of my old face. This one was only about an eighth of an inch different: slightly thinner, higher cheekbones.

I could see Victor. He was only about two yards away from us in the blue direction. The chaos storm was still around him. I saw the acid and writhing mud entering his open chest cavity, entering his mouth and nostrils. He was choking.

I jumped and caught him in my energy-shaped limbs. I yanked him back into the red direction, and we both fell to the deck in a slosh of chaotic goo, flame, and freezing mud. Since the deck was canted over at forty-five degrees, the slop slid down along the deck boards, dripping in a brown fan of filth off the starboard rail.

Victor's torso and trunk had elongated, and his arms had melted off or had been subsumed into his body. His flesh slid through my fingers, running red. Again, he was slipping from my hands.

Again, he was caught up against the starboard rail. Parts of him floated through the bars of the rail and fell to the grass below. I cannot express the ugly horror of it. My boyfriend had turned to sludge.

The chaos-stuff followed him in from the other scene. His legs were shining with blue energy where I had not quite pulled him all the way back into our dimension, and sluices and rivers of fiery slush were crawling after him, slithering across the deck.

Something in the way the slime moved was disquieting; it did not flow like mud or lava. It was more like a nest of centipedes, scuttling on many hair-tiny legs.

There was a hole in midspace, about a yard above our tilted deck. Chaos frothed and crawled and gushed and bubbled in each direction, globes and blobs of fiery mud cascading outward in a sphere, falling in sloppy streams to the deck, gurgling over the smoldering deck planks, flopping and hissing over the side in long muddy icicles.

It covered him up. Victor was somewhere in that mess, half-buried, half-visible, and his body, half liquid itself, stretched and stretched as his head and torso slid down the deck slope, trailing the runny goop of his torso behind him.

Something must have seen my jump up into hyperspace; wefts of siren-music, spinning along more than one axis, ricocheted through the area, whirling like buzz saws.

The shots mostly went wild. The sirens were at extreme range, and the music faded into and out of audibility.

One or two stray notes struck me. I lost sensation in upper and lower parts of my body, and jerked back into a three-dimensional shape. There was blood on my left arm and leg, the points analogous to the wings and tail that had been sliced.

The numbness was only momentary; with an inching, ant-crawling sensation, little ice picks of pain began to play along the nerves of my wounds.

The snap of music knocked me backwards across the deck. My upper senses showed me only pale noise and flashes. I was lying on my back, staring up at our blackened mast. The sails were burning.

"Someone help Victor!" I screamed. My voice was very loud. Instead of trying to outshout a storm, I was yelling over the soft noise of cherry blossom petals in the breeze.

I tried to get to my feet. There was blood on my hands. My blood. My forehead was bleeding. I was on one knee, my other foot braced against the crazily tilted railing, too dizzy to stand further.

Phobetor scuttled, half-bent, across the tilted deck, bending his upper leg and stretching his lower, reaching down to support himself with one hand. The orb and scepter he had been carrying were gone.

Odd. He had been striding across the storm-tossed deck as if it had been a flat carpet; now he could barely walk on a slope. What did it mean?

Behind him, I saw a cloud smother the horizon.

9.

This cloud of mist billowed with alarming speed up the sky beyond the cherry trees. In the space of time it takes a man to draw a deep breath, it had blotted out half the sky. It formed a gray pyramid, and began to part.

Behind it, there was a mountain. The mountain had not been there before: Yet now here it was, appearing from behind an unrolling curtain of mist. Something in the way the mist opened reminded me of a curtain.

No. Not a curtain. A door. A trapdoor.

This was Phaeacian magic. I could see another plane bending in from another segment of dream-space, intersecting with this area. The Phaeacian had folded space.

I looked closer, trying to see the internal nature of what was happening. Something in the composition of the earth and air reminded me, strangely, of that primitive version of Abertwyi town I had stumbled across when I was lost in the snow, back during our second escape attempt. With more senses to analyze it, I could see what it was: a version of man's world occupied not by men. Its mountains and trees and towns were in the analogous locations to their sister spots on Earth, and this made a Phaeacian space-lapse easy to perform between them. I had not known it at the time, but that fishing village I had so briefly seen had been a by-product of Phaeacian magic attempting to close time and space around us as we fled, back then. Now I could see what it was: Our enemies had the power to bend the fabric of the universe to trap us.

The clouds parted like a door opening. I saw the lower slopes of the mountain forested with rank upon rank of black-clad warrior-women on horseback, rifles ready. Field pieces on gun-carriages were placed here and there among the cavalry squadrons, two-inch and four-inch guns of blue metal, with caissons standing by. The beautiful armor-clad women sat ahorse, without motion, without noise, awaiting orders.

To either side of the well-ordered squares of Amazonian soldiers were two loud and ragged mobs of maenads. The vine-clad girls were rollicking and cavorting on the grass, some wrestling, some throwing the discus, many dancing to pounding drums, and bathing in wine, which they drew out of solid rock with their fingernails.

The mist parted further, drawing up the slope, revealing more mountain-side. On the upper slopes were broad designs of chalk cut into the green turf, eerie stick-figure drawings: a man; an elongated bull, crook-legged with crescent horns; a spread-eagle design; a set of curves representing a snake. In the center of each wide chalk drawing, a coven of nymphs stood in a circle, gathered around altar-stones placed here and there across the slope. Some held silver knives or sickles; others held torches. Burned offerings of sheep and cattle lay on the bloodstained altars, and trains of smoke trailed up from them.

On the high slopes, among stands and shards of rock, stood choirs of sirens in austere pale robes of Greek cut, armed with fiddles, recorders, and tambourines. A choir-mistress with a wand stood before them, and the sirens were arranged in a semicircle, three ranks deep around her.

And, on a shelf of rock near the top, above them all, kneeling on an altar-stone, was Lamia. The Phaeacian in white to her right, and goddess of Fraud, Laverna, to her left.

10.

Lamia raised her knife. I saw a huge wash of knotted strands and webs of magic, the force she was using to control the maenads, flex, throb, and begin to turn around that knife. The madwomen had to be controlled by a spell; otherwise, they would have torn themselves and their allies to pieces. Now the spell was heaving itself like a gathering tornado, reaching down to wash over the maenads, readying to fling themselves upon our ship.

With a mechanical precision, each Amazon shouldered her weapon.

The gun crews sent out range-finding pulses of radar energy, which I could feel, useful and innately undreamlike, bouncing obediently off our ship and returning with information to the guns.

The covens of nymphs all raised their torches. With a hissing murmur, the coven-mistresses spoke a word. The flames turned black as midnight, black as pitch, and the shadows of the women began to billow out from them like pools of ink.

The choir-leader raised her wand, and the choir of sirens drew in a breath. Laverna smiled.

11.

Something rose up from the pool of muck where Victor had melted.

And rose and rose, up and up.

It was a dragon. A cybernetic leviathan. An armored segmented wormlike thing, with weapons and projections built along every ring-segment of his long, long body.

The dragon-worm, five hundred yards long, thousands of tons of armed and armored flesh and horn and bone, metal and wire and substances unknown, raised a sleek serpentine head, parted serrated mandibles, and opened a mouth ringed with row on row of crystalline teeth, to reveal a central orb of blazing azure, buried deep in his throat, surrounded by a symmetrical array of boxy muscles and nerves and solenoid coils.

His eye. Victor's eye.

The crystal teeth acted as amplifiers.

What came from his mouth was brighter than the sun. It seemed almost a solid thing, and the main axis of the discharge path was surrounded with concentric tubes of lightning sparks and positronic discharges.

For a split second, all was utterly silent.

In silence, the beam reached across the intervening space and touched Lamia and burned her instantly to ash. The ground behind her sagged, for it was now molten rock. The mountaintop exploded in each direction, sending out tons of ash and smoke. In silence, we saw a shock wave rush out from the point of impact, a wall of dust and rubble flickering outward at the speed of sound, concentric rings of shattered destruction.

Then the sound hit us. It was as if a brick wall fell on us.

12.

Back on the island, he had not found the materials he needed to construct all parts of his body under the sea. That had been a prototype, a toy. This was the real thing. A battlewagon. The real Victor: an adult Telchine, fully grown and fully armed.

A moment before the sound struck, I said nervously, "Leader, what do we do?"

And Quentin answered softly, "Destroy them."

But he was not talking to me. Quentin was in the path of a golden ray of light one of the lesser weapon-ports along the spine of the dragon-thing was shedding. Something large and dark and catlike flickered out from behind Quentin and slithered into, of all places, Colin's guitar. At the same moment, Phobetor (or, I should say, a grinning Colin inside Phobetor's body) was scuttling half-bent across the deck to snatch up the guitar.

His hoof touched a spot where the Chaos muck was still bubbling. Now he straightened up again, standing at an odd angle to the deck, as if it were a flat surface to him.

When the shock wave passed over him, it did not knock him flat. Instead, he grew larger, and the wind swirled around his mane and shaggy hair, and he spread his wings to catch it. And he laughed.

At the same moment when the dragon sheered off the top of the mountain, the siren choir, to save themselves, rotated into hyperspace and unleashed a dire barrage of death music. An all-destroying energy filled the area.

I could see them. This little pocket of dream-space in which we were stranded, this landscape of cherry blossom trees, was surrounded in all directions by a hollow four-dimensional bubble of chaos stuff. Imagine a firm island surrounded by a marshy lake, a solid planet surrounded by vacuum. The sirens jumped off the shore when their part of the island erupted, stepped into space when the planet was under attack.

It was a mistake. The guitar, with no amplifiers and no speakers, woke at the laughter of the demon prince, and jarring electric noise, as loud as the shock wave that heralded its birth, thundered out in all directions.

Colin started to play.

He was not a good player, I admit, but he had energy. He was charged with a sexual tension; his music screamed and roared and reached up with arms of invincible passion, and smashed the barrage of solemn and ornate siren choirs into stunned and broken notes. He rocked.

The death energy was absorbed and began to dance. It fell to our left and right and tore huge swaths out of the ground, toppling cherry trees and quenching the sunlight in those areas. But it did not touch us.

And the chaos, the whirling, maddened chaos in which the sirens had so

foolishly flung themselves, now opened many eyes, which shone and sparkled at the roaring electronic music; and reached out with many hands, all
snapping their fingers to the driving backbeat, and came alive. Chaos came
alive, throbbing with Colin's rhythms.

The sirens attempted to rotate further into higher dimensions, but the
passion and madness Colin wove around them with his music did not admit
the possibility of higher dimensions. There was no place to run; there was no
escape from chaos.

Jerking angular bodies made of chaos substance, horned and clawed and
spurred, rose up, roaring, and they danced to the pounding screams of
Colin's smoking guitar. The devil-things tore the sirens to bits, drew them
down into the muck, and smothered them.

At once the tune changed from a ragged tumult to something wild and
strange and sorrow-torn:

Gold be the hue of my true lover's hair
Rose red her lip, and bright her eyes
I know my love and know despair
She scorns my love, for she is wise.

Wisdom tells her not to be
Enamored of a boy like me
Her thoughts are high; her heart is fine
Too fine to belong to a heart like mine.
I love my love and well she knows,
I love the grass whereon she goes
But I know the day will never come
When she and I will be as one.

And then I felt Colin's music gathering itself out of the air and then enter
into me.

13.

I did not understand what this music-creature was. Unknown energies
thrilled along my nervous system. Something in Colin's driving passion woke
something deep in me, and, all at once, I was aware of a wide area of time

and space, dream and reality, multiple levels of the complex web of unknowns we called the universe.

Admiration. It was not his thanks that opened up my powers; it was his admiration. Hero-worship (heroine-worship?) burned like a fire in him; he touched me with it; I was ignited. He thought I was wise; I became wise. My eyes opened in many dimensions, seeing many things, imaginable and unimaginable.

I saw the final cause, or the for-the-sake-of-which, of the radar beams the Amazons had bounced from us. It was child's play to rotate them into self-awareness and self-being, and send them merrily on their way. False messages were sent to the ranging circuits in the Amazon guns. Shells fell among the maenads, rather than among us.

The army, acting as a unit, had formed an artificial unity-of-purpose. It was like a monad, but larger. I twisted the monad. I sent it to attack the nymphs.

The conceptual unity of the Amazon army was broken at that moment. All those calm, automaton-like fembot women in their black armor now were no longer programmed to act as one. They woke to independent thought: Some fired at the nymphs, some at the maenads, some at us. It was chaos on a mental level.

Too many fired at us. The shells fell. I could deactivate one or two dozen, but many dozens more were still coming.

I reached out with limbs made of energy, took up my friends, sent a line of force into Vanity's ship, found another deck resting deep in another pocket in time-space, and rotated us all through overspace into the pocket.

14.

I do not know what the others saw, what I looked like to them, or what they looked like to themselves. Vanity screamed and screamed. Maybe she could see all of her bones and organs clearly. She folded in half, like a paper doll lifted too suddenly from the flat surface, and her feet were occupying the same space as her skull, brain, eyes.

Something that lived inside Quentin's chest, something bright and pure, seemed to wake up and look around curiously.

I could not move Colin. He seemed solid. I could not lift him out of the hyperplane.

Boom. An explosion went off where we had been standing. The shock wave raced out in three dimensions, but did not reach us. Ripples on a pond cannot touch a bird hovering above it.

I stepped belowdeck into a small cabin. It was paneled with pale wood and lit with a silver lantern. There were barrels lashed to the cabin wall to our left, a small stack of square crates lashed down to the right.

Then I pulled my companions carefully—ever so carefully—down into the plane with me. I made sure all wrinkles were smoothed out, and that they were flipped the right way, not lefthand-righthand reversed.

The echoes of the explosion were ringing overhead. Vanity stopped screaming once her body was twisted from Escher-shape back to normal, but she looked greenish.

Quentin was . . .

I caught my breath. Quentin was made of clay. His face and hair were now composed of pale and dark layers of fired ceramic. . . .

His real body was like the doll he made of Vanity. He had no real body. He was an exiled spirit trapped in matter.

Then he stirred, breathed, and a flush of color came back into his skin. The clay vessel looked like human flesh again.

He said, "Where is Colin?"

I said, "I can't move him. He's back up with the explosion."

He said to me, "Why didn't you bring Victor?"

Vanity said, "Victor melted. He's dead."

Quentin said harshly to her, "Victor is the dragon. He shed his human shape." To me, "Go get him! We are vulnerable only when we are apart!"

I said, "I think it hurts him when I pull him through four-space. He's not built for it."

Vanity said, "Oh! Look! My turn! Mine! Watch this! I can reach him, Leader! There is a path to Victor. Things are calm around him, or something." And she pulled open a switch hidden behind one of the crates.

The deck overhead opened.

Colin, still playing his angry guitar, sparks shooting from his hand, was standing on the head of the dragon-thing.

A hundred guns and emission antennae peeped out from firing turrets that opened along the dragon's armored sides. Tracer fire and directed energy lanced from the huge dragon-shape in every direction. Like some steel instrument of medical torture, the mandibles opened again, the mouth gaped wide, showing a concentric funnel of crystal shark-teeth, the blue orb surrounded by its banks of amplifiers and augmentation-circuits glowed brightly, and the main beam of azure plasma licked out, so bright as to make all the laser fire seem dim by contrast, so loud as to make the other incendiaries seem silent.

The spell that controlled the wild maenads had not dissolved when Lamia died; I saw the strands and wires jerk when that intolerably bright blue flame reached out, and all the maenads screamed and jumped. Zap. All magic gone.

Colin was shouting the harsh words of his song, music loud enough to hear above the din of gunfire, beams, bolts, and bombs:

What genius picked this battlefield?
Here, in the Dreaming, where I am Lord?
You picked unwisely. Your fate was sealed.
Today you die, ladies: You have my word.
For the Father of Lies, you made yourselves whores,
Thought you could cheat Hell? One final lie,
To sucker you into the hell of his wars
But I tell it straight, ladies: Today you die.
For war is chaos, and Chaos is ours!

And, as he sang, the mountainside danced. Break-dancing, I guess you could call it. Slam dancing. Avalanche dancing. And once the rocks and boulders started doing pirouettes and tumbling tricks, the fires started from the incendiaries and explosions of the Victor-dragon wanted to join in. Rolling balls of flame many yards wide, surrounded by billowing black smoke, now hopped and leaped and rocked and rolled all up and down the slope, tossing battalions in the air, quaking with laughter made of yellow flame.

Quentin floated or was drawn upward by a smoke shape that issued from his cloak. Surrounded by wraithlike shapes of mists and motes, Quentin raised his hands and found a white staff in them.

He stepped out onto the deck and stood in the shadow of the giant worm-thing. Pointing his bright wand, he spoke. "Spirits with whom I have a pact: I unleash you from my wrist as a falcon upon my prey. Seize my foes and hold them helpless."

He threw the wand to the deck behind him; it blazed too brightly for any eye to look upon, brighter than a lightning flash, but silent. His shadow was cast upward.

His flesh turned into fine clay, pale and immobile.

The sky from one horizon to the zenith turned black as ink and fell down on the enemy army. This was the real Quentin, too large to fit in any mortal body.

I said to Vanity, "Open a trapdoor beneath them."

Vanity said, "Can I do that? My powers are not working here. Besides, I can't get a door that big."

Victor, speaking over the cell phone in her pocket, said in a small, tinny voice: "I have been stabilizing the matter in the area. Try it again."

The dragon breathed out an azure hurricane. The black sky-stuff rolling over the screaming army turned to a slick black glass. The screams stopped. Movement stopped. I could see dim figures of women trapped inside it, flies in amber.

Vanity opened a trapdoor no bigger than my fist. It was enough for me. I rotated the whole mass of the trapped army into four-space, folded it into two and then one dimension, made it into a point, and sent it through the opening.

When the army reached the chaos, I released the pressure of the dimensional fold.

Colin played a few notes, soft and low. His ragged demon-things now towed the now-fully-three-dimensional black glass mass off into the chaos storm, deeper and deeper. I lost sight of them.

Gone.

No wonder they were afraid of us.

The winged shape of fire seeped back down into Quentin, who turned from fine porcelain back into flesh and blood, and opened his eyes.

19

THE SWIFT GOD, THRICE-GREATEST

1.

Quentin said to Victor, "You should not have killed Lamia. It makes us vulnerable to enemy magic."

An external speaker built into the armor of the dragon-worm crackled to life. "I will attempt to negate any incoming magic, Leader."

"It also might call the Psychopomp. He might come to gather her spirit, to save her from hell. . . ."

Framed in the square of trapdoor leading up to the deck, I could see, against the burned sails and high blue sky beyond, the long metal head of the Victor-dragon, which still had the Phobetor-shaped Colin, steaming guitar in hand, hooves planted wide, atop it. Quentin stood on the deck below them both, and had his hand out. He snapped his fingers, and his wand flew up toward his grasp. The wand was in midair, moving toward him.

Then it happened, too swift to see.

2.

There was a flare of blue-white light. Maybe it was Cherenkov radiation. The head of the Victor-dragon now had a dented furrow bisecting it, and a splash of crumpled armor flying in each direction.

Atop the dragon-skull, at the crumpled end of the furrow, was the figure of a lean man with overly muscular legs. One leg was straight, the other half-bent beneath him. He was balanced for that split-instant on one heel, leaning so far back that his spine was almost parallel to the deck, looking for all the world like a runner sliding into a baseball plate. He was the very picture of speed incarnate, trying desperately to halt his motion. In his hand was a long wand or pole whose edge he had dug into the crumpled surface of the broken armor plate.

There were thin streamers of white smoke and white flame around his heels, and his pale white cloak tails were flying up around his shoulders in a frozen moment like outspread wings.

No, they *were* outspread wings. Wings like white flame. And the white flares of lightning I saw gathered around his heels were wings also.

The pole in his hand was not just dug into the armor. Two long thin snake-heads had shot out from two long thin snake-necks, and had driven long thin fangs into the dragon's surface, like living guide wires or tail-hooks. It would have looked comical if it had not looked so utterly satanic and grotesque. I flinched, seeing those poor snakes, stretched by that tremendous pressure of such abrupt deceleration. . . .

The man had a hat shaped like a flying saucer. It spun off his head when he stopped, striking our mast and rebounding in a spray of splinters. The man's hair was black and loose and flowing, whipped by the wind of his own passage.

All this, I should mention, took place in a split instant of total silence. Then, there was a sonic boom that threw me from my feet.

The skidding figure atop the dragon-head now straightened up, swirling and furling his vast white wings around him. He was a narrow-faced man, with one eye that glittered glee. A patch covered his other eye. His mouth quirked in a crooked half smile.

He hefted the snaky wand in his hand and made a casual gesture.

I saw a blur of burning motion in the fourth dimension.

Without the least struggle or fuss, the Victor-snake fell prone, a puppet with its strings cut. Clashing and clattering across the tilted deck, yards upon yards of snaky folds collapsed to either side of the ship, and spilled in wide arcs across the grass and rock. Victor's fall made an odd ringing noise, as if a giant had shuffled a deck of playing cards made of metal.

At that same time, the eyepatch the man wore caught fire and burned away. The eye socket beneath was filled with a glittering blue metallic orb, the eye of a cyclopes, and surrounded by scar tissue. The man had shot through the eyepatch, like a man with a gun firing through a coat pocket, not taking the time to draw it.

The azure beam flickered out and touched Quentin. Quentin cried out and fell down, choking. The wand that had been flying toward his hand now bounded away at an odd angle and fell clattering to the deck beyond my range of vision. Wraithlike smoke, some sort of choking gas, had replaced the oxygen in Quentin's lungs.

As Victor's huge body fell, the wings blurred into motion on the man's feet, and he stood in midair, motionless while his support fell away beneath him.

The hat, which also had wings of its own, now flapped and flew, light as a hummingbird, lifting itself from the severed wreck of the broken mast, and dropping down on the young god's flowing locks. The shining of the rim of his headgear gave him a halo of steel where the sunlight caught it.

The man looked pleased.

3.

The first person to react was Colin. In his Phobetor-shape, Colin leaped through the air, talons raised, horns lowered, breathing fire, his vast bat wings a hurricane of speed.

Roaring, he fell upon the slim godlike figure.

The slim godlike figure had slipped away and was hanging in the air a dozen yards to the left. The motion was too quick to follow; just pop, and he was yards away.

He gestured with his wand: A Greek temple made of swirls of mist, air made opaque, ripples of shivering twilight, all faded into view, hovering above the deck, with the sudden absurdity of a dream. The temple was complete with Doric columns, a portico and architrave, a solemn altar surrounded by tripods filled with starlight rather than flame.

A system of pentacles and pentagrams were inscribed in firefly light on every flagstone of that hall, diagram within diagram, all scribbled over with Latin, Greek, and Hebrew characters. The Sephiroth were smoldering on the wall behind; images from the tarot cards sparkled in little panels set within the frieze; the zodiac flamed along the roof.

The giant statue that rose, all gold and gleaming marble behind the altar, was of him, Hermes. When he raised his wand, the statue of Hermes raised its wand in the same gesture.

He spoke: "Hermes Trismegistus am I, Lord of all the Hermetic and Hermeneutic Art; I command you and compel you, nude and unhoused spirit, die; I quench your demon heart."

Phobetor fell out of midair as if struck by an arrow. He flopped to the deck, his wide bat wings beating blindly at the deck planks. He quivered, but could not get up. He was not dead yet, but the furry beast face he wore was drawn with pain; the green pinpoints of his demon eyes were extinguished; black smoke poured from his slack mouth.

4.

At the moment that the blue flash of Cherenkov radiation had seared the skull of the Victor-dragon, Vanity had held up her green stone. I saw the edges of the trapdoor above us, the frame leading to the deck, recede in the fourth dimension, an accordion unfolding, while the three-dimensional distances and relations remained the same. Photons or matter entering the trapdoor frame would be teleported across time-space to the other side of the frame with no evidence of any change or delay. Even a yardstick shoved through the gap would feel no discontinuity. From either side, the picture of the other side remained the same.

In the fourth dimension, however, the change was real; Vanity had just put the cabin where we both were far enough away from the landscape outside so as to give it a different set of natural laws. This was the first time she had done it right in front of me; I saw how the green stone actually operated.

It was fortunate, because the next thing the swift god did, after felling Colin, was to move (an invisibly swift wing-blur of motion) to the edge of the trapdoor, draw a revolver—yes, a good old-fashioned bang-bang-type firearm, very mundane and ungodlike: it was a .38 police service model—and shoot Vanity in the head with it.

The bullet lost interest in concepts like inertia and kinetic energy being proportional to the square of the velocity the moment it passed over the edge of the frame. The bullets bounced off Vanity's cheek and shoulder, stinging her about as much as thrown pebbles would have done.

The swift god said in a kindly voice, "Ah, girl of Phaeacian blood, you have been happily raised far from the corruption of the Smuggler-court of the Queen of Thieves. She spurned my suit, but you favor her in look and spirit. Come! I will spare you, if you open this door you slammed between us. I will make you my Queen, and we can rule the wreckage of the universe together. Eurymedusa just died, and I need a replacement busty bride! One of your art to be at my side! I ask only the life of the Chaos-beast there next to you, the one whose cross-section so closely mimics the shape of girl or goddess. I want her people to be at war with Cosmos too."

Vanity said, her eyes like electric flame, her bosom rising and falling with angry breath: "I don't marry murderers on the first date!"

His eyes lit up with inhuman, godlike mirth. "Murderer? Me? Unmurderer, say rather, the one who will make murder as impossible as a five-sided square! Has no one told you how simple, how perfect, how crystalline pure my plan of plans? I intend the cure!"

She said, "Cure for what?"

"For all! All people, all problems, all wants, fears, phobias, discontents, disorders, dissonance! The panacea for the pancosmic all!"

"That's pretty large-scale thinking," Vanity admitted, not taking her eyes from him. "How?"

"I know what Saturn did; I know how to undo and redo his diddling. I thought my ladies told you: I told them to! I will kill you all and unmake the universe. Ah! What a misnomer that shall be: For there will be a second. The duo-verse shall be a universe as well, not merely existing, but being all that exists, all that ever will exist, all that ever had existed. Your deaths will not merely be unmade, but will be made never-to-have-been! My mission as guide of souls, as Psychopomp, as guardian of life and death, will be fulfilled more gloriously, more perfectly, than can be described, for death itself I will abolish. My role as lord of magicians shall encompass a Great Work greater than all workers of the art: The alchemy of all nature shall be transcended— all of base material nature be transmogrified to gold. Do you see? If you help me, I will resurrect you. You and all your friends. The new universe will not have a law of life and death: Other laws will obtain. In this world we have life, and that is all: In that world we will have glory, something above and beyond life!"

Vanity said, "What did Prometheus do?"

The soaring manic exultation seemed to seep from the face of Trismegistus. It was as if he stumbled across a stone while in mid-dash. In a voice suddenly cold and flat, he snapped: "What? What question escaped the portcullis of your teeth?"

"What did Prometheus do to human beings? To make them half-divine?"

Trismegistus shrugged. "Who knows? Who cares? Am I not his greater?"

"Then how can you remake them, in your new universe? How can you remake us?"

His eyes narrowed in anger, but his voice blazed up again like flame, quick, light, gay: "Aha! We have a skeptic in our midst. I can end the war of Order and Madness by combining the best of both, establishing a harmony as Ouranos the all-creator should have done before time was born. Is there

death among the Nameless Ones of Myriagon? There shall be none here. Is
there want or scarcity among the silver-haunted cloudscapes of fair Cimmeria, within the paradises of the dreaming? No more than will be when I am
Saturn, and Time is mine. No matter how small my chance of success, surely
the trial is worthy of attempt, since success will mean infinite bliss and
bounty, not merely for you, but for all creation, and peace as well with un-
creation, the roaring rage of Chaos stilled, Saturn's black crimes undone! Is
it not worth peace, peace between our peoples, peace to embrace Cosmos
and Chaos both?"

"If peace is your goal, why all this killing?"

He smiled a crooked smile. "Because the gods of other things cannot understand the swift thoughts of the god of quickness and quick-wittedness.
Because I am misunderstood. Because the intelligent of this and every world
are mistrusted by the slow of brain. Because I must pull up the roots of this
old Cosmos, so ill-designed, to make the new world from its bones."

She said, "You cannot know it will work, can you?"

He laughed. "Naturally, no one has disnatured all of nature before. De-
stroying and remaking all existence is unique, unparalleled. It is not something one can do in experiment beforehand."

"Well, that's an interesting point of view. I don't want to sound like a
naysayer, but: Would you hire a man to build a house who had no experience
in house building? And a world is bigger than a house."

"Who needs experience? I have theory!"

Vanity said, "Um. Okay. Theory, huhn? Gee. Why don't you give me a
little time to think this through? Come back in a year and a day, and we can
discuss our marriage plans, and—"

"Lie me no lies. I know my children," he snorted, "for I am the Prince of
Actors and Players, Lawyers and Orators and all who live by slyness. Why
don't I kill you now, and finish the discussion when I resurrect the world?
What is wrong for others to do, is not wrong for me."

Trismegistus raised his wand, whispered a command, and all the deck to
either side of him crackled and shivered with a black shadow that passed
back and forth across it. The shadow scrabbled at the edges of the door-
frame, but could not get in.

The swift god said, "Ah, fair girl of Phaeacia, your race alone some power
has that might confound Olympians in wrath. But I am mayhap more than
mere Olympian. I have glanced all unafraid into the Chaos of Old Night; and
Sable-vested Night stared back, not without love, on me; and so I know her
secret lore, her occult craft and all-dissolving alchemy. I know how to unmake

the boundaries of creation, and bash down the walls of time; the walls wherein your ratlike people gnaw their ratlike paths."

The green grass in which the ship lay broken now all rippled, as if the land were a banner shaking into waves. The ground burst into confusion, while little hills of mud and snow and burning lava broke through the earth and shot up to every side. The cherry trees and all the little landscape were suddenly convulsed with whirlwinds of sticky mess.

The green stone in Vanity's hand flickered and lost its color. The gap of fourth-dimensional nonspace between the deck and the cabin evaporated. The laws of nature between the two spots equalized.

The black shadow of Trismegistus' magic snarled and leaped down into the trapdoor at Vanity. She fell beneath its claws, bleeding, screaming, screaming.

Trismegistus pointed his revolver at where I crouched and shot a bullet through my head.

The empty shell of my head. The girl-shaped form of flesh on the deck, at that moment, was a mannequin, an empty outer garment I had carefully left behind me when I moved. It was hollow. The gunshot broke it open like a clay pot.

5.

I had not been twiddling my thumbs while Vanity chatted and bought me time. The initial stroke that paralyzed Victor and sent an azure-burning Quentin, smothering, to his face, all happened before I would move or blink.

But at the same moment when Colin was leaping, with his inspired and impossibly quick movements, onto the god (whose movements turned out to be even more impossible and even more quick), I had slid most of my mass into the fourth dimension and "past" the deck into Victor's body.

6.

My higher senses showed more details about the Swift God. Like a Hecatonchire, he was a fourth-dimensional being. But, where they were thick and blocky, expanding cones in the fourth dimension, he was slim and streamlined, occupying successively smaller and smaller cross-sections. They might be able to turn into giants, but he could turn into a pixie, or a dust mote.

And his geometry was bent the opposite way from mine. His space was Riemannian, where mine was Lobachevskian. Everything in four-space was farther away for me than it would have been through flat three-space; for him, everything was closer.

A ball of shortcuts through space-time was folded around him like an origami rose, confusing and complex to behold.

The spiderweb of moral strands I had seen around Mrs. Wren was nothing compared to the vast webwork I saw now circling the god of magicians, nets upon nets and fields upon fields, streaming away from him in each direction. There were ripples and glances of activity of some sort, furious and restless, pulsing through these webs. Like the eye of a storm, the fulcrum of all these webs was wound around the wand in his hand, so that no moral obligation went straight to nor returned correctly from the web he wove.

He had bent the fourth dimension positively to increase his speed. When he struck Victor's skull, the bend had popped open, and the laws of nature inside had spilled out like burning oil directly into Victor's interior spaces, his heavy armor pointless, useless, a medieval wall unable to keep out a satellite-based missile attack.

Inside Victor's gigantic snake-body, I saw the energy echo of the damage the fourth-dimensional murder weapon had done, and was still doing.

The twisted laws of nature had imposed a twisted moral obligation on the inanimate matter inside Victor's body. Trismegistus had warped the monads inside Victor's huge body, woke them into self-awareness, bribed them to do his bidding, and turned to deal with Quentin.

7.

Matter, in Victor's paradigm, lacked purpose. Atoms simply were what they were, without plan, final cause, reason, or preference. However, from the point of view of the higher dimensions, even apparently random events had final causes, evolutionary pressures directing them toward certain end-states and away from others. Trismegistus had imposed a final cause on the matter in Victor's body; it was now meant to kill him.

Like a game with a bribed umpire, the statistically random microevents, Brownian motions in Victor's bloodstream, nervous system, and chemical system, began to tend toward a fixed outcome. The workings of his body began to manifest a series of "accidents" and malfunctions on a molecular and cellular level.

Little blood clots had formed, blocking capillaries and veins; nerve cells had lost charge or misfired, causing a cascade of neural failures, a seizure; cells hemorrhaged; the statistically random movements of oxygen in the lining of his lungs were no longer even, and the pressures no longer permeated smoothly. Victor's self-repair reactions merely brought more random chance into play, and therefore gave the deliberate accidents a wider scope of action. He had heart, nerve, and lung collapse within the first second; brain misfirings were rapidly erasing all his brain information.

His higher centers of consciousness had been the first things to go; Victor's complex control over his own body, his elaborate defense strategies for dealing with material attacks, had all been bypassed.

His brain had simply stopped. In Victor's paradigm, the mind was merely mechanical brain actions; stop the brain actions, stop the mind. And it is all over.

Except that not everything inside Victor's body was obeying Victor's paradigm.

My little friendly blood-creature, and its gallons of progeny, was not neutral and purposeless matter. Their molecular games had bribed umpires of their own. Its repair-purpose was at odds with the death-purpose Trismegistus had imposed.

Furthermore, my blood-creatures were under an instruction to react and adapt intelligently, to create new strategies, and to perpetuate themselves. On the other hand, the purpose Trismegistus had implanted had been final and straightforward; he had not thought to ask the matter he contaminated to keep trying to kill Victor after Victor was dead. Nor had he thought to order his matter to cooperate with other matter to find any mutually satisfactory solutions.

I saw the solution that had been evolved, an intelligent design springing from the unintelligent motions of purpose-driven matter. I saw a glitter and flash of exchanging utilities, rapid strands of moral obligation running back and forth. A deal had already been struck.

A way was evolved to satisfy both the repair purpose and the death purpose; all the matter that cooperated toward the mutual purpose was helped; matter bits that refused to negotiate or to cooperate spent their energies fighting each other, and were ignored by the majority mass of the body.

I helped the negotiations by nullifying as many as I could reach of the controlling monads of the poisonous death-wish inside those bits of matter cooperating for the destruction of Victor. It took me only a split second, while Trismegistus was striking down Colin.

I saw I was not going to be able to save the huge and armored Telchine battle-body. Part of the compromise was that the death-seeking matter would be allowed to kill that giant body. Too bad. It was magnificent inside, a cathedral on a molecular level, intricate and deadly as one of Her Majesty's Dreadnoughts.

If Trismegistus turned his head, or opened his upper-dimensional senses to look, he would have seen Victor escaping with his life. The shining useful-ness, the reciprocal agreements between the warring groups of molecules, would have been as clear to him as it was to me.

And he would have seen me, too.

But he was blind in one eye on that side, and folded his body back into a three-dimensional solid (all his little forms like nested Russian dolls, one within the other) during the moment when he chanted his death-curse at Colin. (Unable to do two paradigms at once? Perhaps.) So he did not see me. During that moment.

During the next moment, he was talking to Vanity, and she was flashing her eyes and heaving her bosom at him.

I don't meant that the way it sounds, but, gosh, if I had been a superpow-ered mad god, recently escaped from Hell, here to destroy the universe, I would have paused to chat up Vanity, too. I mean, she has that way about her, bright and fiery good looks that draw men like moths to candle flame. And she had undone the three buttons of her blouse again.

And she did what any girl has to do to keep a guy talking: She asked him questions about himself, gave him a chance to brag.

And even a swift god cannot do three things at once.

So, during that moment, I reached into Quentin's body and tried to move the poisonous gas in his lungs into the fourth dimension, while leaving his lungs in three. It did not really work. My upper tendrils and wings and such can manipulate from rather fine energies, but I was not used to dealing with a cloud of discrete particles.

Then I brushed up against a monad that did not belong to Quentin. The gas cloud had a single driving purpose behind it, one set of molecular in-structions that had been repeated by a time-stutter technique onto all the separate cells of Quentin's lungs. The poisonous gas was carbon monoxide, created directly out of the carbon dioxide waste of his exhalations, with an unhealthy seasoning of ozone thrown in for good measure.

I tried to orient my manipulators so as to consider all the monads of the traitor-monoxide as one monad, and negate its purpose. But I did not know what I was doing. Victor's paradigm was one that had been used here, the matter-control of the cyclopes. Had I more time, I could have figured it out.

So I managed to scoop some of the monoxide out of the lungs merely by tilting Quentin in the fourth dimension and bending gravity to make it pour out. When I folded Quentin back into the three-dimensional space, I left a bubble in the lung area, so that the "distance" between any point inside his lungs and the actual walls in his lungs was greatly increased. Any given particle of the swallowed gas cloud now had farther to go to reach the lung wall; the effect was to decrease the density of the monoxide.

It decreased the distance to the oxygen, too. Quentin still could not breathe.

This will sound gross. I put my four-dimensional face inside his three-dimensional lungs and breathed out. I was giving him mouth-to-mouth. Sort of. The wall tissue of the lungs was around me to each side, as if I had put my head in a wet bag, and they were red and blistered from the chemical reactions Trismegistus had created here. Part of the damage had been to turn the cell matter in the lungs into poison.

I unfolded my lungs into the fourth dimension, so that the volume they contained was much greater than any three-dimensional lung. Out I blew, a little Headmaster Boggin of my very own.

It did not seem gross to me, when I saw the utility light up through Quentin's damaged lung.

I reached out with my hand and massaged his heart to make it start again. I felt the unbeating heart jump to life. No, it was not gross at all.

When his heart moved, I saw, outside, that the walking stick Quentin had been carrying now jumped up from where it lay on the deck and struck Quentin.

The internal nature of the stuff Quentin was made of had been disenchanted, turned unmagical, and neutralized, when the azure beam from the eye of Trismegistus swept over him. But his wand had not been in his hand at that moment. The wand was still magical. It was still wreathed around and knotted with lines and webs of spells, set there carefully by Quentin.

The wand struck Quentin's motionless body.

Then it all turned into clay. Quentin's spirit, a shape of dark fire, winged with night and crowned with black stars, fell out from the bottom of his flesh and slid through the deck. It closed upon the black cat-shadow clawing Vanity.

The wand, flying off on a mission of its own, smote Phobetor, who turned immediately back into Colin, a nice, human-looking boy.

A boy without a demon-heart to quench. I saw the web of magic slide away, clawing and strangling, but slipping. Colin swayed unsteadily to his feet, screamed a weak sort of yell, and flopped somewhat unconvincingly at Trismegistus.

Trismegistus, meanwhile, saw Quentin's body turn to fine porcelain, and the beam darted from his metal eye, sweeping down. Both Quentin and the catlike shadow-thing were struck, but the beam must have hit a more vital part of the shadow-cat; it yowled and vanished, whereas Quentin merely staggered.

Trismegistus shrank to half his size and lifted his revolver into the fourth dimension, and shot me.

I rotated my girl-body into place to parry and ducked behind it. The bullet bounced off the skintight Amazonian bodysuit I wore. Tee hee.

A probe (made of some sort of music energy) unfolded from a time distortion in the fourth dimension, and fired a bullet of another kind. This one was an Amazonian space-flattener bullet.

I unfolded out from behind my 3-D cross-section, trying to maximize my volume, so that I would have the largest mass possible to absorb and disperse the damage. Three, four, and five dimensional I became, and, since the restraining weight of the neutronium medium seemed weaker and more flexible here, where the chaos was bubbling to every side, I pushed an inch or two into the sixth.

8.

Odd. What were those tetrahedrons doing here? Each face of the tetrahedrons was made of a five-dimensional plane of time-stuff. Beyond, I saw gravity-lights, refracting the time-shining into four rainbows, which formed, in turn, into many-branching shapes like towers of coral, each angle of which held an interlocking group of hypercube-crystals for an edge, reaching long arms into whirlpools of neutrino-heavy ideograms made of paper-thin five-dimensional thought-energy.

9.

Shock, pain. The shell passed over and into the space I occupied, bypassing the three-dimensional armor, smashing me flat again.

Instead of jumping away from Trismegistus, I jumped at him. The shell went off when I was only two meters from him, and a hot poker of pain went through my shoulder, down my lungs, hip, tail, and out the other side of me.

The music cut into my wings and tail. I smelled my own blood burning, and I fell, three-dimensional again, to the deck. I did not feel the pain just yet. But I could not feel my right arm either.

Trismegistus had to pull all his mass back into the shape he wore, the small shape, because the music burning me was going off so close to him. Colin grappled him for a moment, biting into his neck veins with an unenthusiastic sort of chomp.

During that moment, Victor, our human-size Victor, dressed in a skintight cloth of metal foil, popped out of a coffin-shaped slot or hangar in the tail of the dead dragon body. He was faceless and eyeless, his visage merely a blank mask of bony substance. He reached back inside with a ray of magnetism and manipulated some control. The guns lining the back and sides of the dragon swiveled to cover Trismegistus, and opened fire.

Colin rolled away from Trismegistus and put his hand somehow through and inside me without touching me, plucked out the deadly music with his hand. That saved my life, though it did not stop the pain or internal bleeding.

The music-thing looked like a scorpion made of fire in Colin's hand. He threw it at Trismegistus. The barrage of various heavy weapons lining the dragon armor, now that Trismegistus could not step sideways into the fourth dimension, could hurt him.

Or, they would have hurt him, had he not been able to outrun the bullets shot at him. Trismegistus turned into a blur of motion, but it was a blur localized at about a hundred yards off the port side of our damaged ship, and, with no space-bending techniques at hand, he could not outrun some of Victor's energy weapons, many of which were firing at faster-than-light speeds Newton would allow, but not Einstein.

Colin waved his hand at the chaos muck boiling and seething off the port side. His teeth were red and clenched with pain; his fist was shaking with weakness. His voice was breathy and lacked timbre: "Dream-stuff! Your Prince calls! Dance and play! Rip and rend and slay!"

Evidently, despite his weakness, he was inspired with pain and anger, because the whole environment caught fire, and the liquid earth, which had merely been bubbling and splashing, now erupted as if a million land mines, buried beneath the fluid gunk, had all gone off at once. The whole section of ground in that quarter jumped into the sky; the sky there fell.

The blue metal eye shot out of the mouth of the dragon and floated over to the blind and eyeless Victor. A valve or aperture opened in Victor's brow, and he placed the metal eye half within.

It glowed and rotated. Now Victor could see again.

The metal foil covering his body puffed up with magnetic charge. He moved. He was here, gently picking up both Colin and me.

Then he was down belowdeck. Vanity had been clawed and cut by the beast, and I saw red arterial blood spurting. Quentin's spirit was dissolving and flickering, but it was bent over Vanity, trying to apply pressure to her horrible wounds. His hands were insubstantial, though, and the precious blood simply flooded through them. Tears of fire were burning on Quentin's cheeks. He was too dazed to realize that his hands were only made of phantom-stuff, and could not help her.

Victor's voice came from his chest plate, amplified tremendously to outshout the thunder of the guns and thunderbolts going off overhead: "You'll die without your body, Quentin."

Quentin moaned something, but his wand, up on deck, tapped impatiently.

Quentin's spirit flashed upward through the deck boards and returned with his clay body. The spirit seemed to have great difficulty getting back into it, however. The dark and fiery silhouette was trying to wriggle into it through the mouth like a man putting on a wetsuit, but the spirit was losing fire and color, as if it were fainting, bleeding, dying.

The wand jumped up in the air, and a light came from it. It poked the Quentin-body in the mouth, and seemed to act as a shoehorn. The spirit was slurped inside, a reverse-genie returning to a tiny lamp.

Colin could not stand. He dragged himself on his belly over to Vanity, he bit back a cry of horror and alarm, and he lifted up his hands to apply pressure to her spurting wounds. "Tourniquet!" His voice was desperation. "Tourniquet here, or it is death!"

Victor was having blood drip out of one hand. No, not blood, but his molecular blood-creatures, the ones programmed to heal.

With his other hand, Victor was tearing up long strips from the deck boards he knelt on, which were bubbling and turning into bandages when the beam from his one eye struck them.

Victor's metal cloth suit ripped itself into shreds or tentacles. One strand formed a noose around Vanity's gushing arm, tightening. The spurting stopped. The others, like a hundred-armed hydra of medicine, took bandages, applied them, probed other wounds.

I am ashamed to admit I was too much in pain to move. That does not sound shameful, does it? But the truth was, I was too much in pain to try to move, and I could not think straight. The only thing I was thinking at the time was, *Why are they all looking at Vanity? Why isn't Victor helping me?*

Sometimes the best in people comes out during emergencies. Sometimes not.

Quentin staggered over to Vanity.

I heard Colin say, "Don't look. This is pretty bloody bad."

Quentin made a noise like a whipped dog, a painful whimpering. He whispered, "Darling, don't die. Don't die."

Vanity mumbled something, and made a noise something between a groan and a shriek. I heard gargling. It sounded like blood was obstructing her throat.

My eyes could not focus. I stared at the ceiling. I heard the conversation, but I did not look at Vanity. My imagination was filled with pictures of her soft flesh cut and lacerated, blood and other fluid seeping and spurting from open wounds, white bone fragments sticking from flesh. Maybe the reality was not so bad as what I imagined. Or maybe it was worse.

Quentin said, "What is going on? What are you doing to her?"

Victor said in a cold voice, "Leader, we must wake Vanity back up, so that she can get us out of here before Trismegistus returns. Her body is trying to put her into shock, to release her from pain. Do I have your permission to apply a stimulant?"

"Wh-what? Is it going to hurt her?"

"The pain-signals reaching her brain from her nervous system will increase."

"If, if we don't—"

"Leader, we cannot possibly withstand another attack from Trismegistus. All of you are wounded, and I lost ninety percent of my body mass. Will you give the order?"

I did not hear Quentin's reply; he must have nodded.

Colin said, "Steady on. Steady." I do not know if he was telling Victor to be careful in applying medication to Vanity, or telling Quentin to retain his self-control.

Vanity let out a gasping scream. It sounded horrible.

Quentin: "Darling, I'm here. Don't worry. It will be over in a moment. We need to—"

Vanity: (Something inaudible.)

Quentin: "What?"

Colin: "She said the chaos was in the way. She needs solid reality, something with walls, boundaries, definitions."

Quentin: "Victor, can you stabilize the area?"

Victor: "Yes. But Trismegistus will find us the moment the storm drops."

Quentin: "Do it."

Victor pried his blue orb eye out of his head and threw it upward. I saw it fly up overhead. At the top of its arc, it passed through the trapdoor and shot blue light in a fan toward the starboard side, the side away from where Trismegistus still (I hoped) was struggling with the storm and dodging cannon fire from the dragon-corpse.

Chaotic matter was evidently even easier to command than solid matter. The storm on that side fell quiet with an eerie swiftness.

Vanity mumbled something. A command. I saw the reflection of a green dazzle coming from her position where she lay.

Vanity was clever this time. The floor on which we lay now acted like a platform that shot downward. Deck after deck swooped away from us as we rode the high-speed elevator downward, into ever-vaster holds the *Argent Nautilus* now somehow held within her tiny hull. None of the wounded even had to move.

The square of storm-stuff overhead dwindled to a point, and the falling blue eye of Victor had trouble coming down fast enough, meteorlike, to return to its master's hand.

Slam. A door of steel slid shut behind us. Bang. Another. Boom. A third. Apparently Vanity knew how to run her powers in reverse, and create barriers where none had been before.

Quentin remembered me. He said, "Colin, wish Amelia back to health again. Victor, you concentrate on Vanity."

Colin pulled himself by his bloodstained hands over to where I was. He put an arm around my shoulders to prop me up. I felt a warm sensation enter my body, clarity of mind. Colin said softly, "Okay, Amelia. That is just red ink. Let go of your fear and the pain will let go. Snap out of it."

With my head up, I could see Victor bent over Vanity like a one-eyed ghoul over a corpse. An antiseptic smell and a sense of heat issued from his body, as if he had projected some kind of weird force field to sterilize everything in an envelope around him. He had pried open her chest cavity with several metal tentacles and clamps formed from his suit, and a dozen more tentacles were reaching into the heap of organs, performing a dozen operations with a score of instruments, tiny waldo-hands, molecular engines made of red blood or clear fluid.

Victor had no face. His one forehead-socket was empty. I saw he had perched his one eye on her breastbone, to get a better look at the situation, and it had grown dozens of strands of fiber-optic cable, and these glassy strands had sent little camera-eyes snaking into all her major veins and organs.

I heard the hissing noise of a bone saw.

It was a disgusting sight, much worse than my earlier imaginings.

Quentin was muttering: "Oh, dear sweet Jesus, save her life. Gods of Heaven, of wood, of Hell, save my Vanity, I pray you, if you have ever loved or known love, or if you ever knew horror and pain and fear you wished to flee."

The shadowy cat thing must not have been entirely dead or dissolved, because the black stain on the planks under Quentin's feet now spoke up: "Son of the Gray Sisters, I will restore your dying whore. Merely say the words, *my soul is thine.*"

Quentin gritted his teeth. A look of madness grew in his eyes, brighter and brighter. He said, "Spirit, my s——"

Victor said in a voice of infinite calm: "Leader, please do not be precipitous. Vanity's body is just a broken machine. Fix the machine; she's fixed. There is nothing to it. Give me another three minutes at the outside."

Quentin struck the stain with his wand, "Damned spirit, I suck dry thy last bit of life and grant it to my friend and comrade; let the blood of my lady, shed by you, torture you in darkness forever if you say other than 'I will.' Do you agree?"

Something too dark to see, but reddish around the edges, snakelike, trembled down the wandshaft and embedded itself into the stain.

Screams, screams, screams of pain filled the air. Mingled with the screams must have been the words *I will* because a shower of energy points flowed along the moral lines connecting Colin with Quentin.

Quentin said, "Here is life! Colin, take some as well. Use it on yourself and Amelia."

Colin tightened his grip around me. Suddenly, impossibly, my extra wings and limbs and tendrils were no longer here, and hence no longer in pain. He stroked my face and hair, and brushed the blood away. He stroked my arms and legs, belly, breasts, and thighs, and wherever his hand passed, the blood passed away, too, and the pain was gone. I had had a hole in my lungs with a hypervolume larger than the volume of my whole 3-D body, but that was gone, too, wished away by Colin.

As swift as waking from a dream, and with as little sense or reason to it, the pain was gone. I was hale and whole again.

Victor closed up Vanity. A black fluid, like a swift amoeba, wriggled over her flesh, knitting cell to cell. The wounds closed with no suture and no scar.

Victor picked up his eye in his hand. A blue spark flashed from the iris and struck Vanity's skull. Victor said, "I return bodily controls to you. Wake."

Vanity sat up, stretched, yawned, looked around with her huge green eyes. "What's going on? I've had a bad dream. . . . Quentin . . . ?"

Quentin said, "I am afraid it was real."

I had been lying here for several seconds, while Colin continued to caress my naked breasts and run his hands along my inner thigh.

"Hey!" I shouted, slapping him hard across the cheek.

"Ow!" He shouted back, "Wounded man here!"

"Get your filthy hands—"

"Part of the medical procedure. I am summoning inspiration."

"I'll inspire you, you sick jerk—"

"Madam, I am a trained professional. Now then, for the next part of the process, you are required to start pulling down my zipper with your teeth."

The impending murder of Colin Iblis mac FirBolg was interrupted by a loud noise.

Crash. The first steel door, high above us, had just given way.

Crunch. The second one, too.

Something very fast was coming down the shaft after us.

20

THE SHIELD OF LADY WISDOM

1.

Deck after deck whizzed past us as the platform fell. Some of the decks were crowded with boxes and crates, warehouses. Others held corridors lined with small oval doors and hatches.

Then we started passing decks filled with museum displays, library shelves, rows of obsidian coffins. One deck was a greenhouse, set with water fountains, stretching back as far as the eye could see. Another that flashed past was an observatory, with scores of complex telescopes pointed out a score of portholes and crystal domes, each window opening on a different twilight seascape. We were entering strange territory.

"What is this ship?" I said aloud, my voice hushed with wonder.

"Phaeacia," said Colin.

I gave him a startled look. "What's that?"

"It is all one ship. All of their ships are part of the same ship, folded into different parts of the dream. This is their empire. The ship is larger than the worlds through which she sails."

"How do you know?"

He shrugged. "It is in my heart. I just know. I'm inspired."

Quentin made a choking noise. For a moment, I thought he was laughing at what Colin had said. But no. Quentin's face was pale; his eyes had no life in them.

Quentin was wounded. His body showed no scar, no scratch, but I saw the web of moral obligations radiating from him turning black and curling up. His soul had been wounded by the cat-thing.

I said, "Victor! Do your golden-ray thing to Quentin! Or do something! He's hurt!"

Quentin swayed on his feet and knelt, and put his head to the floor. Then he fell over sideways.

Quentin mumbled something, but his voice, once again, came strangely clear and pristine to the ear: "My part is played. I turn command over to my second."

Vanity shrieked, "Oh no!"

A voice came from Quentin's walking stick. "Milady, my master bade me speak this word once death has silenced him . . ."

Vanity snapped, "He's not dead yet! Shut up!"

". . . He says that, if he perishes still trapped within this false world of matter, the Lord of the Dead will claim his soul and prevent his resurrection; nonetheless, he bids you keep his memory in you, and he promises your memory in him will soften the torments of hell to which he will be taken."

"Shut up!" screamed Vanity. "He's not dead!" She whirled to face Victor. "You fixed me. Fix him!"

Victor said, "He is suffering a software degradation. The electromagnetic envelope where he stores his memory is disintegrating."

I said, "Victor, what can you do?"

Victor turned to me. "For now, nothing. The mission takes priority. Vanity, see if you can get this platform we are riding to dodge; try to lose our pursuer. Amelia, keep an eye on Trismegistus; inform me of his movements. Colin, prevent Trismegistus from approaching through the fourth dimension. You can stop him from using Amelia's paradigm; if he has to come through physical space, Vanity can keep slamming doors in his face. I will sweep for bugs."

I said, "Leader, we can't win without Quentin. Not against the god of magic. We need a magician."

Victor said, "All we need to do is open our lead. Trismegistus had to introduce a chaos storm into the environment to prevent Vanity from using her powers to escape; if he does that again, I can quell it, or turn the storm against him. Logically, he would not have risked doing that if he had some other way to overtake a Phaeacian. Therefore we should be able to outdistance him. If we can hold him off long enough! We'll see about Quentin as soon as we have time."

Vanity stood for a moment, her lip trembling, her eyes bright with unshed tears. Then she nodded at Victor, turned, and knelt on the platform. A hatch hidden beneath the boards opened beneath her fingers. Beneath was a control panel, black with dozens of buttons.

She pushed one. A shunt opened in the shaft, and we were kicked to one side. Our fall was now at an angle. A steel door slid into place behind us. The stone around her neck flared green; we passed another threshold, and another door fell to. Again her stone flared.

She was leaving an alternating pattern of different laws of nature behind us. In one stretch of corridor, kinetic energy was directly proportional to speed; in another, it was inverse; in a third, it was inverse cubed. Another section of the corridor behind us turned black as she lowered the speed of light in that segment to five kilometers per hour; if Trismegistus tried to pass through that area at any faster a speed, he would be outside of our frame of reference, unable to affect us. It was certainly the cleverest thing I ever saw Vanity do.

Clever, but in vain. It was not working.

I said to Colin, "He's skipping out of the plenum. He's just going around the barriers Vanity is setting up. Can you get him?"

Colin looked behind us and saw nothing but dwindling concentric squares as we fell past deck after deck. He said, "I don't see him."

I said, "Look with your heart. Follow my finger. Can you see the direction I'm pointing? There."

Because I could see the slender spindle-shape of the fourth-dimensional being, sliding from dream to dream, parallel to the ship, but in a space skew to our space.

"I see him now. Tiny little thing, isn't he?" Colin made a grabbing gesture with his hand, like a man slapping a fly. "Got 'em. *Ow!* It stung me."

Colin's eyes rolled up in his head, and he fell to the deck. Mist began trickling out of his mouth and nose.

"Colin!" I knelt and put my arms around him. "Oh, dear God, Colin!"

Blue light stabbed out of Victor's eye and bathed Colin. "An electromagnetic field is disintegrating him. I've stopped the field, but I cannot stop the effect," said Victor. "Put the ring of Gyges back on him."

I said, "The ring's broken. Maybe I can try to fix it. Who had it last?"

Colin groaned muddily. "It's all going away."

"What?" I said.

"The dream of the world. All going away. . . ."

Victor said, "It's on his finger."

Foolish of me. There it was. It had a controlling monad, just like a living being. The monad had been forced out of alignment by an Amazonian azure ray, and the internal nature of the ring had turned into something materialistic, dull, and inert.

I twisted the monad back into shape, but the internal nature of the ring did not change. Mending the break in a glass after the water had run out.

"Nothing's happening," I said.

Victor said, "Can you reproduce the effect Miss Daw used to propel you out of the fourth dimension? I've neutralized all energy flows in this area; he should not be able to track us, either by magic or by electronics—"

"Wait! I see something!"

"Report."

"It's the corpse. The giant whatever-it-is inside the hollow horse coffin. The genie in the ring, do you know who I mean?"

Victor said, "The icon representing the ring of Gyges."

"He says there is an object in our future. No one can defeat the God of Speed in a race; no one can outrun him. It's fate."

Vanity said, "Don't listen to him! He's lying! Don't believe it."

I looked at Vanity. She was kneeling, cradling Quentin in her arms. Quentin stirred and moaned feebly. He was not dead.

She said, "Dead people work for the bad guy, remember? The guy with the keys to the underworld?"

Victor said, "Amelia, what were the four steps needed for us to undo an Olympian decree of fate?"

2.

I said, "It is complex, but I can sum it up: Each of us has a part to play. First, I am supposed to give the destiny enough free will to allow it to be changed.

"Second, a destiny is a curse. It uses sympathy and contagion to organize the spirits of the universe to want a certain outcome. To annul that requires magic: Quentin's paradigm.

"Third, a destiny is fixed and inescapable, as dispassionate as a law of nature. That's you. I think you take away the free will I give the destiny-force, so that it acts according to a mechanistic cause and effect.

"I was told that finally, a psychic event of a type and kind unknown must take place at the final step to make it permanent. Unknown to my people! My sister Circe has a blind spot, because of her paradigm: She didn't know what Colin's role was supposed to be." I swallowed. "I volunteered, you know. It was to get that message through that I came into this world, and suffered all this, and met you."

Vanity cut in impatiently, "Do we need that last part? Do we care if it is permanent or not, at this point? If we just temporarily made it possible to outrun Trismegistus, then we could outrun him, right?"

I said to Victor, "There was one thing more: Time-space must be arranged to permit the laws of nature under which these four events may take place. That sounds like a Vanity thing to me."

Victor said to me, "How close is he to overtaking us?"

I looked back. I saw the fourth-dimensional shape of Trismegistus, but he was not behind us, not anymore. He was ahead of us.

3.

I saw an explosion in the fourth dimension, another clash caused by the violent intersection of two mutually contradictory laws of nature. Trismegistus had seized the segment of dream-space through which our elevator shaft was running, and shoved it into the middle of downtown Los Angeles, back on the material plane, Earth. All our running: We had run in a circle, like some wounded game creature.

A flux of crooked morality strands, charged and infused with magic, was issuing contradictory orders to the matter and energy in the area. Nothing knew what the laws of nature were any longer; it was another dream-storm, exploding like a bomb beneath our feet.

At the same time, the line of energy I was using to probe him stiffened with a force of some unknown purport. One of his serpents reared up from his wand, opened its fanged mouth. Musical tension, similar to a siren song, flickered from the snake-mouth, flashed backwards along the strand, and struck me in the face. Musical snake venom in my eyes.

There was a sensation of fire in my eyes, pain. My eyes were filled with tears, but I could still see. Dimly.

It was getting dimmer. I was going blind.

I screamed, "Vanity, get us out of here! He's ahead of us!"

Victor said, "Belay that, Vanity. Create the laws of nature needed to dispel a destiny. There is no point in running."

I was thrown to the ground as the platform came to an abrupt halt. Things to me were half-lit, monochromatic. We were in a green house. The deck to either side of us was spread with wide lawns and jeweled statues, and ornamental gardens in terraces climbed up the sloping wooden hull. The port-holes here were like the windows of a cathedral: a massive rose-window at one end, hazed in rainbows, stained-glass arches marching like sentries away from it.

The green stone around Vanity's neck flickered and went dim. Vanity said, "We are surrounded by chaos, Leader! I cannot back us out of here."

Victor issued a weft of magnetic force that carried him over to the nearest stained-glass window. Without flinching, he shoved his arm through the window, cutting himself badly on the shards. A black fluid squirted from his veins, falling into whatever cloudscape or seascape was beyond the window. I could not see the scene clearly. It was something that billowed.

A beam swept from his eye and ignited the black substance. A bluish flame started up and began to get brighter through the window.

Victor said, "I can try to stabilize the immediate area. Do you have the laws of nature we want?"

Vanity said, "I wished for what you told me to wish for. Is Quentin going to be okay?"

A voice came out of my cell phone. It came out of Vanity's pocket and Quentin's and Colin's coat as well, where they kept their cell phones. I assume Victor could simply hear it.

"Checkmate," came the light, quick, playful voice of Trismegistus.

4.

He continued: "The laws of nature that allow one to unweave a destiny are the same ones, the exact same ones, that allow destinies to be sewn up in the first place. The air of Olympos, so to speak. Our home field advantage. The laws least favorable to Chaos and your powers. A dead zone. Apt expression, eh? Very apt?

"For all this, all this, foolish children, has been ordained by fate. Once fate is set, it must come to pass, soon or late. I had hoped merely to decree your death while I lay at leisure, eating grapes, but your exertions against my incompetent wives and clumsy paramours—in escaping them, your deaths were not escaped, and were in nowise less inevitable, but it was taking long, so very long! I am not the god of patience, but of speed! So now I must run you down myself. It is ended: Now I speak. I decree your deaths, and war, horrific war, to overwhelm the world!

"So I proclaim, Tachys Hermes Trismegistus Chrysorrapis, Diactoros, and Klepsiphron, Polytropos, and Argeiphontes! Swift messenger thrice-greatest of the golden wand I am, messenger of death, guide of souls to hell, thief-prince and many-turning: at whose behest even the wisest, all-seeing, perish! To bring the message of inescapable fate is in my jurisdiction: For I am Mechaniotes the contriver; this I contrive. I am the soul-thief Psychopompos: These steal I."

Even though Trismegistus was outside the ship, what he did next involved a huge section of time-space, and I saw it. Even with my eyesight growing dim, I saw it.

It was the same thing I had seen Mavors do on Mars. Forces flowed into the future and established something there, a cold shape like ice, freezing the energies of time into one rigidity.

It was the destiny of our deaths.

He said, "A life for a life, I demand, by the death of Laverna, of Lamia, of Eurymedusa: your blood to wash her blood from your hand."

A web of moral obligations, many-stranded, complex, dazzling, now wound around the iceberg of energy.

"To deviate from my decree, I do not allow: Time has no will, for Saturn is in Tartarus."

I saw the azure dazzle of cryptognostic particles stream from his eyepatch—but into time, not into space—and negate the free will he had just created. The iceberg of time-energy became as cold and implacable as inanimate matter: a law of nature, from which there was no appeal, no mercy.

Then he threw back his head (I saw it through the walls of the ship) and chanted:

Muse, sing of Hermes, the son of Zeus and Maia,
Lord of Cyllene and Arcadia rich in flocks,
The luck-bringing messenger of the immortals whom Maia bare,
The rich-tressed nymph, when she was joined in love with Zeus!
Born with the dawning, at midday he played on the lyre,
And in the evening he stole the cattle of far-darting Apollo. . . .
As swiftly are all his many-turning contrivances accomplished!

My sight was failing. Perhaps this was due to blindness; perhaps it was the side effect of Colin's paradigm. Whatever Trismegistus did to set the destiny in place, I could not look at it.

5.

Victor paid not the least attention to the voice. He said to me, "Amelia, can you look through time with some new sense of yours and find this destiny waiting in our future? Can you locate the destiny-influencing thing?"

I tried to describe what I had just seen. My words meant nothing to him. In his paradigm, time is not a continuum, but an absolute.

He said, "Perhaps I can negate the electromagnetic entities from Quentin's paradigm. You said you saw what you call morality involved? Which direction is it?"

I said, "It is in the time direction."

"Time is not a dimension," he said, puzzled.

"Victor! I'm going blind. I am losing my sight on all levels. I can't see anything."

The azure light from his eye swept over my face once or twice, with no effect.

Victor turned the beam on Quentin. Quentin shivered, made a gasping noise, like a child might make who cries out during a nightmare.

The voice from the cell phone said, "The god of speech will not deny you now to speak your epitaph, oh no! Choose your *bons mots* carefully. No one will remember your dying words, but me—but then again, since I will be the only being in Cosmos or Chaos to survive the upcoming Apocalypse, no one will recall anything at all, and what I deem to be, real or dream, shall be reality."

Quentin opened his eyes, looking pale and dazed.

Victor said to him, "Cast spells on Colin. We need him to fix Amelia."

Vanity said, "The loudmouth can't get in, I'll bet, to this area of space. If the laws of nature are so solid, all he can do is talk."

The chuckle floated from the cell phones. "To decree is to talk. What god need do more?"

Victor said, "Ignore him."

The voice of Trismegistus slithered from the cell phones again, "Oho! Now is that wise, my wind-up Telchine bot-boy? You don't know what I want; you don't know what I can offer."

Quentin, still lying prone, raised his head, bleary-eyed. He lifted a trembling hand and pointed it at Colin.

The voice from the cell phones said, "Whoops! What's this? A fallen felon spirit thinks now to weave a spoken spell? Do tell! But what if the crafty god of craft, with tragic magic causes a twisted mystic gaff? You can't enchant if you can't chant! Your cantrip might trip! I am an Olympian. This is my decree."

Quentin opened his mouth, but then a series of convulsions shook him; he vomited dryly, his stomach bringing up nothing.

But even with my vision going dim, I saw it. I saw the decree Trismegistus made. It was like a flare of light, bright beyond brightness. It was in the time-direction. The flow of time changed its nature, became useful rather than neutral, and became entangled in a whirlpool of knotted strands of magic. It was a solid block of ice formed in the river of time. It was a fate.

This one was nearer than the death-fate. It was immediate, happening now.

It was within my grasp. I had seen the process several times now, and I knew how to start unwinding fate. I did not know how to finish, but . . .

I knew, at least in part, how to do the work of Chaos.

So with an energy-tendril I touched the fate choking Quentin, pulled part of its nature into a higher dimension, rotated it, replaced it. This rotation acted like a mirror, and the fate became self-aware. It woke up.

It was awake, but not free. The web of magic strands around it forced it to act. I was not sure what it was doing, but, somehow, this thing was making Quentin choke.

I shouted to Victor and told him what I saw.

I said, "We need Quentin to do the next component of the destiny un-weaving spell. How do we save him? How do we save Quentin?"

Victor said, "The enemy must be using the Olympian power to affect us, because the laws of nature here in this space we are in are blocking his other powers from working. Mount Olympos must be likewise defended from ex-ternal attack. All we need to do is outwait him."

Quentin coughed and heaved again. How much could random chance do, once it was no longer random? Make all the air molecules in someone's throat forget their Brownian motions for a moment, and create a partial vacuum?

The azure beam from Victor's eye flickered across Quentin's throat. There was no change. Quentin hacked and spat and could not speak.

I said, "It is not a magical, nor a material effect. We need to have Quentin zap the magic away from the destiny cursing him before you can force cause and effect back into place."

At that moment, steam started to come up out of Colin. His solid body was becoming more and more dreamlike and insubstantial.

Vanity whispered in horror, "Oh my God, he's fading."

6.

The voice over the cell phones called, light and quick and gay: "Oh, Vanity Fair, my Vanity Fair, my ripe young peach with a pert derriere! I will make you a bargain; I will make you a deal. I only need for one of them to die. If you do not decide, then I will."

Vanity yanked the cell phone out of her pocket and stared at it. "What?"

"To start the war with Chaos, the war to end all All. I only need one death. The treaty will break, Olympos will fall, and down will come Heaven, and Cosmos, and all. But you might live, and your fine beau. Just let Hades take Colin to the world below. You get to pick which one of you will die. Will you pick? Or shall I?"

I saw the iceberg-thing in our future stir. It began to orient itself, like a hound catching a scent, from one of us to another. It was coming closer. Death was soon and growing sooner.

Victor said, "Don't answer. Ignore it."

Vanity, her face half-crumbled with unshed tears, threw the cell phone away from her. It clattered off the boards and fell into a flower arrangement.

The voice said, "That was just insane inanity, Vanity. What will you do if I choose you?"

I heard Vanity scream, and saw her fall down. The wounds that Victor had stitched up were leaking again, as if Trismegistus had somehow left something behind in them, something Victor could not see or sense, waiting for some signal from him to rotate back into three-dimensional space.

I could hear her gasping for breath. Hissing. The fate was close, but it did not strike. Trismegistus still was not killing us. He was talking, taunting. He still wanted something from us. What? What did he want?

It got dimmer. I held my hand in front of my face. It was a blur in a blurry world.

I said, "Victor, I'm scared." My voice was shaking.

I could not see where Victor was standing, or what he was doing, but he said, "Don't show fear. You and I have to take care of the young ones, Amelia. You and I."

It was the same thing he used to say to me, back when we were much younger. Back when I was Secunda.

He said, "We're the only ones they can rely on. You and I. Forever."

"What if we don't make it, Victor? What if this is it?"

"Then I shall not have the opportunity to ask for your hand in marriage,

Amelia. I would have preferred to wait till I had something of value to offer you. I have nothing but myself. We have always been together. We shall always be together."

And then he said, in a voice as calm and unafraid as ever he used, "Amelia, my sweet, my brave Amelia, whether we live or die is unimportant. Don't pay it any mind. Concentrate on the task at hand."

There are not many things a man can say to take a girl's mind off the impending prospect of death. But there is at least one.

It made tears come to my eyes, which were already full of tears of pain. For some reason, though, things seemed to get brighter to me. Just a little. Maybe the laws of nature of Olympos had some soft spot in their heart for tears of love.

That's when I saw them. They were so bright, even a half-blind girl could not miss them. Two more icebergs in the stream of time. Larger, much larger, than the fate that was choking Quentin.

Coming closer. I squinted through the pain and tried to see their inner nature.

One was cunning, clever, quick-witted, delighting in lies. The other was disciplined, fearless, steadfast, quiet with menace.

The two fates contending over us. I could only venture a guess: The decree of Trismegistus that no one could outrun him. The other one? The decree of Mavors that no one could threaten our lives without summoning him. Or maybe this was an older, larger, more permanent fate. Perhaps this was the decree of Mavors that no one could overcome him in any feat of arms or battle.

I said, "I can see them. The fates. I can wake them up, but they will still be trapped by their spells."

7.

Spells. I had interfered with the spell the nymphs had used to enchant Colin. How much did I need to interfere before Victor could zap one of them, make it go away? Maybe I could step in for Quentin, just for a moment.

I reached out with a tendril of energy, pointing it toward the flow of time, extended . . .

The voice of Trismegistus whispered in my ear, "Pale Amelia with her hair and heart of gold! The poker game is almost over now. Would you prefer to see, or fold? Just pick for me which one of you must die. I will spare the other four. What do I need four corpses for? The deal is real, and much too good for you to deny."

I shouted back, "None of us will betray the others! We stand or fall together!"

"Ahhhh! You will never imagine how grateful I am to hear you say that, filth of Chaos. With your own mouth you have said it; you are one in the eye of the law; which law I call and now convoke: Hear me!"

My sight was almost gone, but in shadows and blurs, I saw what happened. A tiny dot swelled up in size, became a man cloaked in white, a wand of serpents in his hand, wings on his feet. Trismegistus was now inside with us. My words had somehow invited him in.

With a flutter of his wand, he threw one serpent onto me; the other he threw onto Victor. Both snakes must have had the same paradigm Echidna used. The one on me became as large as an anaconda.

The one on Victor simply grew and kept growing, while Victor pelted it with chemicals, explosives, and energies of various types. It was larger than a freight train when it rolled over him. I did not see what happened to Victor, but his azure light winked out. I think it swallowed him whole.

I was wrapped in a crushing grip. The tendril of energy I was reaching with began to flicker and fade.

I granted it free will, that part of me, that tendril. It yanked free and fell away from me, spinning off into the abyss.

Two hot needles of pain found my neck.

Poison. Music shaped as a liquid. Siren song floated in my veins. I collapsed into three dimensions. No breathing. Bones broken.

As if from a far, far distance, I heard Trismegistus chant: "Primus, Secunda, Tertia, Quartinus, Quentin: by your names of your youth and childhood I call; Victor Invictus Triumph, Amelia Armstrong Windrose, Vanity Bonfire Fair, Colin Iblis mac FirBolg, Quentin Nemo: by the names you named yourselves for you; Damnameneus, Phaethusa, Nausicaa, Phobetor, Eidotheia, and by your names innermost and true, I call, I call, I call to you. Perish now, thou demons foul, who are so fickle and so difficult to kill. Your ghosts nowhere shall abide; you shall perish utterly, and every part of you shall die; it is the Psychopomp who speaks: This is my will. I raise my wand; I now decree. . . ."

My last trickle of vision faded to utter black.

8.

I heard Quentin's voice. "I am in nowise bound by any curse of yours, you who have not named me." His voice sounded strange, so strange. But the curse choking him must have failed.

That meant Victor, somewhere, somehow, was alive, if he restored the normal chain of cause and effect. If the snake was a creature from Colin's paradigm, it was equal and opposite to Victor; it was one against which he had a fighting chance.

The voice of Trismegistus floated like a leaf in the breeze, twinkling and chuckling. "I am the Father of Lies; I know my children. That was a lie. Spirits! I have named him truly! Can he prove otherwise?"

Quentin said, "The name I told my enemies when I was young, Nemo, 'no-one,' is not the name I told myself to myself. In the ring of stones, beneath the moon, with blood I drew myself from mine own vein, I anointed me. That name is my true name, my inner name, my soul name, and you do not know it."

"Do you think you can riddle and argue, debate and expound, with the Prince of Lawyers? You slew Galenthias, my cat: I call on you to render up your life for that. A life pays for a life; that is the rule; you knew and disobeyed."

"You admit that spell is gone from me; and if from me, then from all those whom your words have bound together in one destiny—"

"Oh, this grows tiresome."

A gunshot rang out.

Quentin laughed. It was a sick, forced, hollow laugh, but he still laughed. "It needs to be silver to hurt me. You have damaged my vessel, which is merely made of clay."

Trismegistus said wearily, "Ophion, get him."

The snake relaxed its grip and I was free. I could not extend anything into overspace, and I still could not see.

Quentin cried out in terror.

I tried to get up, but the poison had made all my limbs go cold. I could not rise.

I felt a motion in the air near me. I sensed a looming presence.

A kiss. Someone kissed me.

9.

Colin whispered in my ear, "Wake, sleeping beauty."

Warmth and motion began to filter through to me. Pins and needles stung my limbs.

And wings and tendrils and flukes and songs. I was fourth-dimensional again. Still too weak to get up, but it was something.

I whispered, "Colin! Cure my eyes! I can't see!"

He kissed my eyelids.

Quentin called out one last time, a cry of horror, and was silent. I felt Colin leave my side in a rush of motion. I reached after him, and felt fur and bat-wing leather slide away from my fingertips.

There was a horrid scream: "AMELIA WINDROSE! AMELIA!"

Colin was not calling for me; this was his battle cry.

Trismegistus said, "Oh, come now. Puh-leese."

I heard a dull thump as Colin hit the floor.

Light. The smallest trickle of my vision had returned.

And the brightest objects in time or space or hyperspace around me were the icebergs of fate. I selected the quietly menacing one, the decree of Mavors.

I sent off a tendril to wake the fate, a second one to turn its webs of magic inward on themselves, and a third one to send a message to the fate-thing. *Help me. I woke you up. I am your mother. Help me.*

I was not trying to dissolve this particular fate. I wanted to augment it.

"Ah, where was I?" fluttered the floating tones of Trismegistus. "Ah, yes, brutal murder. Oops. The blond one is getting up again. Hey—here is an idea! Why don't I kill them first, and then cast the spell to abolish any lingering souls or ghosts? Better idea? Much better."

I blinked. I could only see shadows, but I saw the shadow of the slim figure, winged hat and winged shoes, raising his revolver toward me.

There were lumps on the grass and on the deck to his left and right. My friends? One of them was wriggling and writhing. Being eaten by a snake?

I heard the revolver hammer click.

Nothing happened. No bullet.

Click. Again, nothing.

Click, click, click.

"Hmph! That's odd. I didn't think revolvers could jam! I wonder what is wrong with it."

I blinked. My vision cleared a moment, blurred, cleared.

The huge stained-glass window behind Trismegistus formed a frame with him at the center. There was a shadow darkening the glass. Then the glass went black.

Then the ramming prow of a black ship entered. Shards of glass and powder exploded in each direction, and the hull boards protested, bent, snapped, broke inward.

The sea came in.

The whole huge cabin space, where all these lawns and gardens stood, canted to one side. The place where I lay was still dry, but the boards sloped down to a spreading lake of seawater.

The noise was terrible; boards groaned and creaked; waters roared and thundered.

A pair of metal gauntlets, each finger huge as a tree trunk, reached in through the gap made by the ram-ship and pulled an acre of hull away.

I heard the voice of Mulciber, amplified over a loudspeaker, say, "The Master of Cold Iron says for the guns not to fire, so they won't, eh? Mavors, tell your men to use steel."

Slithering shadows, thin and pantherlike, poured quickly from the black deck. Laestrygonians. I did not see what they were armed with, and I could not make out how many there were. They were fast.

Trismegistus was faster. I don't know what he had in his hand. A knife? But he turned into a blur and cut the throats of a dozen Laestrygonians, then two dozen. Anyone who tried to run away from him, it became a race, and he won.

A giant gauntlet, which I saw only as a passing storm cloud, reached into the cabin space and caught the mile-long serpent by the neck.

The other snake, the anaconda-size one, swelled up to something the size of a skyscraper lying on its side. But a squad of Laestrygonians swarmed over it, and blood gushed up from the snake where they were. It thrashed and fell still.

Trismegistus made a noise like a steam whistle, a high-pitched peacock scream. "You sucker! You slew my snakes! Ophion and Serpentine! You are a dead man, Mavors! You, too, lumpity-hump!"

I saw him dimly, a pale shadow with a wing-blur around him, standing in midair.

I saw a silhouette standing on the deck of the black ship, with seawaters rushing in through the broken hull to either side. Even though I could not make out the details, the upright posture, the air of calm command, could not be mistaken.

Mavors said in a flat tone, "Last chance to surrender, Trismegistus. Come quietly."

Trismegistus laughed. "I can circle the equator five laps in the time it takes you to throw your spear at me. Oh, I am sure you could beat me, if I stood still long enough for you to snail on up and poke me. But why should I?"

"Here's why."

Mavors unslung a shield from his back and held it up, and yanked off a cover or cloak he had thrown over it. At least, I assume it was a shield. It was round. I could not make out what was on the shield, but it was something that wiggled like a spider.

Mavors said, his words marching out without inflection, "The other members of your group sold you out. Lady Wisdom asked for amnesty. She's the one who made me promise I'd ask you to give up peacefully. Remember her? Tritogenia? She's the one who carries the shield of the Medusa. She lent it to me so I could get you. Even you can't run faster than you can see."

The shadows representing the Laestrygonians all suddenly stood stock-still. Frozen in place.

The pale shadow representing Trismegistus turned all dark and grainy in my vision the moment Mavors held up the shield. He fell out of the air. When he crashed to the deck, I recognized the noise. Stone. Trismegistus had been turned to stone.

His own men, too. Mavors had petrified platoons of his own people, just to get the shot at Trismegistus. Cold bastard.

10.

Mulciber must have thought so, too, because he said, "As we agreed, you put that damn thing away now. I thought you were going to call out a warning, let us cover our eyes, eh?"

Mavors did not say anything, but his silhouette seemed to be tense, ready. Perhaps he was weighing in his mind his chances against Mulciber. The giant golem Mulciber was in had turrets for sixteen-inch guns, loopholes for other weapons, decorating the crenellations of its massive epaulettes and chest plate.

Mulciber said, "Come on, now. As we agreed. Sure, you can't be afraid of my little toy here, are you? Put away the shield, and I won't shoot you."

A winged figure dropped from the sky and landed behind Mavors. I felt a cold breeze, as if a refrigerator door had just then opened.

I heard Boggin's voice: "My lords, while duly acknowledging the presumption, indeed, I am tempted to say, the disrespect, which may, in some less generous minds, be attributed to my humble words, while lords as august as yourselves are debating the most efficient . . . efficacious? . . . way to betray each other, I feel it is my duty, as a loyal servant of the realm, ah, indeed, loyal to whomever will end up ruling the realm, my duty to mention, a fact which I hope has not escaped your lordships' notice, occupied, as you are, with matters of such import. May I remind my lords that the entire sidereal universe will be destroyed if my children, ah, if the children, are harmed? Might I suggest—although it is not, of course, my place to suggest—might I suggest a quick search of the bodies by medical teams? Yes?"

Mavors said, "Boreas, be quiet. You are only here because you are not loyal to anyone here. A neutral third party."

Mulciber added, in a voice heavy with irony, "Whom we both mistrust equally."

Mavors covered up the shield and handed it over to Boggin.

Boggin took the shield and slid it under one arm. "Sir—if I may—the children's safety is a paramount—"

"You may not. Go."

Boggin hesitated a moment. My eyesight was too blurred yet to see any expression.

I saw his wings spread wide. There was a cold wind, and he was gone.

The statue of Trismegistus wiggled. I saw it open and close its hand.

Where the huge arm was extending inward through the broken hull wall, a peninsula of metal, there came a small motion. A hatch shaped as its thumbnail opened in the gauntlet of the golem. A bent and hunchbacked figure emerged, climbed down a set of rungs. He moved with a limping stride, crablike, over toward where the statue of Trismegistus lay on the boards.

I saw him bend over the fallen figure.

"Not dead," Mulciber said. "No escape for him that way. He's still in there."

Mavors said, "Lady Tritogenia, before handing me her shield, warned me he could work his way out of the petrifaction, in time. A Chaos trick he learned."

"Not in time. Now. He's already working his way out. What a freak he is."

"You can contain him?"

Mulciber crooked his head up at the figure on the black deck above. "I am the master of iron and steel, rock and stone. Stones don't move when I say they don't move. I can keep him bound. You need me to keep him in. I needed you to ensure victory. Deal's over now."

Mavors said, "You assume I am going to let you keep the prisoner. I don't want to see him added to your side."

"Shut up, Mavors. You're an idiot. You think I'd make deals with vermin like him? He killed our dad."

"My dad. Mulciber, if you thought he could put the crown of heaven on you, and keep it from me, you might find a way to forgive him."

"We going to fight now, eh? Is that the plan?"

A man in the green-and-blue scale mail of an Atlantean stepped up behind me and raised his voice. "Sir! One of them is here! Alive!"

Mavors said, "Petrified?"

The man extended a hand to me. "Miss? Can you get up? Are you wounded?"

I did not answer. The man shouted up toward Mavors, "Sir! This one is unconscious!"

My eyes must have seemed closed to him. I merely had my eyelids open a crack, but in a direction he could not perceive. I was looking "past" my closed lids.

Another man, standing in a different part of the cabin, said, "Sir! Two more over here! Wounded, but turned to stone. Not bleeding."

A final man, standing near the mouth of the giant dead serpent, called out: "One over here, too, sir. Turned to stone. I think it is the Phaeacian girl."

A Laestrygonian, with exaggerated casualness, stepped out from a group of petrified Laestrygonians and took a position behind the Atlantean man who was stooping over me.

The Atlantean straightened up and cast a frowning glance at the Laestrygonian.

The Laestrygonian smiled with his huge shark-smile, nodded to him casually, gave him sort of a breezy salute with one finger. "How's it going?" he said in a chummy voice.

Mavors, his voice carrying across the wide space, said loudly, "Mr. mac FirBolg, please desist. I can maim you without killing you. I can overcome your various powers merely by decreeing that they will operate improperly against me. I can decree that I will be victorious if we fight. Don't make me fight children."

The Laestrygonian muttered to himself, "Oh, great. Fifth in command. My choice. 'What do I do now, Leader . . . ?' Okay, do something smart. Smart, smart. Make Amelia proud of your sorry ass."

Mulciber had scuttled around in a circle, so that he could keep an eye on the Laestrygonian, but he was half hunched over, keeping one hand on the chest of the statue. The stone wiggled under his fingers. Mulciber did not look too happy.

The Laestrygonian straightened up and shouted across the open space. "Okay, well, right, then! Let's talk this out for a second, hey?"

Mavors called back, his voice toneless: "There is no basis for negotiation, Mr. mac FirBolg. No matter what your promises, it is too dangerous for you to be allowed at liberty. Your only bargaining power would be a threat to kill yourself. If you thought it was your duty, to sacrifice yourself in order to aid the triumph of Chaos over Cosmos, you would have done so already. You have made an honorable attempt, as all prisoners of war are bound to do, to escape. That escape is impossible. You have no reason to pursue the matter."

The Laestrygonian stood there, fidgeting. He melted and flowed like wax. Now it was Colin standing there, dressed in a black tunic of feathery stuff. He was still fidgeting.

A voice in my head said, *Mother, I will help you. Another battle comes; Mavors will be the victor, for he must be victorious in all melee, but I will delay the victory. Then my debt to you is done.*

I blinked. Who the hell was that . . . ?

Mavors called, "Do you have anything to say, Mr. mac FirBolg?"

Colin was grinning. "Yeah. I've got something to say. Yoo-hoo! Echidna! Can you hear me? I said your name. Here's the guy you were looking for! Hallo, hallo? GET 'EM!"

11.

I saw it through the broken stained-glass window. A whirlpool opened suddenly within the waters behind, swallowing dozens of ships in an instant. Up through the tunnel of air, a figure rose, wrapped in shadow, growing.

Echidna, taller than a mountain, rose up out of the waves behind the ship on which Mavors stood.

Her face was more beautiful than before, made stern and noble by an inner light. But now she wore a tight-cheeked helmet with a nodding plume; a breastplate of barnacle-covered bronze was molded to her rounded breasts and flat abdomen; and in her slim white hands were both shield and spear, each a match for her monstrous size. The spear was taller than a minaret; the shield was a full moon.

Rivers fell from the shining scales of her snake-body, and her serpent colors wavered beneath the waves: green, green-gold, dappled gray and blue, and spotted red.

A monster, yes, but at the moment she was a monster on our side. I cannot tell you how lovely she looked, how proud, how brave.

Her voice was soft and cool as ice: "Mavors, I am your death. My son Grendel, whom you slew, had no grave; nor shall you."

Mavors said, "Retreat, and I shall spare you. I hunt the sons and the daughter of Chaos this day."

"The daughter of Chaos my daughter-in-law was meant to be. That joy died. She and I will know joy again when you fall."

"I am battle itself. I will not fall, save to fall upon you. Let us begin."

He gave a mighty shout and shook his spear. An aura of flame spread from him in all directions.

When she screamed a deadly falcon-wail, the sky turned black, and the waves leaped hundreds of feet into the air. A wild storm erupted.

Mavors cast the spear at her. His spear turned ruby red as it flew, and it shattered her vast shield and pierced her between her round breasts. It should have penetrated her heart.

She plucked it out with a gesture of indifference, flicking it aside, a toothpick. Meanwhile, with her other hand, she drove her titanic spear through the hull of the black ship in which Mavors stood and, with a twist of her hand, shattered the ship as if it were matchwood. Mavors went flying head over heels into the waters. His flame was quenched.

With her fine white teeth, she severed the straps of her broken shield, and tossed it from her, crushing a battalion.

Roaring their battle slogans, the Laestrygonians and Atlanteans rushed to the breach of the hull, casting spears and arrows at Echidna. Many dove into the water, to come to the aid of their chief.

Echidna paused only to breathe flame and poisonous smoke on the men, snatching up a half dozen of them in one tennis-court-size hand to stuff as bloody gobbets into her mouth before she inclined her head to the waters and lifted her huge lace-fluked tail.

Down she dove, seeking Mavors, and a rolling mile of speckled snake-tail trailed in a huge semicircle after her, up out of the waves where she had risen, down into the waves where she dove. Her scorpion sting lolled in the air for a moment, throwing spray high, and then she was gone.

Poisons came from the scorpion tail, mingled with the splash of spray as she dove, and Laestrygonians staggered away from the black rain, screaming, clutching bits of burned and melted faces.

A crewman from the golem shouted down, "Boss! Boss! Should we go save Mavors?"

Mulciber said, "What, him? Kidding, right?"

But the statue trembled under his hand at that moment, and sweat began to roll down his face. "Uh-oh."

Colin turned into a column of flame. The Atlantean next to me flinched back; several Laestrygonians leaped toward Colin in long, loping steps, shooting arrows as they came.

I was almost still too weak to stand, but I was not too weak to do something. I reached up into the heavy substance of hyperspace, the fluid medium thicker than liquid lead, and pulled it down, rotated a mass of it into this space.

A wash of fluid, a small lake, heavier and denser than anything made of matter, flooded into existence around me. Laestrygonians and Atlanteans were swept backwards. The hull underfoot gave way. Everything around me collapsed. Beneath was roaring sea, into which men and splinters were falling, tons of earth, upturned flowerbeds.

I pushed most of my mass into the fourth dimension, and Colin put an arm made of flame around me.

A cloud of dark air, containing the internal nature of Quentin, swept up around us. He breathed. Magic and oxygen were force-fed into Colin, who blazed brighter and hotter, fiercer and wilder.

Quentin said, "My body's turned to stone and I cannot get back into it. Victor and Vanity are both stone, too. Wounded, but frozen. We need to get to them."

Colin said, "Thanks for including me in that spell. When it broke for you, it broke for me. Or did Trismegistus do that by accident by making us all the same for all?"

Mulciber, still crouched over the trembling statue of Trismegistus, called out, "Stop! I can still have my Taloi get you! Gun crew! Stand ready!"

Gun turrets rotated to cover us. A mass of riflemen came out of hatches on the neck, and stood formed into ranges along the epaulettes of the metal giant, field guns and rifles at the ready.

Quentin said, "Colin, can you break the deck between Mulciber's feet where he is standing, if you had to? Get ready."

From the column of Colin, an arm of white-hot fire drew back, and a mass of flame shaped like a pinwheel, turning, began to glow on the end of it, intolerably bright.

Mulciber said, "Oh, come on! Fire doesn't hurt me. I am the god of volcanoes. I piss lava."

Colin said, "Burns decks, though. You might drop your prisoner."

Quentin said, "Sir, we mean no disrespect, but we cannot allow you to imprison us. I am supposing the god of iron and stone is diminished in re-
sources when plunged into deep ocean? Can you make the same boast
Mavors made, and tell us you can maim us without killing us with the huge
guns on your machine?"

Mulciber took a deep breath, and let it out slowly. "This is not a good day.
Should've stayed in bed. Hey! Miss Windrose! You in that mess of flames
somewhere?"

I called back, "I am very well, thank you, Lord Talbot. I mean, Mulciber.
This fire doesn't hurt me."

He squinted and shrugged his huge shoulders, a grotesque rolling motion.
"Phaethusa, you know I've nothing against you. Believe me, I've got nothing
against your kind. But the universe ain't mine to take risks with. I'm going to
have to attack, and I'll hurt you and your friends pretty badly before it's over,
and you all getting yourselves killed is as much bad to me as if I let you go.
You see? You see what I am saying?"

"Sir, I am not going to hurt the world, or let my people in Chaos hurt it. It
is the only world I know. But I am going to be free, and so are my friends!"

"I just want your word on that."

"My . . . my word . . . ?"

"You're old enough to know what it means. You know what I am asking."

I spoke quickly, before Quentin or Colin could tell me not to do so.

And so I said, "I swear it."

He bent over and gripped the statue of Trismegistus with both hands.

Mulciber looked up. "And I decree you'll not survive what comes if you
break that oath, not you nor your friends neither. Agreed . . . ?"

I said, "As long as I am free, I agree."

Mulciber looked back down at the statue of Trismegistus. He looked
quite grim, and wrinkles crumpled up his knotty face.

He spoke again: "Okay. You caught me at a busy time. Your good luck, I
guess. Go. Take your friends. Get a medical kit from some of these bodies lying around the deck here. And if you ever decide you want that job after all,
look me up. Okay?"

FATE AND FREEDOM

1.

The gray waves of the North Sea pitched and rolled the silvery boat, and a cold drizzling fog woven with blowing snowflakes attempted to make us miserable as we shivered on the deck.

The attempt failed. Vanity's face was red with cold, and frost had gathered on the furry hem of her parka hood, and snowflakes on her delicate eyelashes, but delight simply burned from her. In one hand she held her champagne glass. The bottle was tucked into a lump of snow which had gathered beneath the stern bench, since we did not have an ice bucket. Victor was solemn and glad; Quentin could not cease from smiling.

Victor raised his glass, and said in a voice that lacked its usual stern note: "It is too soon to celebrate. The fate of death hangs over us, and we must proceed rigorously and logically. The experiment is still awaiting results." Then he forswore his words by taking a long sip of the bubbling, bright liquid.

Vanity hiccuped, and giggled, covering her nose with her mitten. "Nope! Here he comes. Experimental results. He's looking for the boat."

Across the dark sea the moon sent here and there a slanted pillar of silver light into the heaving mass of snowy waters. The rest of the scene was as dark as the clouds above. A winged shape swept across the waves toward us, and he could be glimpsed only when he passed through one of those curtains of moonlight. His eyes were visible like two sparks of green marsh gas, and when he opened his mouth to cry halloo, the tiny flame of his tongue was bright.

The deck was slightly larger in this version. Like "finding" a space-worthy shape, Vanity found an undamaged version of her ship beneath the wrecked hull. Her ship was all ships.

Quentin said, "The only reason why we let him go off alone was because of the ring. Why is he visible?"

Vanity said, "He can't see us."

Victor, whose eyes these days operated on more than one band of the spectrum, could pick him out. Victor opened his third eye and shot out a bright golden beam, painfully bright in the utter gloom.

Phobetor landed on the stern of the heaving boat and shrank into Colin, who was dressed in a dark sea-coat and sweater.

"You started drinking without me?" were his first words.

"Celebrating!" I said. The champagne had made my face hot, so I threw back my hood and let the snow drift into my hair. I gave him a big and happy smile. "We were sure you'd succeed!"

"Well, you're right about that," Colin said. "The fate that made it so Mortimer was touched in the head is gone. I don't know what you four did here on the boat at midnight, but just when the church-tower clock struck twelve, I flew up to his little barred window and did my hoodoo. Heck, once he was talking normal and stuff, I passed him my cell phone through the bars and let him call his brother Sam the Drayman. He was all crying and laughing so much, I thought it hadn't done anything, and he was still cuckoo, but . . ." He shrugged. "It worked on a small scale. We can undo fate."

Vanity smiled, and her white teeth showed. "And at least one man knows the gods are real. That won't overthrow them. But it is a start."

Victor raised a hand. "Now to save our lives. Everyone ready?"

Quentin took several sticks of colored chalk in his hand and threw them on the deck. In a moment, the snow was swept aside, and the boards were bright with circles and summoning triangles, pentagrams and stars-of-David, all written in and around with Latin and Greek script.

I was feeling a little light-headed and giggly, until Victor swept that azure beam from his third metallic eye across me and removed the alcohol from my bloodstream. He did not bother to sober up Vanity: She had already had Andromeda establish the Olympian laws of nature we needed.

At first our death was far away in the time-stream, but Quentin poked pins in a little wax doll of Victor, which did not hurt Victor in the slightest but sent out a signal that Victor was in danger. His death grew close, curious, hoping for an opportunity to act. This was the curse slaying Lamia had created.

The warning-fate that Mavors had set up came alive within the time-stream, too. We took care of it first. Yes, we had debated the wisdom of having Mavors show up to save us each time we were in an auto accident, or fell down a flight of stairs or something, but in the end we decided we had to take care of ourselves without help.

2.

That left only the death-fate, which closed in more rapidly once the Mavors counterfate was out of the way. Obviously it was more likely that we would die once no protector was around to save us.

The hard part for me was getting Victor to see the direction the death-fate was in: I took his head in my hands and pulled it up out of three-space, and pointed it in the time direction. His brain did not record any activity at that moment. I assume he was unable, by his very nature, to see what I saw. But the blue beam came out of his third eye all proper and normal, and dissolved the huge lump of time-energy.

The hardest part for Quentin was when a voice spoke to him from the cloud. With his hands shaking, he took the champagne bottle and poured himself two glasses. He cut himself with his athame, his witch's knife, and dropped a drop of blood into one.

"Here is the blood shed by she who has offended me," he said, his voice thick. "Here is my anger and my retribution, which I, Fallen and Archon of the Fallen, Master of the Art, have a right to claim. I drown you in the deep."

He tossed the wineglass into the sea.

He held up the other glass. "Here are the sins of Lamia against me. The pain and humiliation . . . the . . . tears I cried. The sound of her hateful voice as she called me a child . . . and molestation . . . ach! Here are her sins. Let the sea, let the great sea drink them, and may they forever be gone and be forgotten, as I forget them. I drown you in the deep."

The second glass twinkled in the gloom as it sailed over the railing and into the snowy sea air.

He said, "I forgive, I forgive, I forgive you."

Then he sat down and put his face in his hands. I think he was crying. Vanity sat next to him on the bench and put her arms around his shaking shoulders.

I said, "What just happened?"

Colin was standing very close behind me. "Didn't you feel it? Trismegistus used the fact that Victor here killed Lamia and her two pals, ap Cymru and what's-her-name, the Phaeacian, to power his curse against us. Necromancy."

The winged bastard probably expected us to kill the bitches. There was a moral component, a vengeance involved. We killed Lamia, so fate could kill us. Big Q, our little Quentin here, just called their bluff and trumped their ace. He forgives Lamia, so her death has to forgive Victor. That's the way I figure it, anyway. Quentin was really shaken up by the time Lamia had him strapped to the table. Maybe he can get over it, now."

"Why is he crying?" I said. I was thinking that boys were not supposed to cry, but I did not say that. It would have sounded like such a stereotype. But I thought it.

Victor said, "Growing pains. Children hold grudges. Adults cannot."

I said to Colin, "I understand four parts of what we must do to unwind an Olympian fate. But what do you do? What did you do to save Mr. Finkelstein?"

He spread his hands. "You're the one person I cannot explain it to, Amelia."

"Try me."

"I turn myself into glass and remember the Real Me, a soul without a body, outside of time, eternal, enlightened, unstained. I think about how Fate has no power over Infinity. And I think of freedom. I am inspired by freedom: In my heart I sing of it. None of my brothers in the dream-universes can do what I do, for they have never been bound, and they do not hate prison half so much."

"I think I do understand." I smiled at him. Sometimes Colin seems sweet.

Victor interrupted the conversation. "Amelia's turn next. We have to get rid of the curse Boggin put on her; otherwise, he can find her whenever he wants."

3.

It didn't work. I could give the frozen time more free will, and Victor could make it act in a neutral fashion, but the moral component would writhe and tangle, and slowly correct the fate back to what it had been.

Quentin said, "I am sorry. If I were more skilled, studied more deeply in the One True Art, perhaps—"

I said angrily, "I thought my parents sent me into the cursed world in order to do this! To find you four, and set about freeing mankind from Lust and Death and War and all the other gods they worship! So was it all for nothing?"

Victor said in a voice as calm and gentle as ever I was to hear him use, "Reality consists of scarcity: No tool is of unlimited use, no good supercedes all other goods, no power is so powerful as to overwhelm all else; otherwise the universe would long ago have been reduced to that one power, with that one tool to that one good."

"What's that mean?" I said to him. Maybe I shouted it.

"It means nothing is perfect. Every rule has exceptions. Every atom in motion has a swerve."

I said tearfully, "It means I will never get away from Boggin?" To Quentin I said, "Why didn't it work?"

Quentin said, "The wording of the oath. You would never do anything to make him ashamed. If you undo his spell, on which his whole reputation and honor depend—he took quite a risk in letting us at large—then he will be shamed indeed. I cannot undo the moral obligation, because the very act of unweaving the obligation is shameful. It is almost as if you took a second oath not to break the oath."

Vanity looked worried. She whispered something to Colin. Colin took me by the elbow and lowered his lips to my ear. "Amelia, don't you even think about trying to sneak away from us, to lead Boggin away. I am not going to let that happen. I want you too much."

Well, that gave me something to think about. The conclusions I came to were not so pleasant.

Why wasn't Victor here, keeping Colin away? I turned my head. Victor was standing, simply standing, in the prow of the ship, looking out into the snowy darkness, the surging waves, his face thoughtful.

As if he had already resigned himself to the idea that I would run away.

22

THE BUBBLE BATH

The magnificent Hotel del Coronado looks out upon the blue Pacific across beaches as tawny-white and perfect as no beach in Europe can be. It is summer here, in Southern California, eternal summer. The sea breeze is always cool and crisp and fresh, and the palm trees are always as green, and know no wintertime.

When ancient poets dreamed of mansions on Olympos, in the aether high above the storms and snows of Earth, they sang of untroubled climes and unchanging seasons, not knowing that the paradise they feigned was here on the West Coast of the New World.

The hotel itself is roofed in sun-baked red tile, topped with cupolas and adorned with quaint architectural flourishes. A dozen white dormer windows peer out from under the frowning brow of a titanic conical dome. Inside, the furniture and decor are stately and Victorian, but here and there are traces of Spanish ornament.

The windows here are nothing like the windows I knew in Wales, broad sheets of shining glass, taller than a man and as wide as an embrace, admitting torrents of southern sun when shut, and the warmest zephyrs when opened wide. The western wall of the room here was more glass than stone, and a second sun shone in the reflections of the pale white floor.

It is worth every penny to stay in a place like this, even if you are counting near to your last penny. Warm days drift by while you walk warm sands, wearing as near to nothing as the law allows, and your limbs turn golden-brown; even being alone is not so much a hardship as it might seem, if you are paid up in your hotel suite through the end of the month, and you are young, healthy, blond, beautiful, and wearing a bikini.

One difficult side effect of being alone, healthy, blond, and young I had not entirely foreseen was the men: Men who want to buy you drinks, buy you food, take you to do their odd style of hopping rock-and-roll dances, and even ask you to shows. It is profoundly amazing how many men, of what age and range of types, will pursue you: men who certainly have granddaughters older than you will smile avuncular smiles while their eyes devour you with ungrandfatherly hunger; boys too young to be out by themselves will strut and posture for you, saying the stupidest things imaginable; crazed men with staring eyes, quiet men with eyeglasses; cheerful or morose men; bald or vain or desperate; men you would never tell the time of day to.

It is amazing how well the worst ones think of themselves, and how little the best ones do.

Some are so bold, it defies belief. More than one man at a café table, during the moment when his date stepped away, would send a drink to my table, and catch my eye, and smile. The most bold was this tall and dark-haired chap with arrogant eyes, who asked me for my phone number while a pouting brunette in a tank top was clinging to his arm, listening. What do such men think I would think of them? That I am eager to be courted by cads? It was at times like these I wished that Victor were near, or even Colin.

Well, perhaps I was more carefree than a woman of proper decorum dares to be, because if the gentleman in question becomes too forward or insistent, you can reach out into the fourth dimension, find his governing monad, and jar it to bring his mind-body duality momentarily out of alignment. It might take only a moment for the human brain to recover from the dizziness, blindness, numbness, but in that moment, you can step half an inch sideways into a direction he cannot see.

You might laugh if I said I often had the sensation of being watched, since a nubile girl frolicking along the beach wearing a mere wisp or two of skintight fabric, making eyes at the passing men, must surely expect to be watched. But this was different from the innocent hungers and lusts of mortal men; I would imagine cold eyes staring at me, puzzled but patient.

It was a terrible life, the way I lived for that week, as lonely as my time chained in the jail had been, despite that there were crowds around me. But it was not without certain compensations, certain gratifications. It was warm.

Warm days yield to warm nights, and you can shed your last scrap of clothing then, and spend lingering hours luxuriating in a near-to-scalding bathtub high in your private room, with all the huge wide windows open to the scent and sound of the sea, the soft, eternal crash and murmur of the waves. The freezing rains and fogs of Southern Wales seem no more than unhappy dreams.

The bathroom in my suite was a palace in miniature: The tub was deep and wide, and the rim was paved all around with a marble so brown that it seemed gold. The steam trickled and played across the mirrors and fixtures of the bathroom, and the shining expanse of the cut-glass doors gleamed like a snowfield.

With those doors open, I could see, across what seemed an acre of carpet and polished wood, the balcony doors of the suite, the wide windows, the moon and summer stars. Beneath the moon, the sands of the beach were as pale as ice; the sea was a shimmering tiger, striped with the reflections of harbor lights, and the noise of the sea waves from the dark waters was like its tiger-breathing, soft and huge.

And bubbles. Lots of scented bubbles. Bath oil. The water was warm enough to gather beads of sweat across my nose and brow, and little breaths of steam from the waters tickled my neck, and my toes (which were resting on the huge ivory knobs of the spigots).

It was a summer night, and I was bathing with the windows open, for the night wind was warm, and carried odors of the sea, the noise of traffic. It made me feel all the more warm and comfy, all pink and nude beneath my layer of scented bubbles, to think of those poor motorists, creeping from red light to red light, going about whatever business men go about, far from their homes.

A cold breeze made me shiver. A drop fell from the steam-bedewed fixture above, and touched my nose. A cold drop. One that had turned to hail as it fell from the ceiling to the tub.

Boreas, his huge reddish wings furling about him, was stepping in through the leftmost window. His hair hung loose and waving around his shoulders. His fierce eyes lingered along the little windows of transparent water gaps in the suds the cooler water had created. A mocking smile touched his lips.

He wore little more than purple silk pantaloons. His calves and feet were bare. His chest was nude. I saw the slide of muscles beneath his fair ruddy skin along his shoulders and arms. His eyes were magnetic, drinking me in. And he had a very small half smile beneath his mustache.

I started to get up. Boreas leaned and yanked the towel off the rack and out of my reach, as well as my flannel bathrobe. He threw them both casually behind him and out the window.

"Well, now, Miss Windrose, we have traveled far from Mare Boreum on Mars, but not so far, it seems, from Los Angeles, have we not?" he said, seating himself comfortably on the rim of the bath. He crossed his legs and folded his hands atop his knee. Very casual, very calm, very in-control.

I shrank down, covering my breasts with one hand and arm, folding my hand between my crotch with the other. The last time I was in this position, it was Grendel Glum trying to rape me with his eyes.

"Turn around," I said. "I'm naked."

He looked skeptical, rubbed the back of his head with his hand, as if to massage an old bruise, but said nothing.

For about the span of time it takes for a startled and badly frightened girl to slowly regain control of her breathing, he sat, staring down at my bubble-hidden body, saying nothing.

Of course, that made it worse. I wondered if he was going to spank me again. He looked like he was in the mood.

I drew a shaking breath, and forced out in a calm voice, "What do you want, Headmaster Boggin?"

A tiny wisp of wet hair had put a tail to the corner of my mouth. I dared not raise either hand to brush the hair away. Boreas idly reached down, touched my cheek, and put the hair out of my mouth.

It was almost shocking, how casually he did that, as if I were his daughter. Or a pet. Someone he had the right to touch.

I said, "Aren't you going to say anything?"

He said, "Miss Windrose, you must have known that your promise to me could lead me back to you. Surely you have had, in that space of time, composed some sort of speech or manifesto to deliver to me. You must have imagined a scene or confrontation something like this, perhaps practicing in front of a mirror what you would say to me. I assume you invented more than, 'What do you want, Headmaster,' or 'Turn around.'"

"Okay," I said, "how about this: I want to know what the real reason is for all this. Tell me why you were keeping the talismans on the school grounds. Where we could find them. Keys to wake our powers back up. Did you want us to escape, for some reason?"

He leaned back slightly and crossed his arms. "Where are the others?"

I said, "You first."

"Are we going to trade question for question?" he said, raising his eyebrows. "You promise to answer one of mine for each of yours I answer?"

I shook my head. "No promises. You can ask, and, if it suits me, I'll answer. But you answer first. Why were the talismans kept where we could get them?"

He said, "My dear Miss Windrose, what did you think I intended? Surely the matter is obvious."

I said, "What is this, a gypsy fortune-teller reading? I tell you what my expectations are, so you can repeat them back to me? Just give me the answer."

Boreas made a dismissive gesture. He said, "The matter is not obscure. There was no other safe place to keep the talismans. As originally designed by His Majesty, Lord Terminus, the boundaries and conditions of the school grounds would have suppressed the several functions of the talismans of Chaos. There was some decay over the years. What Terminus intended as a temporary encampment, I was required to treat as a fortress, and the facilities were not, as one might say, all that one might expect. And where else could I put them? If I threw them in the sea, milord Pelagaeus would recover them; no Olympian would have permitted me to turn them over to another Olympian for safekeeping, because of the temptation, if one of them had the key to open a power of Chaos, to take the chaoticist as well. While the talismans were in my hands, there was little incentive for other Olympians to abduct you."

"And why did they exist there to begin with?"

"Emissaries from Chaos sent them, or they were possessions you had on you when you were taken."

I said, "And what about our education? Lamia thought you were training us in our powers, that you intended to use us in the wars."

"My dear, I hope you are not bringing up an entirely new issue, while my curiosity remains unsatisfied. Where are your companions?"

I said, "Why else would you teach us everything we needed to know to use our powers correctly?"

He frowned.

Boreas leaned, dipped one finger idly in the water.

Steam stopped rising from the tub. The water turned cold. It was no longer comfortable.

I yelped, started to get up, remembered I was naked, and shrank back down again.

It was not icy, but it was no longer warm and inviting. He did not make it numbing, or painful, or coated with ice. Not yet.

"Miss Windrose, I do not wish to pressure you unduly, and yet, in all honesty (if that phrase has any meaning, under the circumstances), I would be remiss in my duties, not to mention personally placed in a very awkward position, if the material universe were to come to a bloody and abrupt end, merely because I was too gentle-hearted to do what it was necessary to do in order to maintain our security. I can make myself be a rather harsh and cruel man, even a barbarian, should circumstances warrant. I leave it to you to determine—yes, that is the word, determine—whether events shall progress in a civilized or in an uncouth fashion. I am, indeed, a terrible person, Miss Windrose. I trust you have not forgotten the messages, written in the language of pain, which I caused to be written on the bodies of Grendel Glum and Mestor the Atlantean, whom you knew by the name Dr. Drinkwater?"

While he spoke, he pushed his hand more deeply beneath the water, and it grew colder and colder. I was staring at his hand in horror. His knuckles, his wrist, his forearm were now below the water level. The suds in that section of the tub were wilting and dying; the water was taking on the crystal clarity only truly cold water can display. I was huddled up against the far side of the tub, as far as the confined space would allow.

The picture I had in my imagination was me, nude, inside a solid block of tub-shaped ice, being carried on his shoulder back to the school.

He pulled his hand back, smiled unpleasantly. The water dripping down his forearm turned white and formed a little glove of frost, which he shook contemptuously to the floor tiles.

"Are you threatening me?" I said, trying to sound stern.

He swallowed a snort. Apparently I did not do *stern* that well. "Ah . . . Not in so many words, Miss Windrose: But to a person of even limited intelligence, I deem the implication would be clear. One might be tempted to say, 'painfully clear'; but, in order to avoid disproportionate drollery, let us simply say, pellucid. Surely the matter is . . . ah . . . pellucid to you, Miss Windrose?"

"You are going to rape and torture me if I don't talk."

A slight tension pulled at the corners of his mouth. Embarrassment? Humor? Temptation?

"Ahem. I had not been planning on any acts of rape. Such things generally turn out badly. Ask my wife. But I compliment you on the fecundity and liveliness of your imagination. I will be disaccommodated if you allow things to degenerate to the more brutal state to which they might devolve. Please consider answering my question."

"I left them. I knew you could follow me; I knew you could not follow them. So they are safe."

"You must have arranged some system of rendezvous, or exchange of messages? Dropboxes, letters to the *Times* signed in code, colored smoke signals, that sort of thing . . . ?"

"You and your people can erase memories. Why not read minds? I thought it would be safer if I didn't leave myself any way to reach them."

"But they can reach you, one supposes?"

"I promised Colin I would have sex with him."

"Hphfnah? I mean, I beg your pardon . . . ?" Disgust, and even anger, broke in his voice. The noise he made was like the snort a large black bull makes when a younger bull comes nosing around his harem. The contemptuous blow of a bull lowering its head to gore an insolent opponent.

"It is like my promise to you. An oath. Colin and Quentin can use it to find me."

"Miss Windrose, sometimes I just wonder what on Earth goes on in that head of yours. Did you actually promise an amorous liaison with . . . Oh, it boggles the mind! With Mr. mac FirBolg?"

"What's so wrong about that?"

"What's so wrong? What's so wrong? Did I really teach you so poorly, Miss Windrose? Have you no sense of propriety, no sense of pride, no sense of self-esteem? Have you no sense? What about taste? Have you no taste?"

I looked at him with my eyes half-closed. "You don't think he's good enough for me."

"I assume, with the natural perversity of teenagers, this will merely recommend him to your favor. But, as a mental exercise, envision a delicate and graceful rose, the fairest bloom of the fairest spring. Now picture a slug dropped on it, leaving a trail of ooze. I am aghast."

"Do you not like Colin so much?" I said, my voice light and airy.

"Mr. mac FirBolg has no capacity to apply himself, and, were he not graced with dangerous supernatural powers, would have no doubt found a satisfactory life as a fast-food-restaurant clerk, or a heroin salesman. But you, you, Miss Windrose, whether born a princess or goddess, common or mortal, you could make of your world what you will of it. You are much too fine a creature for a dull-eyed sluggard like Mr. mac FirBolg. What of your Mr. Triumph?"

"Victor . . . ?"

"Of course, Victor. That he is the only fit man for you, a blind monkey could perceive from half a mile off on a foggy day."

"I really think my private life is none of your damn business, if you don't mind my saying so, Headmaster."

He spread his hands, and "Your promise is a nullity in any case. Promises of marital favors are meaningless outside of marriage, which is a sacred institution. The Great Queen Hera Basilissa established the rules of the universe along these lines, and the rules of magic follow them."

I snapped, "We've gotten a bit off the topic, and you owe me at least three questions! I have a turn coming as well, you know!"

"Not true at all, Miss Windrose! I have been keeping a careful, that is as much as to say, an exact count of questions. Yours, of course, have been remarkably unimaginative, consisting of inquires such as, 'What's so wrong about that?' and 'Do you not like Colin?' and, a brief question, thus: 'Victor . . . ?' You have asked an abundance, indeed, a superfluity of questions, Miss Windrose, and I have answered them all."

"You haven't answered anything yet! What about Lamia's question?"

He looked insouciant. "What about it?"

"Why did you train us to use our powers? You intended to use us to fight your wars. Right?"

"That aspect of it was not entirely beyond my imagination, I admit. However, it was with some care that I took pains to make it appear to the other Olympians that I was not mollycoddling you. Had I placed you in foster homes, for example, and assigned certain of us to be your parents and kin, naturally the ones who got to play at being your parents would be regarded with deepest suspicion by the others."

"So you couldn't afford to treat us nicely as we were being raised?"

"Do not be overly sentimental, Miss Windrose. It ill becomes a woman of your intelligence and character. You were raised perfectly well, better than most. If you feel that the world has treated you unfairly, you have achieved a state of mind well known to all teenagers, but maintained only by adults of a more shrill and self-absorbed type."

I said, "Tell me about your parents."

He tilted his head to one side, his eyes narrowing. But he shrugged and said, "If you will. I was raised by Eos, the Lady of the Dawn, who, while a kindly mother, was somewhat heedless as a woman, and she awarded me numerous bastard half brothers. My father, Astreus, was given a fine rack of horns, and he was, as you might well imagine, quite remote. You should find little ground for envy."

"Would you have preferred to be raised by strangers? Enemies?" I could not keep the bitterness out of my voice. I was thinking of all the birthdays my mother never saw, my first steps, first words, first dance, first infatuation.

"For the isolation of your youth, I am deeply sorry, Miss Windrose, but that was a matter out of my hands. There is a war, you know, between Cosmos and Chaos, between order and entropy, between reason and unreason. This forms the fundamental basis of existence; I do not see how any victory or lasting peace is possible. The most one can hope for is temporary compromises, temporary armistice. You are not the first victim of this terrible conflict."

Strange. I remember Victor saying something of this sort back when we were all aboard the Silvery Ship: that no victory was lasting, no solution perfect.

I asked, "I don't understand how this whole situation arose: Hermes and Dionysus and Athena conspire to overthrow Zeus, and enlist the aid of Chaos: they succeed, and Zeus is killed by Typhon, right? But then Dionysus and Athena turn on Hermes, and someone else shoots him—I forget who—"

Boreas said, "It was the Huntress. The Lady Phoebe of the Moon. We stood on the plains of Vigrid, where the brink of Chaos roared, and the Gates of the World's End had been torn from their hinges, and lay stretched for miles along the plain. To one side reared all the armies of a united Chaos: a fearsome sight." And now his eyes grew haunted with old memory. "I saw phantasmagorical dream-legions from outer realms of eternal night, sons of Morpheus and Nepenthe; I saw fallen spirits from the Abyss, armed and armored with incontestable magic; above them and below, a hundred miles or more in length, the soulless monsters from the Void, with all their engines and molecular alchemies of matter and energy; above and beyond them, nigh-impossible to see or to imagine, were your people, Miss Windrose, creatures too perfect to be threatened or deterred: the uncreated thousand-dimensional superbeings from the unthinkable primordial prereality, before the geometry of space-time was drawn. A sight to stir the soul, I assure you, to look upon those beings, some brilliant with the splendor of eternal night; some wretched and lightning-scarred, yet smoldering with the burned remnants of angelic majesty; others yet with no souls at all, implacable and cold; others far too strange and wondrous ever to be allowed inside a sane universe, too large by far for space itself to hold.

"Yet even they, yet even they were held back by one more terrible still: the great lord whom I will not name, the Unseen One, the Lord of the House of Woe, came forth that day in all his horror, opened the hell-gate, and drove his armies of shadow before him; the dead walked, and the Great Fear was at hand: the dreamlords shrieked and fled like mist; the Fallen spirits cowered, aetherial spear and shield a-tremble in their airy hands; and the cold brains of the war-machines of the Lost would not open fire with their planet-destroying weapons without the support of their allies. Even the deathless Titans of your timeless people, the prelapsarians, were astonished, and they paused, even though they could not be made afraid."

I turned his words over in my mind, trying to imagine the unimaginable. This was the battle my parents lost, the battle when they lost me.

I said, "Why didn't they win? You guys are all so afraid of Chaos that you don't dare kill us. If Chaos is so dreadful, why didn't they win that fight?"

"Fate decreed otherwise."

"That is not a real answer."

"Ah, but Miss Windrose, it is a most penetrating and pertinent, and, if I may say, speaking on behalf of one who fought to defend reality itself against your parents, who wish to impose another condition of being on us, it was indeed a real answer—the very essence of real, so to speak. But perhaps you wish an historical cause rather than a final one? An examination of the mechanism Fate employed to direct events toward the desired outcome? All four races of Chaos fear the Thunderbolt of Jove, and (if I may propose an opinion) for good reason. It is an antique weapon; Chronos himself forged it when Time began."

"But Zeus—Lord Terminus—he was dead at that point, wasn't he?"

"Ah! A most acute and perceptive point, Miss Windrose. Had the inchoate confederation of Chaos been apprised of that most important fact, they might have come to a far different conclusion when they learned that their champion, Typhon of the Lost, had been slain by Lord Terminus."

Boreas smiled, and his eyes twinkled, but his words were cold as he continued: "Oh yes, the dreamlords are temperamental creatures at best; and the prelapsarians are too honest for their own good; and the Fallen Spirits, quite frankly, had several Dukes and archangels of darkness in our pay. (Not that I blame them for that; we found that the Phaeacians were in their pay, which is how they found the Lapses and dark-paths needed to mount their attack.)

"It was only after Chaos agreed to turn over the hostages that they discovered their, what you might call, their oversight, but by then their rage was held in check by the fear that some woeful deed would befall you four. By that time, we had forced you to use your metamorphic powers to change shape into small children, and I am sure the thought of you so small and frail weighed on the councils of the monsters that gave birth to you. Yes. Indeed. I would mock them for their folly, had I not made the same mistake myself.

"You were quite delightful as a child, I assure you, albeit trying at times: but, on the whole, I dare say, you were easier to raise than many mortals find their young to be. Oh, how men must envy the gods, since we can keep loud children stunned with drugs and spells, and, if all else fails, with lessons."

I said, "Why did you do it? The lessons. You taught us exactly what we needed to know to use our powers. I thought we were these wolf cubs, growing up into giants that would eat the sun and moon—why teach the cubs how to hunt?"

"Poetically asked, Miss Windrose. I admire your turn of phrase."

"Thank you. Now answer the question."

He looked away from me and out the window. Maybe he watched the lights of distant vessels on the sea. Maybe he looked at the stars. "I was an educator before I was a soldier, miss. I taught mankind how to break and ride horses, for example. Educators know there are only two types of schooling: indoctrination and education.

"Indoctrination teaches a student how to cleave to a party line, and to recite the slogans and bromides of the accepted conformity. He is taught only how to swallow lies, and there is no assurance he will not swallow the propaganda of foes as easily as that of friends. Such folk are hopelessly provincial to their time and place. Unable to distinguish truth from fable, they swallow both or spit both out, and become zealots, or, worse yet, cynics. The zealot holds that truth can be won with no effort; the cynic, that no effort will suffice.

"Education teaches the art of skeptical inquiry. The student learns the thoughts of all the great minds of the past, so that the implications and mistakes of philosophy of various schools are not unknown to him. And he learns, first, current scientific theories and, second, how frail and temporary such theories can be. He learns to be undeceived by those who claim to know a last and final truth.

"How else was I to deal with a dangerous race of world-destroying monsters? If I taught them to reason, maybe they could be reasoned with."

I said, "Why hide the truth? You did not tell us magic was real, for example, or that there were Olympian gods running around secretly ruling mankind."

"We told you the tales in sufficient detail, that when the truth was ready to emerge, you already knew what you needed to know."

"That cannot be the whole story. Why raise us at all? Why a school? Why not a prison, or an insane asylum? What was the purpose behind all this?"

"Hrmm. Well, would you believe that I am actually the Lord Terminus himself? The real Boreas has long since retired, and is living happily on his pension in Hyperboria. You and your brethren have been raised as the last and only hope of peace between Cosmos and Chaos, and you were taught your powers so that my sons and daughters, squabbling over a meaningless throne, would not have the ability to destroy you? It was done entirely for your own protection, and also to allow the great and altruistic work of universal peace to go forward."

I said, "No, I do not think I would believe that. I suspect, rather, that you would not have had a commodity to sell had you raised us to be totally ignorant, and that we would have been even more dangerous to you than we were, had we been told everything."

"Ah, well, then the benefits of an education in skeptical thinking must already be apparent to you."

"Pellucid," I said.

"Well, then," he said, "try out your powers of skeptical reasoning on this proposition: Without knowledge of your powers, and the ability, should the need arise, to use them, you might have been killed. Since your death would have instigated a war, it was thought best to see to it that you could defend yourselves."

"Why teach us liberal arts? Why raise us among human beings, as humans?"

"You will not believe this now, but in times to come you may. The art and science, poetry and literature, philosophy and thought and myth of mankind exceed the best efforts of the immortal races. Our muses need their artists as much as their artists need our muses. What men had to teach was more rational, fair, and lofty and, in a word, better, than the lessons you would have learned from the Olympians. They are the creatures of Prometheus."

"You wanted us to feel pity for them, a pity you do not feel yourself, so that when the time came, we would not be willing to see the Earth destroyed."

He stood up.

Boreas said in a cool voice, "Do not say 'we,' Miss Windrose. Mr. Triumph has no compassion for mankind; the emotion is unknown to him. Mr. mac FirBolg could not care less about this matter or any other. And your Mr. Nemo is a cold, cold man. He regards morality as a matter of legalisms and maneuver.

"No, Miss Windrose. Much as I wish I could take credit for it, and it would certainly make me seem to be the master of intrigue popular rumor paints (or slanders) me to be, the fact that you have matured into a woman of refined sensibility and noble sentiment, and one moved by compassion for mankind, is a product of your own generous soul."

He put his hand out toward me, as if offering to help me rise to my feet.

There was something menacing in his gesture. I saw in his eyes, his cool and mocking eyes, that he expected no more resistance from me, or that he could overthrow any resistance I might dare to raise, as easily as he once threw me over his knee.

"Well," he said, "at least the adventure was concluded in a satisfactory way. You can carry back many fine memories to comfort you. I speak in an abstract, hypothetical, that is to say, entirely nonliteral way, concerning the retention of memories, of course."

I am sure I must have looked a picture of misery and helplessness, crouching in a cold tub, hugging knees to my chest, dressed in nothing but suds, shivering. But his eyes were not playing over my exposed flesh (as, for example, Colin's would have been). He was looking me eye-to-eye.

Perhaps I did not look so miserable as I should have done, for he said in a thoughtful voice, "The prospect does not seem to dismay you."

"You thought I would fight back?" I said nonchalantly, a proud little lift to my chin.

"Given your history, Miss Windrose, it would be unwise indeed of me to assume otherwise. I also am not entirely convinced of the *bona fides* of your story. My brethren and I have been watching this hotel for some days, depending on which of them was blowing, and have seen no evidence that you are still in communication with your companions. However, as Dr. Fell taught you in science class, absence of evidence is not evidence of absence."

I did not know how to answer that, and I certainly did not want him to follow that line of reason to its logical conclusion, so that was the moment I chose to stand up.

I tried to do that nonchalantly, too, but all I remember is a painful feeling of embarrassment. I wiped some of the foam off my breasts, stomach, and hips, and bent over to wipe it from my thighs and legs.

I am sure Mata Hari could have done it in a more sensuous and less awkward way. I don't know if it actually had the distracting effect I wanted, because I could not bring myself to stare at anything other than his kneecaps.

I felt the water dripping from my breasts and hips, little rivulets snaking down my thighs. I could feel heat in my face. I must have been blushing like a beet.

Boreas suppressed a smile, and his gaze now did travel, up and down and up again, Colin-like. He nodded, a connoisseur expressing admiration for a fine work of art. Again he raised his hand. He said, "Well . . . ahem . . . Very nice. Please come quietly."

I didn't move.

He reached out a hand toward my nude shoulder.

At that moment, I felt nothing but his presence. As if the air around him were filled with nothing but him, huge, immense, masculine, masterful. It was not what I was expecting to feel.

There was a heartbeat in my throat, but I swallowed it down, and spoke before his hand touched me. I wondered if it would feel cold, or warm.

"Are you expendable?" I said.

My voice came out cool and nonchalant. Perfect. I sounded like the woman in control now, regal and mature. If only I could have brought myself to meet his eyes, I would have seen his reaction to that.

"Aha. Now we come to it," he muttered in a light drawl, drawing his hand back.

No matter how hard I stared at his kneecap, I could not read his expression. I still wasn't able to raise my eyes to him, at the moment.

"Come to what?" I said to his kneecap.

"The speech you practiced in the mirror."

I licked my lips, and summoned up the cool, nonchalant voice again. The voice of grown-up Amelia.

Again, it came out of my mouth perfectly naturally:

"You are trying to provoke a response, aren't you, Boreas? You could have walked up to me on the street, or at the store, or in the park. You waited until I was in the bath. You didn't bother insulting Victor. He wouldn't react. But you pulled out all the stops when talking about Colin. The boy you think has no self-control. You think he is listening to us, don't you? You want to draw the others out of wherever they are hiding. Well, it won't work."

Now I did look up at him. That was natural, too.

I was startled, even speechless, by the look of kindness and admiration in his eyes.

He stepped away from me. His red wings opened and folded again across his back, a rustling gesture, as he crossed his arms and looked carefully left and right, up and down.

He said, "Even if your story is true—which I doubt, Miss Windrose— your companions would keep watch over you. To exercise the full range of chaotic powers requires all four of you, and Nausicaa as well; and you need each other for mutual protection. No one else could protect Mr. Triumph, for example, from siren attack. They will come out when I carry you off."

I said, "No they won't."

Cool and calm and regal. I was doing it now without trying.

As if it were the real me.

"Oh? Why not?" His head was cocked to one side, his expression amused, aloof.

"Because you won't carry me off."

"And—?"

"And what?"

"And complete the utterance of your threat. Please keep in mind, however, that I have been threatened by gods and monsters much more malevolent than yourself, older, stronger, and whose supremacy over me I had demonstrable cause to fear."

"Fine," I said. "Here's the threat: If my friends are watching me, they will go to whichever faction among the Olympians who most wants the powers of Chaos on their side. Mulciber, Mavors, Pelagaeus, or even Tritogenia. The only price they will ask is that your head be delivered to them on a silver platter. How popular are you among the Olympians, Headmaster? What would the reasonable course of action be for any Olympian who—?"

He held up his hand. "Spare me further emphasis. My imagination is as fecund and lively as your own, and painted in a somewhat darker stain."

"Well?"

He nodded. "That is a fairly good threat. It is well considered, to the point, and hard to refute or ignore. I will give you a passing grade. There is one counter I can make, however. The other Olympians know I can find you at my pleasure. They will certainly kill me if I leave you at your liberty. To them, at least, I am expendable indeed. If my death is certain in either case, what if I am considerably nobler than you take me to be? I carry you off; your friends turn to Dionysus or Mavors, and demand my head in return for their loyalty. The deed is done. All the orphans of Chaos now work for one faction. That faction overwhelms the opposition, and places its candidate on the throne; and meanwhile, none of you return to Chaos, the peace treaty is preserved, everyone (except yours truly) lives ever after, if not happily, at least inside of a universe that preserves life, order, and structure; a universe with one ruler. No matter how highly a particular chess man values himself, the king must sacrifice pawns to achieve victory."

Boreas was silent a moment, his eyes measuring me.

"Are we really that powerful?" I asked.

"Trismegistus threw four armies at you, my dear girl, and took the field against you himself. I do not imagine your powers will decrease as age and wisdom ripen within you."

"I just thought we were lucky."

"How modest of you. We, the Immortals of Olympos, we control luck. Fate is our ally and weapon. With it, we have conquered the giants and Titans, Typhon and the monsters spawned from Echidna, the Cyclopes, the Hecatonchire, the Phaeacians; the Oceanids, Nereids, Meliades, and Oreads all pay homage to the sons of Chronos. Even the Ker and the powers of Hell bow down. And this omnipotent weapon, Fate, which conquered heaven and hell, ocean and earth, glanced from your breastplate. So, in sum, I am forced to admit, yes, you were indeed lucky, as you say. I am merely at a loss, or so it would appear, to explain that extraordinary fact."

I said, "We were not fighting among ourselves. You were."

"Well, there you have touched on an interesting matter, considering that the very keystone and fulcrum of your present threat against me relies on that fact. Taking advantage of our lack of leadership, so to speak.

"And yet you have not yet answered what seems to be a crucial flaw in the scheme; namely, if contemplating the possibility that you might return to Chaos, or even that the rumor of your liberty might eventually leak out to the Lords of Chaos, creates in me so much terror, or such high sentiment, that the prospect of losing my life holds no more fear for me. My life would end one way or the other, if the ordered foundations of reality were overturned.

"Nor is the danger, so to speak, unreal. I have it on good authority, from my spies among the prelapsarians, that the Green Energy was infused into the Thousand-Dimensional Object, which was moved several inches from its base before its progress was arrested by Phlegon of Myriagon. I know also that Morpheus, riding a steed of silver-white, crossed the moon-path of the Ocean of Untranquil Night, with six million of his phantasms, night-fancies, and long-tailed comets marching and floating behind him; and even now scratches at the windows of the day-world, calling to be let in."

I said, "You will be our emissary."

That caught him by surprise. He stopped his thorough inspection of my thighs, hips, and breasts to jerk his eyes up to my face, searching for some trace to tell him if I were serious.

"What—? I mean, please explain yourself, Miss Windrose."

I said, "I hope you believe that we have no more wish than you to have the world destroyed. We also wish to return to our homes in Chaos, some of us, at least. The only way to accomplish that is to wait until you Olympians settle your succession dispute, and rally behind a throne filled by a king you deem able to hold off an attack from Chaos. Until that time comes, our only hope of continued liberty lies in our willingness to help you deceive the chaoticists, and the other factions of Olympos, into thinking that we children are still under your control. And by you, I mean you, personally, Boreas.

"So this is the deal I suggest. You will be our go-between and emissary to the other Olympians. Anyone who wants to make a deal with us has to go through you, or else we don't talk to them. Not Mavors, not Mulciber, not the Unseen One. Nobody. We talk to nobody without your approval. You are the only one who knows where I am. All communication has to come through you."

I smiled archly. "You can tell them we are filled with affection and loyalty to the man who educated us, if you like."

He quirked an eyebrow. "The ones who were at my bedside in the hospital might not believe that Mr. mac FirBolg is so filled with affection."

"You can tell them anything you want. But tell them this one point: Any faction that tries to pressure, harass, or threaten us will make us go straight into the arms of their opposite faction.

"Tell ambassadors from Chaos that you still have us under tight control, but that we have been moved from the school grounds to another area, and that you occasionally let us out for field trips. If you need our help, in any limited extent, to help put on a charade that will continue to fool the chaoticists, if we can help in a way that will not expose us to danger from you, we will not be opposed to negotiation on that point. We will decide that on a case-by-case basis.

"In the meanwhile, you can now present yourself to the other Olympians as the man who has the children from Chaos in your pocket. I assume you will be able to parley that into some sort of advantage. All you need to do is keep them away from us."

He said, "Let me see if I understand the two sides of your offer. If I cross you, you have my head on a platter. If I help you, I receive a powerful advantage that raises me in eminence above my brethren, and makes me almost equal to my superiors."

I realized in that moment that, nude or not, I no longer felt shy in front of this man.

Exposing everything now, I put my hands on my hips and threw my wet lank hair out of my eyes with a toss of the head. It was one of those arms-akimbo, toss-of-the-head kind of moments. They come up so rarely in life, and it is worth a good nose-in-the-air head-toss when they do. "If your answer is no, go ahead and try to grab me. If the answer is yes, you can just leave by the same window you came in by."

He pondered a moment, stroking his mouth. I think the fact that I flaunted my breasts made him nervous. I was not doing it coyly, or to arouse him, but to show disdain. My lack of fear made him . . . not afraid, exactly . . . but wary. A chess player seeing a coming checkmate.

Boreas said, "If you agree to live without making any obvious use of your powers, I can agree. Chaos has spies and agents among us; we only have a limited ability to hide the evidence of your actions."

I said, "The *Queen Elizabeth* made it to home port, with no record of any deaths, and no scratches on her."

"Echidna's attack occurred in the dreamland waters, not the seas of Earth, and Mulciber's ability to hide evidence, repair damage to man-made things, and erase human memories and records, on this world, at least, is somewhat less limited. Men forget dreams. I insist on your discretion."

I said, "I will not say any words like 'I agree,' because you know how much trouble that causes. But I will remind you that my self-interest is bound up in living as discreetly as possible; I do not want either Olympos or Chaos tracking me down."

He nodded. "Very well; then we have an agreement."

I said, "Not as such. I have dictated terms to you; you have acknowledged that I can carry out the threat I said. And you know it is in our best interest to help you maintain the fiction that you are our emissary and go-between. It is not a deal, not a promise. You have no hold over me."

The look in his eye changed. The chess player's wariness was replaced by a brimming lustiness, a look of confidence and power.

It was like seeing the eyes of a hawk. I started to flinch back. But, naked, dressed in nothing but a memory of cold water, there was nowhere to go.

Boreas strode hugely forward, seized me roughly by the shoulders, lowered his head, and, before I could protest, bruised my lips with a savage and forceful kiss. I was crushed up against his wide chest, and the embrace pushed the breath out of my lungs.

A sensation of warmth and weakness traveled up my spine and spread to my limbs, making them feel tingly and heavy. I am sure I tried to say something, but it just came out as *Mmf—mm, Mm-mm!* I could smell the scent from his body.

Wow. He was a good kisser.

He drew his head back and looked quickly to his right and left. There was moisture on his chest where I had been pushed up against him, little moist droplets.

"Well, your beau is a man of greater self-control than I had given him credit for." He looked left and right again, calling out loudly, "Come out, come out, wherever you are, or I shall surely kiss her again!"

"Don't kiss me again."

He kissed me again.

When he was done, Boreas set me down on the edge of the bathtub, and he stepped back, still looking slightly puzzled that he had not been attacked.

He stepped over to the window and had one foot on the sill, his wide red wings to me.

I put my hands to either side of me on the bathtub rim and pushed myself upright. My feet were flat on the floor, knees together. My wet hair lay heavily along my spine.

I said, "My cell phone number is—," and I told him the number.

Boreas turned his head and looked over his wing-cloaked shoulder. "I can find you at any time."

I said, "Not for long. Good evening, Headmaster."

He looked for a moment as if he were about to question me on that point, but then he shook his head, whether in amusement, or sorrow, pride, or disgrace, I could not guess. He said, "Good evening, Miss W— Amelia."

"What?"

"May I call you Amelia? I did save you from certain dangers you encountered, and have acted to protect you on other occasions. Since this apparently will be my role henceforward, I do not think it improper to ask. May I?"

I frowned. "Headmaster, I do not understand you, and I certainly cannot trust you. I don't understand any reason for anything you do. So perhaps, considering the circumstances, we had best keep our relationship formal."

He snorted. "My reasons for doing what I did are very simple. Pellucid."

"Tell me."

He drew a deep sigh, but his brow furrowed. "My lord Terminus sent his dying message to me. Not to his wife, not to his sons. Me. He was a great man. You have seen how dangerous and willful his sons are; you can guess how powerful his foes in Chaos are. Yet, he ruled them all. Under his reign, there was peace, order, and even some justice. I have done as I have been bid; it is a measure of his foresight that things have turned out as well as they have. Does that explain my soul to you, little girl? I do not think you know the love a loyal follower can feel for a great leader, or know what a leader must do to win that loyalty."

I said softly, "I think I can imagine it. . . ."

"Then farewell for now, Miss Windrose. I imagine I shall hear great things of you in the future."

And he fell from the window, caught the night air in his great wide wings, rose, and was gone.

Colin shimmered and appeared as he yanked the ring of Gyges off his finger. In his other hand, he brandished the truncheon he had from his demon-form, a scepter glittering with black energies. "Next time I kill him! Oh,

God, I swear! Next time! *Pow!* He's a lump of dead meat! I would have done it this time, too, if Quentin hadn't zapped me!"

A segment of the darkness beyond the second window pushed itself into the frame, and when it ebbed, Quentin was standing there, a cloak as dark and weightless as the night sky drawn all around him.

He gestured, and all the windows slid shut. A pressure in my ears told me that all the sounds carried on the winds had been hushed.

Quentin said gently to Colin, "It was well for you that I did. Now then, give me the ring. As soon as the stars are right, I can cast the spell to confound the fate that allows the Master of the North Wind to find her, and let her wear the ring while the spell takes hold. Gyges' ghost will blind even the senses used by Boreas to find her."

In the other room, the fireplace swung open on hidden hinges, and Victor and Vanity came out from the secret passage. Victor was also carrying an Amazonian-style weapon he had constructed. I could see, in the secret room beyond, the slab on which the two duplicates of me Victor had made or grown were resting; one was dressed in my San Diego evening dress, the other in my red bathing suit.

Vanity's eyes were round and wide.

"Wow! I cannot believe you just let him kiss you!" And she marched up to Quentin and slapped his face.

"Ouch." He said mildly, "May I ask what that was for?"

"You are staring at her breasts!"

He offered her the crook of his arm. "Let us go the twenty yards down the secret passage to our rooms overlooking the French Riviera. I will be happy to stare at yours." I saw him put the ring of Gyges carefully in his pocket, and he escorted her out of the room.

There I was in the bathroom, alone with two men who loved me, naked as a jaybird, cold, and wet.

I looked back and forth between them, and they stared awkwardly at each other.

Colin said to Victor, "I'll wrestle you for her."

Victor stepped over to me, seized me by the shoulders, picked me up to my feet, and then an inch or so above that, so I was standing on my tiptoes. He bent his head down and kissed me. Not as roughly as Boreas had done, but much, much more thoroughly.

Wow. He was a pretty good kisser, too. Like everything else he put his mind to, Victor Triumph was driven to excel at this.

When Victor drew his head away, I could barely breathe, and I guess I did not want to breathe any air that did not have the warm smell of Victor on it. I put my cheek up against his chest.

Victor said to Colin, "We have been wrestling. You've lost two falls out of three. No hard feelings, I hope, old sport."

He put out his hand.

For a moment, I was sure Colin was going to spit at him, or throw down his truncheon, or something. But he exercised his self-control, put out his hand, and shook.

Colin said, "Okay. Fine. Maybe the man was right. A half-blind monkey could see it from a mile away on a foggy day."

As he was heading out through the fireplace door, he turned. With a little gleam of impishness in his eye, he said, "Or maybe not. The contest is not over yet. Girls like a man who can push them around, not vice versa."

Victor said sardonically, "You can play with the robot doll of her, if you like."

Colin stepped out behind the fireplace, which swung shut behind him, leaving me alone, gloriously alone, with Victor.

I said, "Now let me put on some clothes."

He said, "Not yet."